Redemption

Book 5 of the One True Child Series

Liminal Books is an imprint of Between the Lines Publishing. The Liminal Books name and logo are trademarks of Between the Lines Publishing.

Cover design by Cherie Fox

Between the Lines Publishing
9 North River Road, Ste 248
Auburn ME 04210
btwnthelines.com

First Published: 2019
Original ISBN (Paperback) 978-1-7321723-7-1
Original ISBN (eBook) 978-1-950502-01-1

Second edition: 2022
ISBN: (Paperback) 978-1-950502-87-5
ISBN: (Ebook) 978-1-950502-89-9
ISBN: (Hardcover) 978-1-950502-88-2

Redemption

Book 4 of the One True Child Series

L.C. Conn

Also available from L.C. Conn

Realm of Dragons: Fight for the Crown

The One True Child Series

Sentinels (Book 1)
Domination (Book 2)
Awakenings (Book 3)

See what they are saying about....

Sentinels:

"An excellent beginning to a fantasy epic. From page one, you'll be swept up into this battle of good and evil with all of creation at stake."

– Jo Neiderhoff, San Francisco Book Review

"…we are committed to following this exceptional opening to a world that seduces our imagination and provides sensitivity to that state of awakening. An excellent overture!" - **Grady Harp, The San Francisco Review of Books**

Domination:

"Once more, Conn weaves her spell, and we are immersed in Carling's spectacular world. Adventure, magic, and romance leave us hungry for more!" — **Tamara Benson, San Francisco Book Review**

"Fantasy is alive and well and exerting its power to enchant and beguile in this novel of foretold destiny." – **Diane Donovan, US Review of Books**

Awakenings:

"Once more, Conn gives the modern young female reader a heroine to look up to. Her prose is accessible, and her storytelling skills shine brightly, leaving us waiting for more in books to come." — **Manhattan Book Review**

"…a sensitive examination of the coming-of-age time of each of our lives but takes that discovery/recognition sequence into the realm of philosophy, a survey of good versus evil/chaos versus order and the

permutations those poles have on each of us." - **Grady Harp, The San Francisco Review of Books**

Guardians:

"Friendship, family, and fate all play a part once more in book four of Conn's engrossing One True Child series. The best thing about this book? The fact that it isn't the last!" — **Manhattan Book Review**

"this exceptional world that seduces our imagination …a very fine series."- **Grady Harp, The San Francisco Review of Books**

Redemption:

"A wonderful continuation of the gripping fantasy saga begun in Sentinels. I've loved seeing the expansion of this world and can hardly wait to see what the sixth book brings." -- **Seattle Book Review**

~

Dedicated to two of the most wonderful and strong
women I know... My Mother-In-Law, Chris, and
Sister-In-Law, Aleta.

Chapter One

The house was deathly quiet, and it suited the moment as Claire Drummond hung up the phone with a frown. She had always known that this time would come, but it still made her heart feel heavy. He was the last of his generation, and now her Uncle Geoff was seriously ill and in decline. The last four years had felt like one long funeral, as her grandparents had passed away one by one. But Lynnette, Grace, and Malcolm had all been there for two of the most important moments in her life since meeting them when she was seventeen: her wedding to her wonderful husband, Matt, and the birth of their daughter Breena a year later.

No matter how much she had come to love her grandparents, Geoff held a special place in her heart. It was her uncle who had taken her in and cared for her since she was ten years old after her parents had been murdered. He had been her strength and support when at seventeen she had learnt about her past, her Talents, and the truth of where she had come from. Then again with her ordeal both in Scotland and back home, until Matt had found her again—even though she had not appreciated it at the time.

Quickly she glanced at her watch. It was almost time to collect Breena from school. Claire grabbed her jacket and scarf and headed out into the bitter cold southerly wind. Clouds, dark and threatening, raced overhead. She shivered as the winter air blasted around her, creeping under the layers she was wearing. The walk was only a short one, but today her feet felt heavy, dragging along as she made her way down the street. She stopped for a moment as the news finally sunk in. A tear escaped her eye and she let it fall unchecked.

Steadying her breathing and calming not only her mind but also her heart, she carried on. Claire brought forth the image of her daughter—her long, dark curly hair that refused to stay in a ponytail for longer than a few minutes, bright blue eyes so much like her father's, and the image of her namesake—Matt's long-passed sister. Sometimes when they were alone together, Breena would look up at her and smile. It had a depth to it that suggested something to Claire, but she always put it out of her mind as soon as she thought it, refusing to face what might be true.

The gates of the school were already open, and children of all sizes began to stream out of them into the waiting arms of parents or walked together for the trip home. The noise of their chatter and squeals of delight turned to shouts and calls of farewell. Claire smiled and waved at friends, promising to get together for a coffee or a playdate with the kids while she waited for Breena to skip out of the narrow entrance. Normally her daughter was very punctual and the wait at the gate was a short one, but today there was no sign of her.

Glancing around, Claire could feel panic starting to rise inside her chest. Today of all days, Breena had decided to tarry. She searched for her daughter in the still-moving crowd of little people, but she was not there. Claire headed in through the gates and made her way to Breena's classroom. Her teacher was at the door, talking to another mother. She smiled as Claire approached, then pointed inside. Looking through the door, Claire found her daughter still sitting at the table, drawing.

"Bree, what are you doing, sweetheart? School has finished," Claire said as she entered.

"Hello, Mum. I just wanted to finish this." Bree indicated the paper she was drawing on. The little girl turned back to her task and the long, wavy black hair fell over her face, free from the hair ties Claire had put in that morning.

"We have to go. You can't stay here after school. How about you bring it home and finish it there?" Claire knelt down and pushed the hair off her daughter's face. "What are you drawing?"

"It's a picture for my friend," she told her mother.

Claire looked at the picture. It constantly surprised her how well Bree could draw, knowing full well she had inherited it from her father and her grandmother. The picture Bree was so determined to finish before going home was clearly of her and a very tall person.

"Who's that with you?" Claire asked her.

"That's my friend—I told you about him. He's funny. He asked me to draw a picture of us." Bree smiled and stood up. "Can I really take it home to do?"

"Yes, of course you can. Come on." She held out her hand for her daughter to take and they collected Bree's bag from the hook outside. As they walked up the street, Claire pondered the person in the picture with a little concern. "So does this friend have a name?" she asked Bree curiously.

"No, he won't tell me what it is, so I call him Mr. Man. He laughs when I call him that." Bree smiled.

Claire took her daughter's hand, and she started to skip beside her mother. Her backpack bounced on her back, and Claire could hear something rolling around inside.

"Did you eat your lunch today, Bree?" She looked down at her.

"No. I told you I don't like cottage cheese and cucumber. It's yucky."

"But you liked it last week."

"Now I don't. What I do like is peanut butter and…" Bree stopped skipping while she thought, making Claire come to a halt as well.

"What do you like with peanut butter?"

"Shh, I'm thinking." Her little finger was pressed against her mouth as she contemplated.

Claire waited, starting to feel frustrated. It seemed her daughter's taste in food changed from one minute to the next and trying to keep up was becoming difficult. Fat raindrops started to fall, landing heavily on the path around them, leaving dark splatter spots on the pale concrete.

"Come on, Bree, otherwise we're going to get drenched!" She tugged her daughter into movement, and they raced down the street together, laughing and squealing whenever they got hit by a raindrop.

After they reached their front door, Bree raced inside and dumped her bag in the living room, then headed straight for the kitchen. Claire picked up the bag and pulled out the lunchbox. Everything she had put in it that morning was gone, except for the offending sandwich. The picture Bree had been so busy drawing caught her attention.

Taking it with her, she walked into the kitchen. Already strewn across the countertop were bread, butter, peanut butter, and three different types of jams. Bree was attempting to spread the peanut butter on the bread, but she seemed to be smearing it on everything else as well.

"You make the mess, missy, you clean it up."

"Yes, Mum."

Claire pinned the picture up on the notice board and looked at it clearly for the first time. It was beautifully done, and Breena had captured her own face very well, but the drawing of her daughter's mysterious imaginary friend gave her an uneasy feeling once more. He was not quite finished, but already she could see some of his features and they seemed almost familiar.

"Mum?" Bree called her.

"Mmm?" Claire broke her gaze at the page and turned to face her.

"Can we go see Granddad soon?" she asked, taking a bite from her jam-dripping sandwich. As soon as Bree could talk, she'd refused to call Geoff by any other name than Granddad. It had made him so pleased that Claire never corrected her.

Her question stunned Claire, especially after the phone call she had received. "Why's that, Bree?"

"I just get this feeling we should go see him." Jam was now smeared on her face, not just the countertop.

"As a matter of fact, my little oracle, we are leaving in an hour and will be there tonight." Claire grabbed a cloth and handed it to Bree. "So, when you have finished eating that sandwich and cleaned up your mess, I want you to go and find some things to take with you. And I don't mean half of your toys."

Claire finished packing their bags and dropped them at the front door on the way to the kitchen as she listened to Bree chatting about her day. The evidence of her daughter's cleaning was still on the bench, with smeared lines of peanut butter and jam heading towards the sink. Claire shook her head and picked up the cloth, rinsed it off and finished the job, then went looking for her daughter.

In her bedroom Bree was sitting in the middle of the floor and staring at a couple of her dolls. She picked one up very carefully and then whispered to it. "I'll take you. I think you will be good on this trip." She placed the doll carefully into the bag at her side and then put the other away on her bed. "You can come on our next trip, to Scotland."

"Come on, Bree. We have to go pick up Dad."

"I'm ready." Bree picked up her bag and put it on her shoulder, then took one last look around her room.

Claire hated the rush-hour traffic that was already starting to build and knew that getting out of the city would be a nightmare—even more so now that the rain had set in. She threaded the small car in and out of the lanes and waited impatiently for the many traffic lights that were determined to delay her. Finally, she made it to the university, pulled into the car park, and took out her phone.

"Here he comes, Mum!" Bree squealed from the back seat.

Matt Drummond was running down the steps from the administration building and splashing across the rain-soaked car park with his bag over his head. He jumped into the car and slammed the door quickly behind him.

"How's my girls?" he asked and then leaned over to give Claire a kiss.

"We're going to see Granddad," Bree answered him from the back.

"Aye. I know, my wee angel." Matt looked hard at Claire. "Have you had any word?"

Claire nodded instead of answering in case she started to cry. "Charlie rang," she said softly, pulling back onto the road and into the madness of congestion.

"Do you want me to drive?" Matt placed a reassuring hand on her shoulder.

"No, you can take over after we stop for dinner." She smiled weakly back at him.

After the stop-start congestion of the city and suburbs that surrounded it, the journey to the village was an uneventful one. The small family only stopped once when Bree started to complain about being hungry and then got back on the road as soon as possible. Once Matt was in the driver's seat, Claire could relax and take a breath. She remembered the first time Geoff had taken her on this journey. It seemed then that her life had been turned completely upside down.

But that had been nothing compared to her first trip to Scotland, where she thought she was going to be on an ordinary excavation. The discovery of the heritage of The Community was still ongoing, thanks to what she had learned in Scotland, but also of her own heritage and learning the purpose for which she had been born. The Talents that the Guardians of the land had given her still had not found their limits, and sometimes that scared her—just as much as the death of Jack at her hands had. And always in the background—supporting and caring for her—was Uncle Geoff.

She had always hoped that one day he would find love again. He had told her once that he hadn't enough time left to train a new wife. Claire knew this was only an excuse. He had found his love and lost her, and he didn't want a replacement.

Claire looked over to her husband and thought the same thing. How on earth could she replace him? He was so perfect for her, always knowing when she needed extra love, when she needed calm. He made her laugh—a lot—and kept her on an even keel. The day she met him was still so vivid in her mind. The first thing she had noticed about him was his eyes, those beautiful, bright blue eyes.

It was a little bit after nine in the evening when they pulled up outside Geoff Brown's house in the village. The porch light blazed a warm welcome with its golden glow, and a curtain twitched briefly, showing a patch of light from the living room. The door was opened before they even reached the steps, and her Uncle Ben and Aunt Charlie came out to greet them.

Ben pulled Claire into a big hug and welcomed her home, then turned to Matt and shook his hand. Charlie was next, with a warm smile and an even warmer hug, and then she guided her into the hallway, telling one of her tall sons to go get the bags from the car.

"Do you want to go straight up, or do you want a cuppa first?" Charlie asked her softly.

"I'll go up. Matt, can you make sure Bree gets ready for bed?"

"Go on up. Don't worry about a thing, my love." He gave her a kiss and watched as she climbed the stairs to Geoff's room.

Claire hesitated at the door. Taking a deep breath, she opened it quietly. The inside was lit softly by a single lamp at his bedside, and what she saw made her heart break. Geoff, who had been so full of life and vigour, now lay quiet and thin. His breathing was even and shallow, his skin a pallid colour. The full head of hair, which had stubbornly remained mostly dark with a couple of distinguishing bits of grey at the sides, was now almost fully white. His illness had ravaged his body, and he was now so wasted away she nearly didn't recognise him.

A chair had been pulled up to the side of the bed, and Claire sat in it. She held his hand and kissed it, his skin dry and thin like paper under her touch. She brought it up to her forehead and did something she had never done with him before—she sought out his subconscious.

As she had expected, Claire found an orderly and tidy mind. Everything was compartmentalised and in its place. She found him with ease. It was almost as if he had signposted it for her.

"I wondered if you would," Geoff said to her as she entered. He stood before her just as he had been when she was a teenager. Tall, with dark hair and eyes, and a grin from one large ear to another, stretched out under his equally large nose.

"Uncle Geoff!" She ran to him and before he could say no, she hugged him close.

"Claire!" Geoff tried to push her off at first, horrified she had created a permanent bond with him, but she resisted until he hugged her back, wrapping those ever-reassuring arms around her once more. They stayed that way for some time, and by the time she did release him, her face was awash with tears.

"That was a foolish thing to do, Kid," Geoff told her as he held her at arm's length. "But I thank you."

"How are you? Are you in pain?"

"No, I'm fine. I find that I am quite comfortable and happy. It's my time, Kid, and nothing you do is going to stop it."

"I know." She nodded.

"Now, have you brought that little firecracker with you? I would like to see her one last time."

"Bree is with us. She even asked this afternoon if we could come and see you."

"Good. She reminds me so much of you. So full of energy and enthusiasm. And Matt—has he been well, not missing Scotland too much?" Geoff asked, holding onto both of her hands.

"No, he is going back in a couple of months. His mother isn't too good."

"Oh, that's not good. I liked Leana. I'll keep an eye out on the other side for her."

"But you don't believe in God and the afterlife."

"Ahh, a human failing it is to change one's mind when the end is nigh." He laughed, then his mood changed. "There is one thing I would very much like you to do for me before I go."

"Anything, Uncle Geoff. Just name it," Claire promised.

"I would dearly love to see John and Jess one last time. Can you call them here?"

She nodded with another trickle of tears chasing each other down her cheeks. Claire closed her eyes and sent the call into the dark reaches of her own mind, and she heard the answer at once.

On either side of her, a man and a woman materialised. John, her father, was in black, and Jess, her mother, in white. They greeted her with a kiss each and then went to meet Geoff. Claire had to swallow a lump in her throat as she watched them greet each other and stood back to give them some time together.

Sitting on a large green leather chair, Claire waited while they talked until she felt a tug at her mind. She grasped on to it and brought it in, and she found she was holding on to Matt's hand.

"I didn't want to disturb you," he said quietly, taking in the scene before him.

"That's all right, Matt. I was feeling a bit alone." He wrapped his arms around her, both mentally and physically, and she cried into his shoulder.

"Hey, I don't want tears in here, thank you. You'll make everything wet," said Geoff's deep voice, and he grasped Matt's hand and pulled him into a hug. They had become close while they stayed at his family's home in Scotland and had remained just as close when Matt came to New Zealand.

"Thank you for looking after her. Make sure you keep it up. And that gorgeous girl of yours," Geoff told him.

"I will always. I promise," Matt vowed.

"Now, I thank you all for visiting me, but I would very much like to wake up for a second and tell Bree goodnight. John and Jess, I have missed you, and it was a very great privilege and honour to look after your daughter. She has become the daughter of my heart."

"It is us who should be thanking you, Uncle Geoff. You have raised her to be such a fine woman." John shook his hand and hugged him one last time.

"Thank you, Geoff," Jess said and kissed him on the cheek.

"Right—the lot of you, out," he said gruffly, trying to hold back his own tears.

Slowly John and Jess faded out, and Matt gave Geoff another handshake. They spoke no words to each other, just nodded.

Finally it was just Claire once more, and Geoff gathered her up again in his arms. "I meant what I said. You are the daughter I never had, and if you were truly mine, I couldn't have been prouder, Claire."

"I love you, Uncle Geoff, and I am proud to be called your daughter. I am so lucky to have had two fathers who have cared so much for me." She kissed his cheek and then pulled away.

"Go get Bree. I want to see her one last time." Claire felt him push her away and she left, very carefully, and finally detached her mind from his.

Geoff's eyes fluttered open, and Bree was by his side in her pyjamas and ready for bed.

"There she is! How are you, my firecracker?" he asked softly and smiled at her.

"I'm good, Granddad. Are you just about ready to go?" Her voice was very low, almost a whisper.

"I do believe that I am, but I waited till I could see you again." Bree climbed up on the bed and gave him a hug.

"Matt, can you go get Ben and the others? It's nearly time," Claire whispered to her husband. He nodded in reply, gave her shoulder a squeeze, and left to go downstairs.

When Claire turned her attention back to the man who had raised her and the child she loved, she noticed that Bree was whispering something to him. Geoff's eyes widened, and he looked at his granddaughter with surprise and love.

Ben, Charlie, and their two boys, Oliver, and Owen, filed into the room, followed by Matt. Ben sat on the other side of the bed and held his uncle's other hand. Geoff smiled and took one last look around the room at all who were left of his family. Bree, still at his side, rested her head on his shoulder, and he closed his eyes.

His breathing, which had been so shallow when Claire first stepped into the room, now began to falter, and become ragged. They watched over him into the small hours of the morning, until his last breath escaped his lips, and he became still.

"Owen, can you and Oliver take Bree out of the room, please?" Charlie asked her son.

Bree reached up and stroked Geoff's face. "Goodbye, Granddad. I love you." She stood up and went around to Owen and held his hand. Before Bree left the room, she took one last look at Geoff and sighed.

Claire was still holding Geoff's hand in hers, and she didn't want to release it. One of the most important men in her life had just left her for the last time, and she felt that a piece of her heart went with him. Tears coursed down her face and dripped onto her lap. A tissue was produced in front of her, and she took it. Finally she let go of Geoff's hand and laid it gently back on the bed by his side.

Matt was there immediately to gather her up into one of his comforting embraces, holding her gently and letting her cry. He stroked her hair and kissed her head. When she was ready, he led her out of the room and down the stairs, followed by Ben and Charlie.

The bottle of whiskey was produced from its high cupboard in the kitchen, along with some glasses. With a measure each, they raised them in salute to the man who had meant so much to all of them. Bree climbed onto her mother's lap and cuddled in, as she had when she was a baby, and fell asleep.

The next few days were a whirlwind of emotions, endless tasks, and cups of tea. And skipping through it all and giving bright smiles and cuddles was Bree. She made sure that everyone benefitted from her sunny nature. Claire had often observed when she was with her friends that this child could make anyone smile.

The day of the funeral, Bree stuck close to her mother all day. Whenever Claire turned around, there she was, slipping her small hand into her mother's larger one. Claire would instantly feel calmer as she looked into her daughter's beautiful eyes.

It was a simple service. Geoff had insisted on that. He hadn't wanted anything too over-the-top or sad. The elders each got up to speak. Claire thought this would have horrified Geoff, as he had often complained about how long their meetings were each month. Claire couldn't face standing up in front of the large crowd that had gathered in the hall, and she had asked Ben to do the eulogy on behalf of the family.

Ben stood up behind the podium on the stage with a few notes in front of him and cleared his throat. Claire noticed how much he had grown to look like his brother, her father, and reminded herself to tell him. He looked out at the crowd and began. Tales of Geoff from a nephew's perspective garnered laughter from the gathered mourners. Ben spoke eloquently and long, something he seemed to have inherited from his uncle. He touched a little on Geoff's relationship with Claire and their history without going into too many details, which had Claire both grateful and a little teary.

The wake was held in the village hall, and it was full of people. He had touched many lives, and they had come from everywhere to farewell him. But the core was the family, and Claire watched them carefully. The boys were now young men. Owen, Oliver, and Hunter, now nineteen, were all at university. The twins were studying architecture, and Ben had great hopes of them joining his construction company. Hunter was following in his father's footsteps and was studying agriculture. He had declared at the age of twelve that he wanted to take over the farm from his father, much to the horror of his mother. The oldest of Claire's cousins was Jasper, and he had just graduated with honours in teaching.

As she talked to them, she realised how much they were like their parents. Owen had his mother's gentle nature and also her Healing Talent, but he confessed to having a phobia of blood. Oliver was more like his father, ready for a good laugh and a joke. He had the Seek Talent. Hunter had Flight and regaled Claire with his exploits in free running, something he had long loved, having been taught by her. Jasper, now twenty-three and with Light Talent, told her he had had enough of study for a while and was about to embark on his own adventures overseas before taking up his first teaching job.

Adam and Addy and their two children had come from the city the day before, and Claire was glad they had. Their twin boys, Cameron and Dominic, were great friends with Bree, and they took her mind off the serious and sad nature of the gathering. She decided she still had a great and supportive family.

At one point, Claire found herself sitting in the corner alone, watching everyone as they mingled. Beth was there, but now the laughter and smiles were no longer forced. She talked to everyone with ease, so unlike the Beth Claire had first met that night all those years before. And she had a flashback to the welcome party and Jack approaching her.

"Claire? You okay?"

She looked up and found David standing before her. He was her mother's twin brother and a great support to Claire. She had taken to him at once with his easy nature.

"Just going down memory lane," she said and smiled.

He sat down beside her. "A lot has happened."

"It has indeed. How's the farm going?"

"Oh, you know, still the same. I can't wait for Hunter to be finished with his studies so I can take a bit more of a back seat. I thought I might take Beth on a trip to Scotland." He winked and smiled at her.

"Do you think she'll be able to handle all the midges?" Claire asked, trying to suppress a grin.

"She'll be all right. Do you think Gerry, Leana, and Gran would welcome a couple of visitors?"

"I'm sure they would love to see you. They always ask after you and your family. You made quite an impression on them."

"We get a card from them every Christmas. Even though it was such a strange trip, I really enjoyed myself."

Claire spotted Addy and Beth talking. "Are they getting on any better?" she asked him with a small grin.

"No, they still have arguments on how to raise the grandkids. I still can't believe that I am a grandfather!" He laughed at the thought.

"Just remind Beth that her mother-in-law also had small issues with her. That might change things a bit."

"Are you kidding me? That would be like a red rag to a bull. Just keep that nose of yours out of it, Kid." He watched his wife a bit more, then stood. "I'd better get over there and split them up before it gets too heated. Come for lunch tomorrow? I know Beth would love to fuss over you for a bit."

"We will. Thank you, Uncle David." David smiled at Claire. She hadn't called him that in years, and he left her with a warm heart.

The afternoon dragged on, and Claire kept herself occupied by cleaning up cups and plates in between talking to the elders about the work she was carrying out for them. With everyone gone, she shooed out those who had volunteered to help clean up, declaring that she needed a bit of time to herself and would finish cleaning the hall on her own. She asked Matt to take Bree back to the house. He kissed her after making sure she was all right and left her to it.

The kitchenette was scrubbed, and the rubbish bags tied and waiting by the door to go out. Out in the main hall, she held a broom in her hands and started to sweep. It was a great time to be lost in her thoughts in the quiet. Memories of Geoff made her smile and cry in turn. The peace and silence of the large room were just what she needed, having had people constantly around her for the last three days. Her defences were down as she reminisced, and she didn't hear the silent footsteps enter the foyer.

She turned in front of the stage to make the final run down the length of the hall when she saw movement. Standing in the doorway was a tall figure with wavy dark hair, now with the touches of time showing, and dark brown eyes that stared at her with such intensity.

"Hello, Claire."

"What are you doing here?" Claire asked.

"I came to give you my condolences." He started to walk towards her slowly.

"I don't think you should come any further, Tony." She leaned on the broom as she watched him get closer.

"I really am sorry for your loss, Claire, for all your losses." Tony stopped and never took his eyes off her.

"Have you been following me all this time?"

"No, I took your advice. I got a job overseas and got back about a month ago. I've only checked up on you once since I returned."

Claire gave him a small smile. "I'm pleased to hear that. And have you gotten over your obsession?"

"I did hope so, but then I read that Geoff died and I found myself halfway out the door to come see you. You seem to be a hard habit to break."

"Maybe you need to go see someone, get some therapy for it."

"Oh, I did that too. I ended up in a relationship with her, and she accused me of transference and then broke up with me. So even that didn't work." He chuckled.

"You're a hopeless case, then."

"Probably. Or maybe I'm just crap with women."

"So, you couldn't just stay away, stop yourself from coming all this way. A card would have done."

He stepped closer to her involuntarily. "I needed to see for myself that you were okay. No matter how hard I try, I still care very deeply for you."

"Ah! You said care, not love," she told him. "There is a difference."

"Yes, there is, but I try not to say it, because if I do…" He trailed away. He was closer now, and Claire did nothing to stop him.

"Your daughter is beautiful."

"Stay away from her, Tony," she told him darkly.

"Don't worry, I'm not interested in her." He smiled down at her. He was close enough to touch her now. "I still remember that night—it haunts my dreams. That kiss."

"This is not helping." She took a step back from him, unsure whether he would hurt her. Slowly she gathered her energy around her and held it in place, ready for anything.

"No, it's not." He ran a hand through his thick, wavy hair. "Look, my offer is still there. If you ever need me for anything, call me."

"I threw the card away. I found it when we were moving," Claire told him.

He pulled his phone from his pocket, dialled a number, and waited. Over by the wall, Claire could hear her phone ringing. She turned automatically to answer it before realising that he had her number already. She turned back to him.

"Hi, Claire. Just a gentle reminder that I am still around." He hit the *End* button on his phone and put it back in his pocket. "There you are. You have my number now. I told you I will always keep tabs on you."

"Are you ever going to stop this?"

"Probably not. If I haven't by now, what's the point?"

"I'd like you to leave, Tony." She carried on sweeping down the hall and when she reached the end, she turned to find he had followed her.

"You are still the most beautiful woman in the world, Claire. Matt is a very lucky man. I hope he realises how lucky he is."

She stood up straight. To her, it sounded like he was threatening her husband. "He does. Every day he tells me how much he loves me and how lucky he is, and I tell him the same right back."

"Good. Because I have tried everything in my power to break you two up, and not once has he taken the bait." He had a grin on his face that made Claire very uneasy.

"Please leave—before I do something I might regret."

"Remember, Claire, I was on that hilltop as well that night. The Talents given to me by the Guardians are still with me. I think we would be very evenly matched."

"Why stand there and throw veiled threats at me, then? Why try to scare me?" Claire asked him, feeling her anger build.

"I'm sorry if I have. It was never my intention."

"Well, you did. You have said what you wanted to say. There is nothing more to talk about." She leaned the broom up against the wall. When she turned back, it was to find him standing only inches from her.

Stepping back hurriedly, Claire tripped over the broom and started to fall. He grabbed her, wrapping his arms around her body, standing her up on her feet once more. She looked up into his eyes and had a hard job pulling away—from both his gaze and his touch—but finally she did both and moved out of his embrace.

"Please, just go," she begged him quietly.

"I think I should," Tony replied. He turned, and Claire watched him leave the hall. He stopped at the door and looked back at her. "I know you were looking at my arse." He smiled and left, his chuckle of laughter floating back to her.

Claire stood staring at the doorway and shook her head, a wry smile tugged involuntarily at her lips. Her own parting words the last time she had talked to him came floating back to her. *Walk away, Tony…stop watching me. My arse isn't that great!*

She finished cleaning, turned the lights off, and headed out of the hall, shutting the door behind her. Out in the cool wintry air, she shivered and pulled her jacket around her more tightly. She hoped the walk would help get rid of any thoughts of Tony that remained. Just the thought of him made her look around. She could feel him still near and reached out with her mind.

Having already been inside his mind once before made it easy for her to gain access again. She walked through the various compartments, looking for one particular part. When she found it, Claire noticed that it had changed slightly. The white filigree box with golden coils was now very glossy and slightly larger. Slowly she felt the surface. It was warm and slick, and she trailed her hand around it.

"Now who is intruding on whose life?" his rich voice spoke from beside her. "And how did you get in here?"

"I just wanted to see it again, and it is amazing what I can do now. I can access any part of you that I wish, not just your brain. If I wanted, I could stop your heart. If you wanted, I could make you stop loving me."

"But I don't want that, Claire. I would rather you stopped my heart. But I know you. I know that you could not hurt me in any way. You proved it on the hill that night. In your own way, you love me."

"Please leave the village. Don't stay." Claire withdrew her thoughts from his and walked down the street. The wind was starting to pick up and the moon was rising over the hill. From behind her, she heard a car starting and then driving down the road in the opposite direction. She listened to it leave with a tear in her eye.

Chapter Two

"Mum, are you going to wake up? It's just about time to take me to school," Bree's urgent voice finally cut through the darkness that was Claire's mind. She opened her eyes and saw her daughter beside her, dressed already, with her backpack on. Looking over at the bedside clock, she saw that it was indeed late. She sat up with a jolt and swung her legs over the side of the bed.

It had been two weeks since she arrived back from the village. It had taken her a little while after the funeral to wind up her uncle's affairs and shut the house up. He had left it to her in his will, but she didn't really want it. It had always been his house, and it would always remain his in her mind.

"Come on, Mum. We have to go." Bree caught Claire's hands in her own tiny ones and pulled her up.

"I'm up, Bree. Let me get dressed and I'll walk you to school." She let her daughter's hands go and shooed her out of the room. The clock ticked loudly in the silence, and she quickly dressed in the first items of clothing she could find: an old paint-smeared sweatshirt and running pants. Since she had come home, this was the way it was. Nights full of dreams and nightmares and days groggy with lack of sleep.

She grabbed the keys off the hall table, pulled on her jacket, and called out to Bree, "I'm ready. Let's go."

Bree walked down the hall and opened the front door. She stood outside on the doormat waiting for her mother to follow. When she didn't, Bree came back in and took her hand.

"Mum, it's okay. The dream is gone."

Claire looked down into Bree's blue eyes and smiled. She cleared her head and took a deep breath. They left the house together, and Claire locked the door behind them. The audible click of the lock shifting into place was also a mental trigger, shutting away the images in her head for the day. They set off together down the street, hand in hand. Bree walked carefully beside her mother instead of her usual skipping.

"Mum, the dreams won't last for very much longer," Bree said, almost in a whisper.

"What dreams? Are you having bad dreams, Bree?" Claire asked.

"No, you are. I can hear them sometimes when you're really tired."

"How can you hear my dreams? They're in my head." Claire looked at her daughter carefully. "Bree, can you do other things?"

"Like what?"

"Do you see things that are going to happen before they do?"

"You mean like Gran and Granny can?"

"Yes, like Gran and Granny."

Bree started to swing their linked hands. "Sometimes. I knew we had to go see Granddad, and I also know we have to go and see Gran."

This news shocked Claire a little bit, and she slowed her child down so they had a bit more time to talk about it before they reached the school gates.

"Gran is sick, and Dad is going to go see her soon. But we aren't going over to Scotland."

"We will have to when she dies," she said sadly.

These words sent a chill up Claire's spine, and she wondered what else Bree saw. How much did she know? They reached the gates in silence, and she kissed her head. "Have a fun day, sweetheart. I'll be right here at the end of the day."

"No, you won't, silly! Aunty Addy will be picking me up today." Bree smiled at her mother, then turned and skipped through the gates without a backward glance.

Claire walked home with Bree's words spinning in her head. This was not normal behavior for a six-year-old child. If she did have Foresight, then how was it that she had developed the Talent so early? A child didn't usually develop their Talents until between the ages of ten and thirteen, depending on when they went into puberty. She knew this as fact after making a study of it—not only when she was learning her own Talents, but more recently for the Elders.

As she opened the door, she heard her cell phone ring from the bedroom, and she ran to pick it up. It was not like her to leave it there. It was normally firmly entrenched in her pocket.

"Hello?"

"Claire, hi. It's Addy."

"Hello, you…what's up?" Claire asked, sitting on the bed.

"I was wondering if you would like to have a girly day out—you know, go get our nails done, have some lunch, and get a facial. What do you think? My treat."

"That sounds like heaven, but I have a lot of work to catch up on. My desk is piled high with papers."

"That sounds like an excuse to me. Plus, Matt rang and asked me to get you out of the house for a while."

"He what?"

"He—like the rest of us—are just a little concerned since Geoff passed. You haven't been sleeping or eating, and he just wanted you to have a bit of fun."

Claire was silent for a while. She didn't like it when people started to organise her life—even if that person was her husband. But there was a kernel of truth to what Addy had said. She had become withdrawn, and she hadn't touched the work on her desk for over a week.

"All right. Where do you want me to meet you?" Claire asked in concession.

"No need. I'm just about to leave and come get you. I'll be there soon."

Addy hung up the phone, and Claire looked at it in her hand. Sighing heavily, she knew she should get up and get ready. Instead, her gaze shifted, and she stared out the window into the street beyond. Rain was now pouring down in great sheets, and small drops splattered on the windows. She watched the trails of water as they slid down the great panes, gaining speed as they went.

The slide into her own mind was so easy, she didn't really know it had happened until she found herself wandering around looking at her life, pigeonholed and boxed in. The aspects she loved most were the biggest—her family, her daughter, and her husband. The blackness that had descended over her was colouring these things with a dark grey shadow that she knew shouldn't be there.

Slowly she walked on, past the glittering orb that was the mainstay of her Talents, and into the surrounds of her subconscious. Immediately she was greeted by her parents, and she felt their love emanating from them and enveloping her.

"It's normal to feel like this, Claire. You've had a bad time of it lately," John told his daughter calmly and carefully.

"It will pass, sweetheart. But you must help it go. You need to remember to set your defences up at night to guard against these nightmares you've been having," Jess told Claire, her hand smoothing her hair from her face.

"I can't remember what they are. It's just feelings of anguish and hatred. I don't know where they're coming from."

"You won't know until you calm your mind and really look hard at it. But it's not the time for that now. You need to leave and go back to the real world, Claire," Jess said kindly.

"Addy is at the door," John told her with a smile. "Enjoy your day. Go have some fun."

Her parents let her go and pushed her gently back to herself. From where Claire sat on the bed, she heard the doorbell pealing its tune throughout the house. She went and answered it. Addy stood there like a brilliant rose amidst the stormy morning.

"You took your time," Addy said as she stepped into the house, looking Claire up and down before greeting her with a kiss. "You are not wearing that, Claire. I refuse to be seen with you in that sweatshirt. Have you showered today, or even yesterday?" She wrinkled her nose.

"I'm not sure," Claire said, shutting the door on the nasty weather that had blown in.

"Right. You go have a shower, and I'll put some coffee on and then pick an outfit for you to wear. Come on. We don't have all day! Our first appointment is in an hour." She shooed Claire into the bathroom and set about the tasks she had laid out for herself.

When Claire emerged fifteen minutes later, freshly showered and dressed in the clothes her best friend had chosen for her, she felt a bit better. Addy always had taken charge with things that needed to be done, without any fuss or hopes of recognition.

"Much better. Now a quick cup of coffee to get you going, and we will be on our way." She pushed a cup across the bench to Claire with a smile.

Claire picked up the white mug that contrasted brightly against the dark swirling contents and took a sip, wincing at the bitterness of it. If there was one thing that Addy did not do well, it was make coffee. But Claire drank it all, grateful that her husband's cousin had taken the trouble to do this for her.

They left for the day, and Claire managed to pull herself up a bit out of the gloom that had come to surround her. It wasn't hard. Addy had always made her laugh, and she had a sense of humour like Matt's. By the time they got back home, Claire was feeling a lot better. There was a lightness in her spirit that hadn't been there for a while, and she hoped it would last.

"Oh look, Claire. Someone has sent you flowers," Addy said as she pulled up the drive.

Sitting on the doormat was a beautiful bunch of the brightest yellow roses she had ever seen. She jumped out of the car and picked them up. A note was attached, and Claire was just about to open it when Addy came up behind her.

"Well, what does it say?" Addy plucked the note from the cellophane wrapper and read it out loud. "*Because you need them.* Oh my God, Matt is so lovely. I have to remind Adam to get me flowers."

"Matt has never bought me flowers. I don't even think he knows that yellow roses are my favourite." She opened the door and put them on the bench, then took her phone out.

"Hello, my darling. How are you?" Matt's voice said in her ear.

"I'm good today. Did you send me these beautiful yellow roses?" she gushed.

"Roses? I didn't send you roses. I asked Addy to cheer you up by taking you out, but I didn't send you flowers. I know you don't usually like cut flowers in the house."

"So, you didn't send them? I wonder who did."

"Maybe it was someone else in the family. I know they've been worried since Geoff passed."

"That's probably it. I'll see you when you get home. Addy is still here, so I'd better get her a decent cuppa before she starts to make it."

Matt's chuckle echoed down the line to her and made her smile. "See you in a few hours. Love you."

"I love you, too." She ended the call and put her phone on the counter. Addy was already placing the roses in a vase of water, and she then carried them along with the small card to the dining table.

"So, it wasn't Matt, then. Maybe you have a secret admirer." She raised her eyebrow at Claire and smirked.

"God, no. You saw the state of me this morning. Who would want that?" Claire laughed and started to make a cup of tea.

"Well, obviously someone does—otherwise he wouldn't have called me so worried. I haven't asked you all day, but now I am going to. What is going on with you, Claire? This is more than Geoff passing away, isn't it?"

Claire was silent for a moment as she laid out the cups and placed tea bags in them. "I'm not sure. I'm having these dreams, but they don't seem to be normal. And before you ask, I can't remember what they are. They're just fleeting images. But I do feel anger and longing, like something has been taken from me." Claire shook her head, trying to rid herself of them once more.

"Have you—you know, gone in to see?" Addy pointed to her head.

"No, I haven't. I might try, though. I'm at my wits' end. I have to do something, Addy, otherwise, I'm not going to be any good for anyone. Especially with Matt about to go back to see Leana. The thought of being like this and having to look after Bree by myself is not sitting well with me. Even running isn't doing anything."

"You could do it this afternoon. I'll watch over you if you like," Addy suggested.

The jug clicked off as it came to a boil, and Claire poured the hot liquid over the tea bags in the cups, watching the water darken as it revived the dry tea leaves within. She pushed the cup and milk to Addy for her to finish it off.

"Would you? What about your boys? Don't you have to pick them up?"

"Adam can get them. He loves using them as an excuse to get out of work. I was worried before we had the boys that Adam would be working so much, he wouldn't see them at all. But he's the complete opposite—he can't get enough of them. It's like I have three kids and not two." Addy looked carefully at Claire. "So, are you and Matt going to have another?"

"It's not like we aren't trying. If it happens, it happens. If it doesn't, then we were only meant to have one. It's not something Matt and I have really discussed. Though I'm sure he would like a soccer team." She sipped her tea and they went to sit at the table.

She picked up the card that Addy had placed by the vase. A flash of an image appeared in front of her. Dark eyes full of concern. Then it was gone. Claire dropped the card in an instant and sat back in her seat, taking a quick glimpse at Addy, hoping that her friend hadn't been watching. She let out a breath of relief when she saw Addy was on her phone, tapping out a text.

The hot liquid from her cup burnt her mouth as it slipped down her throat, and she placed it back on the table. She played with the handle and thought about what she had just seen. It was not the first time she'd wondered if he had placed devices in her home. She knew that he'd had no hesitation in invading her privacy and breaking in before when she lived in the apartment.

"Right. I'm all yours this afternoon. You go do whatever it is you need to do, and I will pick Bree up from school," Addy told her with a bright smile, putting down her phone and picking up her cup.

"You know, she told me this morning that you would be. I didn't believe her."

"Bree said I would be picking her up? How did she know?"

"I think there is something very special about my daughter. You talk to her on the way home and see if you can see it. I have a sneaking suspicion that she's been on this earth before." Claire smiled as she gave voice to what her instincts already knew.

"I will. You have piqued my curiosity. Now, go lie down or whatever you need to do." Addy shooed her away, and Claire did as she was told.

Retreating into her mind, she shied away from her subconscious and her parents, instead heading straight for Crystal. The orb was shining and pulsing with a soft golden light that seemed to dance on the surface and then retreat inside, only to bloom out again on another area of her crystalline features.

"Hello, Crystal," she called to it.

"Hello, Claire. We are not well now, are we?"

"No, we are not. Do we know what is causing it? We want to try and fix it once and for all."

"There could be a couple reasons why we are not feeling ourselves at the moment. One is the loss of our uncle. The other is the disturbance in our dreams, caused by an unknown outside force."

"Where is this force coming from? Do we have any idea?" Claire had found over the years it was easier just to use the collective instead of the individual with Crystal. No matter how many times she had asked it to stop, it always resumed the next time she talked to it.

"That is something we must search for. The tools are at our command. The ones we require are over there." A light shone from one of the compartments Crystal had first made when she entered Claire's mind. Grown from a tear shed by her mother, Crystal had formed and become stronger with the knowledge the Guardians had imparted to her.

Claire turned and walked towards it. There was nothing physical or tangible in the box. It was a metaphor for her to grasp on to, a way of sorting the thoughts she needed before she took on the new information and put it to use.

Slowly she released the information to reach out into her mind. It raced around until it found the right place to do its work from. The knowledge crept into her being, and she immediately knew how to work it. Claire then sought out her dream place and pushed her way into it, past the luminescent barrier that held it.

Swirling emotions and colours whizzed past her, jumbled, and scrambled—not true dreams, just snatches of them. She walked around, looking at each until she found what she was looking for. It was dark, made of up of coalescing black, white, and grey colours, and each time she stepped towards it, it would dance away just out of reach. Following it was getting frustrating for her. It was not a good feeling to have, as it only made the other half-formed dreams move faster than they already were.

Claire stopped and waited. She held out her hand and watched as it passed through the myriad of colours that moved about her. The intense feelings that went with each dream swamped her—joy, anger, elation, depression, the extremes toyed with her hand—until the one she wanted closed in and enveloped her arm. She clamped her hand on it and held it fast.

Peering deep inside, Claire hoped to find what it was that was causing it. The flashes of faces, too quick to understand, assaulted her, trying to break free of her grasp. She held it still with her other hand, and with all her strength she pushed on the monochrome orb, crushing, and crumpling it up until it was a small ball sitting in her palm. The colours swirled angrily, and she could feel it trying to reach out to something or someone. Slowly, she encapsulated it in a ball of light and let it float in the middle of the dream space. Claire watched it hang in place as the other dreams kept their distance, skirting around it as if they were afraid it would still infect them.

Walking back to Crystal, she started to feel the effects already. It was like a dark, stormy night had given way to the beautiful, clear blue sky of morning. Everything felt fresh and clean once more. She stood by Crystal and placed a hand on her glittering facets.

"We feel it already," the orb told her.

"Yes, we do. So much better. We thank you, Crystal."

"We are welcome, Claire."

With Crystal's words still echoing through her presence, Claire left her mind and opened her eyes to the real world to be greeted by Bree's small face, and she smiled.

"Hello, Mum. Welcome back," she said softly.

"Hello, Bree. How was school today?" She lifted her daughter onto the bed with her and snuggled her in close.

"It was good. But I got teased when I said something was going to happen and it did."

"Ah, well, you see, they don't understand, Bree. If they think someone is a little bit different, they pick it up. We have already told you that you come from a special family and that no one can know about the Talents. You can't ever let them see that you have these Talents."

"Even if it means that someone is going to get hurt?" she asked, a little wide-eyed.

"Even if it means someone gets hurt. Unfortunately, sometimes we have to keep things from people—but you don't have to with me or Dad, or anyone else in our family."

"Okay. I won't say anything again." Bree gave a small sigh. "Does that also mean that I can't talk to Mr. Man again?"

"Mr. Man? Why, does he have a Talent?"

"Yes, he does, but he isn't family."

"Ah, but he is special. He is your friend, and if he has a Talent, then it's all right to talk to him. Is he here now?" Claire looked around the room.

"No, silly. He isn't here. I'll tell him you looked for him. He will laugh and laugh." She giggled.

"We can't stay here, young lady, especially if you're going to giggle like that in my ear." Claire sat up and deposited her daughter on the floor beside her.

They walked back out to the lounge and found Addy sitting reading a magazine. She looked up at the pair of them and smiled.

"She's back!" She stood and gave Claire a hug. "I can see it in your eyes—you've done it."

"It's managed for now. I can't quite get rid of it totally, but I hope I have isolated the problem." She smiled at Addy.

"In that case, I'll be going home now and taking advantage of all my boys being together." Addy picked up her bag, and Claire walked her to the door. "By the way, I did talk to Bree on the way back. There is something distinctly different about her, isn't there?"

"I'm pleased I'm not the only one to see it. Whenever I try to bring the subject up with Matt, he refuses to talk about it."

"He would. I wouldn't worry about it, Claire. She is your daughter, after all." Addy gave her one of her winks and left.

The following two weeks passed more peacefully in the Drummond household, with lots of laughter and happiness. Claire managed to catch up on her work and look after Bree and Matt both. The yellow roses faded and were soon confined to the rubbish bin, never to be thought of again, she hoped. But she was not looking forward to Matt leaving them to go to visit his mother, and whenever they were together, she wanted to be as close to him as possible.

"Okay, this is getting a little ridiculous, Claire," he said one night after dinner when the dishes had been done and they were sitting comfortably on the couch. Regardless of what he had just said, he put his arm around her and pulled her closer to him. "What's up?"

"I miss you already. I just want to get as much cuddle time in as possible," she told him.

"I won't be gone long—only two weeks." Matt kissed the top of her head as she laid it on his chest. "Or have you seen something?"

"No, I haven't. You know I don't like using that."

"I know. I'm just teasing." He held her close and worried. Her depressive episode was still in the forefront of his mind. "How about we pull Bree out of school for a couple of weeks and you both come with me?"

"We can't. She's already missed a week of school this term. But it was a lovely idea." She raised her head and gave Matt a kiss, which lingered. His head came down to meet hers and he enfolded her in his arms, pressing her to him.

The same feeling Claire had when she first kissed him came to the fore and she fell into their love, giving herself completely to this man who had not only captured her heart but now was its keeper. He lifted her up off the couch and carried her to their bedroom, kicking the door shut behind them. Carefully he laid her on the bed and joined her there.

So gentle and tender was their joining, his lingering touch sent shivers through her as he caressed her. Their bodies already entwined, Claire joined their minds in that secret and safe place where they shared themselves completely.

Once spent, they lay in each other's arms, still connected in their minds, and just enjoyed being together. Claire sighed contentedly, and he pulled her even closer.

"I remember that first time by the stones, but I also remember the very first time you brought me here," he said dreamily into her ear, referring to their mind sharing.

"So do I, and it keeps getting better and better," she whispered back.

"Claire, my love, I have wanted to ask you a question for a while now, but I haven't found the perfect moment to ask it."

"Ask it." She turned in his arms and faced him.

"Please don't get mad, but I need to know. Do you think those flowers—the yellow roses—do you think that HE sent them?" Claire could see that he was afraid to ask it, afraid of what the answer was, and afraid of her reaction.

"I think he may have. But I don't love him. I love you— always and forever, remember."

"I know, but I can't help worrying. He won't leave you alone, and sometimes that scares me. My imagination runs away with me when I think that he could hurt you, hurt us. Especially now that I'm leaving soon."

"Nothing he does or could ever do could hurt us, Galen." The use of his real name pleased him, and he smiled. It was almost as if she was committing herself to him all over again.

"What on earth did I do to deserve you?" He pushed a lock of hair off her face and kissed her again.

"Whatever it was, keep doing it, because I never want to leave this bed ever again." She moved closer to him and tucked her head under his chin, drinking in his smell and his comforting presence.

All too soon, the days ran out and Claire was driving Matt to the airport. There had already been a tearful farewell with Bree before she left for school that morning. He promised that he would be back soon, and she carefully corrected him and told her father that she would see him in Scotland. Claire could see him starting to anger at this, and she told him to ignore it. She hoped that he had.

"You've got your passport and tickets?" Claire asked as she drove through the traffic around the bays.

"Yep, and I have my book. Stop fussing."

"It's my job to fuss, Mr. Drummond."

"I know, Mrs. Drummond, but there is no need. I have done this once or twice before."

"I know." She stopped at the lights and waited, tapping her fingers on the steering wheel.

"Why are you so on edge?" Matt asked with a little concern.

"I don't know. We've done this many times, and yet this is the first time I feel nervous. Stupid, isn't it."

"Just a bit. You don't have anything to worry about. I will ring you the second I get to Glasgow."

The light turned green, and Claire moved off and turned the corner to the airport. They reached the set down and pickup lane, and Claire parked. She had wanted to park and go in with him and wait till he had to go through customs, but Matt hated paying for parking and told her to just drop and run. She got out of the car as he grabbed his bags and then kissed him soundly.

"I love you," she told him earnestly.

"I know. I love you, too. I'll call as soon as I can." He kissed her once more and then headed into the terminal.

Claire got back into the car and left the airport, not looking forward to the drive home. As she waited at the lights to turn back onto the road that ran along the bays, she noticed a dark-coloured car behind her. She shook her head and told herself she was being silly.

For a week, Bree and Claire muddled along together, forming their own routine to fill the days. They both missed the male presence of the house, and Bree tried to make her mother laugh with tales of Mr. Man.

In the early hours one morning, Claire woke with a jerk as the telephone rang by her head. She fumbled with the light and answered it. "Hello," she croaked.

"Claire, it's Matt."

"Sweetheart, is everything okay?"

"No. Mum's gone. She died about an hour ago."

"Oh, Matt, I'm sorry. Are you…no, of course you're not okay. We'll come over straight away."

"Please, I need you. I need you both." Claire could hear the tears in his voice and wished she was there.

"We'll be there soon, sweetheart. I'll make the flight bookings as soon as I get off the phone. Go be with your father. You need each other more now."

"I will. I love you." He hung up before she got a chance to say it back, and she sat on the edge of the bed. Getting up, she grabbed her dressing gown and pulled it on against the cold night before padding her way barefoot to the study and her computer. The cell phone was still in her hand, and she almost dropped it when it began to ring and vibrate again.

"Claire, it's Adam. Hey, I'm so sorry about Leana. Robbie's just called. Now, I don't want you to worry about a thing. I have already made a call and have hired a private jet for us all."

"Adam, don't be ridiculous. You don't need to do that," Claire protested.

"Of course I do, and it's already done. It'll be faster, and I have all this money, so why not use it for something good? I'm not taking no for an answer. Just be ready to be picked up around ten in the morning. We should be winging our way out of New Zealand by twelve, hopefully."

"All right…you've twisted my arm. I'll be ready, boss."

"See you in the morning. Go back to bed and get some sleep," Adam told her, knowing full well that she wouldn't.

"Yeah, right. See you at ten." She hung up on him and went to the closet to get some suitcases out.

Claire spent the remaining hours until nine packing for both herself and Bree. Her daughter got up early and gave her mother a hug. Claire felt that it was her way of saying *See; I was right*. She told her to go pack some things to do on the plane.

After an urgent phone call to Bree's school explaining the need for her to be away for a couple of weeks and another to their neighbour, asking to keep an eye on the place, Claire was ready. They were dressed, packed, and waiting by the door when two cars pulled up outside.

Adam, with his long stride, was at the door in no time—with a smile, hug, and kiss for them both. Her childhood best friend and ex-boyfriend remained a very good friend. She was grateful he was there for her at that moment and was also glad for his strong arms to carry the bags out to the car. Claire and Bree hopped into the rear car, and they were whisked away to the airport in style.

With only a couple of stopovers for fuel, they were soon landing in Glasgow amidst a beautifully sunny late summer's day. Hire cars were already waiting for them when they left the airport, and they drove the well-worn trip to the house nestled in the arms of the valley. Claire followed Addy and Adam, feeling like she was home again in the wonderfully rugged countryside of Scotland.

The ford stood in their way as they turned from the main road, and Claire felt even more relaxed once she had crossed it. Adam drove on, and Claire made her way a bit more cautiously, especially with the large old oak coming up.

"Mum, can we stop by Breena's tree?" Bree called to her mother from the back seat.

"Why not? Dad will understand." Claire smiled at her daughter in the rearview mirror.

Claire stopped the car just before they reached the tree, and Bree hopped out. She walked slowly to the trunk of the old oak and placed a hand on it. A feeling of recognition was emanating from the tree. Claire watched her daughter closely and remembered another little girl with the same hair and eyes standing under the same tree, and she smiled.

Bree climbed back into the car, and they drove up the track to the house. She could see Matt waiting for them. The sight of him took Claire's breath away. He looked so tired and sad, but he managed a smile and raised his hand in greeting to her.

The driver's door was open as soon as she had put the handbrake on, and Claire quickly turned the car off. Untangling herself from the seat belt, she leapt out the door and ran the short distance to him, wrapping her arms around him.

"How's my girls?" Matt asked into her hair, a catch in his voice. She hugged him harder until he complained he couldn't breathe.

Then Gran was there, still upright and unbent, healthy and hale for her age. She had a worn smile on her face as she greeted her great-granddaughter first. Taking Bree's small face in her hands, she kissed her forehead.

Matt picked up his daughter and held her close. She reached up and placed a hand on his cheek. "I missed you, Daddy."

"I missed you, too, my wee angel." He carried her into the house with his arm around his wife, where the rest of the family were waiting.

Robbie and Fiona greeted them as they walked into the living room, and Robbie's face went white when he saw Bree. Claire saw her daughter put a finger to her lips to quieten him, and he looked at Claire with a raised eyebrow. Gerry gave Claire a kiss and took Bree from Matt's arms.

"Granda, I have something for you. I drew a picture on the way here," Bree told him.

"That's all right, lass. You can give it to me later. I just want a cuddle with my best girl." He sat with her on his lap, and she snuggled in to his shoulder. Claire was busy with the talk in the room, and when she next looked over, Bree was fast asleep.

The next morning, Claire woke and had to remember where she was: lying on a mattress on the floor of the living room with Matt snoring softly at her side, his arm resting over the top of her. She moved closer to him, enjoying the warmth of his body against her, and closed her eyes again. It was but a moment or two before she heard the door open and soft footsteps come into the room.

"Daddy," Bree whispered softly. Claire waited to see what she wanted, knowing that when she failed to wake her father, she would come around to her.

"Daddy, you have to wake up," she said a bit louder. There was still no response from Matt. "Daddy, wake up!" She was pushing on him now and her voice was a normal pitch.

"Mmm…what is it, Bree?" he mumbled back to her.

"We have to go up to the stones," Bree told him.

Matt rolled over and looked at his daughter and then at his watch. Claire opened an eye.

"Bree, it's five in the morning. We are not going anywhere. Go back to bed," Matt told his daughter.

"Dad, we have to be up there before the sun rises. Please get up. Mum is already awake." She looked at Claire and smiled. "Instead of walking, can we take the other way?"

Matt turned to look at Claire. "Do you know what she is going on about?"

"No idea. But I get the feeling we should." Claire had a faraway look in her eye and could feel the pull of the stones.

"I'm not going to get any more sleep, am I?" he asked no one in particular as he sat up. "Go wait in the kitchen, Bree, so we can get dressed. I hope you didn't wake Gran."

"No, Granny is still asleep." Bree left them alone, and they both started to dress.

"What is it with these damn stones? Normally when we come home, you two are off up there straight away," Matt complained as he pulled a jumper over his head.

"I think you are about to find out," Claire told him and slipped on some shoes.

Outside, the predawn light was marching across the sky, the air was cool and clean, and Claire breathed in deeply the faint smell of heather and earth. Matt picked Bree up and pushed off the ground, rising high and hovering, waiting for

Claire to join them. Together, they flew to the hill and rose up beside the tumbling spring, the water forming white ribbons as it descended the steep and rocky side.

At the top, Claire landed lightly beside the big rock that hid the stones and rounded it. She had been back many times since that horrible night, but what she had to do then still haunted her.

The stones stood proudly as they had for many eons, thrusting up from the earth and covered in lichen. They hummed to Claire their collective energy, and she reached out to touch one of the entrance stones. Underneath her hand, it was cold and smooth, but she felt the energy flow into her and smiled.

Matt reached her side and put Bree back on the ground. On impulse, Claire clasped his hand in hers and looked deeply into his eyes. Immediately the stones recognised him and welcomed him with their song. Matt's eyes widened as he felt what Claire had felt the first time she touched the stones. Bree took his other hand and then placed her free one on the opposite entrance stone just as the first ray of sunshine hit the tops of the circle.

In that orange glow, figures emerged, one for each space between the stones and all facing the centre. They wore long, dark robes with hoods covering their faces, and they were chanting. Their arms raised up and pointed inwards as they slowly moved together into the centre, the chanting reaching its crescendo, until only one stood before the family.

"Welcome, Galen; welcome, Breena; welcome, Carling," the figure spoke and gestured them into the circle.

Hand in hand, they walked together at a measured pace till they reached the robed figure. They joined hands and formed their own circle as the sun rose higher on the horizon.

"Galen, you can now see what has been hidden." A bony, white hand raised up over Matt's head, and he looked at his daughter. He thought at first that he was seeing double as another girl stood behind Bree. As he watched, the other child grew before his eyes, and in her place was a beautiful young woman—one he had seen before, but always thought was a figment of his imagination.

"Galen." This woman smiled at him. "Do you not remember me?"

"I...I...I don't know," he stammered and looked at Claire to see if she was seeing the same thing.

"Carling, my sister. I have missed you." Her hands were resting on Bree's slight shoulders, and their daughter looked from her mother to her father.

"Galen, this is Breena." Claire managed to gain his eye. "The Guardians granted her this when she joined them. She helped me that night and I sent her to you when I fled."

"I don't understand," he told Claire.

"I will leave you now. Breena, your time here is short." The hooded figure moved to the entrance of the stones and vanished as it passed through.

"My brother, is it so hard to remember that night? I came to you and told you to wait, even though I disagreed with Carling on her decision."

"I thought you a figment of my imagination," he told her. "Is that really you?"

"Yes, Galen." She moved to her brother, and he let go of little Bree's hand and then Claire's to take his sister's.

Claire stood with her daughter and watched the reunion as it played out in front of her. Once Matt had stopped staring at Breena, he gathered her up in his arms and held her close.

"When you passed over, I thought that was the last time I would see you. I don't know how this is possible," he said into her long, flowing hair.

"It is possible because this is what I asked for." She broke the embrace and held on to his hands. "There is information I need to pass on to you to help you in the next few days."

Breena looked over at Claire and her niece. "I'm sorry, Carling, but your task is not yet finished. This time it will take you far and wide to complete it."

Claire's heart sank at this news. "What is it that I must do?"

"It will be revealed to you by one who is close to you," Breena told her. "My little one." She smiled at her niece. "You have your own task. This is why some of your Abilities have already started to bud. Galen, my brother, the Guardians have granted certain gifts to you to get you through what is to come."

"What are these tasks, Breena? What is it that we must do?" Matt asked her.

"I cannot tell you that—but remember, whatever happens, you are a family and are connected."

"I need to know something, Breena. Are you part of our daughter? Because sometimes I see you in her eyes," Claire asked.

"Yes, a small part." She smiled cheekily. "And that is only possible because of what you and Matt did that morning— when you joined for the first time in the entrance of the standing stones."

Matt looked at his wife and they both blushed. Claire reclaimed her husband's hand and stood with their daughter. Breena's demeanor changed.

"Tomorrow, at our mother's funeral, I need you and Claire to stay behind after everyone has left. She has a message for you. It was something she saw before she died, and she cannot pass on until she has told you."

"Why can't we see her now?" Matt asked.

"She must complete this task first before she can join us here at this sacred spot," Breena told her brother and looked at the position of the sun. "I must go now and prepare Mum for tomorrow. She's not in pain anymore, Galen," she said quietly as she ran to the small family and hugged them one more time.

They watched her turn and walk through the entrance of the circle and disappear. The sun now hit the centre of the stone circle, and the day was warming. A small wind blew around them, bringing with it a cleansing breath of air. Matt was stunned by what had happened and could still feel the stones singing to him.

"Is this what it is like for you when you come up here?" he asked Claire.

"The stones or Breena visiting?" Claire asked back, taking hold of their daughter's hand, and leading them out of the circle.

"Both, I suppose."

"That's the first time I have seen her since that night," Claire said quietly, her words seeming to float on the breeze. Once outside, she let go of their hands and made a circuit of the stones, touching each one in turn. "As for the stones, yes. They pull at me and feed me their energy. They help to heal and cleanse me. It's very hard to ignore them sometimes when I am back at the house, but I try my hardest to. I know if I spend too much time up here, I feel like I will be lost to them. My own energy will be fed back into them, and I would only exist with the Guardians." She stopped and faced her family once more.

Matt could now understand the faraway look that she sometimes had when they visited his childhood home. With Bree beside him, he walked to Claire and gathered her up in his arms, holding her close. Together they picked Bree up and started to hover above the ground. He took them down the hill and back to the flat land at the back of the house, then he held on to them for a moment longer after they had landed.

Bree wriggled free of their grasp and started to skip back, stopping along the way to pick wildflowers for Gran. Already they could see movement in the kitchen windows, and Claire knew it would be Gran baking up a storm. She smiled contentedly.

"What's that for?" Matt asked her, his arm now around her shoulders as they walked slowly back.

"I was just thinking I could live here quite happily." Claire let out a great sigh at the thought.

"Could you, now? Well, I never got a chance to talk to you last night about it. I have received an offer from Glasgow University. It's a permanent position, which means we would have to move to Scotland."

"Oh. When did this happen?"

"I stopped in before I came up here and caught up with them. A couple of days later, I got a phone call from the head of the department."

"When do they need an answer by?"

"He told me that it could wait, and that the job was mine whenever I wanted. I know it would be a great upheaval for both you and Bree, so I want you to be sure." He stopped and circled her waist with his arms. "I chose to follow you to New Zealand, so don't think that there is any pressure now to return the favour."

"Well, I wasn't thinking that, but now I am." She smiled up at him and laughed. "I love you, Galen Matthew Drummond, and I would follow you to the ends of the earth and back, forever and always. If you want this job, then take it. My home is where you and Bree are." She reached up and kissed him.

Chapter Three

Throughout the rest of the day, Claire kept catching Matt staring up at the hill where the stones were hidden. She knew their pull and tried to distract him. As they were going to bed, she sat and waited for him to join her. She had decided that he needed to know how to defend himself from them. He slipped under the covers and looked at his wife, cross-legged and hands resting on her knees.

"You have to try to ignore the pull of the stones, otherwise, it will make you mad. That was part of the problem when they were opened up to me."

"How? The only Abilities I have had to deal with my whole life are Flying and Art. I don't even know what's going on up there." He pointed to his head.

"I can help, and you need to trust that what I'm going to do will help you control it."

"I trust you, Claire. You know that."

"Okay. Just lie still and don't fight me." She leaned over and placed her hands on his head.

His eyes were not on hers, but on the beauty of her body. The way she smelled aroused him, and he grinned involuntarily up at her.

"This is not going to work, Matt, if you are focused on that right now." She looked down at him.

"I can't help it." He grinned back at her.

"I will sit on you if I have to."

"No, don't do that. It would only make it worse." Matt took her hands off his head and kissed each finger.

He made love to her with a frenzied energy. The need to have her was urgent and driven by the desire that had built up inside him. They climaxed together with a great passion, their bodies and minds linked. She lay in his arms, their bodies heaving with the exertion and gleaming with sweat.

"Now, do you think we can go back to what we were doing before?" she asked him.

"Not yet." He kissed her long and hungrily. So deeply he felt for this woman that he thought his heart would explode from it. He took her again, his hands touching every part of her, exploring her as he hadn't done for years. The drive to have her completely gnawed away at him and consumed him until they lay sated.

"My God, I love you," Matt told her as they lay panting.

She rolled onto her side and rested her head in her hand, tracing a finger over his chest and down his stomach. His eyes shone brightly as he watched her.

"If I had known that the stones would do this to you, I would have taken you to them long ago," Claire told him.

"I'm pleased you didn't. I don't think I have the stamina to keep that up." Matt was still breathing hard.

"Time to get you some training, then. But first, my love, you need to learn how to put up your defences." This time she didn't bother using her hands but made her way into his mind through their connection.

Claire walked him through what he needed to know before giving in to his advances again. He was a quick learner and managed to keep her out when she tried once more.

The morning brought with it driving rain and squally winds racing down the valley. Dark grey clouds hid the tops of the hills in a thick blanket, blocking the sun from the house. The weather reflected the mood inside. Everyone was quiet and polite. There were no raised voices, no running up and down the stairs. Even the children were subdued, picking up on how the adults were feeling.

Bree sat by her mother in the dress her Gran had sent her. It was a pretty dress with roses on the skirt, the kind of dress Claire would have hated to wear as a child, but Bree loved it and it suited her.

Addy walked into the room, stopped dead when she saw the girl, and then walked out again. As she put Bree's hair into a ponytail, Claire frowned at the behaviour but said nothing of it to the others in the room. A few minutes later, Addy was back, and in her hand she held a red ribbon.

"Here. I think she needs this." She passed it to Claire, who looked at the long, satiny material for a moment and then remembered. She smiled up at Addy and then tied a bow on Bree's ponytail.

"There," Claire said. "You're all done. Go play with your cousins for a bit, and don't get anything on that dress."

"Yes, Mum. Thank you, Aunty Addy. I like the ribbon." The girl gave Addy a sunny smile and walked calmly out of the room.

Gerry had watched the whole thing from his chair by the fire and raised an eyebrow at the pair of them. "I thought I was the only one," he said quietly.

"No, Dad. You weren't. We have seen it for some time now, only some of us have been a bit slow in accepting it." Matt looked at his wife and smiled.

Robbie came into the room at that moment, looking very pale and shaken. "Are you trying to give me a heart attack?" He looked at Claire. "I thought...well, for a moment I thought I had seen..."

"Yes, Robbie. We know," Gerry said with a smile.

"It's remarkable." Robbie sat down and let out a breath, the colour returning to his cheeks. The hair that was always long and flowing was now tied back neatly, and his beard had been trimmed. The wild, woolly, frenetic man who used to be on the television now sat like an elder statesman.

"Addy, can you go check on your Gran? We have to go soon," Robbie said to his daughter.

"I'll go, Addy." Claire stood up and smoothed the skirt she had on. "Sit. You have had two to get ready."

Claire mounted the steps to the second story and knocked on Gran's door. She waited a moment and then knocked a little louder.

"Come," Gran called out.

Claire opened the door and found Gran sitting on her bed, dabbing her eyes. "Are you all right?" She went and sat beside her.

"I'm fine, dear. Just getting the tears out of the way now. I didn't think she would go. I thought she would get better, but the doctors said that the infection had taken too much of a hold on her."

"She's not in pain anymore, Gran. Breena told us," Claire said quietly. "Up at the stones yesterday morning, she came to us and let us know that Leana is all right."

"Little Bree? How could she know?"

"Not our daughter, Gran, but Matt's sister."

Gran's surprised expression was soon turned to understanding. "That would explain it all. Before she died, I had a vision: a young woman was standing beside Leana. She had long, dark curly hair and brilliant blue eyes, much like Matt's. She wore a sapphire-blue dress, trimmed with silver. That was our Breena?"

"Yes. She really likes that dress."

"Well, I never. She would have been so beautiful. Gerry would've had a hard job beating the boys away." Gran laughed at the image.

"I don't think he would've had any worries in that department. She would've known how to deal with any situation."

The door pushed open, and Little Breena stood in the doorway. "Mum, Dad sent me to remind you that it's time to go." She looked from her mother to her granny.

"And there is the spitting image of her. My wee angel, look at you. You are as pretty as a picture."

"Thank you. Daddy calls me that."

"Where do you think he got it from?" Gran smiled as she stood up and took Bree's hand, then the three of them went downstairs.

At the front door, they were all assembled, waiting for Gran. Once all were in the cars, they left the valley. As they passed the old oak tree, the first rays of sun came out and shone down on them. The ford was running high with all the rain that had fallen, and Matt sped up to make sure they made it through. Claire saw the look of relief that passed over him when they got to the other side.

Every house and florist shop around the area had been bought out of roses—in all colours, shapes, and sizes. Leana's coffin was bedecked with a blaze of colour that draped down the sides. In front of the lectern in the small church was a display of some of her work. The service was simple, and the church was packed. Matt was the only one who made a eulogy.

"Mum would have hated the fuss. Her family and her work were the two most important things to her. When my sister Breena died so young, it tore her apart. It tore our whole family apart. But we made it out the other end. Mum got better, and her work flourished once more. She doted on her granddaughter so much, and she loved my wife as if she were her own." He looked up and caught Claire's eye. "My parents renewed their great love for each other, and these last years were the happiest for her. She told me every time we visited or called, *Matty, my life is just rosy*. We'll miss you, Mum."

At the graveside they gathered, just the family. The rest had been asked to go on to the hall for the wake. They all linked hands as they waited for the priest to say his piece. Instead of dirt to throw into the grave, rose petals sat in a beautiful basket. They all picked up a handful and together scattered them over Leana's coffin. By the time they had finished, there was no wood to be seen, but a beautiful carpet of colour.

When it was all over, Matt stayed where he was, and Claire asked Gerry to take Bree with him. She went and stood by her husband and held his arm. Sunlight streamed from the sky and the day had become still. And they waited.

Once the graveyard was quiet, they wandered around the headstones. So many different names could be found etched on their cold faces, although some were hidden through the wear of time. A great sense of history descended on Claire. The history in the area was incalculably long, and it made her feel small and alone.

"Claire," Matt whispered to her, and she looked up. Under a great yew tree in the corner of the graveyard stood two people, and she recognised both.

Hand in hand, they walked over to Leana and Breena, stopping just under the first branches. Leana beckoned them on, and Matt let go of Claire's hand and ran to his mother.

"I don't have long, Matty," Leana told him quietly. "Claire, come closer, my dear." Claire walked into Leana's embrace and felt the chill of it.

"You have to be quick, Mum," Breena told her, looking around.

"I had a vision and it scared me, but I was so far gone at the time. Your little family is going to be tested once more, and you cannot let it break." She looked directly at Claire. "There is too much to lose if you do."

"It was tested once, and it didn't fail," Matt told her.

"Yes, before you were married. But I see trying times ahead, and Little Bree needs to be protected."

"What danger is she in, Mum?"

"I don't know. I just see that she needs protection. And you have to work together."

"We will, Mum—always," Matt promised earnestly.

"Good. Now it's time for me to go. I liked the rose petals, by the way. I always found the dirt to be a bit of a slap in the face to the departed." Leana kissed them both and then took Breena's hand.

"Don't worry, Galen. I'll look after her," Breena said as they slowly disappeared.

Claire hugged her husband and let him cry his last tears for his mother. They stood under the yew tree with its branches hanging low, almost as if it were enfolding them in an embrace of its own. With the sound of voices, Claire saw the gravediggers coming to do their job. She gently guided him out of the graveyard and walked down the street to the hall. A shiver escaped her, and she held tighter to Matt's arm.

"You all right? Are you cold?" he asked as he placed that arm around her, pulling her closer to him.

"No. Just the day, I guess." But Claire had felt something else, like a brush against her mind. She sent out searching threads that snaked around the area. Only one gave a slight tingle of recognition, and she followed it. It was shut off and hidden from her in a moment, but what she had felt resembled a mind she had touched before, and she set her guards up against him. He was learning.

Later that afternoon, Claire sought Matt out, and they went for a walk around the house. She linked arms with him and laid her head on his shoulder.

"I didn't want to tell you earlier, because we had just seen your mother, but Tony is here somewhere," she said quietly, trying not to move her mouth.

"Here? Where?" The tone of his voice alerted her to his change in mood.

"I don't know. I only felt him briefly, and he has learned how to block me. Matt, there is nothing we can do but protect ourselves and those around us. One of the pieces of information I came across in the library the last time I went in there had a method of protecting an area."

"Do you think it will work?"

"I hope so. But I'm going to need your help. The last time I was in there was when I ran from you. The overload of information was too much, and I still haven't found a way to be in a library comfortably for too long."

"Do you want me to stand guard?" He stopped walking and held her in his arms.

"Yes, please. I need you to be linked with me and get me out of there if you think I've had enough. I'm hoping I can get the information I need before that happens."

"Anything you need, my love. This connection thing we have—will that work over long distances?" he asked her.

"It should do. It's a bit like Dream Messaging, except you could be walking around with me talking in your head."

"Oh, that's all I need—a nagging wife with me twenty-four hours a day." He smiled, chuckling.

"I do not nag, Matt! You take that back."

"No. I'm extremely lucky in that department. Actually, I'm lucky in all departments. Two of the most beautiful and wonderful girls in the world love me."

"And don't you forget it." She reached up and kissed him. Even though the day was a sad one, Claire had never felt more loved, and she stored it away in her memories for safekeeping.

"When do you want to do this?" he asked her as they resumed their walk.

"I was thinking tomorrow. Addy was telling me that she and Adam were thinking of taking the kids out somewhere, and she asked if they could take Bree with them."

"Sounds like a good idea to me. I know she loves this place, but a bit of time away will be good for her."

"Good. I thought so too, so I said yes."

"You were so sure that I would agree?"

"Of course," Claire said smugly.

Matt and Claire waved Addy, Adam, and the children off the next morning, wishing them fun for the day. Hand in hand, they walked inside and into the kitchen to clean up after the rushed breakfast. Gran was already there wiping down the table, and she looked up at them both as they walked in. A small smile and a twinkle appeared in her eye as she watched Claire, but she said nothing.

"Where's Dad?" Matt asked.

"He and Robbie are in your Mum's studio, packing up her things. He wanted to know if there was anything in there that you wanted," Gran replied.

"There are a few things. I won't be long, Claire." He gave her peck on the cheek and left them.

Claire turned the faucet on and filled the sink to wash the dishes when she felt Gran's eyes on her. She looked over her shoulder but found Gran merely repositioning the chairs back to where they should be.

"Have you two been back up to the stones?" Gran asked her, bringing the last of the dirty dishes from the table.

"Bree, Matt, and I went up together the other day," Claire said as she plunged coffee cups into the hot water.

"That's not what I mean, and you know it, Claire." Gran was leaning against the bench, watching the younger woman.

"No, Matt and I have not been up there alone since—"

"Oh, aye. I know. Look what happened as a result of that."

Claire stopped what she was doing. "Breena is not fully there—only a part."

"Am I going to have to drag it out of you, girl, or are you going to put an old woman out of her misery and tell me the whole story?" Gran picked up a cloth and started to dry the dishes stacked up on the drying board.

Claire related to Gran the tale of their meeting Breena in the circle that morning and how Matt had been given the gift of the stones. She related it all to her and felt a bit sad that she couldn't tell her Uncle Geoff.

"What does it feel like, the stones?" Gran asked as she ran the cloth over another cup.

"It's like static electricity, only safer and more intense. They hum with the energy they hold. When I touch them, they feel alive, and they heal me—spiritually and physically."

"I must admit that I am very envious of you, Claire. I wish I could feel it one time." She put the cups she had dried away and came back to start on the bowls. "You say they heal you physically?"

"That's right." Claire wiped the bench and let the water out down the plug hole.

"That would explain it." A knowing smile crossed the old woman's face, and that twinkle was back that Claire had seen earlier.

"It would explain what?" she asked.

"Oh, nothing. Just the change in you since you have been up there. Almost like you were glowing."

"Glowing from windburn, you mean." Claire chuckled and completely missed the wide smile that Gran had broken out in. "Is there anything else you would like me to do? Only I was hoping to get into the library this morning."

"No, you go. I have a bit of baking to do, as the tins are getting low. What do you fancy?" Gran asked her.

"Anything you make is good, Gran, but I do have a hankering for your shortbread."

"One batch of shortbread it is, then. Off you go." She shooed Claire from her kitchen and locked the secret she held from the younger woman away in her heart.

Claire found the three men in the studio along with Fiona, who was sitting in the corner, perched on a high stool and cradling a cup in her hands. They were discussing a picture they had found, and Claire didn't want to get in the middle of it. She walked over to her aunt-in-law and pulled up another stool.

"Have they managed to get anything done?" Claire asked as she looked around.

"Not really. All they seem to be doing is moving one pile to another and then back again," Fiona said as she smirked.

"At least they're being kept busy," Claire responded with an equal smirk.

"I think it will take them all day to do. Hopefully," Fiona replied with a conspiratorial grin.

"How has Robbie been since he retired?"

"Impossible! It's hard enough getting a good role at my age, but having him hanging around is even worse."

"He needs a hobby. Have you suggested he write his memoir?" Claire asked, still watching the trio.

"Yes, and we have also had offers for a biography. But he doesn't want his life down on paper. I told him that it would happen when he's dead anyway, and this way we can enjoy the profits from it."

"So will you ever retire?" Claire turned her attention to Fiona.

"Me? Never. I say that getting a job is hard, but there are more and more roles out there for older women. I might even let my hair go grey." She laughed and flicked her deep auburn hair off her shoulder.

"What are they looking at?"

"A picture. Apparently, Robbie and Gerry were arguing about whether Leana had actually drawn it, then Matt saw it and got all excited by it. Now I have no idea what is going on."

Matt looked up and grinned at Claire. She suddenly got a very deep sinking feeling. He took the frame off his father, hid it behind his back, and walked up to his wife.

"Do you remember, my darling wife, that day on the hill at the dig? The day that I came to your rescue?"

"I vaguely remember it. But as I recall, you not so much as rescued me but laid him out so I could finish him off."

"If I hadn't flown up that hill, who knows what might have happened," Matt said and grinned at her.

Comprehension dawned on her. A sketch pad left lying on the ground and returned to her. A page ripped from the pad and stowed in a bag. She looked in his eyes and did not want to look at the other pair that she knew was behind his back.

"The day before you left that night, I found it in my bag. I took it to Mum and she framed it for me. But with everything that happened after, I completely forgot about it." He produced the simple wooden frame from behind his back and presented it to her.

Claire took it in her hands and stared at the blue eyes she knew were there. Those sad, devastated eyes of disappointment with the tear hanging from the lashes and the reflection of a younger version of herself in it. She hung her head as the old feelings welled up inside her and threatened to overwhelm her.

"Hey, Claire, it's all right." He held her shoulders.

"I'm fine. I just don't like remembering that day. I had made you so mad at me, and I was feeling sorry for myself."

"If you don't want it, Claire, I'll take it," Fiona offered, looking at the picture. "It's absolutely beautiful and so full of emotion. Did you do this, Matt?"

"No. This is all Claire's work," he said proudly. "And sorry, Aunt Fiona, this is going up in my office." He took the drawing back from Claire.

"I didn't know you could draw, Claire. I remember your lamentable sketches of the site. But this is just stunning," Gerry said, standing behind his son.

"Maybe you could do another. This time a happier version," Matt suggested. He tucked the picture away in a box and then turned back to Claire. "Now if I remember, we have a date in the library." He held his hand out to her, and she took it in her own.

"The library—do you need a hand?" Gerry asked hopefully.

"No, not this time, Dad. Anyway, you have your hands full here," Matt said.

Gerry rolled his eyes and went back to work. The couple headed out of the house, leaving their elders to their rummaging and cleaning. They crossed the farmyard under a warm summer sun and stopped outside one of the outbuildings.

On the outside, it looked like any other farm building you would find in Scotland. But inside was a totally different matter. Inside was light and hermetically sealed with an air filtration system. The walls were lined with bookshelves and specimen drawers, all holding treasured writings of the ancients that had been found and passed down the centuries. The information that was contained in this room was a hundred times larger and more important than those in the archives of The Community.

As soon as she stepped in, Claire had the air knocked out of her as the information assaulted her mind. Like a sponge, it sucked hungrily from the tomes surrounding her. She stumbled, and Matt caught her and carried her to the table. He lowered her onto the metal chair and looked her in the eye.

"Claire, try and set your mind," he urged her, worry tinging his tone. Matt was happier when she nodded and closed her eyes.

Kneeling in front of her, he tried to reach Claire. He called out and tried to surround her with everything he could. Having only just received more Abilities and unsure of how to use them properly, he felt like he was floundering. Matt felt the energy flying around the room. It was almost tangible, and he could almost smell it. He dived into the flow of it and watched in amazement at the capacity of his wife's mind.

How long they stayed that way, Matt couldn't tell—until a hand pressed down on his shoulder, and he tore himself away from the ebb and flow of the energy. He looked up and saw his father.

"Before you wear yourself out, let me help," Gerry said, frowning.

Matt nodded and stood up on cramped legs. He held on to the table and found that his father was right. His strength was just about spent. Gerry had already taken his place, standing behind Claire.

"What is it you were doing?" Gerry asked him.

"Trying to slow the flow of information. Claire said that it overwhelms her. She's already set some boundaries of her own."

Gerry nodded and placed his hands on Claire's head. Matt could immediately see the strain on his father's face as he lent support to his daughter-in-law. Matt sat heavily on the other chair and waited. The smell of food at his elbow caught his attention, and he started to eat. He appreciated how hungry Claire got when she used more than one Talent at a time. He never realised until now how much energy she used and how heavy it left a person feeling.

Claire's mind was like a tempest, a great tornado of thoughts and images, as the information flew into it. She tried to hold it back, to limit how fast she absorbed it. Matt was there. She could feel him trying to help. She used his energy to shore up the defences where they were weak until she felt him pull back from their efforts.

Almost as soon as he left, another joined her. The presence of Gerry was battered and attacked from all sides in the rushing energy. She helped him find his place and set him to work, careful not to draw too much from him.

Soon the great onrush was slowing. The urgency lessened, becoming a steady trickle. She looked around her and found that the task was coming to an end, and she sighed. Claire found Gerry in her mind and walked up to him. He was staring around him at the immensity of information that had invaded her mind.

"Thank you, Gerry."

"You're welcome. This is an awful lot of information to have opened yourself up to. It was dangerous to try this with only Matt's support. He told me what happened up at the stones."

"I tried to be careful with him. But I think I underestimated this Ability. I have never been able to find anything that can help me stem the flow when it rushes at me."

"It sounds like you need to do your own experimenting and figure it out for yourself. You are truly Guardian blessed. The amount you can retain and hold for Recall is amazing."

"I feel like an overstuffed cushion at the moment, like I'm splitting at the seams. Once all this is sorted, then I can make sense of it." She looked at the mess around her, and her stomach gave a very loud grumble.

"I think you might have to come out now and have something to eat," Gerry told her pointedly.

"I'll see you out there." Claire gently pushed him away from her mind.

Before she left, Claire found Crystal and sat on the ground in front of the great orb. The light that moved around her faceted exterior was now flickering and circling at great speed.

"Are we too busy for a conversation, Crystal?"

"We can manage a few words, Claire," the orb responded, although a little distracted than normal.

"Good. We need to know something from the new information, and we were hoping that we could access it now."

"We know what we need. We will have it ready for us soon. We need to eat, Claire. Our body is changing, and we need to feed it."

"Yes. We will go now. Thank you, Crystal. We know we have set ourselves a great task."

With that, she opened her eyes and was back in the library. She sat and listened to the silence of the room. For once there was no hushed clamouring for attention. Her vision was clear again, and her mind stilled. Claire saw both Matt and Gerry watching her, and she smiled up at them.

"Thank you—both of you—for your help. I'm sorry I set you such a hard task, Matt. I should have known better."

"I was holding my own, but I'm glad Dad came in when he did." Matt pushed the plate in front of Claire and watched as she ate.

"So, what is this all about? I could see you sorting through it while we were in there. What are you searching for?" Gerry asked them.

"Tony is around. He's learning quickly how to control his Abilities, and I remembered that I had seen something on placing a protection on an area. I want to protect the family— make this a special safe place, away from prying eyes," she told him between bites of her sandwich.

"Do you think he means to harm us?" Gerry asked her, concerned.

"I don't know what he's doing. But I know he has managed to deflect my Seeking and hide his mind from me. I just want to be sure that we're all safe."

Claire picked up another sandwich and took a bite. Inside this room, it felt like the outside world was far away, but she knew that in just a few steps, she would be back there with all its problems.

"Mum wanted me to tell you the shortbread was ready if you wanted some," Gerry told her as he picked up the empty plates.

"Oh, yum!" Claire stood and held out her hand to Matt. "You coming, or am I going to eat it all by myself?"

"You usually do." Matt smiled and took it. As he stood, he was overcome with a wave of tiredness he had never felt before. Claire could see he was trying to hide it from her. She took his hand and gave it a squeeze, letting him know he would be alright. All the while she was slowly transferring energy to him as they walked back to the house.

That night, Claire lay by his side listening to his even breaths. Her eyes were wide open and staring up at the ceiling as she drew on her energy and slowly released it, trying to send out her search as softly and lightly as possible. She was hoping that he hadn't hidden himself. The feelings she got back were of ordinary people and a few with some Ability. She was just about to give up when a small touch passed her. Backing up the path, she found it. Tiny and wrapped up on itself, it was there.

Careful not to disturb it, she took in the surroundings and smiled slightly. It was the same cottage that he had been in all those years ago, when he had revealed his Talents to her. Withdrawing the search, she didn't want to alert him to her presence. As she rolled over, she set her own protections in place to hide her mind from him.

Chapter Four

Crystal's persistent and pestering calls dragged Claire from a deep and satisfying dream. With great reluctance and regret, she struggled to set it aside to go find the glittering orb. The lights that had been flickering fast earlier in the day were now back to their normal languid orbiting of the crystalline body.

"We are sorry to wake us, Claire, but we have found what we were looking for. We know that we were anxious to find it as soon as possible so we can lay the protection down."

"Thank you, Crystal."

"It is located there, Claire." A nearby box was illuminated, and Claire removed the lid and peered inside.

The information did not act like any other she had come across. Instead of knowing instantly once it was fed into the right part of the brain, this information battered against her, almost like it was fighting something already. She watched it and followed as it pushed against her defences, her subconscious, and finally it entered her dream state.

Claire slipped into the area, and a kaleidoscope of colours swirled around her in great agitation. In the centre, the tight ball of the dark dream still sat, but now the protection information encased it, ripping at the light that Claire had placed around it, and tearing it into glittering shards.

A scream rent through her mind as the protection attacked the ball itself. A deep, painful scream that split her thoughts and chased them far from her. It echoed through the deep reaches and came bursting from her. The pain emanated out and speared her over and over. Claire's body went rigid and her hands clasped to her head, her voice tearing in her throat.

Hands held her; voices, scared and shouting over her screaming, tried to reach her. Her eyes rolled into her head and she fell into a comforting embrace. Her mind went blank. She had no idea where she was, or even who she was. But people were there.

"Claire, come back to us, sweetheart." A woman was kneeling beside her, dressed in white. Claire knew who she was. She could recognise her and grasped on to her.

"That's it, Claire. You remember now." The man was there, strong and calm. He picked her up and carried her to a safe place, with the woman walking beside her.

The man was John. She remembered his name. John placed her on a blanket on the ground and held her still while the woman held her hand. Claire looked into the eyes of the woman in white and remembered mist. Soft, caressing mist that would wind around her with comfort. Jessica.

"You're nearly there, Claire. Just a little bit more," Jessica encouraged.

Over this woman's shoulder stood a younger man with dark hair and piercing blue eyes. He ran towards her, calling her name. There was an attraction she felt for him—a deep-seated attraction that she knew they both shared, one that bonded their souls together.

This younger man knelt beside her mother—she remembered now. Her mother was before her, and the man who held her was her father. But who was this other man, the one who looked so worried? His hands now stroked her hair, and he took her from her father and cradled her in his arms.

Her hand reached for his face to wipe the tear that was tracking down his cheek. The instant she touched him, she knew who he was, and relief flooded her. Claire buried her face into his shoulder and gave a great sigh. The pain ebbed away from her, and she felt her body relax into his embrace. The comfort of her family filled her and renewed her spirits.

"Galen," she whispered.

"Yes, I'm here." He kissed her head and smoothed her hair. "I'm here." He looked at John and Jess. "What was that?"

"We don't know. There was just chaos and screaming—both from Claire and from somewhere else," John told his son-in-law.

"It was that dark dream," Claire said softly and pushed herself up. "Crystal woke me. She had found the information for the protection. When I released it, it didn't act the way it should have, and it searched out the dark dream. The one I told you about that I had confined, the one that had caused the depression."

"I remember," Matt said, still holding on to her.

"It tore it apart, and when it did, there was a scream and pain. So much pain." She rubbed her eyes with the heel of her hand.

"It's gone now, sweetheart," Jess told her daughter.

"Mummy?" The small voice came from out of the darkness that surrounded them.

John looked up and was moving in a moment, racing into the black and disappearing. They looked where he had gone and waited. When he returned, he was carrying a small child, who smiled at her.

"I found someone special." John was beaming from ear to ear.

"How is this possible? She is only six!" Jess looked at her daughter.

"You haven't told them?" Matt asked her. When Claire shook her head, he looked surprised.

Bree was there in a moment, hugging her mother and father. "I was scared," she told them.

"We're safe now, my wee angel," Matt comforted her. "Breena, these are your grandparents, John and Jess."

The little girl stood in front of Jess and held out her hand. Jess reached out and pulled her close, looking at her hard, memorizing each detail. Then she embraced her granddaughter.

"An explanation is in order, Claire." John sat down beside his wife and waited.

With help from Matt, Claire filled them in on what happened at the stones and why Bree's Talents were already forming. By the end of the telling, Claire's strength was returning, and she was itching to find out what had happened to her.

"I think we should go back now. The others will be wondering what is going on. Your screaming brought everyone running," Matt told her.

"My screaming?"

"Yes. It was loud enough to wake the dead." He looked up at his in-laws as soon as he said it.

"Don't worry, Son. This piece of us was never dead in the first place." John smiled at Matt's discomfort.

Claire stood with help from Matt and held out her hand to Bree. When her little hand slipped into her own, she felt even stronger.

"Bring her back to visit us often," Jess said to Claire.

"I will, Mum, and thank you. I don't even want to think about what would have happened if you weren't here."

"Matt would have been. It didn't take him long to get here." John smiled.

"I have to protect my girls," Matt said seriously.

"Yes, you do." John clasped Matt's hand.

Within moments, they were back in the real world. Claire could hear people whispering. The light was on and she could feel her body again, the sweat chilling her skin. Slowly she opened her eyes and winced at the brightness of the overhead lightbulb. Her throat felt dry and sore, and the tickle of it sent her into a coughing fit.

Steady and gentle hands helped her into a sitting position, and a glass of water was produced and forced into her trembling hands. She greedily gulped down the cool, soothing liquid and finished it off within moments. Faces stared back as she looked around her, seeing people in dressing gowns and pyjamas.

Claire got up and staggered to the bathroom. She heard Matt trying to explain and calm everyone. She leaned against the sink and turned the tap on. Cold water ran over her cupped hands and she raised them, splashing her face and cooling the back of her neck. The shock of the water helped to wash away the pain and anguish that had become almost incapacitating. As she dried her face, she heard footsteps pass beyond the wooden door in the hallway outside, and she sighed.

Slowly Claire tugged the door open slightly, making sure there was no one around before slipping back into the living room. Matt was waiting for her, a smile with concern in his eyes, ready to comfort her and reassure her. She thanked her lucky stars that the fates had brought him to her. Claire climbed into bed next to him and he enfolded her in his arms protectively, her head resting on his shoulder. She could hear his heart beating in his chest, faster than normal.

"I'm sorry I scared you."

"I didn't know what the hell was going on. I think I'm going to be deaf in this ear for the next week," he said, rubbing it.

"Was I that loud?"

"Pardon, can you repeat that? I can't hear you," he teased her, laughing.

"Stop it." Claire laughed softly, which brought another cough.

"Do you want some more water?"

"No, I'm fine." She settled back into his arms.

"Get some sleep while you can."

Even though she tried, Claire could not sleep. She lay awake until the sky outside began to change. The orange glow of the clouds as they caught the sun's first rays stained the room with their ruddy light, and she shivered. Matt moved restlessly beside her, and she carefully lifted his arm off her. Standing slowly from the mattress on the floor so as not to wake her husband, Claire dressed quickly and quietly, using the Stealth Talent. On silent feet, she crept from the room and made her way outside into the early morning light. She rose into the air and floated up the hill to the standing stones. They thrust their way towards the sky, greeting the morning eagerly.

Claire touched the first stone and let out a sigh as the energy flowed into her. She turned and sank to the ground with her back and head against the stone, arms resting on her knees. Her eyes closed as she felt the events of the night slip away.

"Thought I would find you here."

"Good morning, Tony. Did you sleep well?" She didn't need to open her eyes to know who it was.

"What did you do to me last night?"

"I did nothing. I am not responsible for your dreams, Tony." She opened her eyes and saw him leaning against the rocks.

"Something happened last night."

"I was taking care of a bit of housekeeping. Up here." She pointed to her head. "I've had an infestation for some time now, and I finally found a way to rid myself of it."

"I worked hard on that."

"I bet you did. You've learnt a lot, haven't you?"

"It looks like I still have a way to go. Any chance I can get into that library down there?" Tony asked, using his thumb to gesture towards the house and outbuildings.

"Sorry. It's a family-members-only sort of place. I don't think it will help you much. And how do you know about it, anyway?"

"I have my ways."

"Stay out of my head, Tony," she told him with raised eyebrows.

"You started it. I felt you last night searching for me."

"Just as I felt you the day of Leana's funeral."

"Touché." He shot her a small grin and a nod of the head.

The sound of the spring babbling between them punctuated the silence that stretched out in the early morning. The sun was well up now, and the orange light faded out of the clouds as they returned to a steely grey. Claire breathed in deeply the clear air of the hills.

"Where are you, Claire?" Matt's voice sounded loud in her head.

"I'm here at the stones. I'll be back soon."

"I'll be waiting, my love," he said as he faded from her mind.

"He's very loud, isn't he?" Tony asked as he watched her.

"Matt is new to this. And stay out. A girl has to have some secrets."

"I thought you didn't like secrets."

"I don't, so when I get down there, I will be telling Matt all about this conversation. You do know he wants to beat the living shit out of you?"

"If I were in his shoes, I would, too." He looked up at the clouds as they shifted across the deepening blue sky.

"Was there anything else you would like to discuss while you're here?"

"No. Just wanted to connect with a human being for a while." The waves of loneliness coming from him were immense. She tried to see what exactly it was that he was missing.

"Don't go there, Claire. You won't like what you see," he warned and shifted position.

Claire stood up and walked over to him. The pity that welled up inside her for this man made her feel very sad. She reached up her hand to him and he caught her wrist.

"I don't want your pity," he growled roughly.

"You wanted to connect with someone. I'm here."

"But I can't have you, remember? What I want doesn't matter anymore."

"What is the matter? What has made you so sad?" she asked, searching his dark eyes.

Tony let her go and moved further away. "Soon. You will know soon enough." He looked at her one more time, his brown eyes ringed with dark circles, and then walked away behind the rocks.

Claire followed him and watched as he walked down the other side of the hill. His shoulders were hunched, and his hands pushed into his pockets. She reached out to him with her mind.

"I do care, Tony. I hope I can help when the time comes."

Tony made no response in return. His emotions were raw and ragged, but not for Claire. She understood that she was somehow his way to heal and get back what he had lost, and felt his hate at the thought. Then his defenses were slammed into place with some force, leaving Claire feeling a little shaken.

Claire sat at the table with Matt, a cup of hot coffee in her hands. She sipped it, feeling it warm her from the inside, and sighed as she put it down. Her mind was still on Tony.

"I think I should put the protection on the house this morning," she said.

"Do you think you'll be up to it?" Matt asked her, worried. "You didn't get much sleep last night."

"I'll be fine. I want to do it before Tony does anything. He was up there this morning."

"Tony was at the stones?" Matt's jaw started to clench at the thought. "Did you talk to him?"

"Yes, I did. He seemed so lonely."

"I don't care if he has lost everyone in his life. Was he there when I called to you?" he asked in a voice he was struggling to control.

"Yes. I can handle him, Matt."

"Why didn't you tell me that he was there?" His tone was deep but rising.

"For precisely this reason. I didn't want you going up there half-cocked and getting into a fight with him." Claire's own temper was now rising to match his.

"What? Don't you think I could take him? Do you really think of me as such a complete weakling?"

"No, Matt, I don't. I just know what he's capable of and I don't want you getting hurt."

"You are calling me weak bastard!" He stood up suddenly, the chair he was just sitting on flying back behind him, hitting the wall with a loud crash. "I always suspected you had feelings for him. Why don't you just run off to your boyfriend?"

"Because, Matt, I love you, you asshole. Not him."

"Claire, calm down. Matt, please don't do this now." Gran had entered the room, hastily tying the cord of her pink dressing gown around her.

"Now I'm an asshole for wanting to protect my wife?"

"I can protect myself. I have for many years, since before I even met you."

"I gotta get out of here!" Matt snarled as he made for the door.

"Now look who's running away!" Claire yelled at him.

Matt spun on the spot, raised his finger, and started walking back to her. "Don't you fucking dare throw that in my face, Claire. You were the one who ran away, ripping my heart out as you went. You didn't have the guts to face me that night, didn't trust me enough to know that I would love you no matter what." Matt stood close to her at that moment, his face bright red with anger and disappointment.

Gran pushed them apart, and before either one could react to her actions, she grabbed Matt's hand and placed it on Claire's stomach.

"Feel, Galen. Feel what is growing inside your wife. This is what you two have to fight for. Now stop behaving like children and think of your own bairns."

Matt's eyes widened as he felt the tiny spark of life hidden inside Claire. It was a tiny pulsating glimmer under his hand, softer than a butterfly's kiss. The redness of the heat of his anger dissipated and was replaced with the paleness of shock.

"I'm pregnant?" Claire asked in disbelief.

Matt nodded and kissed her, his hand still on her stomach, linked to the tiny child. He released Claire and turned to his Gran.

"How…? When…?" He couldn't find the words.

"Why ask me?" Gran replied with a smile.

Matt turned back to his wife. Claire, trying to find the seat behind her, nearly fell on the floor. He was with her in a microsecond, making sure she didn't fall.

"I believe the stones may have something to do with it. Remember, Claire, you told me that they heal you."

"But that was only a few days ago, we…" She blushed and looked at Matt.

"I don't want to know the particulars. I saw your face yesterday and could see it then. I haven't gotten to this age and not picked up a trick or two. And before you ask—no, I did not see it in a vision." She kissed both her grandson and his wife. "Now, say you're sorry and be happy. Congratulations."

"What is all the noise down here?" Gerry demanded, coming into the kitchen.

"Ask your son. He was doing most of the yelling," Gran said as she took the kettle from the hob and moved to the sink.

Matt and Claire sat looking at each other with their hands linked, tiny smiles on their faces and no need for words. The argument was forgotten, and happiness and calm descended upon them.

Later that morning, Claire made a circuit around the outside of the farm buildings and the house. Her brows knitted with the concentration she was using to form the protective barrier. As she understood it, the protection would stop others from prying and eavesdropping. If Tony had been using his new Talents this way, then it should stop him from listening in.

She closed the circle and checked it by standing outside and trying to contact Matt, who was standing in the centre of the yard. Claire faced him and sent out a thought, waiting for his reply. After a moment or two, she stepped through the barrier and sent the same message.

"Boy or girl?"

"Don't care," Matt responded with his voice and a rather large grin.

"Well, that worked," she called out aloud and walked up to him. "I'm sorry about this morning. I should have told you."

"I don't want to talk about that." He threw his arm around Claire's shoulders and walked her back to the house. "We only have a couple more days until you fly home with Bree."

"Yes, back to normal life. How long are you going to stay on?"

"I was thinking another week. There are still things to discuss with Dad. It'll be easier once everyone has gone. Then, I thought I would go to Glasgow for a bit and take up that job offer, if you're sure."

"I couldn't be more certain of anything else." She slipped out from under his arm as they entered the living room.

"All done?" Gerry asked them, and Claire nodded.

"Right. Well, we have a long drive back to London, so we had better get going. I will ring later and check up on you, Mum," Robbie said, getting to his feet and kissing his mother on the cheek.

Everyone stood, and the farewells went on for a good while. When Robbie came to Bree, he picked her up. "Now, don't you go getting too big on me, lass."

Bree giggled as his beard tickled her face. "I won't, Uncle Robbie." He let her down and she went to Fiona.

Her great-aunt knelt down beside Bree, and the little girl threw her arms around her neck. As Claire had observed before, Bree whispered something in Fiona's ear as they embraced, and her great-aunt's face flickered through the gamut of emotions. Claire had often wondered what she said to people to get this reaction, but in the next minute, she decided she didn't want to know. This was one secret she was willing to let lie.

Chapter Five

"Breena," a soft voice called in the middle of the still, dark night. Bree had been lying awake and waiting for this call since she was put to bed. In the single bed by the door, her great-grandmother lay snoring softly. Bree rolled over and faced the door. She'd had to try hard to pretend to be asleep when Granny came up for the night.

"Breena," the voice called again. This time, standing at her side was her Aunt Breena, dressed in a long, silver-trimmed blue gown that matched her eyes.

"Hello, Aunty Breena," Bree whispered the greeting.

"Hello, Bree. Did I wake you?" Breena sat on the bed beside the little girl.

"No. I didn't go to sleep. Thank you for coming to help me."

"They asked me to look after you, and it's my pleasure."

"I knew he would pass on my message. We better go, Aunty Breena." Bree got out of the little camp stretcher bed. She was already fully dressed, even down to her shoes.

"Get your jacket. It's going to be cold tonight, and it's a long walk to the ford," Breena suggested.

Bree did as she was told and put it on. Before they left the room, Bree tiptoed to Granny's side. She searched her mind and found she was lost in a dream of her youth. A handsome man was walking beside her, and she felt very happy.

Standing on her toes, she reached up and gave her Granny a kiss goodbye and then opened the door, which for once did not give is customary protesting squeak.

Out on the landing, she stopped and looked at the closed doors around her. Granda was next. He was in the room next to Granny. When she entered, she could already feel the disturbed dreams he was having. There was no light, only dim greyness full of sadness, very much like the dream that had pestered her mother. Bree reached up and stroked his hair. His breathing immediately steadied, and he lay still. The little girl sighed. She didn't want to go and leave them behind, but she had to. If she didn't, then things would change, and the outcome of what was to happen would be disastrous for her family. She kissed him gently and then turned to go.

She went to her parents next—now moved from the living room and into her father's old bedroom. They slept so peacefully, the fright of the night before and the argument she had heard them having forgotten. They were happy, and Bree smiled knowingly. She was sure she would enjoy being a big sister. Lifting off the floor, she floated onto the bed and carefully snuggled between her parents.

Bree didn't want to go, but the last thing she wanted was for anyone that she loved to be hurt—and they would be if she didn't leave them now. She kissed them both and floated out of the room with one final look back. She sighed and headed for the stairs. As Bree passed Addy and Adam's room, she felt guilty for not saying goodbye, but she had to get going. Time was running out fast.

Out of the house they walked together, hand in hand. Two peas in a pod they were. The child and the adult incarnated together, but now separate. Bree waited until they were out of the farmyard to look back at the house.

"Aunty Breena, can you explain to Daddy where I've gone and why? Please tell him not to worry and that I love him." She looked up and met the blue eyes.

"Yes, of course, Bree, if you want me to. I don't know how Galen will take it, and I bet he will yell at me."

"Only for a little bit."

They walked on past the protection line and Bree took a breath, holding tightly to her aunt's hand. The moon lit their way down the track, and the wind tousled their hair. Their steps quiet on the gravel path, they said not a word to each other. The silence of the night was oppressive and heavy.

The old oak tree came into sight, silhouetted against the night sky. To some it could have looked ominous and creepy, but to these two travellers, it was inviting and comforting. Their steps lightened and quickened as they approached it. With willing and loving hands, they both greeted the tree, and it answered them back with a welcoming feeling.

"He misses us," Bree said.

"I miss him," Breena replied, leaning her head against the rough bark.

They sat and communed with the spirit inside the tree for a while until a car could be heard coming down the main road. Bree and Breena walked down to the water's edge and waited. The headlights scanned the bitumen in front of them before pulling into the track and stopping near the water.

Breena picked Bree up and held her close, then slowly lifted off the ground and floated across the river—just above the flowing water. A dark figure got out of the car and stared at the ethereal figure of a woman and child coming towards him. Even in the moonlight, Bree could see that he was pale and shaking.

They reached the other side, and Breena brought them back down to the ground and walked towards the car. She stopped and let her niece down, holding her hand once more.

"Who…? Are you a ghost?" the man stammered, taking a step back from the pair.

"Yes." Breena smiled sweetly. "But not a scary one, I hope!"

"I… Um…I…" he stumbled, struggling to find words that would work in his mouth.

"That's all right. You have come to take the girl?" Breena asked.

He nodded and switched his eyes to Bree, then back to Breena. "I have. But I was supposed to get her from the house."

"We have saved you the trouble. You wouldn't have been allowed to pass the ford anyway. If you harm Bree or touch her in any way that is not caring and kind, then I will find you and haunt you for the rest of your days. That is a promise." Her voice was lowered and full of all the threats in the world.

"I'll look after her. I promise. She won't leave my sight." He was shaking violently now.

Breena crouched down in front of Bree. She zipped up her jacket and gave her a hug. "I want you to be very brave and behave. Don't give them any reason to be angry with you."

"I won't, Aunty Breena. Look after Granny and Granda." She hugged her aunt again. "I love you."

"I love you, too, our wee angel. I'll try to keep an eye on you when you are not in our lands." Breena stood again and held on to Bree's hand for a moment longer as she spoke to the man. "You will not remember me, but you will remember my threat with dread."

The man's eyes glazed for a moment as the girl walked to his side. His eyes focused and when he looked around, Bree tugged on his jacket, and he looked down.

"What's your name?" Bree asked politely.

"I'm James—James Boyle."

"Hello, Mr. Boyle. I'm Breena Drummond. Are we going now?" she asked him so casually that he blinked a couple of times before answering.

"Ahh, yes, I believe we should. Hop in." James opened the back door and Bree climbed in. "Into the booster seat, please—it's the law."

The girl rolled her eyes and climbed into the child seat that was strapped in beside her. James climbed into the car and pulled the seat belt across her, clicking it into place. He climbed from the back seat and shut the door, slipped into the front, and reversed the car, heading back down the road.

Claire woke to brilliant sunshine streaming through the windows. Below, she could hear the familiar sound of Gran moving about in the kitchen. Stretching slowly with contentment and not wanting to wake Matt, Claire got out of bed and dressed quietly. Walking on silent feet was second nature to her now, and she crept out of their room and into the hall. When she passed Gran's room, she peeked in to see if Bree was still asleep. The little camping cot at the end of Gran's bed was empty except for the crumpled bedding, so Claire made her way down the stairs. When she entered the kitchen, Gran looked up and greeted her warmly. "Good morning, Claire. Did you sleep well?"

"Yes, thank you, Gran. It was a wonderful sleep. I thought at one point Bree had climbed in with us, but she wasn't there this morning. Is she in the living room?"

"No. I thought she was with you." Gran stopped what she was doing and stared at Claire in confusion.

A cold feeling descended over Claire. She immediately sent out searching thoughts and followed them to her. Claire found her daughter in the last place that she expected.

Quickly, she rushed to the boot room and pulled on her shoes. Before she left, she called to Gran, "Tell Matt I'm going to get her."

Claire did not bother running on the ground but launched herself up in the air and away. She flew in a direct line to the cottage over the hills, where she had felt Bree's life force. Her anger at Tony's audacity was starting to overflow, and she was ready to face him with everything she had to get her daughter back.

The cottage came into view, and it was as she remembered, complete with the still-overgrown garden and rusty gate. Claire landed at the door and thumped on it as hard as she could. Inside, she could hear movement in response to the echoing thuds and she waited, ready for the fight that must come.

The door opened wide, and Tony held it, standing off to one side. "Claire, come in."

"Where is she, Tony? Where is Bree?" Claire hadn't moved. Her fists were clenched, and she was shaking.

"Come in, Claire," Tony repeated, reaching out and closing his large, strong hand around her upper arm, pulling her inside. "There's not much time."

Claire stumbled slightly, and when she managed to straighten herself, she stood her ground, facing him. "Tell me. I know she's here. I've felt her here."

"She is here, Claire. And I'm sorry, but I had no choice." Tony looked sad and haunted, but he still held on to her arm. "Please forgive me."

A sharp, stinging pain attacked between her shoulder and neck. Claire turned and found another man looking at her with a syringe in his hand. The room started to spin around her, and she felt her legs giving out. The last thing she saw was Tony picking her up in his arms before everything went black.

Matt woke with a start at the sound of his grandmother's urgent call. The spot beside him in the bed was empty and cold already. The door burst open, and Gran stood framed in the doorway, panting, gasping for breath. She was pale as a sheet.

"Gran!" he cried out in surprise.

"It's Bree—she's gone. Claire has gone to find her," Gran told him quickly, trying to catch her breath.

Her words took a moment to sink in, and he was quick to move when they finally did. He leapt out of bed and started to dress, struggling to climb into his jeans.

"Where did she go?" he demanded.

"I don't know. Claire left and I came up here immediately." Gran turned so he could have privacy.

Matt sat on the bed, halfway in the process of putting on a jumper. He pushed out with his thoughts, trying to find her with the connection that they already had, and he came up against a blank space. It frightened him.

The stairs he took two by two, and he was outside in the cool air before he knew what he was doing.

"Matt, what is it?" Adam stood at his side, Gerry walking towards them.

"I don't know. Someone…Bree…Claire…" His panicked breathing was getting in the way of his words.

"Calm down, Son. Take a deep breath." Gerry was at his side in a moment, a calming hand placed on his shoulder.

"Bree is missing, and Claire went to look for her. Did she say anything to anyone about where Tony was staying?" He looked at the pair of them, but they shook their heads, shocked to hear that Tony had been around them.

Gerry closed his eyes and concentrated, but he received the same blank space where Claire should have been. He opened his eyes and pulled out his phone.

"I'll call the police. Gordon will know what to do," he told his son.

"I can't wait for the police, Dad. I have to find them," Matt said urgently.

"I know, Son, but we won't be any use going off and doing something stupid. If Tony was the one who took them, then we'll find him and get the information out of him. Remember, Gordon is one of us." Gerry started to dial.

Matt watched his father go back inside and turned to look at the spot Claire had been just the day before, asking him a very special question with a radiant smile on her face. She had tried to teach him some basics, had put the information into his head. Now it was time to put them to the test. He went into his mind and found what he was looking for. He handled it gently, turning it this way and that, and then absorbed it.

The searching fingers spread out from him like a web, covering the hills and surrounding valleys. Pinpoints of vibrations came back to him from ordinary people, but he was looking for a specific person. Then he found him.

Adam grasped his shoulder when he came back to the real world. He looked at his friend and knew.

"You've found him. I'll drive, you navigate." The set of his face matched that of Matt's, and before they could tell anyone else what they were doing, they were heading down the track at great speed.

Flying through the ford with streaming walls of water on either side and onto the main road, Matt directed Adam. An image of a cottage with an overrun garden and a rusty gate was in his mind. He knew exactly where that was—he had passed it many times. Adam stopped just before they got to the cottage, and they both got out of the car.

"How do you want to do this?" Adam asked him.

"Beat the living crap out of the bastard, get my family back, and get home. Hopefully before he manages to use his Abilities on us. You don't have to do this, Adam. You have to think of Addy and the boys."

"And you have Claire and Bree. No, we do this together. She is my best mate, after all," Adam told him, clasping Matt's hand in a handshake.

Carefully, they jumped the fence and made their way to the door. Matt raised and lowered the tarnished brass knocker, hearing movement inside. The door handle squeaked as it started to move. Matt and Adam put all their weight on it, slamming it into Tony's face as he opened it. They burst into the room and were on him before he could gather his senses. Adam held him down while Matt sat on top, fists flying.

"Where…are…they…?" Matt yelled over and over, landing punch after punch with each word.

Tony did nothing to defend himself. He waited for the two men to tire themselves out, covering his head with his arms. The pummeling he was taking hurt, and he could feel bones breaking under the force of the blows. Matt's yelling was starting to lessen, and he could feel him backing off.

Matt fell off the prone body of Tony and sat panting. His knuckles were red and bleeding, his breathing hard. Tears streamed down his face. He sat looking at Tony with no pity or remorse, only disappointment in himself that he couldn't carry on hurting this man who had stalked his wife all her life.

"Are you done?" Tony moved slowly as he sat up. Feeling the bones in his ribs moving, he winced. Running his hands over his injuries, he healed himself quickly, then sat looking at Matt. He ran his tongue over his teeth, checking for loose or missing ones. "Do you mind explaining yourself as to why you came bursting in here and beat me up?"

"Where are they? Where are Claire and Bree?" Matt asked quietly, still breathing hard.

"Claire? How should I know? You're her husband. Shouldn't you know?" He stood and was suddenly face-to-face with Adam.

"Bree is missing, and Claire went to find her," Adam told him through gritted teeth.

Tony offered his hand to Matt to help him up. Matt pushed it away and stood by himself.

"The mere fact that I have not used my Talents on you gentlemen must not be lost on you. If I had taken Claire and Bree, don't you think I would've defended myself a bit better than I did?" He went to the kitchen and got himself a glass of water before taking a large gulp. He swirled the liquid in his mouth, spat it out down the sink, and washed it away.

"If you don't have them, who does? Who are you working for?" Adam asked him.

Tony ran his hands through his dark, wavy hair and stared Adam in the eye. "I used to work for your father, remember? Then I worked for Jack. I left for a while and had a life of my own. Then, my wife was murdered, and my son held to ransom. All I had to do to get him back was to follow Claire again. Report where she was, who she was with."

"So, who is it that has her?" Matt stepped towards him; his anger still not sated.

"It's your father, Adam." He didn't take his dark eyes off Matt's blue ones. "Marcus Ryder."

"Dad? But why? I don't believe you. Why would Dad want Claire? We changed him."

"Obviously not well enough. All I know is that he has my son, and I want him back." His voice lowered and took on a menacing tone.

"And we are just supposed to take your word for it?" Adam challenged him.

Tony turned and pulled out a laptop from a bag on a chair. He opened it and tapped on the keyboard, then turned it to face the two men. There were a few seconds of silence before Tony's voice came out of the speakers.

"I don't deal with monkeys. I want to talk to the man in charge. Put him on now."

"*Hang on.*" Static sounded in the pause, then another man came on the line.

"Anthony, this is not how things are supposed to go. You of all people should know that," the slick, unmistakable voice of Marcus Ryder blared out of the speakers. "All you have to know—my old friend—is that I have your son. And all you have to do to get little John back is to track Claire. It's something you've been doing for a while now, anyway. I want to know where she goes and what she does. If you get a chance to bring her to me, then please do. Sooner rather than later, Anthony."

"Why do you want her?"

"Oh, Anthony, I don't have to spell it out, do I? It's none of your concern. Get me Claire and you get John. Call on this number when you have something to report."

The line clicked, and Tony shut the laptop. He placed it carefully on the table and turned back to Matt and Adam, leaving a finger still resting on the top.

"I have every conversation with him recorded. I always make sure to report only to him—old habits die hard. He was not happy when I let a prime opportunity to take her slip through my fingers. The night of Geoff's funeral, when she was cleaning the hall."

"She told me you were there," Matt confirmed for Adam's sake.

"I don't understand why or how. She made sure that the suggestion could never be lifted—also the other one she put on him herself," Adam insisted.

"My guess is that Jack found someone who could do it. Someone in the States, possibly. There are whole communities of people with Talents over there." Tony sat down at the table.

"This changes nothing. You were still here watching her. If you hadn't, then they both would still be with us!"

"If I hadn't, I would have lost my son. He has killed before—you know this. Not just adults, but kids as well. What would you do if our roles were reversed?" he demanded of Matt, his voice rising.

"Claire would have given herself up before I could do anything." Matt rubbed his face, clearing it of the drying tears.

"You're probably right. She has guts, that girl," Tony said with a smile.

"Where do you think he's taking them?" Matt's voice still had an edge to it. He didn't quite believe Tony was as innocent as he was making out.

"Ask your friend there. Marcus is his father, after all." Tony's eyes turned darker as he asked Adam, "So where, Adam? To the States? Back home to New Zealand? Tell us where to begin looking."

"How the hell do I know? I didn't even know he had been changed." Adam paced around the room. "One thing's for sure: if he was getting Claire and Bree out of the country, it would be on a private jet. There's no way he would risk going commercial." He pulled out his phone, flipped through to a number, and dialed.

Matt lowered himself slowly to sit on the side of the table opposite Tony. He kept a wary eye on the man, expecting that any moment he would lose his calm exterior and make an attack.

"Did you get it out of your system, or do you need to carry on a bit more?" Tony asked Matt.

"Pardon?"

"Claire told me you wanted to kick—no, she said that you wanted to 'beat the living shit' out of me. I just wondered if you were finished."

"You're an asshole."

"I've been called worse."

Matt winced as he tried his knuckles, bending his fingers and wiping the blood on his already splattered shirt. He checked the cuts, causing them to start bleeding again.

"Do you want me to heal those?" Tony offered.

"No. I don't want anything from you."

"Don't be stupid. They'll get infected." He stood up, walked around the table to Matt, and held out his hand. Matt looked up at the tall man, thought for a moment, and then presented the damaged hands to Tony. It only took a moment for him to heal the cuts and reduce the swelling.

Tony walked over to the sink and got a clean cloth, wet it, and then passed it to Matt to wipe the blood off. He went to the fridge and got three beers, handing two off and taking a long swig from the third as he sat down once more.

"This doesn't make us mates," Matt told him as he opened his own and drank heavily from it.

"Wouldn't dream of thinking it—mate." Tony drank deeply again.

"How old is your son?"

"Six." The single word seemed almost to stick in Tony's throat.

"Same age as Bree. I would've done the same," Matt admitted.

They both watched Adam talking on the phone and pacing. When he came close to them, Matt passed him the third bottle from the table.

"I can help find her, you know. I can get hold of them." Tony leaned forward, resting his elbows on his knees.

"I don't want you anywhere near her. I've never wanted you near her. Why couldn't you stay away?"

"I did. I was married, had a kid of my own. I didn't want to come back and find her. I was happy and content with my life. I had moved on—just as Claire asked me to. And I never wanted to hurt her in the first place. I'm not the baddie here, Matt. Can you trust *him*?" He nodded towards Adam.

"With my life. With my daughter's life and with Claire's life, I trust him. He's been hurt by his father as well."

"Oh, I know what Marcus did to his son. I don't think he remembers, but I was one of the ones to deliver a beating to him. I don't know about the others who did it, but I always guarded my blows to him. No father should ever put his child through that."

"Okay, he has a flight chartered. It leaves in two hours. Can we make it to Glasgow in that time?" Adam said, switching off his phone and looking at Matt.

"No, they've got too much of a lead. Best we can do is follow. Did you find out where they're going?" Matt asked eagerly.

"Yep. Auckland is their destination, but he will be taking them somewhere remote. I know most of the properties he owns, and I've got someone digging a bit to see if his portfolio has changed in the last couple of years."

Matt stood up, downing the rest of his beer, and put the empty bottle on the table. Tony stood up with him and watched the pair of them carefully.

"I don't want to see you anywhere near us ever again. You got me?" Matt told him with some heat, but his tone changed slightly. "But I do hope you get your kid back."

Adam and Matt walked out of the cottage and back to their car. Tony didn't try to stop them or even talk to them. He waited until he was sure they had left before getting his phone and dialing a number.

"You have them both. Where is Johnny?" he demanded.

"Anthony, don't be like that. You will get your boy, but you have to do one more thing for me. I want you to keep my son and that fool Claire is married to out of my way. I already know they're on my trail. I have people at the office as well."

"We had a deal, Marcus."

"I know, but deals change all the time. Just think of this as an addendum to the clause of release. Just remember where you come from and what I have done for you. You owe me, Anthony."

"Yes, and you better remember that I know where all your skeletons are buried, Marcus. See, you're not the only one to play that game."

"Just do as you are told if you want John back." Marcus's voice became steely and flat before the line went dead.

Adam and Matt drove up to the door of the house and got out. Gerry and Addy came running out to meet them. Addy took one look at the pair covered in blood and her face turned white. "Is that his blood?" she asked anxiously. "Please tell me that is his blood!"

"What the hell did you two do? I told you not to do anything stupid. Is Gordon going to find a body out there?" Gerry yelled at Matt.

"No. Some is his blood, but some is mine. He's fine. He healed himself." Matt walked past his father and into the house. He headed straight to his mother's studio and rummaged around behind one of the cabinets, pulling out a full bottle of scotch.

He opened the bottle as he entered the kitchen and got down a couple of glasses, handing one to his father, one to Adam, and pouring himself a good measure.

"I didn't know she still had one," Gerry said, taking a sip.

"There are a couple more. I'll show you where another time." Matt swallowed the contents in one and placed the glass on the bench.

"Are you going to tell me what happened out there?" Gerry asked.

"We found him, we threw a few punches, he healed himself, and he told us that Adam's father has them. He also told us that Marcus has his son."

"Tony has a son?" Addy asked with some surprise.

"Yeah. He won't get him back unless he does what Marcus asks," Matt replied.

"And knowing my father, he won't let a valuable asset like Tony get away too easily," Adam said.

"Right. Let's get packed and on the road," Gerry instructed as he headed towards the door.

"I don't think you coming is a good idea, Dad. I would really rather you stayed here and looked after Gran." Matt saw the disappointment on his father's face. "Please, Dad. I couldn't stand it if something happened to you."

"All right. You go find them and look after yourself." He pulled his son into a hug.

"I will, Dad." Matt fervently hoped that it would come true.

Chapter Six

A deep, constant hum droned through Claire as she stirred from a deep sleep. Her mouth felt like it was full of cotton wool, and her head thumped painfully. She couldn't remember what had happened, and she rubbed her eyes. The droning sound continued to press in on her mind, and it didn't help with the pain. Finally managing to pry her eyelids apart, the light from above made her blink and wince as they began to sting. Carefully Claire lifted her head, taking in her surroundings.

Confusing images met her. She was strapped to a long couch-type seat in a cylindrical area. Comprehension dawned on her as she realised she was on a plane very much like the one she had traveled on from New Zealand to Scotland. She tried to rise but found that her restraints were tightly fastened.

"Help our guest up, will you, Mr. Carter? I believe she'll be more comfortable sitting up," Marcus's drawl came to her.

A large man in a black suit rose from a seat in front and made his way over to her. With a few clicks, the belts were released, and he offered his hand to help her up. She gracefully took it and pulled herself to a standing position. Her head began to swim, and Claire felt dizzy. With a gentleness that defied his size, he steadied her until she was ready to stand on her own. This man was younger than her, and she remembered him. It had been his face she saw standing behind her with a needle.

"Stealth, I presume?" she asked the young man politely in a whisper, giving herself enough time for her mind to come to terms with all that had happened.

"Yep," he answered with a whisper.

"Come and sit with me, Claire," Marcus called to her. "Mr. Carter cannot play chess to save his life."

She moved past Mr. Carter and sat down in the large, comfortable lounge chair opposite her captor. Marcus was resetting a board and turned the white pieces towards her.

"Now, no cheating, Claire. I would like a proper game. Please start," Marcus urged her.

"I'm not really a chess player, Marcus. I think you will find that any game against me will be very one-sided," she said thickly through a dry mouth, giving a small cough.

"Mr. Carter, fetch our guest a drink. What would you like, my dear? I can offer you wine, champagne—but you prefer a bit of scotch, don't you?"

"Water will be fine, thank you," Claire said to Mr. Carter.

The large man went to the rear galley and returned with an unopened bottle of water. He placed it in front of her with a smile, and Claire returned it with her thanks while hastily opening it before drinking deeply from it, finishing it off in only a few gulps.

"Are you hungry? We will be served very shortly. I hope you like salmon," Marcus said, looking at her.

Claire couldn't decipher his demeanor, but she kept up the polite attitude toward him. She decided that playing it such was better than panicking and wildly using her Talents in such a confined space.

"Salmon would be lovely. Thank you, Marcus." She picked up a pawn from the board in front of her and moved it up a couple of spaces.

Marcus made his move, then sat back and waited for Claire. She, in turn, was undecided, trying to remember the rules. Her hand hovered over another pawn, and she changed her mind several times before making her choice.

"You really don't know how to play." His eyebrow arched in amusement, and he moved another piece.

"I only ever played it with Uncle Geoff at Christmastime over a bad frozen dinner."

"Yes, I am sorry for your loss. Geoff Brown was a great adversary. Our working together was much like chess."

"But he managed to keep me safe." She watched the board and the move he had just made and immediately countered.

"I was still able to get a few people near you."

"But I sent them on their way. That reminds me, how is Richard these days? I believe he had a nervous breakdown and was in a bad way."

"Yes, he did. I am afraid to say that the last I heard, he had managed to drink himself to death. You really did a number on him."

"Well, he had it coming. I mean, who goes to talk to someone with a large stick in their hands?" Again, she quickly followed up his move, taking his rook.

"I thought you said you couldn't play." Marcus moved in his seat as he stared at the board, his eyebrows now knitted together.

"Lucky shot, I guess." Claire concentrated on the board and from somewhere in her brain, strategy after strategy began to play out, showing her each and every move she could make in great detail and the resulting outcomes. She chose to ignore them.

They played the game out in silence, and Marcus was very pleased when he won. He reset the board and presented her with the black pieces. His smugness really grated on Claire, and her own ego got the better of her.

This game was faster, their moves more calculated, and Claire had him worried. She could see his brows growing closer together with each of her moves as she kept up the pressure, taking piece after piece. Instead of conceding defeat, he wiped the board of the remaining pieces like a little child throwing a tantrum.

Claire sat back and watched his face revealing his emotions as he fought to get himself back under control. He looked up at her, trying hard to smile, but only managing a snarl.

"Just a gentle reminder that my Talents have increased slightly. I don't know if the information got through to you about them, but they have far surpassed that of a Chameleon," she told him sweetly, referring to the almost mythical state of allowing one to take on many Talents.

"Then why have you not disabled us all?" he asked curiously, watching as Claire reset the chess board after Mr. Carter had picked up the pieces that had fallen to the floor.

"Because unlike you, I don't like throwing my weight around. Plus, the air crew may have questions about what happened. Mr. Carter, will you please go sit back down? I am no threat to Mr. Ryder at the moment." She smiled as she saw Marcus look up and nod to his bodyguard. "He may have Stealth, but I can still keep track of him. Where is my daughter?"

A stewardess appeared from the back carrying two plates, and she placed them in front of Marcus and Claire. She then produced two glasses and poured some champagne for each of them before retreating to her seat in the back.

"Please, eat," Marcus directed her.

Claire found she was feeling very hungry and ate the meal with great enthusiasm. Once finished, she placed her cutlery on the plate and sat back, waiting for Marcus to finish.

"You're not drinking. It's very good. Only the best will do," he encouraged her, scraping the plate of the last morsels of food.

"No, thank you. I'm not a champagne type of girl," Claire told him. "If I could have another water instead."

"Help yourself," Marcus said moodily and indicated the small fridge down the back.

Claire stood and made her way to the back of the plane. As she passed Mr. Carter, she smiled sweetly at him and he responded in kind. The galley was small, and Claire found the fridge easily. When she looked up, the stewardess was watching her. She mouthed a few words, and it took Claire a moment to figure out what she was trying to say. "Are you okay?"

With a small nod, she smiled at the woman and got the bottle of water out of the fridge. Claire made her way back to her seat opposite Marcus.

"You haven't answered my question," she stated as she settled herself back in her seat.

"No, I didn't. She is safe."

"Where?"

"That's all you need to know for now. She is safe and on her way to New Zealand." His tone had a note of finality about it and Claire clenched her jaw trying not to respond in a way that could be adverse.

Claire stared out the small window at the clouds below, watching the sunlight play over their tops. The blue sky above seemed like a dome over the world. She tried to send her thoughts out to find her daughter, but her mind was still so muddled and confused with whatever she had been given that she finally gave up. Instead, she turned her attention back to Marcus.

"There's something I would like to know. You are what, over one hundred and seventy now? Maybe even older? That would make you part of the first generation of our people to have been born in New Zealand. What were your parents like? Where did they come from?"

"This is not a subject I like to talk about, Claire. I'd really rather we don't talk at the moment," he answered sullenly.

"But this is the perfect opportunity for you to tell me your story. All I've ever had is second and thirdhand information about you. You know I couldn't even find you in the archived genealogy lists."

"You won't, either. I believe all the information about my family was taken out of the files. I'm the last of my line, so there's no need for the lists."

"But you're not the last. Your grandsons Dominic and Cameron are."

"They are not of my line. Adam is not a true Ryder. After what he did to me—betrayed me—Jack was more my son than him. It was Jack who found someone to undo what you two did to me."

"It could have been worse. The original plan was to kill you. I'm now starting to regret Adam talking me into saving you." Claire laced her fingers together and rested her hands on the table.

"You and your kind are weak. That's why you didn't go through with it, Claire. You couldn't face killing me." His lips twisted into a sneer that hinted at triumph.

"That's correct. The thought of taking your life was very hard for me. And it nearly destroyed me when I eventually took Jack's."

Marcus's eyes widened at this news. *Nobody told him the truth about how Jack had died*, she thought. Claire expected Tony to have reported back to him with this news, and she immediately regretted telling him.

"You killed Jack? I don't believe you," he scoffed. "He fell down a cliff and smashed himself to pieces."

"That's how it was made to look." Claire tried to remain calm as she watched him carefully digesting this new information and waited for him to respond.

"Well, I will be having words with certain people about how they report things."

"I wouldn't blame Tony. He didn't see it. He was out cold when it happened." She hoped this lie would protect him.

"Two men against one slip of a girl and she came out the victor. I don't believe it," Marcus sneered.

"You know, women's liberation has come a long way since you were younger, Marcus. But you know all this. You lived through it. It must have been a fascinating time."

"Yes, and I am looking forward to turning back the clock." He reached out and placed a hand over hers. "Women belong in the kitchen—or on their backs in the bedroom."

"You disgust me." Claire pulled her hands away from him, secretly pleased that he had touched her. She now had the connection she wanted.

"We have quite a few hours until we land in Auckland, Claire. I suggest you use it to change. I took the liberty of selecting some clothes for you. They're in the back. There's a shower there as well. You might like to freshen up." Marcus dismissed her with a wave of his hand, turning his head to look out the window at his side.

In Glasgow, Adam and Matt were waiting for their charter flight to be ready. They sat in an exclusive lounge usually reserved for VIPs and waited impatiently. The delay in their travel had been annoying and frustrating for the pair. But it was about to get slightly worse.

Through the doors strode Tony, impeccably dressed in a business suit with no tie but the collar open on the crisp white shirt. He wore dark glasses and carried a bag. There was no hesitation in his actions as he confidently placed his bag on an empty seat near Matt and took off his sunglasses. There was no evidence of the beating they had given him only a few short hours earlier.

"I thought I told you I never want to see you again," Matt growled through gritted teeth, not even bothering to get up.

"And I told you that you're going to need me to get to Claire and Bree. I had a very nice chat with your dad, Adam. I think you can guess what he said." Tony paused, his body tense and ready to react. "I want that bastard dead—no offence."

"None taken. I'm beginning to think the same thing. I should've let Claire kill him back then," Adam replied slowly.

"I know how bad she took it when she killed Jack, so this time it's my turn." Tony sat down.

"You're not invited, Tony. The manifest only has our names on it," Adam told him.

"I think you'll find that it has been updated." He sat back in his seat and crossed his long legs.

The easy manner in which he was acting only served to feed the frustration Matt was feeling at the delays. He looked at his watch, trying to calculate how much lead they had on them already. It would be not quite twenty-four hours before they could even begin to be on their trail again once they landed in New Zealand. He stood and went to the window, looking out but not really seeing the busy airport beyond.

"Matt, I've been at this game longer than you. I have the skills to find them. Actually, I have already put some of them in motion. I have set someone to follow them the moment they leave the airport. When we land, we'll know where he's keeping her," Tony told him.

"You'd better be right. If he harms one hair on either of their heads, it won't be just Marcus who gets hurt," Matt threatened.

"It's not just Claire and Bree who are in danger, Matt. I have just as much interest in making sure this works out as you do."

Warm water cascaded down, washing away the remains of whatever they had drugged her with, along with the feeling of the unknown. The body washes and hair shampoos were beautiful smelling, but Claire did not enjoy them. She worried what Matt was doing and while she was alone, she made an effort to send out a message. Her mind sought his, and she almost cried with relief when she made the connection.

"Matt, thank God. It's Marcus. He has me. And I don't know where Bree is. He won't tell me." She called frantically.

"We know he's behind it, Claire. We're following you. Adam and I are in the air on our way to Auckland. We got delayed." He sounded frustrated and anxious, and it worried her more.

"Hurry, please. I can keep him occupied, but I don't want to do this by myself. I need you."

"Hang in there, Claire. I love you. Keep yourself safe."

"I will. Please take care looking for me. I'll try to keep you informed on where we are and if I can get any information about where Bree is. I have to go. I only have a few moments. I love you."

"I'll see you soon, my love," Matt said, and they broke their connection.

Claire was just about to turn the water off and step out of the shower when someone else touched her mind. She pulled back for a moment and then recognised him.

"I heard your conversation. Matt didn't tell you everything."

"You bastard, Tony. Why did you do this?" she demanded. Even though it was only a mental conversation, her hands were balled into fists ready to fight him.

"This is important, so shut up and listen. I had no choice. Marcus has my son—no questions, I'll explain later. He has my son and I want him back. I'm with Matt and Adam and I'm coming along. You are not to touch Marcus—he is mine. You owe me that. Now get dressed and get back out there. Otherwise, the bodyguard will break down the door."

The break was a clean and clear one, and when she came back to herself, there was a banging on the door.

"I'll be out in a moment," she called out testily, and it stopped. She dried herself and opened the garment bag the stewardess had given her. She was shocked to see some of her own clothing inside. Wasting no more time, she dressed and returned to her seat.

"Do you always take so long in the bathroom?" Marcus asked her as he sipped his drink.

"Not always, but I felt like I had some extra filth to wash off me." She sat back in her seat and crossed her legs.

"Would you like a drink?" he offered, not even batting an eye at her veiled insult. Whether he had understood, she did not know.

"No, thank you. I think I will stick with water. I prefer a clear head when dealing with people like you."

"You just have to get to know me, and then there won't be any misunderstanding about my personality."

"Oh, I know your personality, Mr. Ryder. Character and moral groundings are a completely different matter. I noticed that you haven't tried to Charm me."

"What would be the point? With your Talents the way they are, it would just be a waste of my time and energy." He flashed her that sneering smile once more.

"What I would like to talk about is how you managed to break the suggestions Adam and I put on you."

"I'm surprised Tony didn't tell you. After all, it was he who found the one who could do it," Marcus replied, obviously trying to bait her.

"Well, Tony and I don't really talk that much. It goes more along the lines of me telling him to stop following me. But I suppose if he's being paid to do it, then he will keep on doing it." Tony's words were still echoing in her head. The revelation that he had a son was a surprise to her.

"Tony has served me for a very long time. He was a watcher on your parents before they died." Marcus eyed her over the rim of his glass.

"Oh, that I know. He told me that he and Dad were friends once, and that he was devastated when he died. And if you try to tell me that he was the one to carry out your orders, I won't believe you. I've been inside his head," she told him, trying to sound casual about the topic.

"What an experience for him. That would be the closest he's ever been to you. Has he been inside yours?" The smirk he wore was clearly designed to suggest something else.

Claire just sat and stared at this man who had caused her so much pain and misery since the age of ten. She refused to rise to his bait, understanding that this was how he had fun. Claire decided she did not want to play his games anymore.

"When you can talk to me intelligently, Mr. Ryder, then I will listen to what you have to say."

"Don't tell me you are a prude, Claire? He's a good-looking man. You haven't thought what it might be like?" This time, she refused to look at him and kept her thoughts to herself. But still he wouldn't let up. "Have I hit a nerve, Claire?" She saw the delight in his eye.

Anger and hatred rose up and constricted in her throat. She bit back several comments she could have made and tried to remain calm. The energy boiled inside and was pushing to be released, and Claire worked hard to keep it under control.

"At least tell me that he told you he has a son."

"No, he didn't. I told you, we didn't really open up to each other, and it's been years since I've seen him last," Claire told him.

"That surprises me. I felt certain he would have told you about him. His name is John, by the way. So sweet how he named him after your father."

"Not really surprising. He looked up to my dad," she retorted calmly.

Marcus sat back, laced his fingers together, and held them against his lips. Every time he tried to get a reaction, this girl—no, this woman—would bring it to an end, not taking the bait he so carefully laid out. He decided that Claire had developed into a worthy adversary for him and he was going to enjoy breaking her—spiritually, physically, and mentally. His plans were all in action now with one more piece needing to be put in place—then it would be checkmate and she would grovel at his feet for mercy.

Chapter Seven

The plane landed with a slight jolt and a squeal of rubber meeting the tarmac. Green grass and mud flats passed them by before the plane slowed and taxied to the terminal. Claire looked at Marcus, waiting for the instructions that she knew he would give her.

"Here's your passport, Mrs. Ryder." He reached into an inner pocket of the jacket he was wearing and retrieved it, tossing it onto the table in front of her. "We have just returned from our honeymoon. I hope you understand how to act as we go through customs?" Marcus smirked suggestively.

"You will have no problems from me, Marcus," Claire replied with no emotion.

The plane came to a stop and the stewardess opened the cabin door. Claire stood with Marcus and Mr. Carter and moved to leave the plane.

"Ma'am, your handbag." The stewardess looked down at the bag and then back up to Claire. She raised an eyebrow at the woman as she handed it to her.

"Thank you! I would lose my head if it wasn't screwed on right. And thank you for taking such good care of us on the flight. Marcus, dear, I do think she deserves a very big tip. Don't you?" Claire turned to her captor and smiled sweetly.

"If you insist, darling." He reached into his jacket for his wallet and pulled out a twenty-dollar note.

"No, sweetheart. That's not enough." Claire plucked the wallet from his hands and pulled out considerably more notes than Marcus would have liked, handed the near-empty wallet back to him, and gave the cash to the woman. "Treat yourself to something very nice," she told her cheerfully, then descended the stairs, leaving a stunned Marcus and a very happy and hopefully hushed flight attendant.

Claire waited for the two men to join her, and they walked into the terminal, passing through customs and border control without any mishap. Claire made sure to play her part well, fawning all over Marcus and clinging to him. She had decided to play the blonde bimbo trophy wife, but the one thing she refused to do was kiss that horrible man.

A black car pulled up in front of them as they exited the terminal, and Mr. Carter opened the door for Claire to get in. She sat in the back with Marcus beside her, staring out the window as they drove out of the airport.

"That was not a nice thing to do, Claire—giving away my money," Marcus grumbled.

"She deserved it. Also, she kept asking if I was okay." She picked up the handbag the woman had given her and opened it. Inside were a few bits of makeup and a cell phone. She pulled it out and handed it over to Marcus. "You should be thanking me."

"You could have kept this and I would be none the wiser. Why?" He held it in his hands as if it would explode and looked at her with surprise.

"I don't need cell phones to contact the people I love." She continued to stare out at the suburbs of Auckland as they whisked by. The sun was still high in the sky, but grey clouds were threatening.

The pocket of Marcus's jacket started to ring, and he answered it. "What?" he demanded, still staring at Claire. "Good—send it through."

Shortly after he had disconnected the call, the phone beeped. He opened the text and started to chuckle. "Your daughter is very pretty, Claire. She doesn't look like you, though. That's a pity." He turned the screen so she could see and laughed at her reaction.

The photo he showed her was of Bree sitting strapped into an airplane seat. She was smiling, and her blue eyes were sparkling. There was a date and a time stamp on the photo—it had been taken only moments before. Her anger rose once more. *How dare he touch my daughter!*

"Now you have proof that I have her, I expect you to behave yourself," he told her, turning the phone back so he could gaze at the picture.

Claire sat mute, unable to speak. Her energy was percolating away inside, starting to reach its boiling point. It would be so easy, she thought, to take them all out right now and go find her daughter. But the *what ifs* started to form, and they kept on until she felt like her mind would collapse with the weight of them.

"I'm okay, Mummy. James is a nice man. Aunty Breena made sure that he wouldn't harm me," a tiny voice spoke in the back of her mind. She reached for the connection and held it close to her, sending her love and comfort to her daughter.

"Oh, my sweet, I'm so sorry you have been caught up in this. What happened?" Claire asked.

"I knew they were coming, so I called to Aunty Breena to help me, so they didn't hurt anyone. Mummy, I have to be in New Zealand. I can't do what I have to do in Scotland," Bree replied carefully.

"What is it you have to do, my sweet?"

"I can't tell you. The Guardians won't let me."

Claire swallowed hard, silently cursing the Guardians and their secrecy. She wanted so desperately to help her daughter and protect her, but she was being hamstrung at the first turn.

"You stay safe, my wee angel, and behave, okay?"

"Yes, Mummy. I love you."

"I love you, too."

The connection faded so slowly she didn't realise it was fully gone. Talking to Bree that way had calmed her down, and she sank further into her seat and fell asleep.

"Hello, Mr. Man," the small girl's voice rang merrily like a tinkling bell in Tony's mind.

"Hello, You," Tony replied. Somehow her voice made him feel calm and almost happy.

Over the last six months, she had come visiting him in his mind. At first, he thought he was going mad, but then just as quickly he realised that this child was special. He had managed to ascertain that she was six and that she loved to draw and to laugh. But there was one thing that he hadn't been able to discover, and that one thing was her name. She had told him that she couldn't give it to him. As a result, he just called her "You."

"Mr. Man, would you like to know my name now?" You asked in a shy voice.

"I would love to know your name if you're ready to give it to me," he told her.

"If I give you my name, you have to promise to do something for me—something really, really, really important. Will you?"

"If it is in my power, You, then I will make that promise."

"Do you promise?" she asked again.

"I do promise," Tony told her with a smile.

"Good." The word sounded like a gong, and he suddenly wondered what he had got himself into. "My name is Breena," she declared.

"Breena? Claire's Breena?" He felt so shocked. Once it wore off it, didn't seem so surprising to him.

"You made me a promise, Tony, and now I would like you to keep it."

"How do you know my name?" he asked, suddenly confused.

"I know a lot of things. I have known your name all my life. Do you want to know what it is that I want you to do?"

"I think we need to have a very serious talk, Breena. I need to know some things first."

"But you promised, and I can only pretend to be asleep for so long," she told him, the childish voice suddenly sounding so grown up.

"Okay, it can wait. What is it?"

"I want you to teach Daddy how to control his Talents. He shouts when he talks to Mummy, and that's going to be bad later on. Please," she added.

"I don't think your father will want me to do that. He doesn't like me right at the moment."

"No, not yet, but he will. One day you two will be great friends, like you and Mummy are," Breena said brightly.

"That is a different kind of thing, Breena."

"Well, you are. Sometimes I wish you grown-ups would just listen and understand." Breena was feeling frustrated that he didn't take her seriously.

"I'll try to keep my promise, but he will not like it."

"Good, but don't tell him that we have talked. He won't like that at all."

"No, he wouldn't."

"Johnny is okay. Mummy will look after him when we are together, which will be soon," Breena told him gently.

"Thank you, Breena," he said, and then she was gone.

Tony opened his eyes and looked around the plane. The two men he was traveling with were tucked away in their own little corners. Adam was reading—or it seemed like he was—and Matt was chewing on his thumbnail, his eyes wild. His body was tensed and wound up like a spring ready for release.

For a start, he was going to have to get Matt to loosen up before he even attempted to train his Talents. He studied the younger man. *Not that much younger than me*, Tony thought, but still closer to Claire's age than his own.

Standing up, he went to Adam first. "Beer?" he asked him.

Adam looked up at this mysterious man who had invited himself along on the journey back to New Zealand. "Yeah, thanks," he said, then he went back to his book.

"You want one?" Tony asked, turning to Matt, and waiting for a reply. When he didn't get one, he gently touched Matt's shoulder.

Matt flinched away from him and turned angry eyes up to look at Tony. "What?"

Anger radiated from him in great arcs of energy. Tony stepped back from him and then asked again, "Would you like a beer?"

"No." Matt went back to brooding.

Tony headed down to the galley and brought back two beers and a bottle of water. He placed the water in front of Matt and sat opposite him, opening his own bottle and taking a long swig.

"Fuck off," Matt told him quietly.

"No. I won't, thanks. You and I have to have a little chat." Tony placed his bottle in front of him.

"I'm not in the talking mood right now. I'm trying to work out how to get my wife and child back."

"I know you are. You are also expending a lot of energy doing it. Also, when you talk to Claire, can you turn your voice down? I would much prefer I wasn't privy to your private conversations."

"You what?" Matt demanded, turning his full attention to Tony.

"I know you don't mean to, but your voice is being sent out for the whole world to hear. You need to work more on keeping it intimate. I can help if you like," Tony replied gently.

"I don't want your help. Claire has given me all the help I need," Matt spat at him.

Tony began to curse both Claire and Breena. Without either of them, he would be sitting at his comfortable house with his wife Maddison and their boy Johnny, enjoying semi-retirement. Now he was grieving for the wife that he'd loved more than he'd realised, was fighting to get his son back, and chasing—yet again—the woman who had started it all.

"Really?" Tony turned to Adam. "You've heard him, haven't you? Mr. Mind Touch and Charm?"

Adam looked up from his book. "Those are my Talents. You would know that, having worked for my father. But yes, Matt, I have heard you talking to Claire. It's like some bizarre one-way telephone conversation. Don't look to me to help— my Talents are very limited."

"That leaves me," Tony said, leaning back in the seat and drinking his beer.

Matt stared at him with fire in his eyes. Tony could see that this was the last thing he wanted to do—get assistance from him. He could see all the emotions as they flicked across Matt's face. The realisation that he was going to have to trust him, and that finding both Claire and Bree was going to be nearly impossible without Tony's help.

"Yes, Matt, you are going to have to trust me. I know you don't right now, but does it help for me to say that I don't want Claire in that way anymore?" Tony asked gently.

"Not really. How can I know that's true?" Matt narrowed his eyes as he asked the question.

"Have a look inside. I have nothing to hide." Tony indicated his head.

"You would trust me to go in there and not do any damage to you?" Matt asked eagerly, sitting forward.

"I don't think you would. You're not like that. Anyway, Claire once offered to change me so I didn't love her anymore, but I told her no. Even though I don't love her in the romantic sense anymore, I still love her and care for her like an older brother. If she had taken that away, I would've had no hesitation in taking her to Marcus when I had the chance. So, if you go in here and change me in any capacity, then you change me, and I don't think you would like what I would be capable of. Marcus asked that I delay you getting to New Zealand. So far I haven't acted on his orders."

"Claire asked you that?" Matt said, thinking back to what Claire had offered Tony.

"She said she could stop my heart or she could stop me loving her. I told her I would rather she stopped my heart than take that away from me. The ability to love is what's keeping me going. She once told me something else. She said that love is stronger than hate." Tony stood and picked up his beer. "I'll let you think on it."

Matt watched him leave and move down the plane to sit. The words he had told him sounded like something Claire had once told him, and Matt was beginning to reevaluate everything. Claire had always said she could handle Tony, and this new piece of interaction between them surprised him. He had always thought Claire had somehow liked being the centre of this man's attention in some strange way. She had asked him to trust her on it and he hadn't. The argument in the kitchen had proved that.

The walk was a short one, but it seemed a long time to get to where Tony was sitting. Matt sat opposite and held out a hand. Tony raised an eyebrow, took the proffered hand, and shook it.

"If this is the only way to get the people we love back, then I am willing to listen," Matt told him. "But after this is all over, you go your way and we will go ours."

"Believe me, I want nothing more."

"what do I have to do?" Matt asked with some trepidation.

Tony took a deep breath, but before he had a chance to say a word to Matt, another voice broke through.

"Thank goodness for that," Bree thought in his mind. He made a mental note to himself to have words with the young girl about boundaries.

Gran climbed the stairs, her knees protesting greatly as she went. Gerry's idea of making the studio a bedroom for her started to seem like a good one. She reached the landing and opened the door to her room. The fuss of the morning had got to her, and she felt tired and old. There was nothing she could do to help her family, and it was breaking her heart.

The door swung open, and she looked at the small camping cot at the end of her own bed. The blankets were all pushed to the end and the pillow had fallen to the floor. Some of Bree's toys were scattered under the tiny bed, and Gran bent down to pick up a doll and held it to her.

She looked out the window and wondered where both Bree and Claire had gone when a cold draft wafted past her. She shuddered involuntarily. Turning slowly, she was confronted by a vision of a beautiful woman in a long sapphire blue gown, which set off the young woman's eyes and dark curly hair.

"Hello, Gran," Breena greeted her grandmother.

Gran placed a hand on her heart and gasped in surprise. When she felt her heart wasn't going to leap out of her chest, she took a step towards Breena.

"Breena?" she said in an almost whisper.

"Yes. I have to tell Galen something. Can you call him up here for me?" Breena sat on Gran's bed and waited.

"I can't, my sweet girl. He's not here. Is this something to do with Bree and Claire?"

"Yes. I promised Bree that I would explain to Galen. She knew he would need an explanation."

"We need that explanation. We're going spare thinking about it. Can't you tell us, then we can pass the message on to him?" Gran begged.

Breena was still a moment, cocking her head as if she were listening to someone. Finally, she nodded. "Aye. I can do that, Gran."

"Gerry! Addy!" Gran called out. "Gerry, Addy, I think you should come up here, now!" She went and sat down beside Breena, just looking at her.

Heavy footsteps on the stairs reached the two women, and Gerry called out to his mother-in-law, "What's the matter? Are you hurt?"

They rounded the corner and stopped dead in their tracks. Gerry's face went white, and the breath was knocked out of his lungs. He reached out and steadied himself against the wall to stop from falling to the floor. Addy stood behind him, looking over his shoulder, with her mouth hanging open.

Breena stood and rushed to his side, throwing her arms around his neck, hugging him enthusiastically. Gerry pulled her off and held her at arm's length.

"It's me, Da."

"I can see that, lass. But I don't understand how!"

"It doesn't matter how at the moment. I have important news for you." She released his grip, took his hand, and led him over to Gran. Once he was seated on the bed, Breena stood by the window and looked at the three of them, feeling nervous.

"Bree was taken by those who took Claire. She wanted me to tell you that she's fine and being looked after properly. I actually made sure of that."

Gerry's face was turning red. "Where have they gone? And why?"

"Please, Da, sit down and listen. Bree knew they were coming for her and asked for my help."

"How did she know? She is only six!" He was running his hands through his thinning hair and dreading having to ring his son to let him know.

"How do you think, Uncle Gerry?" Addy spoke for the first time. "Our Bree is a very special girl."

"No, she is too young. This just cannot be," he stumbled, shaking his head.

"I know it is hard to come to terms with, Da, but there's more, I'm afraid. Please sit," Breena urged him.

Gerry got his emotions under control and sat as Breena had asked. This young woman who stood before him was his daughter. He had known the moment he laid eyes on her. There was no way he could explain how he had known. It was as if she had grown before his eyes in the perfect world he had once hoped for.

"You have to go to the library and do some study, Da. I know for you that won't be a hardship, but you're going to have study your own Mind Touch Ability. You have to push through the barriers that limit it in the modern world. The

Guardians will guide you. Claire is going to need all the strength that you and Gran can send her when she performs her task."

"Are we to go to New Zealand, then?" Gran asked with a little hope in her voice.

"No. You are needed here, at the stones. You and Da are to be the focus for the Guardian's power."

"Is there anything I need to do to prepare?" Gran reached across to the young woman and clasped her hands. She was surprised by how warm they were.

"No, Gran. There is nothing more for you to prepare for. The memories that you hold are to be your strength and your shield, the happy ones. It is important for you to hold them close to you, the memories of love and caring."

"I have plenty of those." She smiled.

"Bree, what do I have to do?" Addy asked, as she had begun to feel left out.

"Addy." Breena turned and hugged her cousin. "They need you in New Zealand. They need your strength and your Abilities. It's time to dust them off and get them working properly again. You know who you must turn to. I know it won't be easy, but she will be able to help. Claire is going to need you. Please look after my sister."

Addy nodded and hugged Breena one more time. "I wish we could have grown up together, Bree. I think we would have had a lot of fun together," she said wistfully.

"Aye, we could have," Breena replied as she smiled back.

Gran stood up from the bed and joined the two women who were her granddaughters. She took Addy's hand in hers and then looked at Breena and Gerry. "I think you two need a moment alone. Come on, Addy. Let's go get you and the boys packed." As they left the room, Gran smiled and closed the door gently.

Chapter Eight

Matt wound down the window of the car that had picked them up and breathed in the chilly winter air of his adopted home. He was feeling a bone-weary tiredness he had never experienced before. Sleep was something he had readily sacrificed on the plane, in order to go through the endless exercises Tony had put him through. Even though he had tried his hardest, he still held back from Tony, unable to trust the man fully. It made things more painful than they needed to be, but the result was satisfying.

Pain was also what was sustaining him: the near physical pain of being parted from his wife and daughter. Also, the pain of outrage that someone could enter their lives and hurt them in this way, combined with the anxious pain of having to work with Tony. It was all taking its toll on Matt. His eyes were red and bleary, his face looked drawn and pale, and he felt his spirits were at the lowest they had ever been—even worse than the night Claire had run from him.

"Wind the window up, will you, dude? It's fucking freezing!" the driver called to the back seat where Matt was sitting. "Just 'cause you come from a cold climate don't mean we all do." He laughed at his own attempt at humour.

The man who had met them at the airport was a friend of Tony's, and he had been introduced him to them as Nikau. He was a muscular man with tattoos on his arms. His hair was cropped closely to his head, and he wore black dress pants and a black jumper with the sleeves pushed up. Once in the car, he had reported to Tony on what they'd seen. Matt had listened in and was impressed with the way this man handled himself.

"There were three with Claire. She didn't look scared. In fact, she looked like she was pretty much in control. Marcus sat in the back with her, and his bodyguard, Greg Carter—nice kid, we looked at recruiting him last year—sat in the front."

"What was wrong with him?" Tony asked.

"Too much of a loose cannon. Lots of issues and a bit unstable to be really reliable," Nikau answered.

"Sounds perfect for my father," Adam chimed in from the back.

Matt saw Nikau's eyebrows raise in surprise at that news, and he looked across to Tony. "Anyway, they sped away and headed down Highway One. I have a tail on them, and they should be reporting back in about an hour. So, where to first, boss?"

"We go to my place first, and then we can work out from there. Any word on Johnny?" Tony asked hopefully.

"Nah, sorry, boss. I've been trying, but I can't get any info from any source inside his camp. It's like nothing I've seen before."

"Thanks for trying, Nik." Tony's voice sounded tired and resigned.

The rest of the trip was made in silence.

An hour later, they pulled up the long drive of a house that was hidden well away from the road. Outside the front door, a bright yellow car was parked.

"Who's here, Nik?" Tony asked, suddenly very tense.

"Don't panic. It's only Tia. I sent her ahead to get everything ready. She's even got the books for you to look at."

"Great. You couldn't have sent someone else?" Tony asked, slowly undoing his seatbelt.

"Hey, I can't help it if my sister still has the hots for you. But she's the best administrator we've had, bro, so don't piss her off."

"Well, well, well. The stalker has a stalker?" Matt said, laughing a little.

"Shut up, Matt," Tony said testily as he exited the car.

The door to the house opened, and a beautiful woman came out to meet them. Her long hair was a riot of colours—blue, red, and pink—and was pulled back from her face, showing off her big brown eyes. She had a ready smile, and Matt watched with amusement that her eyes only tracked Tony.

"'Bout time you lot showed up! I was about to send out a search party," Tia greeted them. "Come in. It's nice and warm inside."

Once inside, Tony made the introductions to Tia. She gave Adam and Matt's hands a firm shake and told them that dinner would be ready soon.

"You didn't have to do that," Tony told her.

"Of course I did. You don't eat properly. Everything is on the desk in your office ready for you to look at." She left them with a smile and went to the kitchen.

"You two are business partners?" Adam asked Tony and Nikau.

"Yep, have been for what—fourteen years now?" Nikau answered.

"You didn't think I could do what I've done on a wage from Marcus, do you?" Tony laughed slightly, pouring himself and the other men a drink and handing them round. Matt noticed that Nikau declined his.

"There's a lot of demand out there for people of our skill set. Plus, Kiwis can pretty much go anywhere in the world.

They love us out there," Nikau continued as he sat back, resting an ankle on his other knee.

"Who's tailing them?" Tony asked. The mood inside changed slightly, and Nikau became all business again.

"You were lucky. Our best op had just arrived back from overseas when you rang. I've got Michael Kelly on it."

"Good," Tony replied, nodding.

"Come and get it," Tia called from the kitchen. Matt found that he was starving and couldn't remember when he last ate. He followed everyone else and sat at the table between Adam and Tia.

The table was laden with food, and he enjoyed it immensely. Nikau and Tony talked shop over dinner, and there was little left of conversation between Adam and Matt.

"So, you are her husband?" Tia suddenly spoke in a quiet voice.

"Pardon?"

"You are Claire's husband?" Tia repeated.

"Yes, I am."

"What's she like?"

"I'm probably the wrong person to ask," Matt said. "I'm biased."

"Do you know why she has such a hold on Tony?"

"I think he would be the best person to ask that. From what he has said to me lately, I don't think there is much hold anymore."

"Really?" She looked at Tony speculatively.

The ringing of a phone brought them all to silence. Nikau answered it and walked away from the table. They watched him leave, and Matt found he was holding his breath. Letting it out slowly, Matt waited for Nikau to return.

"Did you know, Adam, that your dad had a place near Midhurst, by Mt. Taranaki?" Nikau asked as he resumed his seat.

"Hang on." Adam got out his phone and started to scroll. "Yeah. He bought it two years ago, and he's had it extensively remodeled."

"Well, that's where he's taken her. What do you want to do, boss?" Nikau asked, turning to Tony.

"See if Michael can get a closer look at the place. We'll stay here tonight. I can't imagine that he will keep her there for long." Tony looked at Matt. "Does that sound all right?"

"It's your show. As you said, you have the expertise in this. What can an archaeologist do?" The hand Matt had resting on the table was clenched in a very tight fist.

Daylight was starting to dim as the sun began to settle over the horizon of rolling hills and old Macrocarpa trees, bent from the prevailing winds. The car threaded its way up a narrow road, dipping and rising with the terrain. The clouds overhead began to change from a deep grey to a coral blush with purple hues. Claire watched the New Zealand landscape roll past her and wondered how much longer this journey was going to take.

Ahead, a large house could be seen in and out of the trees that surrounded it. The gardens looked immaculately kept with flat, lush grassy areas and plenty of trees, some waiting for the onset of spring to burst into life. Smoke trailed out of the prominent chimney, and lights shone from the many windows on the ground floor.

"It's not much, but I'm very proud of how it's turned out. It was almost derelict when I purchased it," Marcus said, watching Claire.

The car turned up the driveway and stopped at a set of very large iron gates. The driver pressed a button from a remote attached to the sun visor and the gates swung open on silent hinges. Inching forward until he could drive all the way through, he pressed the same remote to shut them, closing out the world with a loud and final *clang*.

Mr. Carter was at her door within seconds of the car stopping, and he held his hand out to assist her. Claire took it and smiled. A flash of a belt hitting a bare back came to her from the touch, and she almost flinched from it. No wonder this boy was working for Marcus. Adam suddenly came to her mind.

"Thank you, Mr. Carter." Claire smiled at him, and for the first time, it wasn't forced.

"Shall we go in?" Marcus asked as he strode off in front of her.

The door opened for him, and he went in without waiting for Claire. She climbed the steps and entered the large hallway that greeted her. The décor was tastefully done. It was almost to the time period of the house, but with a few modern twists. She followed him into a large reception room, and he told her to sit.

"You can't object to a drink now that we're here." He moved to a small bar in the back of the room.

"No, thank you. I don't drink," Claire said, trying to remain calm.

"Yes, you do. You drink—oh, what is it called—one of the well-known Scottish whiskies."

"I would rather not, thank you." She sat down, crossed her legs, and put her hands together. "Water will be fine."

Marcus looked puzzled for a moment, and Claire delighted in it. She had just made part of the dossier he had on her obsolete. She could see him wondering what else was wrong in her information.

"What exactly are your plans for my daughter?" She accepted the glass of sparkling water from him and sipped it.

He sat opposite her and took a draft of his drink. "Nothing for the moment. She is just a bargaining chip to get you to behave. I have found her a useful tool."

"Too bad you didn't use it on my parents. They may still be alive now." Claire placed the glass on the table that separated them.

"Ah, yes. That could have been handled a bit better. I really did like your parents—very down-to-earth people. And your mother was beautiful. You look just like her."

"I've been told that before. What is it exactly that you want me to do?" she asked.

"We will get to that. Shall we just relax and wind down for a moment? I always have a hard time after travelling for so long."

"That's what happens when you get old, Marcus."

"Do I look my age?" Instead of being offended, he looked slightly amused at her comment.

"It may be starting to show a little around the eyes."

Marcus let out a little chuckle. "I heard you had a wicked sense of humour."

"That would be from Tony, wouldn't it? He's the only one of your cronies I've had the pleasure of meeting—except Richard, of course."

"Are you quite sure about that?" He raised an eyebrow and enjoyed the momentary surprise it caused. He admired how quickly she recovered from this little bit of information.

"If you're referring to your son, then that was a long time ago. Anyway, I've been able to pick your people out long before they even get near me. There is a certain—oh, what's the word I'm looking for? There's a grubbiness in their thoughts that gives them away."

"And Tony? Does he have that—grubbiness?" He finished his drink and dangled the glass in two fingers.

"I really am not interested in talking about Tony."

"Is he really that much of a sore spot for you, or do you secretly fancy him and wish you had chosen him over your husband?"

"I'm surprised that in all your long years on this earth, you've never really loved anybody except yourself. Or is it too painful to watch them grow old in front of your eyes and pass away? You've already lost one son. How many other sons and daughters have you watched pass away? How many grandchildren—or even great, great, great grandchildren—do you have?"

Marcus stood and went to pour himself another drink. The bottle clinked loudly against the crystal glass, and she could tell he was annoyed. He lifted the glass to his mouth and swallowed it in one go before hastily pouring another, then rejoining her.

"That is a very touchy subject, Claire, not one I think I will elaborate on." He gave her a steely look. Claire could see he was trying to hide his reaction to her question.

"So do you still see them, or have they been wiped from your genealogy as well?" She knew she was goading the bull and wondered how he would take it.

"I think that this conversation is over. You may be more comfortable in your rooms. I will have your dinner sent up to you. Such a pity—I was looking forward to a nice meal with you. We may have to try again tomorrow." He stood up and looked at her. "Goodnight, Claire."

Claire got to her feet and held out a hand to him. It was not something he was expecting, and he took it automatically. "I'm sorry I hurt your feelings—though I didn't know you had any. Goodnight."

She turned before he had a chance to reply and walked out of the room. Mr. Carter was waiting for her at the door and showed her the way upstairs. The rooms were sumptuous and beautifully appointed, done in very subtle colours with white being the main. For her use was a sitting room with a fireplace that was already dancing merrily with bright orange flames, a bedroom, and a bathroom with a deep claw-foot bath.

Mr. Carter was turning to leave when Claire stopped him. "I can't keep calling you Mr. Carter. What's your first name?"

"Greg, Mrs. Drummond."

"God, no, don't call me that. Please call me Claire. It would make me happier if there was someone who was at least a little bit friendly here."

"Have a good night, Mrs…Claire." He gave her a shy smile and left the room, closing the door behind him.

Claire took the opportunity to have a good look around the room. She was almost certain that it would be bugged in some form, either by microphone or video. Not finding anything in the sitting room, she moved to the bedroom. It was the same—either they were well-hidden, or he had decided she didn't need to be monitored, which she doubted. In the drawers and wardrobe she found clothes in her size and felt a bit creeped out that someone had bought these things with her in mind.

The bed looked lovely and soft, and she sat down on it. The silence was deafening in the room, and she sighed. Marcus had mentioned dinner—at the thought, she started to feel hungry. The thought had crossed her mind to reach out to Matt and Bree, but she didn't want someone walking in, so she decided to leave it until later.

The curtains were drawn, and she pushed herself off the bed and wandered over to them. Parting them, she found a pair of French doors, which led out to a deck. When she tried the handles, she found them locked, and there was no key in the holes. Outside it was dark, and it was very hard to see anything beyond a few feet.

A knock came at the door, and she called for them to come in. Greg opened it and carried in a plate with a silver cloche over the top. He placed it down on a small table and moved it in front of one of the comfy chairs beside the fireplace. From his pocket, he pulled a fresh bottle of water.

"Thank you, Greg," she said as he removed the cloche. "It looks wonderful. Do you know if I'm allowed the key for the French doors?"

"Sorry, Claire. Mr. Ryder won't allow it. Just ring when you want the plate taken away." Greg indicated to a button by the door before closing it softly behind him, leaving Claire to eat alone.

Later that night, Matt was tossing and turning. He just couldn't settle knowing his girls were out there somewhere and in danger. Finally, he resigned himself that sleep would elude him and slipped from his room to get a glass of water. When he finished and walked back to his room, he tried to be as quiet as possible so as not to disturb anyone else. As he turned into the hall, he saw a dark figure step into Tony's room. Feeling curious, he crept up to the door and listened.

The voices were muffled, but when he concentrated some, they became clearer—as if the door was open a crack and he could hear what they were saying.

"You can't be here," Tony whispered, almost with a groan.

"I don't care. He can go take a flying leap into Lake Taupo, for all I care. He's my brother, not my keeper, and he asked me to come up here."

"Not that I don't appreciate what you're trying to do, Tia, but..."

"No buts, Tony. You need this. You deserve it," Tia crooned.

Matt could hear kissing sounds. He moved away, but he found that the sounds followed him—even to his bedroom, where he had firmly shut his door. He had managed to transfer their conversation, and it was now firmly in his head. With all the speed he could, he reversed the process to stop hearing their lovemaking.

It brought to mind his own wife, and he reached out to her in his loneliness, hoping that she would reply. Claire came to him the instant he had the thought of her.

"Matt, are you here yet?"

"We've landed. I don't know where the hell we are, but its Tony's place. Oh, by the way, he invited himself on our little rescue mission. We were told you're somewhere near Mt. Taranaki."

"Tony is with you? I hope you haven't done anything stupid, Matt."

"Not too much. We had words, but he and I have come to an uneasy truce." Matt didn't tell her that Tony had been helping him. "Is Bree with you?"

"No. I don't know where she is. I'm so worried about her." Panic was creeping into her voice.

"I know it's going to be hard to deal with. Let me come to you," he said softly and carefully.

Matt slid through the space between them and found himself in her mind. She ran to him and clasped him to her. Matt sank his face into her hair and breathed deeply. This was definitely one advantage of their Abilities that he enjoyed. Even though they were miles apart, they could still be together. He stayed with her all night, and they slept together. Matt felt her rouse in the morning and lay beside her, watching as she woke. He loved it when he got the chance to be awake before her, seeing her blue eyes open and be the first thing she saw in the morning. She stretched beside him and gave him the most heartbreaking smile.

"Good morning," he said gently.

"It is indeed a good morning."

"For the moment," Matt said sadly.

"Let's make the most of it, then." She pulled him down to her and laughed wickedly.

Once they were finished, Matt decided Claire deserved to know what he had heard before he called to her. "I heard something very interesting last night," he started.

"Mmm, what was that?" Claire stretched, luxuriating in the peace he brought her.

"Tony with his business partner's sister."

Claire looked at him, fully awake now. "Really, Tony with a woman? Thank God for that."

"I thought you'd be upset," Matt confessed.

"Oh, I am so heartbroken that my stalker has found someone else!" she said dramatically. "Is that better?"

"Much." He laughed at her sarcasm.

"So, what is this woman like?" Claire asked, her curiosity getting the better of her.

"I knew it!" he exclaimed, then defended himself from her slaps. "She is very pretty, and she can cook. She cooked the most beautiful lamb roast with all the trimmings for us last night."

"Is that right? Even better than mine?" Matt knew she was baiting him, but he took it and ran with it.

"Oh yeah. So much better than yours. You always manage to make it go dry. This was juicy and done to perfection." He looked sideways and saw the outrage on her face. "Ha, you deserved that." He smiled and kissed her until she relented.

"Are you able to show me what she looks like?" she asked, obviously still curious about Tia.

"Really, I can do that? How?"

"Never mind. I can find it." Matt could feel her rummage around in his mind until she found what she was looking for. It was the memory of the dinner, and she played it a couple of times.

"She doesn't take her eyes off him, does she? What did you say her name was?"

"Tia, and I remember someone else doing that," he whispered in her ear.

"Wasn't just me. I seem to remember catching you looking at me as well." She played the memory again and watched Tony this time. "He doesn't even notice—or he is avoiding looking at her? What is his problem? Oh, Matt, if he could find love, I would be so happy."

"He did. Didn't you know? He was married. Marcus had her murdered and took their child. Tony has a son who's six."

"What? How do you know this?" Claire didn't seem as shocked by the news as Matt thought she would be.

"He told us. He wants to be the one to take Marcus out."

"No wonder he had loneliness emanating from him when I saw him at the stones."

"Oh, shit. I remember saying I didn't care if he had lost everyone."

"You weren't to know, sweetheart. We were having a fight at the time." She laid her head against his shoulder and looked at the freeze frame of the memory. "They look good together. You feel up to a bit of matchmaking? He deserves to be happy."

"What do you want me to do?" he asked, resigned to the fact that she would nag him about it until he agreed.

"Just get them together as much as possible. You know, like Addy did with us."

"She didn't," Matt protested.

"Oh, my dear, sweet, darling husband, you were blind back then, weren't you? Addy orchestrated the whole thing from day one. She caught us sneaking glances in the mirror at each other after you picked us up from the airport. She told me."

"That little—"

"Shh. It worked out for the best." She kissed his cheek. "Just talk to him about her—or whatever you blokes do."

"Yeah, I'm not doing that. Getting them into the same room as each other is easy enough. She follows him around like a lost puppy. But guys don't do that—all that chatty stuff."

"Just encourage it, then." She smiled and then put the memory away where it belonged.

"Is Marcus treating you okay?" Matt asked her with concern.

"Yes. I feel like a princess locked away in a tower. I have everything I could want and I can't escape. Not until my prince in shining armour comes to rescue me."

Matt looked around and then down at his wife, pointing to his chest. "Me? A prince in rusty armour is more like it."

"Your Talents! We never got to practice with them."

"It's okay. Tony has insisted on training me. Oh, bloody hell. I forgot to put up my walls so they don't hear me."

"Who, Tony and Adam? Don't worry. I invited you into my mind, so they can't hear anything." She got a faraway look in her eyes and then came back just as quick. "No, they wouldn't have heard anything."

"Thank Christ for that. You had me worried for a while."

"Would have served you right." She laughed a little.

"Pardon? I'm not the one conspiring to get rid of her stalker by setting him up with a woman who's obsessed with him."

"Well, you got me there. Anyway, Tia seems perfect for him." She became alert then and was listening to something else. "I have to go. Someone is at my door." She gave him one more lingering kiss.

"I love you," Matt whispered when they broke apart.

"Love you too." Claire's voice carried with him as he travelled back to his own mind and body.

Chapter Nine

Bree held on tightly to the hand of James Boyle as they walked through the crowded duty-free area, before they reached border control. James had been very kind to her and made sure she was looked after the way she should be, just as her Aunty Breena had asked him to. They lined up with the rest of the people off their plane and waited their turn.

When they reached the head of the queue and an officer became available, James fumbled with their passports and documents. He handed them over to the woman at the desk and she looked at them, particularly reading the court document that allowed Bree to travel with him.

"Uncle Jamie, I'm tired," Bree said, tugging on his sleeve. He immediately picked her up and she cuddled into him, laying her head on his shoulder.

The officer looked up and smiled at the little girl. "Oh, aren't you so sweet. You're lucky to have such a handsome and caring uncle," the woman behind the desk said, eyeing James up and down. Bree nodded to her. The officer smiled and handed the documents back to James. "Welcome home," she said, sending them on their way.

Without really realising he was doing it, he carried Bree through the rest of the airport and out to the waiting car. He made sure she was buckled in securely before climbing into the front passenger seat.

"Poor you—stuck with kid duty. Bet she was a nightmare," the driver said to James as he pulled away from the curb.

"Actually, she was a breeze. She slept most of the way, and when she was awake, she was a sweetheart."

"You're having me on, right?"

"Not at all," James replied.

"Hello, sir. I'm Breena Drummond. What's your name?" Bree asked from the back.

The driver glanced over his shoulder at the girl. "I'm Andrew Malloy," he replied gruffly.

"It's very nice to meet you, Mr. Malloy. Are you a friend of Jamie's?" she asked.

"Sort of. We work for the same man."

"Mr. Ryder. He has my Mummy," Bree said sadly.

The driver quickly looked back at her again and then up at James. "What have you been telling her?"

"Nothing. She told me the same thing when I grabbed her. She has been calm as a cucumber this whole time. No tears, no screaming, nothing. Man, it's really unnerving," James told him with a shake of his head.

Bree looked out the window and smiled to herself. The whole act was hard to keep up, but it was going to be worth it. The asking of their names was very important for her. With their names she could gain access to their minds, much like a touch would do for her mother. Thinking of her mother made her sad, but right at that moment there was more of a pull towards her father. She settled into her seat and pretended to drop off to sleep.

Within moments, she had found her father and looked through his eyes at the people around him. Very subtly, she made him go outside so she could talk to him.

"Hello, Daddy. Are you mad at me?" she asked, feeling anxious at his response.

"No, my wee angel. I'm not mad at you. Only angry at the man who has done this to our family," he replied with some relief in his voice.

"Good. I thought you were going to shout at me."

"Are you all right, Bree? Are they taking good care of you?"

"Yes, they are. James Boyle is very nice. I just met one of his friends, but I'm not sure about him. His name is Andrew Malloy. He's driving us. I don't know where they're taking me," Bree said, making sure she said their names carefully so her father would remember them.

"That's all right, Bree. We'll figure something out."

"Good," she replied and yawned in his ear. "I'm sleepy for real now. I love you, Daddy."

"Do as you are told and sleep well, my wee angel. I love you, too."

The deep sigh Bree made heralded the end of their connection, and Matt stood in the brisk winter wind, feeling the cold seep inside him. The heat of his anger was again rising up, and he desperately wanted to hit something. His fists were clenched, and his breathing was becoming faster.

"I have a punching bag in the gym," Tony said behind him. "You're welcome to use it. Actually, I would prefer you used it. I don't have the energy to heal a gnat at the moment."

"I suppose you heard that?" Matt replied through a clenched jaw as he turned to face Tony.

"No, actually, I didn't," Tony said. "Not much, anyway. Whoever you were talking to was well-guarded, and you did a great job of muffling."

Tony led Matt around the back of the house and into a shed. Inside was a fully kitted-out gym. Weights, benches, machines, and contraptions of all sizes and uses were placed around the stark, white-painted room. In the middle was a large punching bag hanging from the ceiling by a fairly sizable chain.

"There are some gloves over there. Put them on. I'll spot you and you can tell me what has got you so riled up," Tony instructed him.

Matt walked over to one of the benches and picked up a well-used pair of red-coloured sparring gloves and slipped them on. Tony checked to make sure they were in place properly and then held the bag for Matt to hit.

The first attempt at punching the bag was pitiful, and Matt knew it. Tony encouraged him to hit harder. Matt threw another punch and Tony stopped him. With a little bit of guidance on how to throw a good, solid hit, Matt carried on. Soon the sweat was pouring from his brow, and he wiped it away with his sleeve. The image of his daughter in the hands of faceless men spurred him on further, and the hits came faster and harder. Claire was now the focus. His girls were in danger, and he was in there hitting an inanimate object. The more he hit, the more the tears came to him, mixing with the sweat that dripped from his stubbly chin.

Finally exhausted, he crumpled to the floor and lay on his back. Sobs came as thick and as fast as his fists had just moments before. Leaving him there to compose himself, Tony went to get him a towel and a drink of water. When he thought Matt was ready, he sat cross-legged beside him, undid the gloves, and took them off. He handed the water and the towel to the man he used to be so jealous of but now could sympathise with.

"I know how you're feeling. I want to kill him, too. You've got a good arm on you," Tony told him, placing the gloves to one side.

"I've been in a few pub brawls in my time," Matt told him.

"We will get them, Matt. I promise you."

"Damn right we will." Matt wiped his face again on the towel and his wife's request came back to him. "I don't mean to pry, but last night I, um, saw Tia—"

"Don't mention it to Nik. He jokes about it, but he would murder me."

"Does that mean you two are…an item?"

"Not really. She would like more, but at the moment, I don't have it in me to give her what she deserves. Don't get me wrong. I like her a lot, but Maddison was special."

"I know that feeling, like your stomach is in knots every time you see her?" Matt asked sympathetically.

"Yep. I never really had that when I thought I was in love with Claire. I'm sorry about that, by the way."

"Don't mention it. I understand." Matt stood up and felt every muscle protest. He knew that the next day would be worse. He offered his hand to Tony and pulled him up.

"Now I don't mean to pry, but was it Claire you were talking to before?" Tony asked him.

"No, it was Bree. She has come into her Talents early. Something to do with the Guardians. Don't ask." Matt held a hand up when he saw Tony about to speak. "I don't understand it myself."

"Bloody hell, your family is strange."

"She's with two men. She got their names for me. A James Boyle and an Andrew Malloy. They ring any bells?"

"Not to me, but Nik might know. Come on. We'll go ask." They walked out together. Somehow the relationship between the two men had changed in the gym, a lot more than Matt realised.

Claire stood looking out of the bedroom window at the changing world outside, still wrapped in the bathrobe she had hastily pulled on only a few minutes ago. Beyond the glass, the sun was trying to shine through the swiftly moving clouds.

The large Macrocarpas bent in the gusting wind, swaying over the hedge that marked the bottom of the garden.

When Greg had entered after a polite tap earlier, she was still in bed and was annoyed at having her conversation with Matt interrupted. As a result her mood was already grumpy and noncompliant.

"Tell him that I have a headache and feel sick," she replied after refusing to go down for breakfast.

"I'm sorry, but he won't like that, Claire." Greg had grimaced as he said it, and she felt sorry for him that he had to be the one to carry the message.

Now she felt doubly stubborn. She had not made a fuss or even tried to get away—even though she'd had ample opportunity—so if he wanted to see her, Marcus would just have to come to her. Claire knew she was being stupid and obstinate, but today she felt bolshy and decided he needed to see for himself what she could do.

"I understand you are ill. Do you need a doctor?" Marcus asked as he strutted into the sitting room.

"No, I don't. I just need fresh air." Claire stalked from the bedroom to meet him and stood in the doorway between.

"I am afraid that is not possible, Claire. You know why. We can't have you flying off, now, can we? Breena could get hurt." He placed his hands in the pockets of his trousers, a smug grin on his face.

"Oh, really? Okay, how's this for size?" Claire immediately disappeared and then flew to stand behind him, then reappeared and whispered in his ear, "Shall I show you what I did to Richard?"

Marcus jumped and spun around to face her at the same time. Claire's smile was just as smug as his had been only moments before.

"There are many other things that I can do now besides the normal Talents of flying and shrinking you down to the size of a mouse. For instance, I can now do this." Claire concentrated hard. She had only done this twice before and that was a while ago. She wanted it to look like she had been doing it for years, so carefully concentrating she masked the great effort that it took to pull it off.

She waved her hand and a vase that sat on the mantle above the fire across the room, flew straight towards Marcus. He ducked out of the way and Claire caught it. She hefted it in her hand, feeling the weight of it.

"Just as well you ducked. That could've left a very nasty mark on your head. And that wouldn't do, would it? Maiming that face of yours." She raised an eyebrow at him.

"I think I have just about had enough of this!" Marcus said, pulling out his phone.

"Oh, I'm only getting started. There are a few things we need to talk about before you go phoning anyone, Marcus. Please take a seat." She waved her hand again and prayed that the chair she was focusing on would obey. Claire thanked her lucky stars when it sprang across the carpet and scooped Marcus up into in.

As she moved past it to sit in her own chair, she turned it around so that he was facing her. Claire sat carefully and adjusted her robe to cover her legs.

"First of all, Marcus, you do not summon me. I will come down for breakfast when I am ready. If I want to, I will have it up here in the rooms you have so kindly provided for me. Secondly, I want my daughter brought to me at once. I know she is in the country; I can feel her. And thirdly, I want Tony's son here as well. I don't know where you're keeping him, but he better be here today. And don't think you can pull a fast one on me. When I see him, I'll be able to tell whether he's John or not. Do we understand each other?" Claire stared him in the eye.

Marcus had completely underestimated her. This forceful woman was not the meek and timid creature he had been led to believe she was. This Claire was very together, very dominant—and he was impressed. His hope for his plan was increasing as he imagined what they could do together if only he could get her to see things his way. All these thoughts flickered through his mind, and he was totally unaware that Claire could not only read them on his face but hear them as well. They made her want to shudder in revulsion.

"I'm waiting, Marcus. Do you understand me?" Claire demanded again, suppressing the shiver that threatened to give her away.

"Yes. I do. I will have both children here by late this afternoon. You have my word." Marcus stood. "Would you like breakfast in here this morning or will you be coming down?" he asked her graciously.

"In here, please. Just a cup of tea and two pieces of toast, thank you." She stood and watched him leave.

Within seconds she was at the door, shutting it behind him. Her hands began to shake and her stomach began to cramp. The nerves she had been holding in check decided they needed to be on the outside, as she rushed to the bathroom and was sick.

She was washing out her mouth and spitting when she heard a voice at the door. She put the towel on the rail and straightened it out.

"Just a minute," she called out with as strong a voice as possible.

In the sitting room, Greg was setting out her breakfast. He looked up when she entered the room and took in her pale face.

"Are you all right? Should I get the doctor?" he asked.

Claire appreciated his concern but waved him away. "No, I'm fine. Just the use of my Talents sometimes gets to be a bit much. I hope I haven't made things too bad downstairs for everyone."

"No. He was whistling after he told me what you wanted. He seemed very happy," he told her pointedly.

"Oh, dear. That can only mean one thing: I overdid it. Never mind. Thank you for bringing me breakfast. I'll bring the tray down myself later."

"I can't let you do that, Claire. Mr. Ryder's orders," Greg told her at the door. Greg left her to it, shutting the door behind him. Claire looked down at the toast and felt her stomach heave again. She poured the contents of the teapot out into the very delicate cup and watched it darken. Carefully she lifted the black tea to her lips, took a small sip, and swallowed slowly. There was no movement down below, and she attempted another sip.

She sat back in the chair with the cup held between both hands. The tea was staying down, and she was pleased. Knowing she had to eat something after using her Talents, she picked up a small triangle of toast, ignoring the butter that sat on its own little dish, and took a bite. Claire suddenly realised there could be another reason she had thrown up—and it had nothing to do with nerves.

After managing only two small pieces, Claire sat with her hands on her stomach and could feel the tiny life inside her. She had done this when she found out she was pregnant with Bree. It made her feel connected with her child, and this one was no different. The child inside her was growing, the heartbeat stronger than the last time she had felt it. She smiled. If she was getting morning sickness with this child, she knew it would be a boy.

"Change of plan. We're not taking her to the cabin, but to his place in the 'Naki," James told Andrew as he pocketed his phone.

"Bloody hell, I wish he would make up his mind." Andrew slammed on the brakes and swung the car around to face the way they had just come from.

"Will you shut up? You know he likes bugs," Greg said quietly.

"I don't bloody care. We're halfway there already. Now we have to drive all the way to Tara-bloody-naki. Next petrol station it's your turn to drive. I'm sick of being a taxi service for bloody kids."

"Andy, watch your mouth in front of the kid."

"I told you. I don't fucking care." Andrew sank in his seat, his hands barely resting on the steering wheel.

"It's okay, Mr. Malloy. I don't mind," Bree said from the back.

Andrew was just about to yell at her when he saw her face. She was smiling sweetly at him, and his whole demeanour changed. He turned back to face the road and was quiet.

Bree was thankful she had calmed him. She didn't like it when people were shouting around her. It made her feel scared, and now was not the time to be afraid. She settled herself down and looked out the window, but it was not the scenery she saw. She sent out her feelers and found that her mother lay in the direction they were now heading. Her sensors picked up her father shortly after. He was closer to them, but further north, and she found Adam and Tony with him. There were also two others with them—a man and a woman. Bree smiled when she felt the spirit of the woman. Tony did not know what was coming his way.

Inside the house, Nikau was trawling through the computer looking for the names Matt had given to Tony. Tia was sitting at the other desk going through the emails, checking in with their clients and watchers. She suddenly sat up straight and shivered.

"What's up your butt?" Nikau asked his sister.

"Don't know. Just a goose, I guess, walking over my grave." She shuddered again, feeling like someone was watching her.

"Hell, don't let Mum hear you say that. She'd do her nut."

"Mum should stop listening to that old trout down the road who thinks she's Mystic Meg. I'm sick of hearing about how my husband is just around the corner and I should be ready to rush into his arms. Bloody bullshit, if you ask me," she muttered, tapping the keyboard a bit hard as she answered a query from a client.

"Yeah, and don't tell her you've been in Tony's bed already, either." He looked sideways at his younger sister, trying to get a reaction out of her.

Tia remained tight-lipped. She hoped he was just fishing and not really stating a fact.

"Got one." He hit the print button and then carried on clicking through the files. "So have you?" he asked, barefaced.

"What?"

"Don't play innocent with me. You have, haven't you?" he carried on with his prying.

"You just passed the other one." Tia pointed to the screen.

Nikau cursed loudly and went back a couple of screens until he came to Andrew Malloy.

"Bloody hell, I wouldn't let my kids near that one." He hit the print button and picked up the two sheets of paper, showing them to Tia.

"God, he's an animal. What the hell is this guy thinking?" She looked at James's sheet. "This one is a bit better. Only a small rap sheet, for nothing really major. But this other one…where the hell did Ryder drag him up from? I'm glad it's not me giving Tony this information." She handed the pages back to her brother and resumed typing.

"You still didn't answer me, Sis, but I will get the truth out of you."

"Piss off, Nik." Tia did not look up from the screen she was watching.

Nikau left her and headed out to the living room, where the three men were waiting. He handed the sheet to Tony and waited for the response that he knew would come.

"Really? This is correct?" Tony looked up at Nikau.

"As up to date as possible, boss. That first one isn't too bad. I mean, I wouldn't let him babysit my kids, but the other—" Nikau made a face.

Tony passed the pages on to Matt and watched him read the information. He could see Matt's face turn redder and redder as he scanned the page on Andrew Malloy.

"Fucking hell!" Matt let out an explosive breath. "He's been up on murder charges four times and never been convicted? One of those a child! Rape, wounding with intent, drugs, domestic violence. Oh my god, Claire cannot find out. If she knows Bree is with a man like that, it would do her head in."

Adam took the pages off Matt and read them himself. "We need to get them now. We can't wait." He looked at Tony.

"We're still waiting for Michael to get back to us. Have you heard anything yet?" Tony asked Nikau.

"Not yet. I'm expecting a report from him in about an hour." Nikau checked his watch.

"Soon as he calls, I'll speak to him, okay?"

"You're the boss."

"So are you—stop calling me that."

"Yes, boss." Nikau chuckled and left the room.

Outside, the wind had died down, and the sky became a deep blue that had chased almost all the clouds away. The late winter sun shone on the bright little pinpoints of yellow daffodils that had decided it was their time to bloom. Some bushes were ablaze with colour, while others were still in the middle of their winter sleep.

Claire tried the French doors in the downstairs formal living room and found them locked. She wanted fresh air—needed it, having always hated being cooped up inside. When she had finally come down the stairs, the ground floor was quiet. There was no sign of Marcus or Greg anywhere, so she wandered. She found where the kitchen was, and beside it was a TV room with multiple chairs, the downstairs bathroom, and at the back of the house, a few bedrooms. Towards the front of this massive house was the living room Marcus had brought her to the night before, a formal dining area, another sitting room, and a room with Greg standing outside.

"You can't go in there. He's working," Greg whispered to her.

Now Claire found herself back in the living room. The bookshelves were full of curiosities and knickknacks—or as she liked to think of them, dust collectors. The books she had avoided, but she was so bored at that moment that she stepped closer to them. The pull was strong, but not as urgent as the library back in Scotland.

Standing in front of them, she could tell which book thought more of itself than the others. This was new to her, and carefully she explored the categorising that was going on in her mind. Her fingers ran over the spines on one of the shelves, and she could almost feel that they were alive under her touch. She stopped on one. It was giving off an *I-don't-care-if-you-touch-me* feel, and she pulled it from its place. Flipping through the pages, she could tell that the words didn't want to be read. Claire was fascinated by this new development and sat down on the nearest seat, thankful that Crystal had managed this Talent somewhat.

The book dangled from her hand as she stared out into the winter garden, lost in her thoughts. Two worries were on her mind: the first was the welfare of Bree and Johnny, and the second was what Marcus had planned. She fervently hoped that her performance earlier in the day had not encouraged him even more.

Footsteps on the polished wood floor in the hall bought her out of her reverie, and she placed the book in her hand back on the shelf. Before he even stepped into the room, she turned to greet Marcus, steeling herself for whatever he might say to her. Instead, she found Greg.

"Mrs. Drummond, Mr. Ryder wishes to see you," Greg said formally. "If you could follow me?" He gestured towards the door, and Claire followed him.

"We are back to being formal again, Mr. Carter. I take it I'm not going to like whatever comes next."

"I don't know, Mrs. Drummond." His back was straight and stiff, and there was a slight limp to his step.

Claire brushed his mind with a feather-light touch, and her heart sank when she discovered his pain. Because of her familiarity with him, he had suffered at someone's hands. Not a severe beating, but one bad enough for him to revert to his ancient memories of a father standing over him, with a large belt in his hands.

"I'm sorry I got you into trouble, Mr. Carter," she said softly, hoping nobody was listening.

"Not your fault," Greg replied. The pain he was in was etched around his eyes.

From the back of the house, a phone started to ring and was stopped as soon as it did. Tony stood and waited for Nikau to enter, hopefully bringing the news he was desperate to hear. The tension inside him was building. He'd had enough of sitting around waiting for intel. He wanted to be out there himself, doing something.

Nikau strode into the room with a hastened step. He still held the phone to his ear and was listening to someone talking.

"Yeah, okay. Tony's here now. He wants the information first." He passed the phone over to Tony and stood waiting to hear.

"Michael, what can you tell me?" Tony's heart started to race. This was what he was trained for. This was the work he loved, and now he had the chance to use it to protect those he loved.

"I've managed to tap into the security system. I thought Marcus would have upgraded his systems by now. He's still using the outdated one. That girl of yours is something else. She just gave Marcus a couple of ultimatums, and he's caved. She told him if he didn't get her daughter and your kid there by this afternoon, then she would let loose. I'll send it through. You're going to enjoy her performance. But—and there is a 'but.' He has brought forward a plan that he had in reserve. He's speaking in some sort of code because I can't understand what he's saying," Michael told him quickly, seemingly out of breath.

"Good. Send everything you have through. The more info we have, the better prepared we'll be. Great job, Michael. Stick with it. There'll be a big bonus in it for you." Tony tossed the phone back to Nikau.

"Apparently, Matt, your wife has taken on Marcus and had a victory. Michael's sending some vision through."

The double doors to Marcus's study stood wide open and Claire could see him leaning against his large desk, waiting for her to enter. His suit jacket was discarded, and the tie he had on earlier was now hanging on the back of his chair. She wondered if this was casual attire for him, or if he ever just relaxed. He stood as she walked into the study, and the doors closed behind her.

At her back stood two men she had not seen before, dressed in the same dark suits that all his people wore. She turned her attention back to Marcus, who was smiling now.

"I would like to introduce you to someone you will be getting to know very well. This is Dr. Peter Cashin. He is my personal doctor. The reason Peter is here is that we understand that you were not very well this morning—in fact, you were vomiting."

"Yes, I did. But I'm fine now. I believe it was just a reaction I had to something particularly nasty," Claire replied, looking him dead in the eye.

"Well, whatever it is, I would like to make sure you are all right. When I told Peter about it, his first reaction was to ask if you were pregnant." He paused and looked at the doctor.

"Claire, I would very much like you to take this test. Just follow the instructions on the box, but already having one child, I think you know what to do," the doctor said, presenting a box to her, which she took automatically.

In her hands was a pregnancy test that could be picked up at any pharmacy. She looked at it for a moment and then at the two gentlemen in front of her.

"You can't be serious! Just because I blew chunks doesn't mean that I'm pregnant. And anyway," she said as she waved the box at them, "these things aren't really accurate."

"Humour us, please," Peter said in that condescending tone only a bored doctor could inflict.

Claire could not think of any way to get herself out of the situation. "Can I at least use the toilet, or do you want me to do it here in front of you?"

"In there." Marcus smiled at her, indicating a door to her left.

Inside the bathroom, Claire locked the door behind her and opened the box. She pulled out the stick and sighed. Knowing the outcome still did not make this any easier, but she had her doubts that this test would work, as it was only a matter of days since she had conceived.

With the deed done, she waited for the result, watching with a nervousness that was misplaced. The control line came up and then nothing. The line that she was supposed to see indicating pregnancy refused to show itself, and she smiled in relief. She opened the door with the test stick in hand and joined the men in the study.

"I'm sorry to disappoint you, but I told you I wasn't pregnant." Claire handed the test to the doctor, and he looked at it, then showed it to Marcus.

"This is most disappointing. I had it on very good authority that you were pregnant," Marcus told her, still looking at the stick the doctor held out.

"Sorry. They were wrong. Can you tell me who was this authority?"

"A group of specialists." Marcus was a bit hedgy with his words, and Claire understood that there were those in the room who did not know anything about the Talents.

"Well, I suggest you go back to them and clarify their findings. Is that all? Can I go now?" she asked him, feeling very confident in herself.

"Yes, but I would appreciate a candid conversation with you this evening. Just the two of us," he said to her.

"It's your house." She turned and waited for one of the men still standing there to open the door for her. When they didn't, she looked back at her captor.

“Open the door for Mrs. Drummond,” Marcus told them, and they obeyed immediately.

Chapter Ten

The air outside promised a frost for the following morning. The temperature was dropping like a stone, but the sky above was still and clear blue. Matt was walking in the garden, trying to get his emotions under control. He was so proud of his wife and the way she handled herself, but the audacity of Marcus and what he was putting them all through was still hard to bear.

The antics of a small bird twitching in the bare trees caught his attention, and he stopped to watch. The tail was fanned out and it swooped and dove for small insects, twittering as it went. Claire had often tried to tell him the names of the birds, and this one was more than easily recognisable. It took its name from the tail it used to make such wonderful manoeuvres: a Fantail. He watched a little more until a door opening from the gym startled it, and it fled.

"I wouldn't trust those buggers if I were you," Nikau called out. "I hate them. They are messengers of death."

"They look harmless enough to me," Matt replied, turning to face him.

"Yeah, well, you're a Pakeha. You know shit about the spirituality of our land." He shoved his hands in his pockets and joined Matt out on the grass.

"Do you know ours?" Matt asked him straight.

"Enough not to mess with you." He laughed at the challenge. "Tony sort of explained it—from his side, anyway. I take it your lady is pretty special in that area."

"Just a bit," Matt agreed and smiled. "Tell me more about it—about your lands."

"Another day when there's time to answer all the questions. If you really want to know, talk to Tia. She loves a good discussion on our heritage," he said with a grin.

"I get the feeling that I'm being set up for something here, so I won't, if it's all the same to you."

"You're a smart one. I thought I could slip that one past." Nikau chuckled. "It's bloody cold out here. I'm going in."

"Don't know what you're talking about! This is summer weather where I'm from," Matt told him and laughed.

"You Scots are crazy." He waved at Matt and headed inside.

Sounds from the gym caught his attention. Matt wandered over to the fogged-up door and opened it, thinking Tony was inside. He stopped as it shut behind him when he saw that it was Tia instead, punching and kicking the bag in the centre of the room. Her movements were fluid and calculated, and he realised that there was a fierce and aggressive part of her that he never wanted to get on the bad side of.

Tia caught him watching her and stopped, still bouncing on the balls of her feet. Her hands were up defensively, wrapped in tape only instead of the sparring gloves he had worn earlier. He suddenly felt himself weak in comparison to this woman.

"Did you just come to perv or did you need to speak to me?" Tia asked as she took a sip from the open bottle of water near her feet.

"No. I actually thought you were Tony," he told her, walking further into the gym and taking a seat on one of the benches.

"Tony only does his exercise at night." She wiped the sweat from her face, still watching Matt carefully.

"Does he come back often?" Matt asked.

"No, not really."

"Not as much as you would like?" He smiled at her.

"Is it that obvious?" Tia dropped her fighting stance, picked up the bottle of water again, and came to sit near him on another weights bench.

"Just a bit. Claire likes you."

"How would Claire know me? I've never even met her, and I doubt Tony would have said anything."

"We have a special way of communicating." Matt indicated his head.

"Oh, that. What's it like?"

"It takes a bit to get used to it. But it has its advantages."

"It can't be easy for you, working with Tony." A brief look of concern crossed her face, and Matt figured she wasn't one to let her real feelings out very much.

"No, it's not. But it seems it could be getting easier."

"Come again?" she asked, clearly confused.

"Well, if he's with you, then I don't have to worry about him hanging around anymore."

"But he's not with me," she said sullenly and took another gulp of her water.

"Not from what I heard last night." He raised an eyebrow at her.

She spat some water and spluttered. "You heard?"

"I may have been eavesdropping a little. That was very impressive, by the way—the workout, I mean," he added quickly and blushed a little.

"Got to keep my hand in."

"Are you one of his stalkers as well?"

"Was. And he calls us Watchers. I don't do it so much these days. Being a female has its advantages, but sometimes—"

"You got hurt. Sorry, I'm prying," Matt said, suddenly concerned for her.

"Nah, it's all good. He sent me out on a job that was dangerous. He didn't want to, but I made him. I wanted to prove to him that I could do it. My mind wasn't really on it and I got caught. He saved me. He won't let me go out anymore." Tia stood and stretched.

"That's so I don't have to rescue you again," Tony said from the doorway. Neither had heard him enter.

Matt turned and watched him as he stood at the door, looking only at Tia. He suddenly felt like a third wheel as the tension thickened between the two of them. He watched as Tony picked up a towel from the stack by the door and brought it over to Tia. Her eyes, as dark as his, never left his face. He thought for a moment there was a spark in Tony's eyes that belied what he had told him earlier, but it was gone so quick, he couldn't be sure.

"That's what happens, Tia, when emotions get in the way." Tony handed her the towel. "Anyway, you're more use to me on the books. You're the only one I can trust them with."

"Flattery, Tony? Gee, I'm touched." The sarcasm in her voice wasn't real. It masked the deeper feelings she had for him. It was a defence mechanism that she held tightly against herself.

"I think I'll go find a beer somewhere," Matt said to the pair, and when they didn't answer, he left them alone.

Inside, he headed straight for the fridge and pulled out a cold beer. He cracked it open, then headed into the lounge. From out of the study, Nikau came looking for Tony.

"Sorry, I've not seen him. I've just come in." He lifted the beer in salute to Nikau and drank a gulp. He hoped that Nikau did not find Tony or Tia for a good while yet.

Her little face was trying to see out the front windscreen as they passed through the gates and into the property that held such a large house. Bree could feel her mother inside, watching the car pull up outside the door. She was in a hurry to find her, but first she had one more thing to do. She waited patiently for Jamie to open her door after she had unbuckled herself. He lifted her out and placed her carefully on the gravel.

Waiting until Mr. Malloy came around the car, she stepped towards him and held her small hand out for him to shake. He was a nasty man. She could feel that, but he needed saving, just like all the rest. At least she could start him on the path that would set him right.

The large man looked down at Bree and scowled at her. He was tired and in no mood for little kids and their funny ways. But something made him take her hand in his, and he shook it. Inside, there was an immediate, small change. With the touch came the image of the last person who had cared for him—the image of a grandmother he had fought with and ignored, but who still loved him. It wasn't her fault he had been placed with her. He saw her heart break at the things he did, but still she loved him. His eyes widened at this image, and he felt a loss and an urge to find her. Bree let go of his hand and smiled up at him.

"Thank you for bringing me safely to my mother, Mr. Malloy." Then she took James's hand, and he led her inside.

James looked down at his charge and smiled. "Now we're going to meet Mr. Ryder. Please don't do or say anything silly," he warned her.

"I won't, Jamie. He's not interested in me." She smiled back.

James escorted Bree into the large room and found Marcus sitting in one of the high-backed lounge chairs, his legs crossed and his hands resting on his lap. When Bree looked at him, she felt his anger and his disdain for her emanating in waves. She did not like this man, especially knowing that he was going to hurt her mother.

Marcus looked at the small child and gave her a smile that held no warmth in it whatsoever. "Hello, Breena. I hope that while you are with us you will behave and not cause any trouble."

"I won't, Mr. Ryder. My mum will make sure of it," she told him with her head held high.

"Let's hope she does. I don't like children, Breena. As long as you stay quiet while I am around, then all will be fine. Do you understand?"

"Yes, sir," she said quietly.

"Good. Mr. Boyle, take her upstairs to her mother. Mr. Carter will show you which room." He dismissed them and James led her back to the stairs.

"Hi, James. This way," Greg told him, and he gave Bree a small wink and a cheeky smile.

"Good to see you again, Greg. How's he been lately?" James asked.

"Secretive. He doesn't confide in me, mate, but I don't think it's going to end well for—" He trailed off when he looked at Bree. He knocked on the door he was standing beside and opened it. "In here."

Bree still held onto James's hand as she entered the room and found her mother waiting for her. She let go and ran to her waiting arms, holding on tight. Her mother smoothed her hair and kissed her over and over, checking to make sure she was okay. All the while, James and Greg stood in the doorway watching them.

When her mother finally let her go, Bree went and stood in front of James, and he knelt before her. She kissed his cheek and put her little arms around his neck.

"Thank you for looking after me, Jamie." She released him and went back to her mother.

"Bree has told me that you were kind to her. Thank you," Claire said to him.

"It was my pleasure. She's a very lovely girl," James replied. "I hope to see you again, Breena." He gave her a smile and left the room.

"Is there anything I can get you, Mrs. Drummond, or your daughter?" Greg asked them.

"I think a cup of tea for me and a glass of milk for my daughter. Thank you, Mr. Carter. And some biscuits if you have them."

"Certainly. I'll be right back." He left the room and closed the door behind him.

They passed the afternoon together with Bree on Claire's lap, not moving from the seat in the living room beside her bedroom. Bree sent a quick thought to her father and let him know that she was with her mother and was safe, and she felt his relief knowing that they were together at last.

Bree looked up at the sound of a car on the gravel drive. "He's here, Mum," she told Claire. They stood, getting to the window in time to see two men at the front door.

They could hear footsteps in the hall downstairs; then they stopped. Soon afterwards, there were more footsteps coming up the stairs that came to a halt outside their door. Claire placed herself between the door and her daughter, ready for anything that may occur. The door opened, and Marcus himself led a little boy inside. A smile was plastered over his face, as he looked pleased with himself that he'd achieved what she had demanded from him.

The child was taller than Bree, and he had dark hair and eyes. The resemblance to Tony was there, but she had to be sure that Marcus was not trying to pull a switch on her. Claire sought out Tony's mind, brushing it slightly like a light knock on a door. She was relieved when he answered her call.

"Claire?"

"I need you to do something for me. Are you able to look through my eyes?"

"Of course. What do you want me to look at?" he asked curiously.

"Just do it," she said impatiently.

"All right. I'm doing it now."

There was a shift of vision for Claire, like a visor had been lowered over her eyes. She felt him gasp and his emotions ran wild.

"Thank you, Tony. I'm sorry, but I had to be sure."

"Look after him, Claire," Tony begged as his raw emotion flooded over her.

"I promise I will do everything I can to bring him back to you."

Tony broke the connection with a lurch, and Claire took a moment to recover.

"I take it you were confirming his heritage?" Marcus asked when Claire came back to herself. "How is Tony?"

"How very astute of you, Marcus." She turned her attention to the boy, kneeling in front of him. "Hello. I'm Claire. I'm a friend of your father's, and this is my daughter, Bree."

Bree walked towards the boy shyly, which amazed Claire, as she had never seen her daughter be shy with anyone. Normally, she would have taken his hand by now and led him off to play some game.

Claire reached out to take his hand, but Johnny flinched away from her touch. She looked up at Marcus, then stood and faced him.

"What have you done to this boy?" she demanded quietly.

"Me personally—nothing. But naughty boys who don't behave themselves need to be punished. Otherwise, they grow up to be spoilt brats," he sneered.

"Your men did this with your permission. How dare you lay a hand on a child. Didn't you learn anything from Adam? You and I have very different views on how to raise children."

"I do very much like this protective side of you, Claire. It bodes well for our children. We would balance each other out nicely. The dynasty we are going to create will dominate the world within a generation or two." There was a mad gleam in his eye and an aura of lust coming from him that had nothing to do with Claire, and she stepped back from him. Marcus chuckled. "I have done what you demanded, Claire. The time will come when you will have to do what I want. I will see you at dinner." He turned and left the room.

Bree's hand snaked into her mother's, and Claire looked down. "How about you and Johnny go play over there by the windows?" Bree nodded, then released Claire's hand and took Johnny's.

As they passed, Johnny looked up with those dark eyes— so much like his father's—and gave her a smile. Claire reached out and brushed her hand over his head. The images that came to her were worse than anything she could have imagined.

This small boy had been through so much in the last six months. He had watched his mother die at the hands of a stranger, been dragged from her side, and taken to a strange land. The punishments he received were over the top for such small transgressions. And he missed his father.

Claire saw the memories he clung to—the laughter and smiles, the love and the playful nature of his mother. A tear came to her eye when she saw Tony and the woman he had married, the love they had for each other seen through their son's eyes. The feelings of security and safety in a world he had thought would be that way forever.

This angered Claire. The injustice of the situation flared like a white-hot burning flame inside her, and she wanted to hurt someone badly. She looked around her and her eyes fell on Greg Carter, but she dismissed him. He had already suffered enough under a brutal father and now an even more inhuman boss. She sent her thoughts out and found a man whose mind was littered with the bloody and damaged bodies of his victims.

She grasped on to his mind and began to squeeze. He was a man who took pleasure in hurting people, and now she was determined to hurt him. Gripping tighter, she compressed his memories, his very nature, anything she could to bring as much pain to him as he had brought to his victims. She heard him scream, both within his mind and from somewhere within the house.

"Mummy?" Bree stood in front of Claire and took her hand. "Mummy, that is enough. He is not the one to be punished."

Claire slowly released her grip, removing her thoughts from that disgusting man. She stood panting from the effort she had used to hurt him in a misguided sense of vengeance. It had not satisfied her. It had not released the outrage she felt. The screaming diminished, and she heard feet running around the house.

Looking towards the door, she saw Greg staring at her, concerned about what was going on. At her side, her daughter was pulling her to a seat, and she made her sit down. Bree climbed on her mother's lap and held her tightly, and Claire could feel the soothing nature of her daughter bleed into her soul, calming her. She hugged her daughter back and the tears that had started when she witnessed the memories of Johnny kept flowing.

Over by the window, the little boy stood watching the mother and daughter. He was stiff with fright and trembling all over. Claire deposited her daughter on the floor and rushed to his side.

"I promise I will never hurt you. I promise I will get you to your father." She bundled him up and hugged him.

At first he fought her, pushing against her to get away. Claire could hear the silent screaming in his head, terrified of the unknown. The longer she held on to him, the less his fighting became. Slowly he became limp in her arms, and she carried him to the couch. Sitting down, she cradled him while she cried. Bree climbed up beside them and held his hand.

Matt was sitting back on a chair, his legs stretched out in front of him and his hands behind his head. He stared at the flickering flames in the fireplace, watching them dancing over the charred wood on the grate. His eyes were closing with the warmth of the room, and he was just about asleep when he suddenly sat up, scaring Adam, who was sitting nearby.

"Claire!" he cried out both with his voice and in his mind, searching for her.

He was confronted by a maelstrom of emotion and energy. It battered him, and he struggled to get a hold on anything. It picked him up and dashed him about. He felt like he was on a roller coaster, and his head reeled with the force of it. Within this storm, a bright spark joined him. It spun around, steadying his spirit, and waited until everything had calmed down.

The spark transformed into Bree, and she took her father's hand. Matt was breathing hard, and he picked her up and cuddled her close.

"Are you all right?" he asked her, checking her for injury.

"I'm fine, Daddy, but Mummy needs you." She kissed his cheek and then wriggled her way out of his grasp. She took his hand and walked him through the gloom.

Claire came into view, crouched on the ground and holding something in her arms. Matt gasped when he realised she was holding a child, and his heart caught in his throat. Carefully he went to her, knelt beside her, and lifted her head. Tears coursed down her face, and sad blue eyes looked back at him.

"Matt."

"Shh…I'm here." He stroked her face, wiping the tears.

"Matt, this is Johnny. Careful—he has been so hurt. That bastard hurt him so much. I couldn't find Marcus to hurt back, but I found someone who was just as evil. Matt, I nearly killed him. I had his mind in my hands and I squeezed it. I wanted them to hurt as much as this boy has been."

"It's all right, Claire. I'm here. I'm here now." Matt tried to take the boy from her, but she refused and clung tighter. He felt a wave of relief in the fact this boy was not a manifestation of their own child Claire was carrying.

Bree placed a hand on her father's shoulder. "He needs his daddy," she said simply and quietly.

Matt wasn't sure if he was doing it properly or even if it would work, but he sent out a request for Tony to join him. The brush he got back was urgent and hurried, and then he was there standing over them, taking in the family scene.

"Claire, Tony is here. Let him take Johnny and look after him," Matt said quietly to his wife. When she didn't answer, he looked to Bree. "Go get your grandparents."

Bree left, and Matt completely missed the anguished look on Tony's face at the task he had sent his daughter on. Claire still refused to release the boy, even to his father's care. Matt watched as Tony begged her for his son—pleaded with her, but she still shook her head. Bree was back with Jess and John closely following, taking in the scene, John's eyes resting on Tony.

"Claire, sweetheart, look at me." Jess pushed both Matt and Tony out of the way and took her daughter's face in her hands. "You did what you thought was right. You need to give him up. He needs his father, Claire. Give the boy to his father."

Claire blinked at her mother and nodded slightly. Jess gently took the limp body of Johnny from her daughter and handed him to Tony. The look of recognition between them sparked, and Jess narrowed her eyes.

Bree took Johnny's place and cuddled her mother. Matt was with them, his arms circling them both as Claire let go a sob, then another. Tony lowered himself to the ground and held his son, worry all over his face. He looked up at them.

"Why isn't he waking up? I can't reach him," Tony cried out in fear for his son.

Jess came to him and placed her hand on the child's head, gently searching for the problem. Carefully she left and pulled her hands off.

"He has a lot of damage. He has experienced some very bad trauma, and his little mind is having a hard time dealing with it. Just talk to him. What's his name?" she asked gently.

Tony flicked his eyes up at John and then back to Jess. "His name is John." He looked back at his boy and smoothed the hair from his face.

"It is you," Claire's father said, coming to stand behind his wife. "You're Tony, aren't you?"

"Yes. It's been a while, John. Jess," he acknowledged them.

"You don't seem so surprised that we're here. I know Adam had a hard time accepting it," John said as he joined Jess in front of him.

"Nothing surprises me about Claire anymore. She is a remarkable woman," he said, not looking up at the couple who had meant so much to him in his early years.

"I didn't want you in our lives back then, and I don't want you here any longer than you need to be." Jess stood up and turned her back on him.

"Grandma?" Bree reached out to Jess, and she went to join the little family.

"This is not Tony's fault, Mum," Claire told her quietly. "He's been watching over me since you died. I never knew until I first met him seven years ago."

"You did that?" John asked him.

"I made a promise to you at your grave. I promised to watch her and make sure she was being looked after," he told John.

"We've had our differences, but he is our friend. He's helping us," Matt informed Jess. Tony looked over and caught Matt's eye. They nodded to each other, a mutual respect growing between them.

"You were right, Tony. I do love you in my own way. As a brother. An annoying, pestering older brother." She smiled at him.

"Not so much of the old." He looked down at the son he was rocking and cradling in his arms. "Johnny, please come back to me. I need you."

Claire disentangled herself from her family and knelt in front of Tony and Johnny. "Do you trust me, Tony?" she asked, turning his face to meet her eyes.

"Always, Claire," he said, and she saw that he meant it.

With a nod, Claire placed a hand on Johnny's forehead and the other on Tony's temple. Claire closed her eyes and concentrated, trying to make the connection between father and son. She was just about to give up when she found it—a tenuous link that the boy was holding on to. She fed it with energy and bolstered it between them. When she retreated, Claire sat back and watched.

Fluttering eyelids were the first movement he had made since they all arrived in Claire's mind. Tony held Johnny closer and called his name softly. Brown eyes met brown eyes and they smiled, both relieved as they found each other once more. The boy threw his arms around his father's neck and held on tightly. Claire turned to give them some privacy for a moment.

John came up to his daughter and put his arm around her. "You are not a bad person, Claire. How can you do something like you have just done and still be bad? Your problem is that you care and feel too deeply. You take on others' problems as if they're your own. You need to be careful how you react to it. Especially now."

Claire placed her head on his shoulder and held her hand out to her mother. "You know about the baby?" Her mother nodded and smiled.

"He is beautiful and will be amazing. Another special child to join our family." Jess looked at Bree, now in Matt's arms, and included them in the family hug.

This talk brought to mind the conversation she'd had with Marcus earlier. "Matt, he knows—Marcus knows I'm pregnant. He got me to do a test, but it's still too early for it to show. He has people with Foresight."

"Let's not worry about it for now," Matt told her with a small smile.

They broke apart when they heard a noise from Tony. "Johnny, I would like you to meet some people who are very important to me." He held the boy's hand and they walked over to them. "This is Jess and John," he introduced the couple to his son. "They took me in when I had nowhere else to go and taught me all the important stuff. I never thanked you when you were alive." Tony held out his hand to John, and he took it and pulled him in for a hug.

Tony turned to Jess. "I learned from you as well, Jess. You taught me how to be protective and supportive of family. I never sought your acceptance. I never thought I deserved it."

"I could tell you were being secretive, that there were things about yourself you were hiding. I just felt I couldn't trust you," Jess told him honestly.

"And you had every right not to. Marcus was paying me to spy. There was nothing I passed on that I thought was out of the ordinary. I never appreciated what was offered to me. For that, I'm sorry."

"I can tell you are being truthful now, Tony, and I appreciate it." She kissed his cheek. "Maybe if I had accepted you back then, things would have been different."

Tony blushed slightly at the olive branch Jess was offering and just nodded. He then turned to Claire, Matt, and Bree.

"Johnny, these are my friends. They're trying to help me find you."

"You are with Bree and me at the moment in the real world, remember?" Claire asked him.

Matt put Bree down, and she walked to Johnny and took his hand. "I would like to be your friend, if you would like," Bree suggested, and Johnny smiled back.

"Thank you, Claire. I feel happier now that I know he's in good hands. We'll get you all out of this mess. You have my word on it," Tony promised.

That night with dinner done and the children safe in Claire's room, she sat in the living room with Marcus. This was the conversation he had promised her earlier in the day. Claire sat holding a cup of tea while Marcus poured himself another bourbon. He sat down opposite her and crossed his legs while he sipped his drink.

"My people have never been wrong with any of their visions. I have had multiple Foresight people tell me that you are pregnant and that this child will have amazing Talents. Just as you yourself have," he told her.

"I don't know what to tell you, Marcus. You saw the test yourself, and it was negative." She blew on her cup and sipped it.

"There is an explanation for that. The pregnancy is so new that it can't be detected yet. Am I close to the mark?" he asked as he took another sip, not once taking his eyes off her.

"Nowhere near it. I don't know these seers, but they really need to re-examine their visions. Matt and I have been trying for five years to have another child, and if it hasn't happened by now, then it's not going to."

"Or maybe you just need the right partner, Claire. We could make beautiful babies together." He gave her one of his leering grins and it turned her stomach.

"Are you trying to make me sick? Because you are going about it the right way."

"With you as their mother, there will be no stopping them, and as their father, I will have full control," Marcus continued on as if he hadn't heard her.

"Your success as a father so far is such a stunning effort. Jack was a roaring success as a total mental case, and as for Adam, you made sure you drove him away."

"They were mistakes. This time round, I will be more hands-on with their rearing."

"You never did answer my question—have you had any other children in your long, long history?" Claire was tempted to filter through his mind and his memories but shied away, not wanting to delve into his insanity.

"Cards-on-the-table time. I tell you something truthful, and you tell me something truthful," he suggested.

"I already know what you will ask me. So it's a moot point. Another question: why did you have my parents killed?"

"That one I can answer. It was simple, Claire. Because of you," he said seriously.

Claire finished her tea and placed the cup on the coffee table. She sat back in her chair and clasped her hands together to keep them from shaking. Looking him in the eye, she could sense that he was telling the truth.

"No comments, no smart-arsed remarks?" Marcus asked her with a hint of a smile as he swirled the bourbon in his glass.

"What can I say? You tell me my parents died because of me; I am just waiting for the explanation. I presume there is one?"

"Even before you were born, I had the first inkling that you were going to be special. I've tracked your life with great interest, Claire. I hoped that your parents would have seen sense and gone along with my plan. They had no idea how special you were. I offered them a lot of money for you, but they refused everything I had to give them."

"You tried to *buy* me? No wonder they refused. What exactly was it were you told that made you think that I was 'special'?" Claire tried to swallow down the anger that his statement had aroused.

"I was told that your Talents would far outstrip those of any other with our Talents, past or present. That you, Claire, will come to possess all of the Talents, some of which have not been seen for centuries. Thank you for the demonstration this morning. It just confirmed it for me."

"How were you told?"

"The same way I was told you are pregnant. With your help, I know I can raise your son correctly and guide him properly with the Talents he will possess."

"We're talking in circles here. If there is nothing else you can tell me, then I cannot help you. You know what my answer is going to be—what it has always been. I do not want—and will never want—to be a part of your grand design. What you want to achieve is madness. People will find out we have Abilities, and we will be hounded just as our people were in Scotland and America."

"Is there nothing I can do to change your mind?" Marcus finished his drink off with one swallow and leaned forward in his seat.

"No. We will stop you, and it won't be just me this time."

"There are those beautiful, innocent children upstairs, sleeping so soundly and peacefully. I would hate for something permanent to happen to them," he said slowly, his voice low and dark.

"Are you really that naïve, Marcus?" She looked around her. "We are alone. I could stop you now."

"But you won't. There are things that we have to achieve first." He took his phone out of his pocket and switched it on, then handed it to her.

"You are a complete bastard." She threw the phone back at him. The image of her daughter fast asleep with a man standing over her, a knife at her throat, burned into her vision.

Claire stalked away from him and ran up the stairs. A large man was exiting her room when she reached the door, and she spat in his face. Inside, she shut the door, turned the key in the lock, and leaned against it. She slowly walked into the bedroom, where a single bed had been put for Johnny and Breena to share, and checked them both.

They were sleeping peacefully, a beautiful dreamless sleep of the innocent. Claire sank to the floor beside them and thanked whatever god was looking after them. It was all getting to be too much for Claire. Every time she thought she had the upper hand, he dragged her down again.

Chapter Eleven

Claire woke to the sound of little voices talking, and she smiled to herself. They were trying hard to be quiet and let her sleep, but as most children do, they did not realise how loud they were. She did not mind, and she lay still listening to their chatter. It was the first time she had heard John really talk to anyone. Bree was good at getting people to talk.

Another reason for staying still and quiet was that Claire was waiting to see if she was going to be sick. There was no cramping stomach, no nauseous feeling, but still she waited. She moved a bit and finally sat up, and relief flooded her. She stood up and found the two children watching.

"Morning, Mummy. We're hungry," Bree spoke for them both.

"I bet you are. How about we all get dressed and go downstairs for breakfast?" They didn't need to be told twice. In short order, they were waiting for Claire at the door.

Just as she was about to unlock it, Claire heard shouts and running feet throughout the house. Carefully she opened the door, then told Bree and Johnny to stay where they were. She peered over the banister and saw a man running by.

"Get Mr. Ryder now!" someone called from the back-door area. The noise sounded like a scuffle between men, and Claire started to descend the stairs.

From the rear of the house, Greg came running and turned to the mount the stairs. He stopped dead in his tracks when he saw Claire coming down, and then he carried on.

"Get back to your room, Claire, now," he hissed as he passed, then disappeared down the hall.

She didn't hesitate at his warning and ran back to the room, shutting the door behind her and locking it. She shooed the children back into the bedroom and closed that door behind them. More shouts could be heard, and then there was silence. Claire pushed the children into the en suite bathroom.

"Bree, lock the door behind you and do not open it unless it is me." She shut the door and waited to hear it lock.

At her door there was urgent knocking, which quickly escalated to thumping. Claire sent a thought out to see who it was and found a very agitated Marcus waiting on the outside. Claire stood on the other side and called out.

"What do you want?"

"I want you out of that room now," he called to her.

"Not until I get some assurances. I want you to promise not to hurt the children."

"I can't promise that, Claire. It all depends on the answers I get." The edge to his tone left her no doubt that Bree and Johnny could be in some danger. She called on her energy and created a light in the palm of her hand. She threw it, expanding it as it went, and filled up the doorway between the sitting room and bedroom.

Taking a big breath, she turned and opened the door. Marcus looked past her at the shimmering light, and his face darkened. He grabbed her by the arm and dragged her out of the room, marching her down the stairs and to the rear of the house.

Greg was standing guard outside a room, and he opened the door as soon as he saw them coming. Marcus pushed her through the doorway, and she found herself face-to-face with a man with blood dripping from his nose and cuts to his face, being held up by two other men. The man looked up at Claire slowly, his eyes nearly swollen shut, and then slumped between them.

"Heal him," Marcus demanded.

"You'd better get me a big breakfast, then," Claire told him as she prepared herself.

Her hands scanned over the man's face, and as they did, his cuts started to heal. The further along his body she scanned, the more injuries she found, and healed them as she went. Claire made sure to take her time. The beating he had taken wasn't too bad, but she wanted to make sure there were not any more dangerous injuries to his internal organs.

When she finished, Claire stumbled back from him. Marcus caught her by the elbow and guided her to a chair. Once she was sitting, he stood in front of her.

"Do you know this man?" he demanded.

"No, I haven't seen him before. Why should I know him?" she asked, breathing deeply, trying to regain some of the energy she had expended.

Marcus crouched down in front of her. "Are you sure, Claire? This is very important for the survival of those children up there—and also your own." The way he talked was even and calm, but the stony stare he was giving her showed her how dangerous he could be.

"I've never seen him before," Claire repeated to him emphatically. She stole a look at this poor man and felt sorry for him.

"Mr. Carter, take Mrs. Drummond to the kitchen and get her some breakfast," he said, still looking down at her. "Stay there. I may have need of some of your other skills."

Claire left the room and followed Greg to the kitchen. Sitting at the counter, she placed her head in her hands and watched as he moved about the room, making her toast and tea. Within minutes, he laid it before her and waited with her. Claire ate it hungrily and asked for more.

"Who is that man in there?" she asked him.

"They found him just outside the grounds. They think he works for a guy named Tony Benning." He poured her another cup of tea and then buttered the hot toast.

"How did you come to work for that man?" She couldn't bring herself to say Marcus's name.

"I was on the streets. My dad was—well, not the nicest person in the world, and he kicked me out when I was fourteen. Marcus took me in and trained me. Be careful, Claire. He will hurt you."

They were interrupted before Claire could ask any more. A large man entered, seeming jittery and slightly jumpy. "He wants her," he said, not looking at Claire.

"Right, Andrew." Greg looked at Claire with sympathy.

They went back into the room, and the man was bloodied again and crumpled on the floor. He spat blood out of his mouth and raised an eye at their entrance.

"If you keep hurting him, I will not be able to keep healing him," Claire told Marcus.

"I don't want you to heal him this time. I want you to go inside his head and get what I want out of it," he spat at her with arms folded and burning eyes still on the intruder.

"Don't you have your own people for that job?" She looked at him, and then she remembered. "Ah, yes; you don't like people with Mind Touch. Adam told me."

"You may have placed a barrier between my men and those children, but there are other ways to get into that bedroom," Marcus said menacingly.

Claire stared at him for a moment longer and then crouched beside the prone man. She placed a hand on his bruised head and very gently tested his mind.

"I'm not going to hurt you," she said to him gently. "I'm sorry I have to do this."

"Do it. Don't resist him," he said back with resignation. "I will not willingly give him what he wants."

Pushing through into his mind, Claire made sure she could hear what was still going on around her. Inside, she met the undamaged version of the man at her feet. He walked towards her with his hand outstretched to shake, but Claire refused to take it.

"I can't shake your hand. Please don't take offence. It's just something that would be a bad idea. I'm Claire."

"I know. I've been watching since you got into New Zealand. I'm Michael—Tony sent me to keep an eye on you. Are you able to get word to him with this Talent of yours?" he asked her.

"I can, but you can talk to him yourself."

"No, I'm afraid this is the end for me. Nobody survives once Marcus has decided you're a threat. Don't worry, I knew the risks going in," he told her without any regret or remorse.

"What do you want me to tell Marcus?" she asked with great sorrow that this man had given his life in tracking her.

"Tell him I work for Tony and that I've been here for a couple of days. That Tony knows where you are and that the kids are here as well. That I don't know what his plans are. I was only told to watch. Keep him on his toes, Claire. You're doing a good job managing him and looking after those kids."

Claire repeated out loud what Michael wanted Marcus to know. After a moment's silence, she heard Marcus ask where Tony was based and whether he was close, and she asked Michael.

"No. He isn't nearby. I will not give that information to him. I'm loyal to Tony. He showed me another way to live. Tell Tony that I'm grateful for all he's done for me."

Claire gave the man his assurances that she would do as he asked and then gently broke the connection. She placed a hand on his for a moment and whispered her thanks. Only after she made sure Michael had heard her did she stand to face Marcus.

"He won't tell me where Tony is. He said that he was too loyal to him and I won't go digging in his mind for it. He will only resist me, and I don't want to be responsible for permanently damaging it. I would rather he died with his mind intact."

Stepping over Michael, she headed out of the room.

"Claire, I have not finished yet," Marcus called to her and followed.

"I will not do what you want, Marcus. I can't do that. I will not go there again."

"You will do it, Claire, and you will continue to do it as many times as I want you to. You may even begin to like it," he told her as he came closer.

Her hand raised and moved swiftly to slap his face, but he caught her wrist and pushed her against the wall.

"Do you want to try that again?" He asked in a low growl as he pushed his face nearer to hers. "Because I like it a bit rough."

Claire turned her head away from him and squeezed her eyes shut as he brought his face closer to hers and licked her cheek.

A force welled inside her and she repelled him, sending him crashing into the wall opposite her in the small hallway. At first he was shocked, but that soon changed to a leering smile.

"Oh, we are going to have fun together," he said to her, then walked back into the room and shut the door behind him.

Claire stayed where she was for a moment and then headed to the kitchen, starting to gather some food to take to Bree and Johnny, when Greg entered.

"Let me help you," he said and started to put together a tray for her to take. "I warned you. It might be easier just to give him what he wants."

"I will not do that, Greg. I cannot give myself to him."

Greg handed her the tray and gave her a sympathetic smile. "I'll walk you up, just in case."

As Claire was about to shut the door on him, he put his hand out and stopped it. "I wish my mother had been as protective of me as you are with those two." He let the door go and walked away down the hall.

"Tony, Michael's late checking in," Nikau said as he came into the gym.

Tony stepped back from the punching bag he had been holding for Matt, who stopped mid-punch and turned to Nikau. Adam sat up from the weights bench and waited for the news.

"By how much?" Tony asked, looking at his watch.

"Two hours. He was supposed to call at eight, and it's now ten. I gave him a leeway just in case, but he's never late."

"I can't find him," Tony said, coming back to himself.

"They're on the move. Claire and Bree. Marcus is moving them," Matt told them urgently.

"Shit. This is not the news I wanted today." Tony headed to the door with Matt and Adam following closely. "Nik, get in touch with Jasper—see if he can get any information, then get someone else out there. If they've left, then I want Michael back…whatever you can find of him."

"Jasper? I hope that's another guy called Jasper and not my kid brother," Adam demanded, catching up to Tony and swinging him around.

"He came to me. Marcus had already tried to recruit him. If you thought he was safe from your father just because he is your half-brother, you really don't know your father very well. He's Claire's cousin, from her mother's twin brother. You do the genealogy." Tony shrugged off Adam's hold and continued into the house.

"Jas is in the States." Adam chased after him.

"No, that was the story he wanted to put around to the family. He wasn't exactly going to shout it from the rooftops that he was coming to work for us, undercover in Marcus's organisation."

"I glad I'm not the one to tell David," Matt piped up.

"No one is telling anyone anything, got it?" Tony rounded on the pair. "We can't protect him if everyone knows. And believe me, he needs protection. It's a sure bet that Marcus will use him the first moment he can. If you have a problem, Adam, with Jasper's decision, take it up with him. Right now, I am more concerned with my son, Claire, and Bree. Do you want to argue some more, or can we get some work done?"

Adam stalked off, muttering under his breath. Tony turned to Matt, who held up his hands.

"Hey, I don't have a problem. He's old enough to get himself into whatever trouble he wants," Matt told him as he headed to his room. "I'll go pack."

Matt sat on the bed and tried to contact Claire, but he found she was being blocked. He tried again and again, but there was no connection to grasp. Bree brushed his mind, and he held onto it closely.

"Mummy's is being blocked. James is holding her. He has Strength Talent. He won't hurt her. I won't let him. We're in a car going somewhere."

"Do you know where they're taking you?"

"No. Do you want me to find out? I could ask James—he would tell me," Bree offered eagerly.

"Only if it's safe for you to do it. I don't want you to get into trouble."

"I won't."

There was silence as Matt waited for his daughter to return to him. It had only been a matter of minutes since they found out, and now the worry became even harder to bear. He was supposed to protect his family, and here he was sitting around, waiting for other people to do something.

"We're going to be near the village. He didn't want to tell me, so I sneaked a peek in his mind. There was an image of the village and a place nearby."

"Well done, Bree. Don't let them know you can do these things. As long as they don't know, I can keep in contact with you and Mum. Is she okay?" he asked, trying to keep the worry from his words.

"I think she is. Something happened this morning and she wouldn't tell me what it was. She even blocked her mind from me so I couldn't find out. She looked scared when she came back into the room."

"When you can, give her a hug for me. Look after yourself, my wee angel. We're coming to get you," he told her encouragingly.

"Love you, Daddy."

Matt drew in a deep breath and let it out slowly, then unclenched his fists. He punched the mattress underneath him a couple times and let out a silent scream of frustration.

Within ten minutes, they were throwing their bags into the back of Tony's car. Adam had already placed his preference of being in the passenger seat by the age-old tradition of putting dibs on it. Tony was still giving instructions to Nikau, and Matt was about to get in the back seat when Tia came running out of the house.

"Here—you'll need this." She pushed a package into Tony's hands.

"We can stop and get something to eat, Tia. You didn't need to do this," he told her.

"Yes, I did. Don't get yourself killed." She reached up and pulled him down to kiss her. Tony's arms reached around her and held her close. When Tia pulled away, she ran straight into the house, leaving him standing there watching where she had gone.

"You better marry her, mate. Otherwise, I'm going to have to do something nasty to you." Nikau grinned at him.

"I think you just got caught," Matt called to Tony over the roof of the car, grinning before getting in and shutting the door.

Without her Talents, Claire felt very uncomfortable, and she shifted in her seat again. The hand that was clamped on her arm was beginning to feel heavy, and she looked at the man who was assigned to curb her Talents. Bree had told her that this man was James and that he had looked after her on the way back to New Zealand. He had been polite enough, but the pressure of his grip told her that he meant business.

"Not long now, Mrs. Drummond," he told her, continuing to look out the front windscreen.

There was no point asking where they were going. He had already refused to answer the question. So had the driver, whom she recognised as the jittery man from earlier in the day.

Bree had called him Mr. Malloy. Greg was sitting in the front passenger seat, and he was just as closed-mouthed as James.

The massive Lake Taupo passed them by, and Claire couldn't help but compare it to the lochs of Scotland. The land of her birth still held a special place in her heart, but Scotland was becoming more and more her home. Every time she went there, it became harder to leave. She thought of moving there when Matt took up the job offer, and she found her heart was well and truly happy at the thought.

Mr. Malloy pulled over behind the car in front, in which Marcus was travelling with Johnny. She had not liked the fact that he had split the children up, taking him where she could not keep an eye on the boy, but she could do nothing about it. Greg was out of the car and opening her door within moments of it stopping, and Claire and James exited.

They were in the middle of nowhere, amidst hills that were covered in native bush with the lush green grass of grazing paddocks surrounding the small group. A cold wind blew through the narrow gully and whipped Claire's hair across her face. Pulling her jacket closer around her, she worried that they had stopped somewhere too remote. She watched Marcus's approach with dread.

"Don't look so worried, Claire. I'm not going to hurt you." He grinned at her, then looked at the scenery. "You don't know where we are, do you?"

"Not exactly—somewhere between Taupo and Napier," she replied, still feeling very uncomfortable.

"This spot, Claire, I thought might have held some very special memories for you. Or maybe Geoff never told you where it happened."

"Where what happened? Are you going to get on with this, or are we just going to freeze on the side of the road?"

"He didn't!" Marcus crowed and laughed at her. "Another secret he kept from you. Your guardian liked to keep so many secrets, didn't he, my dear? This, Claire, is where your parents died. Their car was a blazing inferno after they crashed over that embankment." He pointed to their right, and Claire looked stricken.

Marcus came and stood very close to her. His hand moved a stray strand of hair away from her eyes, and then he ran his finger down her face and neck.

"I will comfort you, Claire. Just give yourself to me and I will make sure you are never hurt again." His finger continued down, skirting her breast and down her stomach.

Claire stood her ground and refused to yield and make him feel like she feared him. She looked him in the eye disgustedly.

"Mr. Boyle won't be with me all the time, Marcus. You keep this up and I will really will have to do something about you," she said through gritted teeth.

"Now, don't be like that. We are going to get to know one another very intimately, Claire, whether you like it or not. And you and Mr. Boyle here are going to be constant companions from now on." He turned away from her and headed back to his car.

"Mrs. Drummond, we have to get back to the car," James said softly, feeling embarrassed at having witnessed this confrontation.

Claire turned with James, still with his hand on her arm. He assisted her into the car and gave Bree a wink.

Chapter Twelve

Tony pulled the car off the road and onto the gravel drive that led to the farmhouse. This was not a place he honestly thought he would ever be visiting, but Adam had insisted they stay there. One thing he was grateful for was that they were expected. He did not fancy facing David unannounced. He parked the car and sat looking at the large old farmhouse.

Adam was already out of the car and running up the steps. The door flew open, and Addy, with her flaming hair, flew into his arms. Matt patted Tony's shoulder encouragingly and exited the car, to be caught up next by his cousin once she'd let go of Adam.

Tony climbed out from behind the wheel and closed the door. He made his way slowly up the steps, still uncertain of his welcome. Addy turned to him with suspicious eyes and a handshake. The door to the house opened and David stood there, his large frame taking up most of the doorway. Tony turned to him and David advanced. The next thing Tony knew, he was flying through the air and landing at the bottom of the steps, his jaw throbbing with pain and sparks swimming in front of his eyes. Matt helped him up and he rubbed the spot where the large fist had connected with his face.

"That was very satisfying. I've been waiting to do that for a very long time, and since Claire isn't here to stop me—" He held his hand out to Tony.

With a wary eye, Tony took the offered hand and shook it. David's grasp was very firm, and he returned the pressure.

"No hard feelings?" David asked.

"None at all. I don't blame you. You were just looking out for Claire. I was a bit of an arsehole back then," he responded.

"Come inside, all of you." David spied Matt and pulled him into a bear hug. "How are you doing?"

"As good as can be expected. The girls are fine. I talked to them a little while ago."

David raised an eyebrow at this piece of news. "I thought you could only fly?"

"We have a lot to catch up on." Matt patted David on the shoulder and moved past him, entering the house.

The reunion continued inside, with Cameron and Dominic leaping on their father as soon as he walked in. Beth brought up the rear, greeting her son warmly, and gave Matt a sympathetic smile and embrace. Then she turned to the stranger who entered behind everyone else. Her face, at first curious, blanched when she recognised him. "You—you work for Marcus. I remember you," she said shrilly.

David came to her side and reassured her. "He used to, Beth; used to. He's here to help look for Claire." Then he looked at Tony. "We trust him, Beth." David sincerely hoped that they could.

"Can I trust you, Claire?" James asked her quietly. He looked at her and then at the two men sitting in the front of the car.

"Yes. I promise I won't do anything." Claire was desperate to have her arm back and feel free for just a moment.

James took his hand off her arm but kept it near in case Mr. Malloy or Greg should turn around. Claire rubbed where he had grasped and stared out the window. Her anger was still with her, just under the surface, and she kept it there. It fed her and made her stronger. She would get away—with or without help from her husband or Tony. She would protect the children from this monster of a man.

Mr. Malloy followed the lead car with Marcus onto a turnoff that Claire recognised, and her spirits started to lift. Home was not far away, but she knew Marcus would not stop in the village. She watched the very familiar landscape pass and they made another turn, this time onto a little-used back road that would take them around the village. She had run these roads and knew them well. She knew the farms and the families who lived on them.

They turned onto another back road that took them up into the hills and the bushlands that covered them. The sun shone sporadically through the thick canopy above. The bush thickened under the trees the further they followed the meandering road up the slope. She recognised Henry's Gully and was feeling very happy. There was only one house up this way, and she knew exactly where it was located. She also knew that her Uncle David was familiar with it as well.

"I spent a lot of time in this area," Claire said to no one in particular. "This is Henry's Gully. It makes for a challenging run. I would try to do it once a week. But I don't suppose I would be able to run it while we're here."

"No, I don't think Mr. Ryder would allow that," Greg told her.

The house came into view, and Claire could see that some changes had been made. A large fence now circled it with heavy electric gates at the entrance. It seemed the old house had Marcus's stamp all over it. The gates closed automatically after they had driven through, and Mr. Malloy pulled up beside the other car. James placed his hand back on Claire's arm, flashing her a regretful glance.

Inside had just been remodelled. Claire could still smell the distinctive odour of fresh paint, and the floors shone with the fresh polish. It was a typical cabin with an open plan downstairs and bedrooms to the back and above. She noted that there was a door under the stairs and remembered another cellar, shivering.

Claire moved to the couch and James went with her. He was to be her shadow, and she knew this could get very awkward. Bree came and climbed up onto her lap and Johnny sat at her other side. She placed protective arms around them both and watched the busy movements around them.

Presiding over it all was Marcus. He stood in the living area, barking out orders to the men he had brought with him. Then he turned and faced Claire and the children.

"I hope your stay here will be an enjoyable one. I am sorry to disappoint you by saying I will not be here. I have far more palatial accommodation. I will be checking in every day, however, and I may even come to visit. I do hope I will be welcomed accordingly. I will leave you in the capable hands of Mr. Boyle and my other men. I will be taking Mr. Malloy with me, Mr. Boyle." He gave James a significant look, and he nodded his agreement.

Marcus gave Claire one last leering glance before he disappeared out the door with Mr. Malloy on his heels. Claire waited until the car could be heard leaving down the drive before she let out a deep sigh of relief. She turned to face James with an expectant look.

"Not yet. There are some here who are truly devoted to him. Let me get them out of the way first," he whispered, and it gave her hope. "Mr. Carter, can you assemble all the men, please?"

In all, there were six men, including James and Greg. They formed up in front of them and waited for James to give the orders.

"Mr. Jones, Mr. Hewson, and Mr. Watson, you will be on the night shift, so go get some sleep. Mr. Carter and Mr. Wilson, you will be on days along with me. Mr. Wilson, please take the perimeter. Mr. Carter, you will be in the house watching the children."

The men nodded an acknowledgment to their orders and went about their business. James kept his hand on Claire until he was certain that the men on the night shift were well and truly settled down.

"So which man is to relieve you?" Claire asked as he released her.

"None. My orders are to stay with you at all times. I think I'm being punished for something," he replied.

Claire sent the children off to play under the supervision of Greg while she relaxed on the couch. It felt wonderful to be back to herself. She stretched out and closed her eyes.

"I don't mean to interrupt, but why are you not trying to escape? I've heard that you have amazing Talents—unlike anyone ever before. If I were in your shoes, I would've taken the first opportunity to get myself and those kids free."

"There is method in my madness. There's a task that we have to perform, and it hasn't happened yet," she told him, still leaning back in her seat, eyes closed.

"*We?*" he asked.

"Yes, *we*. I am not alone in this, James. I have never been alone in this. The support of family is a wonderful thing. It's something that Marcus doesn't understand."

"When he recruited me, he told me that I would be joining a family," he told her with a note of sadness.

"Were you another lost boy of the streets?"

"No. My family already worked for Marcus, so I didn't think anything of joining him. The further up the ladder I climbed, the bigger and the nastier the jobs became. That was when I started to question whether I'm in the right job. He's dangerous, Claire. He will hurt you."

"He can try," she said quietly and with some determination.

Bree and Johnny were playing in the late afternoon light. In the gully with the hills surrounding them, the sun disappeared around three in the afternoon during winter. Bree was her usual chatty self, and Johnny didn't seem to mind.

"In Scotland, it's summer now. At Granny's, there are wildflowers in the field and the sheep are so friendly. But I really like it in the spring with the lambs. Their little tails waggle like a puppy's. It's really funny. What about where you live?"

"It's home," Johnny replied with a shrug. "Do you live in Scotland?"

"Not yet, but we will be soon. Daddy is taking a new job there, so we'll be moving. We live in the city. Where do you live?"

"I live in a little town near my grandpa and grandma in the mountains." Johnny started to tremble, and a tear escaped his eyes. Bree came and held his hand, waiting until Johnny had composed himself. "Grandpa said boys shouldn't cry, but Dad said if I wanted to cry, then I should just let it out," he told her with a hiccup.

"I like your dad. He's funny," Bree said quietly.

"He is. Mom was too. She used to tickle me and read me stories. I really miss her, Bree." Johnny gave a great sniff, which included moving his shoulders.

"What if your dad got you a new mum?"

"Why would he? And I don't want a new mom. I want *my* mom."

Greg couldn't keep silent anymore. He walked over to the two children and knelt on the ground beside them. Johnny immediately became tight-lipped and tensed up.

"Relax, kid. I'm not going to hurt you. If your dad got remarried and she was really nice, then if I were in your shoes, I would love her as if she were my own mum," Greg told him gently.

"What if she's really horrible?" Johnny asked him with a small, quiet voice.

"Then you need to tell your dad so he can do something about it. From what I've heard of your dad, he's a pretty cool guy." Greg looked around to see where Mr. Wilson was. "Sometimes I wish I could work for him instead of Mr. Ryder."

Bree came and put a hand on his shoulder. "If you wish for it hard enough, it will come true. My Gran always told me that. She said that the fairies would hear you and they will answer your wishes." Bree said it so seriously and with such feeling that Greg couldn't laugh at her.

"I will try that, Bree," Greg replied just as seriously.

Mornings were becoming harder and harder for Matt without Claire beside him. He lay in bed listening to the birds outside in between the snores of Tony, who was in the next bed. He sent out a small search to touch Claire's mind and found her still asleep. They had talked the previous night and he'd found out where they were—and that Marcus was not with them. She had also told him about the man named James, who was supposed to suppress her Talents. He wondered again if he was the same James that Bree had so much faith in, and if he would, in fact, help them.

Getting out of bed was a sore task after the workouts that Tony had bullied him into. He stretched and pulled at the muscles, trying to get them to work properly. Matt dressed quietly and left the room. Downstairs, he heard the unmistakable sound of a chair scraping on the floor and headed towards it.

In the kitchen, he found Beth already up and preparing for the morning breakfast. The coffee machine was full of ground beans, pans were laid out on the stove, plates were on the table along with cutlery, and she was standing looking out the window with an apron tied around her still-trim waist.

"Good morning," Matt greeted her softly and then cursed himself for making her jump.

She turned with her hand on her chest and gasped, but smiled when she saw him.

"I see your Stealth is in force." She laughed. "Come in. Don't just stand there. Would you like something to eat or drink?"

"Not at the moment—thanks, Beth. I heard someone down here and I couldn't sleep. Is there anything I can do to help?"

"No, there's nothing. It's all done apart from the cooking." She looked around the room.

"Well, at least let me do that—you do so much already." He had heard from Addy shortly after arriving that she felt useless, as Beth wouldn't let her daughter-in-law do anything.

"What else is there to do but look after everyone? Now that Hunter is at university, there is only David and me in this large house, and he's usually out in the fields all day or puttering around the farmyard." She sat down at the table, and he joined her.

"I thought you and Charlie did a lot of things together?"

"Oh, you are so sweet, Matt. There's only so much we can talk about before we run out of conversation. Plus, she's busy with the medical centre. When Claire was younger, we had something in common, but now, not so much," Beth said sadly with a sigh.

"There's always Addy. She really is a wonderful person and she just wants to help. I hope you don't think I'm butting in, but Claire and I were talking last night and she wondered if you remembered what it was like with your mother-in-law."

"Yes, you two are butting in, and yes, I do remember. Trust that girl, always thinking she has to fix things," Beth said with a smile.

"What is she fixing now?" David asked, coming into the room and kissing his wife. A pang of loss ran through Matt and he shook it off, knowing soon they would be together again.

"Claire. Trying to fix things between Addy and me," she told him, patting the hand he had rested on her shoulder.

"I've been trying that for a while now. Your wife is as bad as her mother was," David said pointedly at Matt. "I'm going for a run. I shouldn't be too long," he said to Beth, depositing a kiss on top of her head and pinching an apple from the fruit bowl on the table.

"Mind if I join you?" Matt asked before he even thought about it.

"Sure. I'll meet you out front."

Matt ran upstairs and almost started to regret the decision immediately, but now that he had committed, he didn't want to back down. He changed and pulled on his sneakers, then left the sleeping form of Tony to his restless dreams and went to join David on the steps of the house.

Dreams were not what disturbed Tony's sleep. There was a concerted effort to break into his mind, and he did not know where it was coming from. Pressure built up against the barriers that he was trying hard to bolster, and it was becoming harder and harder to stave off the attack. His energy was almost spent, and he knew soon they would break in and trample through his mind.

A spark of light appeared above him and he tried to move it. He tried everything in his arsenal of Talents to get rid of it. But it would not budge. Music soared from its depths, and Tony could feel the waves spread out, reenergising him. He stood and watched this tiny spark and waited for it to finish its work. Then he watched with a smile as it changed its form into the little girl, Bree.

"Why didn't you call for help?" she asked him with a frown.

"I was doing all right," he told her defensively.

"Not from where I was standing." She smiled at him with a strange glint in her eye.

"I have been meaning to talk to you, Bree, about boundaries and wandering into my mind uninvited."

"I know—but I know you don't mind, really," Bree replied sweetly. "But if you don't want me to, then I will knock first."

"That would be better. Sometimes grownups are thinking things that children—especially little girls—shouldn't know about."

"Like what?" she asked, cocking her head to the side.

"That's something for your mother to discuss with you. I'm not even going to attempt that minefield." Bree started to skip around him until he caught her and made her stop. "How is Johnny?"

"He's sad. He misses his mum and you." She looked up and stared him straight in the eye. "I told him that maybe you might get him another mother, but he didn't really like that idea...until Greg said that if she was nice, he should love her as his own."

"Who's Greg?" He sat down beside Bree, and she climbed onto his lap.

"Mr. Carter. He's nice, but sad inside too. I wish everyone wasn't so sad. I wish we could all be happy again." She flung her arms around Tony's neck and held on tightly.

"We will be happy again, Breena. We will all be happy again when this is over," he told her gently.

"But then we will be moving to Scotland, and I won't see Johnny again for such a long time. And you won't see Mum."

"I thought you told me that your dad and I would become good friends?"

"You will, but you won't see each other until..." she stopped talking and pulled away.

"Until what, Breena? Your mother doesn't like secrets, and neither do I," he told her gently.

"I know. I'm not allowed to tell you what I see. But it will make everyone happy." She looked up at him again. "I can tell you that you will marry again, Tony, and she will love Johnny just as her own—and you will have a daughter together."

"That's enough, Breena. I don't want to know any more." He placed her on her feet and stood, then started to walk away from her.

"But you have to know, so it can happen. I'm supposed to tell you who it is." She raced after him, trying to keep up with his long strides.

"I can't, Breena. I can't love again. The two most important women in my life have been taken from me. I can't risk it again."

"But you have to, Tony. Tia will never be happy again if you don't." Bree stopped and stamped her foot in anger. "You cannot stop it, Anthony Benning. It has already been written in the book of destiny." Her voice sounded loud in his mind, and he covered his ears. There was also another tone above it, a more mature woman's voice he recognised.

"Who are you?" he asked her.

"I'm Breena," the child in front of him said.

"No—who is with you?"

"That is the correct question. I can't give you the answers if you don't ask the right questions," Bree said, and her answer infuriated Tony.

"Just tell me, Breena. Stop talking in riddles."

"I am Breena, and I am Breena," the dual voices spoke together.

"The older Breena—I only want to talk to the older one," he told her, and his vision shifted.

Hand in hand they stood before him, so alike and so beautiful. The older Breena he recognised as the woman he'd fought on the hill by the stones, and he took a step backwards.

"There is nothing to be afraid of, Tony. I will not harm you. This time," she said with a cheeky smile.

"How can you be here?"

"It's complicated. I can let you know if you want." Breena held up a hand and was about to release the information when he stopped her.

"No, I don't think I need to know that. Why are you here?" he asked her.

"We thought it would be easier if the image of Bree were in your mind and not me. The Guardians have worked very hard for this to happen, and it took the sum of all our knowledge to achieve it. There are things that have to happen, and it was one of my tasks to make sure that you and your son are happy in the years to come. An arrangement was made with the Sentinels of this land for a joining. That joining is you and the woman Tia. Your daughter will be a peacemaker and a very influential person in the world to come. She will be the sum of two peoples, with their Abilities entwined in her."

"Tia? She doesn't believe in her people's spiritualism," Tony said with some disbelief.

"She will come to know it very shortly. She is also the mother that Johnny will need. Bree cannot tell you, but I can. Johnny has a very special destiny, and he will need to be cared for by two very loving people to achieve it. That's why it is important that Tia is in his life and yours. You cannot change your fate, Tony. It has already been decided for you," Breena told him.

"I think I would like you both to leave now. I have a lot to think about," he said politely, watching as the two merged into one person again.

"The people who were attacking you are going to try again," Bree told him. "They're trying to make you weak. I have something here that will help you." She opened her little hand and released a tiny spark. "It will protect you from them, and they will not be able to break in. I'm sorry if we made you sad or angry." She cocked her head to the side again as she looked at him.

"Just surprised, Bree. You should go now," Tony told her.

Before she left, she floated up and placed her arms around his neck, then kissed his cheek and he closed his eyes. All too soon the feeling of her hug began to diminish, and he was left with her whispered words floating back to him.

"Goodbye, Tony."

The final note of her voice drifted away, and it felt like she was saying goodbye to him for good. This little girl he had never met in the flesh had come to mean so much to him, and he was feeling the loss already.

Bree's giggling woke Claire up. She sat up and watched her daughter, who was asleep in the bed next to her. She was curled up, and her long, dark hair covered her face. Claire brushed it aside and smiled, pleased that she was having such a good dream. She rolled over and found James sitting in the chair he had placed there the night before.

"I hope my alarm didn't wake you," he said softly, so he didn't wake the children.

"No, it didn't." Claire felt uncomfortable having this stranger watch her sleep. Even though he seemed so nice, she knew that he was still working for Marcus.

"Good. The night shift men are still out there, so if you want to use the bathroom before they come in, I would hurry. I promise, I will not harm the kids."

"Thank you. I will." Claire got up and made use of the time she had, quickly showering and changing from the clothes she had slept in.

When she came out, James was standing by the bathroom door and immediately took her arm. He put a finger to his lips and pointed to the hallway. Male voices were talking outside their door. She couldn't quite make out what they were saying, and she did not recognise them.

"I don't like them," Johnny said with eyes wide, looking at the door. "They hurt me."

James reached his side before Claire could and scooped him up. "They won't hurt you while Greg and I are around, kid. They won't dare," he told Johnny as he sat down on the bed, trying to comfort him.

Claire began to reevaluate what she thought of him once more. At first she had thought that he was just being kind, trying to get her cooperation. But now it was all changing.

"If we needed you to help us, would you?" she asked carefully.

"I would, Claire. I know Greg will—he and I have already talked. I wouldn't trust anyone else, though. They all like their work just a little bit too much, if you get my drift."

She nodded her understanding and felt a bit of relief. They just had to make it through the time until the task was presented before her. This holding pattern was getting a bit much for her, and she started to pace. She knew there was a timeline, and she wished she knew what it was. Then her eyes rested on her daughter.

"Bree?" she said, touching her mind and trying to look like she wasn't using her Talents.

"Mum? We can talk in front of James. He is going to help us," Bree said seriously.

"I know that, but this is something I want to talk to you about alone. How long until the task, do you know?"

"How can I know that, Mum? I'm only six!" Bree responded with a slight giggle.

"How about the Breena side of you? I know she's in there with you."

"It tires her to talk this far. She has just been talking to Tony. But I'll check for you."

This news surprised Claire. The talk Bree had had with Tony and the image of the picture she'd drawn at school swam before her eyes. The tall figure who looked familiar was, of course, Tony.

"Oh, dah. Of course it was." Bree laughed at her mother's sudden realisation.

"Don't be cheeky, young lady. What did Breena say?"

"She's here but can only stay for a short while." There was a shift in Claire's perception, and Breena was there.

"Hello, Carling. Please be quick," she said breathlessly.

"Can you tell me how long until this task is done?"

"Not long now—days. Please be patient. Everything must be in place."

"What were you talking to Tony about and why was Bree involved?" Claire demanded.

"It is important for the future, Carling. That is all. Bree had to be there—he would have remembered me and not trusted what I had to say. I have to go. Our love is with you always. Remember, please."

"I will, Breena." Then she was gone.

Claire was looking out the window at the blue sky above. The lawn below was still encrusted with a white frost, and she could see where the men had walked, leaving their footsteps dark against the white. Mist clung to the sides of the hills enshrouding the trees, but the birds still sang their sweet songs at the top of their voices.

"When you're ready to go down, let me know. Greg will be getting breakfast soon," James told her.

"I'm hungry, James." Johnny looked up to the man beside him.

"So am I, but it is up to Claire when we go down," he told the boy gently.

Johnny jumped off the bed and walked over to Claire, taking her hand. "Claire, please. I'm so hungry."

She looked down and smiled. "Then we had better go." She turned, still holding his hand, and Bree took his other one. "We're ready, James. Let's go face this day."

Chapter Thirteen

The grey horse snorted at the arrival of David and Matt, and the latter stood watching as his wife's uncle gave the horse an apple from his pocket. David rubbed the long nose and patted the neck of the horse affectionately.

"Claire used to love coming to see Janie. I believe that this horse was the first friend she made in the area. The old girl has missed her visits and the apples she would bring her," David told Matt. He then put his hand in the other pocket, pulled out another apple, and tossed it to Matt.

He caught it in one hand and looked at the glossy red surface of it, then walked slowly up to the horse.

"You haven't had much interaction with horses, have you?" David asked him.

"You've seen the farm. There are only sheep and a few cows on it. Not much call for horses, and who would look after them, anyway?"

"Just give Janie the apple—she's seen it now," David said.

The horse was snorting and moving her head up and down. Matt held out the apple, and the horse took it gently from his hand. He reached up and patted her neck, and the hair under his hand felt coarse to his touch. Janie nudged him to see if he had another apple for her.

"I think you've made a friend, Matt." David laughed.

"Claire never told me about this."

"She probably wouldn't have, since it was a hard time for her. And how was she going to tell her husband that this was the place she had her first kiss—with her ex?" David told him with a large grin.

"Really? Here?"

"Yep, exactly where you're standing right now." David laughed at the face Matt pulled. "Come on. I'm starting to get hungry for Beth's pancakes." He slapped Matt's shoulder, and they ran back to the house.

By the time they got back, everyone else was up. Tony was outside on the phone, looking pretty serious. Matt told David that he would see him inside and to save him some pancakes. He waited until Tony was finished and asked him what was up.

"Your daughter! Once she's in your head, she doesn't let up, does she? Oh, and your sister, too—they tag-teamed me," Tony told him with a huge sigh.

"You want to start again and give me a proper answer?" Matt asked, looking slightly bemused.

"I was under attack last night—we'll talk about that later. Bree came in, and I don't even want to start thinking about how she managed to stop them. Then your sister was there, telling *me* that I have to marry Tia, to make sure that Johnny has a great future and that our daughter will be something big."

"Okay, then who were you talking to on the phone?" Matt asked curiously.

"Nik. I was asking his permission to date his sister."

Matt started laughing and kept on laughing. "You what? You do realise that you just made Tia mad? She's not going to like the fact you asked Nik's permission, as if she's his chattel. Tony, ring her now before Nik can talk to her—otherwise, you're going to be in so much trouble." Matt slapped his back and walked inside, still laughing.

The battered ute drove to the base of the hill and turned the corner away from Henry's Gully. Its engine seemed to be running a bit rough, with blue smoke pouring from the exhaust pipe. The two people inside seemed as mismatched as any could be: Addy, with her flaming hair, and David, with his receding hairline and grizzled, unshaven face. David turned the wheel and headed up a track that was barely there. They bumped along it slowly, before he pulled up and they got out.

"You ready for this?" he asked her.

"I was born for it, David," Addy replied confidently.

"Right. Then let's go. Stick close. I don't want to lose you." He chuckled.

"As if. I may be rusty, but I can still out-track you, old man." Her clipped English accent made the fighting words sound even funnier.

They took off up the track with David still laughing at his daughter-in-law. The sound of the bush around them was the only sound that could be heard. The track soon became mud and they skirted around it. Even the most skilled Stealth user would leave footprints in the type of mud they had come across. The terrain began to rise and the going became tougher. The bush started to close in, but they made their way through with as little disturbance as possible.

Once they reached the top of the ridge, they followed it around until they managed to get a good view of the house halfway down into the gully. Addy let out a breath to calm herself, and she watched the compound below.

"Bit out of breath there?" David asked as he crouched beside her.

"You wish. How's the heart holding up?"

"Never better. What do you see?"

Addy squinted and focused her gaze. "One guy walking the fence, one car out in front, and sorry…I left my x-ray specs in the car."

"You're enjoying this, aren't you?" he asked with a smirk.

"Of course! Away from the kids and the hubby, trekking around in the dirty forest—what's not to love? We have movement."

Down below them, a door opened and two children ran outside, followed by a man in a dark suit who had a ball in his hands. Addy and David watched as he played with them in the afternoon sunshine.

"That must be Greg Carter," David said. "Claire said he and one other were the only ones she trusted with the kids."

"Yeah, the other being the one who is supposedly suppressing her Talents. I wish I could talk to her right now."

"Send out your thoughts. She may pick them up," David told her.

"I don't think it works like that," Addy replied, but her mind was on Bree as she watched the little girl play.

Down on the lawn, Bree stopped and looked up into the bush, staring at the spot where they stood. The hair on the back of Addy's neck stood to attention and she shivered. Bree went back to her game, skipping along after the ball.

"Come on," David said quietly, obviously affected in the same way as Addy. "We have to check further up."

The pace David set was not hurried as they circled around the house until they came to the head of the gully. From somewhere ahead, they could hear water tumbling over rocks as it made its way down the shortest possible route to the stream below. The sodden ground under their feet tried to catch at their shoes and halt their footsteps. All around them was the sound of wetness, from the running stream to the squelching mud, to the *drip, drip* of water falling from the tree ferns and larger trees that surrounded them.

David put out a hand to halt Addy, and they crouched down. A voice called out and was answered by another, echoing along the gully. Addy pointed one way and David the other, indicating the direction the voices had come from. Heavy footsteps through the leaf litter and undergrowth could be heard nearby. Addy lifted up the hood on her jacket and tucked her bright red hair underneath it. David smiled at this action, not saying a word.

The footsteps stopped, and they could hear something scraping at the earth and debris. "Over here—is this one?" A loud shout came from uncomfortably close by.

More steps rushed towards where they were hiding. David raised one, then two, and finally three fingers. The skills that had long gone unused by Addy were flooding back to her, and she could almost smell these men that were tramping around out there.

"Yep, that's one. The next should be close by. Spread out and see if you can find them. They may have fallen or even broken off. Make sure you search thoroughly. He wants all of them uncovered and dug up." The man spoke with a deep, gravelly voice.

David motioned for Addy to stay where she was and started to creep towards the voices. The activity of the men grew, and she waited with increasing nervousness for David to return, trying to imagine what they were looking for up there in the hills.

When David returned, he indicated with his hands to go back down the trail. Addy didn't need to be asked twice and led the way. The trip back to the car seemed to take no time, and when they reached it, she waited for David to talk about what he had seen. He made her wait a little longer as he drove out of the bush and back to the road.

"I made a sketch." He pulled a small pad out of his pocket and handed it to Addy. "Look familiar to you?"

She looked at the small drawing he had made of a little plateau on the side of the hill. Over the drop-off, a small stream ran and beside it, some rocks jutted out of the earth. The sketch didn't include the trees that grew there, but it did—as he suggested—look very familiar.

"All that's missing is the stones," she said quietly.

"That's what I think they're looking for." He looked at her for a moment before returning his gaze back to the road.

Marcus walked into the cabin just as they were sitting down to dinner. The smell of his cologne presented itself to them before he reached the table and sat down.

"Good evening. I hope you all have had a pleasant day." He looked directly at Claire, and she stared back at him.

"Yes. Thank you, Mr. Ryder. All is quiet here," James told him.

"I know, Mr. Boyle. I am getting the reports. Thank you." Marcus flicked him an annoyed glare. "Mr. Carter, why don't you take the children upstairs to have their dinner? They can watch a bit of TV if they wish."

Greg didn't argue and hurried them along up the stairs, leaving Claire and James sitting at the table with Marcus. The atmosphere immediately changed in the room. It had gone from an almost happy evening back to the feeling of oppression and darkness.

"Please eat, Claire. You must keep your strength up. That child you are carrying needs to grow strong and healthy." The smile was back, but it was very fixed.

Claire picked up her knife and fork, but before eating her own food, she leaned over and began to cut up James's for him so he could eat as well. Marcus chuckled at the sight.

"Isn't she so sweet, Mr. Boyle? So thoughtful, always thinking of others before herself. You have a kind heart, Claire, but you should think of yourself before others once in a while. I can always replace Mr. Boyle," he said darkly, a veiled threat to not get too comfortable around his man.

"And I would do the same for the next person you put on guard over me. He can't cut up his own food without taking his hand off me. And if he did that, you would not be sitting there for very much longer."

"Threats, Claire? That's not really necessary, is it?" Marcus asked her.

"As a friend of mine once said, 'You started it,'" she replied as she began to eat her own meal.

"Where is the third man who is supposed to be on this watch?" Marcus asked, still watching Claire.

"Mr. Wilson is eating his meal in the bunk room. He said he hated being around kids," James told him, picking up his fork to begin eating.

"Therefore, swap him out. Do I have to organise everything myself, Mr. Boyle?" Marcus demanded of him.

"The men on the other watch are not suitable for looking after children, Mr. Ryder. I told you that when you asked me to head this up."

"Sentimentality has no place in my organisation. These are the men I picked to help you, and I picked them for a reason. To keep Claire in line. Now, if you are not up to the job, I can easily replace you with perhaps Mr. Malloy instead." Marcus looked pointedly at James and Claire felt the threat heavily.

"I am up to the job, Mr. Ryder. I will make sure that Mr. Wilson is working to order."

"Good. You do that. Let's just say that this is your second and only chance left to prove yourself."

"Thank you for the opportunity, Mr. Ryder," James said as he continued to eat.

Marcus stood and went the cabinet on the opposite wall, unlocking it. For a brief moment, James unconsciously let go of Claire's arm. She took that second and crept into Marcus's mind. What she saw there filled her with horror, and she tried to hide it. The mouthful she had just taken stuck slightly in her throat at the thought of it, and she tried to steel herself, preparing for what was to come. He poured himself a drink and brought it back to the table, waiting for the pair to finish eating. Claire noticed he was looking very pleased with himself, and she was not looking forward to spending an evening in his company.

Greg came down the stairs shortly after they had finished eating, carrying the plates from the children. He took them into the kitchen, then came and cleared the table off.

"Thank you, Mr. Carter. It was a lovely meal," Claire told him with a smile.

"You are welcome, Mrs. Drummond. The children are watching a movie," he told her.

"You have left them alone?" Marcus asked with an arched eyebrow.

"The windows and door are locked. They cannot escape, Mr. Ryder," he told his employer.

"Go get Mr. Wilson, please. He can babysit while you finish off the rest of your duties," Marcus said dismissively.

"Yes, sir." Greg left the room.

"Claire, shall we make ourselves more comfortable?" Marcus held out a hand to her, and she took it reluctantly as he led her to the living area and sat beside her on the couch.

James stood uncomfortably behind them with a hand still on her shoulder.

With her hand limp in his clasp, Claire tried to make herself comfortable, but he was sitting very close to her. He raised her hand to his lips and kissed it.

"You are looking very lovely tonight—so beautiful. You seem to be positively glowing. Women change when they're pregnant, and I find it very enticing."

"You are deluding yourself, Marcus. I'm not pregnant, and I am getting very tired of this conversation. How about you tell me what you really have planned for me?"

"And spoil the surprise? No, I couldn't do that. But I do have one surprise for you, my dear." He reached into his pocket and pulled out a small box. "Open it. I saw it and thought of you. You deserve the very best, Claire, and I can give it to you—anything you want."

She held the box in her hand. "Anything?" she asked as she held the box in her hand. "As long as it's what you want me to have. I don't want this and can't accept whatever it is."

"Now, don't hurt my feelings. All day I have been looking forward to giving you this gift. Open it," Marcus urged her.

She raised the lid and nestled inside was a gold filigree ring in a Celtic-inspired design with diamond insets. It sparkled in the light from above, and he plucked it out of its cushioned seat. He held it up and smiled as he placed it on the ring finger of her right hand.

"We can transfer it to the other hand when your divorce comes through," he told her softly, then leaned in to kiss her. Her head automatically pulled away from him and he stopped. A hard, flinty glaze came over his eyes but left just as quickly. Marcus tried again to gain a kiss from her, and she moved again.

"I can't, Marcus. You can't make me do this," she said to him, her heart thumping in her chest with fear at what was to come. The hand on her shoulder squeezed a little tighter.

Marcus let go of her hand and held her face tightly, his fingers digging into the soft flesh of her cheeks.

"Oh, you will, and I can. This is going to happen, Claire. You cannot stop it." He planted his lips on hers and then slipped them down past her jaw, nuzzling her neck as he went, his hands roaming her body roughly.

Claire opened her eyes and saw James looking at her with outrage and anger. She shook her head and hoped he understood not to do anything that would get him in trouble. *Enduring this is nothing,* she told herself. As long as Bree and Johnny were safe, she could retreat into her mind. She held an image of Matt before her, and along with it the feeling of his love for her. She focused on him, hoping that he would understand as she blocked the world out and shut herself away.

The brightness of the sun shining in the window woke Claire, and the night before came flooding back to her. Her body rejected the thought with a sudden lurch from her stomach. She ran to the bathroom and threw up into the bowl of the toilet. Tears streamed down her face, and her body shivered in the cold. She could still feel his rough touch on her skin, feel the hands clenched around her body as he took her. A new wave of nausea hit her, and she expelled it.

After she cleaned up, Claire turned the shower on to the hottest setting she could stand and stood under the flow, scrubbing at her skin and trying to get the stench of his cologne off her—until she was red and raw. She sat in the bathtub with the water raining down on her and cried, her body shaking with the sobs that escaped her lips as well as the anger and outrage that were building up inside.

Claire felt a brush on her mind and recognised it as Matt. The thought of telling him what had happened was too much, and she blocked him. The persistence of her husband kept up and she kept knocking it back. She could feel his frustration before he gave up. She rested her head on her knees and let the hot water flow over her.

Another brush—this time from Tony. For one moment she thought she could open up to him and tell him what had happened, but she knew that would be betraying Matt. She again pushed back against his request, sending a loud message of *Go away*. She felt him pull back and leave at once.

The door opened, and she could hear movement inside the bathroom. A window opened, and the steam from all the hot water started to shift and eddy in the morning breeze. She huddled herself behind the curtain of the shower and hoped the person would go away.

"Claire, there is a towel and a robe for when you're ready," James said softly from the other side. "I have also brought your bag so you can dress." When she didn't answer, he left and closed the door behind him.

Flashes of the night before rose in her eyes, and she remembered. A hand grasped in support, also to hold her prisoner. She saw eyes filled with a murderous stare and the frustration of being unable to stop it. And she cried some more.

Eventually the hot water began to cool, and the contrast on her heated skin made her shiver. Standing, she turned the water off and pulled the curtain back. On the vanity sat a fluffy white towel. She picked it up and wrapped it around herself. The shivering continued. Claire dried herself and pulled on the robe James had brought to her, and then steeled herself as she opened the door to the bedroom beyond.

James was sitting in the chair where he had been the night before, dressed more casually than he had been previously.

Claire saw darkening bruises on his wrists. He followed her gaze and pulled the sleeves of his jumper down over them.

"Did I do those?" she asked.

"It doesn't matter. They don't hurt. Why wouldn't you let me do something to stop him?"

"You wouldn't understand." She sat on the bed and stared at the clouds racing across the sky through the window.

"Try me. We want to help you, Claire."

"This is something I have to do myself, and because of that, there are things that must be done—things that have to happen." A tear ran down her cheek from her red-rimmed eyes.

"Bree has been asking for you since she woke," he said.

Claire didn't answer him but continued to cloud-watch. She remembered a day when she was younger, lying on the grass in the park with her father and mother, watching the clouds sail overhead and finding animals in them. A happier time, a more secure time in her life—before it had been turned upside down and shaken for good measure.

"Claire, can you hear me?" James was in front of her, concern written all over his face. "Claire, you're frightening me. Tell me what I can do to help."

"Nothing. There's nothing you can do."

"She's blocking me as well," Tony said with a frown.

"I told you something happened last night. I could feel it. Can't we just go in there and get her? Stuff all this nonsense about a task. She's being hurt," Matt urged.

"Try Bree. See if she knows."

"Bree is six. Do you really think Claire would allow her to see anything?" Matt said, running a hand through his hair roughly.

"No, but Bree may be able to get through to her mother. Claire is blocking us for a reason. Matt, you need to be calm. Talk to Bree. Or if you want, I will."

Matt glared at Tony. "Leave my daughter alone."

"I'm not the bad guy here. I'm not out there tracking them—I'm here with you." Tony placed a hand on his shoulder, trying to be supportive.

"Fine. Just stay out," Matt warned him, shrugging off Tony's hand.

Matt called out to Bree, and his daughter came running at his call. She threw herself at him and buried her head in his shoulder.

"Daddy, something is wrong with Mummy. She won't let me see her. I can't talk to her like this. I'm scared."

"It's all right, my wee angel. It will be all right. Mummy is tough. Do you know where she is?" Matt asked, trying to stay calm for his daughter.

"She's in another room. James is in there with her. But he didn't hurt her, Daddy. James is trying to help her."

"Who was it, sweetheart?" Matt asked, dreading the answer.

"That man, Marcus. He came last night, and we were sent to our room to watch TV. I heard a noise, but Mummy wouldn't answer me."

All sorts of scenarios came to Matt in a flash. Most of them he did not want to think about. If something happened, then it had to be bad, if Claire was shutting herself off from everyone she loved.

"What about Breena—could she help?" Tony's voice said behind them.

"I told you to stay out, Tony." Matt placed his daughter down and took her hand.

"I know, but I can't. What about Breena, Bree? Could she get through to your mother?" Tony asked again.

"I don't know, Tony. She was pretty tired last time." Bree bowed her head and shuffled her feet a moment, and then looked up. "She'll try, but she can't promise anything. Daddy, she told me to tell you to send all the love you can to Mummy. She needs it right now."

"Thank you, Bree. I will. Look after yourself and Johnny," Matt told her as he knelt at her side.

Bree hugged him once more and then went to Tony. "Johnny is getting better. I told him that you weren't far away."

"Thank you, Bree," Tony said and faded from Matt's thoughts.

"I better go, Daddy, so Aunty Breena can talk to Mummy. Remember to send your love to her. She will make sure Mummy gets it."

"I will, my wee angel." With his promise made, she left him, and once more Matt felt alone and helpless.

Claire was still sitting on the bed where James had left her to resume his own seat in the corner. The silence was deafening between them, and he was worried and angry with himself for not doing anything during the long, horrible night. He had lied when he said his wrists didn't hurt, but he wanted it as a reminder of what she had gone through—a talisman to keep so he could remember, and when the time came, beat the hell out of Marcus.

This woman who had endured what no woman should have to was strong, he could see that—both in her personality and her Talents. She had given herself to Marcus and not put up any fight to protect not only her children, but himself as well. He could not figure her out. Why, when they could both have defeated Marcus then and there, had she not done anything? Why had she not stopped him from doing anything? She was a puzzle that no matter which way he turned, he could not solve.

Claire went to the window and opened it. The cool, wintery air blew in and mixed with the warm air from the central heating. She closed her eyes and her mind wandered from the forested hills of New Zealand to the bare, grassy ones in Scotland. She could smell the subtle fragrance of heather on the wind and she longed to be back there. Scotland was home for her now, she could feel it. She needed it; she longed for it.

"It will be home soon, my sister." Breena was beside her, linking her arm through hers. "It will be over soon, I promise."

"Breena, I let him—" Claire clung to her sister and cried bitter tears of a pain from deep within.

"I know, Carling. I know." Breena comforted her, holding her close. "One more day is all there is. Tomorrow night it will be finished. Look—I have a gift for you."

Breena held out her hand, and inside was a rose. A deep buttery yellow rose, with a single dewdrop that clung to one petal and glistened like a diamond. She showed it to Claire, who took it into her own hands and held it close. The perfume from the deep golden centre was intoxicating, and she breathed it in deeply. It calmed her and stopped the tears.

"This is from Galen and Breena and everyone else, including myself, who love and care for you, Carling. This is for you to hold in your heart, to keep you from your dark thoughts. Remember, no matter what happens or what harm is brought to you by others, this will never die."

Cupping her own hands underneath Claire's, she pushed the rose to her heart and nodded. Claire held it to her chest and pushed it slowly inside. The love that was held within the beautiful rose spread out and surrounded her heart, giving her strength and courage.

"Thank you, Breena," Claire whispered, feeling it spread out within her.

"Don't thank me. This was Galen and Tony's doing. You are not alone, Carling—we are with you always." Breena hugged her sister again. "Now go. Bree is worried about you."

Breena left her with the hint of heather in the air and a smile on her face. The tears were now dry, and her heart lifted. She was determined never to doubt her husband's love again.

Chapter Fourteen

James could sense the change in Claire before she had even turned around. The room suddenly seemed brighter and the air less cool. There was also something else he couldn't quite put a finger on. He was on his feet as soon as she looked at him, and she was smiling.

"Thank you for being patient, James. I'll get dressed and go down now." Claire moved to the bag and took it into the bathroom with her.

When she came out, there wasn't a hair out of place, and not a hint that she had been crying. She carried herself as if the night before had not happened, and this frightened James even more. Claire stood at the door and waited for him.

"Are you coming? Or are Marcus's spies going to have a field day about the fact that I am unrestrained?" she said when he didn't move to her side.

"What happened? One minute I thought you were going to throw yourself out of that window, and the next you are all smiles and happiness." Confusion was coursing through him, and he stayed where he was until he got an answer.

"Believe me, I will be killing Marcus for what he did to me, then bringing him back and killing him all over again." The coldness in her voice chilled him to the bone. "But at the moment, I'm being helped through this. Please let this be the last time you refer to last night."

James nodded and joined her at the door. As he went to place his hand on her shoulder, she took it and linked arms with him. "I don't like feeling like I'm being held down or steered like a ship. If we're friends, then let's act like it."

"What about Marcus?" he asked with concern.

"He will get his due tomorrow night. And I'm very much looking forward to it."

As they left the room, James was overcome with a complete sense of the unknown. This change had skewed his views, and it was messing with his head. He hoped that the confusion he was feeling wasn't too obvious, because he felt he was losing complete control over the whole situation.

Downstairs, Bree and Johnny were sitting at the table drawing, and Claire dropped a kiss on her daughter's dark curly head. She sat next to Bree, making James move his hand to her shoulder. He apologised with a small smile when she looked at him.

"Mummy, I'm so glad you're up. I've made you a present," Bree said with a sunny smile and pushed the paper over to her mother.

Claire looked at it in amazement. It was the yellow rose, complete with the dewdrop, from her meeting with Breena. It touched her deeply that Bree had been so thoughtful as to give her a visual reminder of what now lay surrounding her heart. She pulled Bree onto her lap and hugged her close.

"Thank you, sweetheart. I love it! When we get home, I'm going to frame it and hang it on the wall for always." She gave her daughter another squeeze and kissed the top of her head.

Looking across the table to Johnny's drawing, she was surprised to see that he, too, had an artistic Talent. The subject of the drawing was more surprising to Claire, though, and she smiled at it. It was a beautiful drawing of Bree with her cheeky smile.

"You draw very well, Johnny. Was your mum very artistic?" she asked the boy.

He looked at her with his sad brown eyes and shook his head. "No, I just like drawing." Johnny carefully folded up the page and put it into his pocket without showing it to Bree.

Claire was wondering what else he was going to be good at as he grew. The likelihood that he would inherit any Talent from his father was remote, according to all the research she had done into the Talents. They were more likely to be passed down via the female line than the male. She put the matter to one side. There was no use thinking about it until he was older.

There were far more important things to do for the moment, and she put Bree back on her own chair and went to sit on the couch. The lingering memory from the night before made her shudder, and she made herself sit in the same spot she had been.

James sat down beside her and carefully removed his hand from her shoulder. She leaned back in the seat and closed her eyes, then reached out for Matt.

Not a word was spoken between them as they ran into each other's arms. He kissed her deeply and long, hoping to drive out any pain that may have lingered. She pulled him into their special space in her mind, and they were soon one. Desperate to blank out her memories, she clung to him forcefully, tears of joy and happiness springing to her eyes.

Matt decided he didn't want to know what had happened to her, decided that if this is what she wanted, and then he would give it to her without question. He trusted her completely and loved her even more. The energy he used to show her overwhelmed them both, especially when she joined hers with it. They floated on their love and rejoiced in it, savouring each and every moment.

The words now seemed less than the emotions they were feeling, but he said them anyway.

"I love you."

"I love you, too, Galen," she whispered back and held him close, knowing that she would soon have to let him go. "Tomorrow night. It will be over tomorrow night," she told him.

"Are you sure? Will you be okay until then?" he asked, caressing her face.

"Yes. I have the rose to hold me until you can hold me in person."

His hand trailed down her body and rested on her stomach. "And the baby?"

"He's fine. Nothing has hurt him."

"Him? You know we're having a boy?"

"Yes. One of each, unless you want more?" she asked him with a shy smile.

"Let's just see how this one turns out." He kissed her again.

A noise made her sit up and listen. "I have to go. Something is happening. I'm sorry."

"Don't be. Go—we'll talk later," Matt said, then pulled his mind from hers.

With a jolt caused by James clamping his hand on her arm once more, she came back to herself in time to see Greg being pushed further into the living room by Mr. Wilson. Claire stood as he followed Greg in.

"There she is. Did you have fun, darling, last night with the boys? I heard you all the way down in my lonely bunk. I reckon it's my turn, don't you?"

"Jonah, you got it all wrong," James said.

"No, Jamie boy. You and this sweet-looking peach here were having lots of laughs with Greg—or was it one of the others?"

"It was not any of us, you bastard. It was Ryder," Greg growled at him. Claire could see the muscles under his shirt flexing, ready to pounce.

"He wasn't here last night." There was a tiny touch of uncertainty in his eyes as he said it.

"It's all right, Greg," Claire said. "Can you please take the children out to play before it gets too late? I think I need to have a little chat with Mr. Wilson here about what happened and what's going to happen."

Greg looked at James, who nodded his agreement. As they disappeared through the front door, taking the ball with them, Claire turned to James.

"Do you remember me asking you a certain question yesterday morning and your answer?" she asked him.

"Yes, I do, Claire. Are you asking me now?"

"Indeed I am. Just this once, and then we have to go back to normal."

"What the fuck are you two on about?" Jonah asked.

In answer, James looked him in the eye. Very deliberately and with a great deal of show, he released Claire's arm and stood back from her.

"Just one thing. Claire. Don't make the change too obvious. I don't want to have to try and explain it away."

"Anything for you, James," Claire said, walking towards a stunned Jonah.

"Don't you touch me!" he cried out.

"Just a little. It won't hurt—I promise." Claire's hand touched his lightly and she was in immediately.

The mess of this man's mind was highly evident. It was like walking into the worst teenage boy's room imaginable. There was clutter everywhere, and she soon regretted looking at some of it. Jonah Wilson had not matured much past the age of fifteen, and there had to be a reason for it.

Trying not to touch anything that was there, she picked her way through the mounds of discarded memories until she came to one that might help her. Looking at it and replaying it, she could see him being bullied, not just by bigger and older boys but by girls as well. Claire saw signs that his stunted mental growth had started much earlier than his formative teenage years, so she dug deeper.

Over in one corner, piled high, was a mound of children's things. Toys and clothes, memories of a father who had abandoned him and a mother who blamed him for it. His mother had been a drunk who didn't much like him, and the boy who had gone through all this knew it. He had put up with her name-calling. *She's just drunk,* he had told himself. *When she's sober, she's better.* Those thoughts echoed through his childhood memories. He had put up with the occasional beating, justifying that he had deserved it in some way.

Then Claire found it. The one memory that had damaged him forever. When she watched it, she felt great pity for this deficient man. His mother had ruined him with her hatred and callousness. He had woken in the middle of the night with her standing at the side of his bed, in her hand a syringe. With her other, she was grabbing at his arm, trying to find the best place to insert the needle.

A struggle had broken out between them, and Claire watched as Jonah shoved his mother across the room. He had fled that night and never looked back. He tried to find his father, but nobody would tell him where he had gone. And soon after that, he was introduced to Marcus's organisation.

Claire stopped the memory and held it in her hand. She brought him to her with a bit more force than she really would have liked, but she wanted to impart how much she could damage him. He stood before her, not sure what to expect, and watched as she replayed the memory.

"Your mother was not a nice person, Jonah. You didn't deserve to be treated that way," she said gently. She let the memory play some more. "I can do two things at this point. I can modify this memory and take some of the pain away, or—" She stopped it there at the exact moment his mother had the syringe raised, ready to plunge it into his arm. "I can take this little light of mine, and let it shine all the way to your heart." Claire let the light flicker in the air a little so that his attention was on it fully. "What's it going to be, Jonah?"

"What do you mean by *modify*?" He watched the light with fascination as it danced on the palm of her hand and changed colours rapidly.

"I can make this memory disappear and be replaced by anything you like. But remember, it has to fit in with the rest of your life. I'm sorry—I can't make your father suddenly reappear."

"Could you make her die before she tried to do that? She did anyway. I went back the day after and found her. The needle was still in her arm."

"If that's what you wish me to do." Her hand closed around the light and hid it from sight. He looked up at her.

"Would you have killed me?" he asked. It was not a demanding question, but asked so simply, it seemed like that of a child.

"Possibly. Do you wish me to modify the memory?"

"You know the answer."

"But you have to say it—I can't until you do. It's the way it works."

"Yes. Modify it, take it away."

Claire reclaimed the memory and held it in between her hands. With effort, she changed the scenery, even the room itself. The woman she placed in another part of the house for the boy Jonah to find. And when she was done, she handed it back to him.

"How come I can still remember what happened?" he asked, confused.

"Because you need to absorb it. Take it to your heart and let it play out." She watched as he looked at it for a moment and then clenched it to him. Jonah didn't so much as absorb it, but thrust it upon himself and with that action, he cried out in pain. His eyes widened, and a change came upon him. It was only a small one, but it was there.

"There is something else, Jonah. You will tell no one of this. And you will do exactly as James, Greg, or I ask you. I am not going to put myself or the children at risk because of you. Do you understand?" she asked him carefully.

"Yes, Claire. I do."

Claire impressed upon him with great emphasis that this was what he must do. The suggestion was implanted deeply in his mind, and she left with more care than when she went in.

"Are you feeling okay, Jonah?" Claire asked him, stepping backwards to stand beside James.

"Yes, Mrs. Drummond, I am. Thank you. Can I get you anything?" he asked politely, as he seemed to be coming out of a fog.

"Not at the moment, thank you."

"How about you make one more round of the fence line, Jonah, and call it a night? The others will be up soon," James suggested.

"Not a problem, James." He left via the front door and James turned to Claire.

"I hope you didn't overdo it," he told her.

"No, but can I have something to eat? I'm starving," she said, realising she hadn't had anything all day.

Matt raced down the stairs and burst into the kitchen, skidding on the polished floor in his sock-covered feet and crashing into one of the chairs at the table.

"You better have a good excuse for acting like a child, Matthew Drummond, or you can clean my floors!" Beth told him with a raised voice.

"I do, Beth—promise. Where's David and Tony?"

Beth looked at her watch. "David should be on his way back from the top paddock, and Tony is in the living room, I think."

"Thank you," Matt said and left the kitchen. He had just reached the entry when the front door opened, and Jasper walked in.

"Matt. Good to see you," Jasper said, shutting the door behind him, not in the least surprised to see him in his parents' house.

"What are you doing here?" Matt asked.

"Um, this is the family home still, isn't it? I mean, nothing major has happened since I've been away, right?" He dumped his bag by the stairs and shook Matt's hand.

"Some things have changed, Jas."

"Oh, you know," Jasper said slowly.

"Yeah, I know. What the hell were you thinking?" Matt asked him quietly.

"Later…let me talk to the olds first."

"I'm going to love seeing that conversation. Your dad is going to freak out, and as for your mum—man, you'll be lucky to survive until dinner."

"Jasper! You're home!" Beth came rushing into the hall and embraced her son.

"Hey, Mum!" Jasper said as he picked her up.

"Put me down! What are you doing home so early? You weren't due back for another month! Did you get in trouble?" she asked, concerned.

"No, Mum. Look, I will tell you everything when Dad gets in."

"You are in trouble, aren't you?" Beth persisted.

"It depends on what your opinion of *trouble* is," Jasper relented.

Just at that moment the back door opened, and David called out a greeting to Beth.

"We have a problem, David," she called back to him, watching as he came up the hallway.

"Jas, good to see you, Son!" He pulled him into a bear hug. "What's this trouble you've got yourself into?"

"How about we go to the kitchen and grab a beer, Dad? I think you're going to need one."

"That serious, huh? All right...let's go." He headed back the way he'd come and went straight to the fridge.

Matt followed them, accepting a beer from his wife's uncle. Leaning against the counter, he opened it and took a swig while waiting for the fireworks.

"Um, I'm not sure where to start," Jasper began, and then took a large gulp from his bottle. "I never went to the States. I've been in the city the whole time."

"Why?" David asked, leaning back in his chair and rubbing the stubble on his chin.

"I think I can tell you that. Pass me a beer, Jasper," Tony said, entering the room.

"What have you got to do with it?" Beth rounded on him.

"Mum, leave it," Jasper told his mother.

"Don't talk to your mother that way, Jasper," David warned.

Jasper got up and grabbed another beer, handing it to Tony. From the hallway, Adam and Addy appeared. He looked at them and grimaced.

"Great...an audience. I was hoping to do this quietly," he said with a strained voice.

"Tony, would you like to start?" David asked him.

"In April, Jasper sought me out. He had been approached by some people and made an offer," Tony started.

"What people, what offer?" Beth asked with fear.

"Beth, let the man talk," David said calmly.

"The people were Marcus's. The offer was to join them," Jasper told them.

There was silence in the room as David and Beth took in this new information. David slowly sipped his beer and watched his wife as she sank down into one of the other chairs, letting out a breath.

"I take it you declined their offer?" Beth asked hopefully.

"No, he came to me. He told me that he had been approached and asked for my advice," Tony explained.

"How did you know how to contact Tony?" David asked. Matt was amazed at how calm he was being, considering how he'd felt about Tony.

"I heard you talking about him when you came back from Scotland. When I helped Matt and Claire move, I found a card she had thrown out. I kept it. I don't know why, but I'm glad I did." Jasper told them, all the while playing with the label on his bottle.

"What happened after you talked?" David stared at his son. Jasper returned his stare and finished off his drink.

"Tony asked me if I wanted a job. I love the idea of teaching, but he offered me more than I would earn in five years. And when this is all over, I promise that I will go teach," he told his mother.

"What exactly did you ask my son to do for you?" The stony stare he had given his son was now a murderous one as he turned his gaze to Tony.

"His brief was to get into the organisation and tell me what he learned. Anything he could find out, no matter how small or stupid. Marcus was so over the moon to have your son working for him that I managed to sneak another couple of agents in under the radar. At no point was he in any danger. He had the best handler looking out for him—me—and when I wasn't available, there was Nikau, my business partner."

"So why the deception? Why tell us that you went to the States?" Beth asked Jasper.

"I didn't want you to worry about me. Everything had to seem like it was normal here. I discovered that Marcus was doing up properties left, right, and centre and that he was gearing up for something big. When Claire and Bree were taken, it all sort of fitted together. But that's not the reason I came home. They've approached Hunter."

"Did you know this?" David demanded, his voice rising as he turned to Tony.

"No. This is news to me, David. I swear. When did this happen, Jas?" Tony was suddenly worried.

"I got lazy and I bumped into him. He told me after he demanded to know why I was still in the city. Apparently, Owen and Oliver have as well. I don't know what has happened with them, but Hunter is running scared. I told him to come home, and he said he would...only, now I can't contact him. I called Nikau and he's looking into it."

"Shit." Tony pulled out his phone and walked out of the room.

"When did you see him last?" Matt asked.

"Yesterday. That's why I'm here. I went round his place and have called him, but there's no answer. I didn't want to trust my phone. If they have him, then they may be looking for me as well."

David changed his gaze to Adam and pointed at him. "If you had let Claire kill Marcus all those years ago, this wouldn't have happened."

"You can't blame me, David. We did what we thought was right. She didn't want to kill him, anyway." Adam's face was starting to redden at the accusation of his stepfather.

"The blame game is not going to change anything. Beth, have you got something of Hunter's?" Matt called across the pair of them before it could get out of hand.

"Yes, in his room." Beth disappeared and when she came back, she was holding a soft toy.

Matt took it from her and held it close. He sent out a broad net trying to find any trace of Hunter. The net spread far and wide. The hit, when it came, was in the city still. He homed in on the signal and found exactly where he was.

"He's in our old apartment," he told the room.

Tony walked back in just in time to hear it. "I'll get Nikau on it in a minute. There's something you should know. Marcus's heavies are all being taken out of the city. In fact, from everywhere he can get them. Something is going down soon."

"Tomorrow night," Matt told them, and they turned to him questioningly. "Claire told me. I was coming to find you when Jas walked in. She said she doesn't know what's going to happen, but that it would all be over tomorrow night."

"Get me another beer, Jas," David told his son. "This is what's going to happen. Tony, you get my youngest boy to safety—that's your first priority. First thing in the morning, Tony and I are going to set up a vantage where they were digging yesterday. There must be a reason he sent his men to that spot. Addy and Matt, set up on the other side of the gully.

Make sure you get a good view of the house. I want to know what's going on. Matt and Tony can be our communication."

"What about me, Dad?" Jasper asked.

"You stay here with your mother and Adam." David looked at his stepson. "This is not a punishment, Adam. You have Mind Touch, and I need someone here. If he's bringing in more muscle, then he could target this place. Please, look after your mother for me. I'm trusting you."

"You have my word, David," Adam told him, looking a bit disappointed not to be more involved.

"What about the boys? I don't want them in harm's way," Addy interjected.

"It's too late to get them to the city, Addy. They'll have to stay here. We'll look after them," Beth said, putting an arm around her. "We're all family. We need to stick together."

Tony made another call to Nikau and reported back over dinner when his partner returned his call. "Nik and Tia are already on their way to the city. They're going to pick Hunter up and bring him here to us. Beth, Nik may look a little scary, but he really is a pussycat at heart. Feed him some of your wonderful cake and he will do anything for you. He loves his food."

"And who is Tia?" Beth asked.

"Tia is someone very special, Beth," Matt put in before Tony could say anything.

"Oh, yes? Tell me more." It was obvious that she was enjoying the blush that was creeping up Tony's face.

"According to Bree, she's the woman that Tony is supposed to marry," Matt said, grinning.

"Your daughter is as interfering as every other female in this family, from what I can see," Tony said into his plate.

"Really?" Addy asked with just a touch of outrage.

"Don't start, Addy. He's right. You had a hand in getting Claire and me together—admit it." Matt grinned again. "And as for you, Beth, Claire told me about what happened when she ran away from Scotland."

Beth rounded on Matt from one side and Addy from the other. He had them both talking at the same time, basically saying the exact same thing. On the other side of the table, David and Adam were both laughing at him.

"You're on your own with this one," David told him.

"Addy, how did you and Adam get together?" Matt asked, trying to be heard.

"We didn't have any help whatsoever, thank you very much," she replied indignantly.

"Are you sure about that? Adam, is there anything you want to tell your wife?" Matt asked him pointedly.

"No. There's nothing, mate," he said quickly, shaking his head.

"Adam, darling, dearest," Addy said sweetly. "You can tell me."

"You're dead, Matt," he said directly. "Claire may have said something to me, but she just said she knew someone—she never told me who."

"Claire? Really? You think you know someone."

"That just proved my point," Tony said, scraping his plate with a piece of bread.

"Okay, we've established that we all have interfering wives," David said, ignoring the stares coming from the two women at the table. "I want us up early tomorrow, and I'm talking about before the sparrows even have a chance to think about farting."

"Don't be absurd! Sparrows do not fart," Beth scoffed as she started to clear the table. Jasper automatically jumped up and helped her.

"Yes, they do. Every morning before the sun comes up," David told her. "That's why they make so much noise in the morning."

"That is the most ridiculous thing I have ever heard. If they farted, then that would make them jet-propelled, especially if they fart like you in the morning," Beth told him with arched eyebrows.

Everyone looked at her for a moment before collapsing with laughter. Beth just looked at them, with no idea what she'd said to make them laugh so hard.

Chapter Fifteen

Drizzly rain fell lightly from the dark clouds that seemed to hover over the top of the hill. It drifted on the breeze that was starting to blow in and coated everything in a wet blanket, seeping into every nook and cranny. It even got through the smallest of spaces in Matt's clothing as he set himself up in the position David had given him. He crouched with Addy, watching the house in the dark. The sky had not even started to lighten when they reached their position, and all they could see were a few windows glowing in the inky valley. Somewhere across the gully, an owl called out its mournful call, and it echoed around the hills. The stream below them gurgled and spluttered off the rocks and stones of its bed as it made its way down the hill to meet the river near the village.

"What do you really think of David's theory about the stream?" Addy asked in a hushed whisper.

"That it's like home? I don't know. His sketch is similar, but there can't be anything in it. How did it feel when you were there?"

"I didn't get near it, and anyway, I never got any feelings from the stones like you and Claire have." She sounded a little jealous about that.

"Yeah, well, look what happens when you do." He mumbled it so quietly that Addy couldn't make out his words.

"Sorry?"

"Don't worry about it," Matt told her, trying to brush off the irritation that had suddenly arisen from the subject.

"Did Claire really talk to Adam about me?" Addy asked after a short spell of silence.

"Yeah, she did. She said since you had been working hard on getting us together, she wanted to return the favour."

Tony sat on the wet ground. He was already feeling miserable and exhausted, having taken several calls during the night, and gone downstairs to meet Hunter, Tia, and Nikau in the early hours of the morning when they arrived. He calculated that he had only gotten about two hours' sleep. Now he was in the wet bush, staking out a small patch of dug-up earth, waiting for something to happen. David was off scouting out the area, but Tony figured there wasn't much to see in the dark.

He sat still, listening to water dripping from the lush green tree ferns and the first initial hesitant bird calls, quickly followed by the mournful louder call of the Morepork owl. It had been a very long time since he had been in the bush. He really hadn't liked it the first time, and he didn't like it now. It was wet, muddy, and—in this case—eerie.

There was a feeling he got from this gully that set him on edge. He would have said it was almost like the stone circle in Scotland, but it was more intense than that. Like it was anticipating something was going to happen. Nikau, only a few hours before, had commented to him that he already didn't like the main valley. Tony now wondered what he would make of this.

Growing up on the streets, Tony had never really given spirituality a thought. It hadn't figured highly in the scheme of trying to survive, or even necessary. But now that he was older, his Talents had been increased, and he was a father. The Guardians had a future in mind for him, and he wasn't entirely sure he wanted it. The message Breena had given him was very precise and direct, and he started to think of Tia.

The comparison of this woman to his wife was stark. Maddison had been intelligent, calm, hard to anger, loving, and supportive. Tia, on the other hand, while still intelligent, was emotional, feisty, and knew exactly what she wanted and how to get it—and more like Claire than he really cared to admit. He knew he was definitely not ready to get into a relationship. It was too soon. But now that Breena had put the idea into his head, it had taken hold and he was thinking about her more.

When Tony had talked to Nikau and asked his thoughts on the matter of him dating his sister, he wasn't entirely sure that her brother was happy about it. The life Tony led could be a nomadic one and putting down roots again would be hard for him. When he was married to Maddison, he would leave her every other month to deal with work. She had understood that going in, but Tia was a bit more passionate in displaying her feelings, and that worried him.

Nikau had finally relented and grudgingly agreed that it was all right with him. When Tony eventually did ring Tia, he found that Matt had been right. He should have called her first. The ear-bashing he received from her about going behind her back and asking her brother was something he endured, keeping quiet until she was done. They had hung up with him left feeling confused as to whether they were starting a relationship or not. That was until earlier this morning.

When they had arrived at the farmhouse there had been a whirlwind of activity. Tony had given up his bed to Nikau so he could have a few hours' sleep. Hunter had grabbed the couch in the living room, and then it was just Tony and Tia sitting at the table in the kitchen.

She had taken his hands in hers, and when he looked into her eyes that were as dark as his own, he felt peace. There was a click in his mind that this was right, and the time was right. Thoughts of Maddison and Claire were left out in the cold, and he took Tia to his heart and held her close for that moment in time. But now doubts were creeping in. It was still too soon after Maddison.

"Are you asleep?" David whispered to him, breaking his thoughts.

Tony jumped at the words. "No, just thinking."

"That girl is beautiful. You better snap her up before someone else does," David said, lowering himself down beside Tony.

"That is what I'm trying to do. Have you noticed how women always think they know what is best?"

"You're only now figuring that out? Boy, have you got some training to do. My best piece of advice I can give you is to just say *Yes, dear* when you are in an argument, even if you know you're in the right. Then make sure she feels that you have understood her point of view."

"Maddison and I never argued. I think that was because she took on all the day-to-day decisions. I wasn't there a lot, though I tried to be," he said with some regret.

"I never liked you before this. I always thought you were a selfish bastard who wouldn't leave Claire alone. But since you've come here, I've changed my mind. Thank you for getting Hunter back here, by the way."

"Both your boys have their heads screwed on right. That's down to you and the way you raised them. I wish I'd had parents like you and Beth. I may have turned out different."

"Who were your parents?"

"My birth mother I met once before she died. She was raped by the scumbag who was my father. She gave me up when I was born. She told me all about him, and I went looking for where he came from. I found out he was from this village and that he had been exiled. I went and saw Lilith Brown when I was there supposedly watching Claire and Geoff. I wanted to know who Thomas Burton was and what he was like. She was not happy when I told her who I was and how I came to be. She didn't want to believe me until I showed her my birth certificate." Tony pulled the neck of his jacket closer to him, trying to stay warm.

"Okay, so you're HIS son. Man, you would have shaken Lilith's world with that piece of news." When David saw the look on Tony's face, he chuckled. "Lilith didn't tell you, did she? She was in love with him. He was the reason she had a falling out with Geoff for all those years. Your father was expelled from The Community, but Lilith loved him and wanted to change him. She blamed Geoff for his going and subsequent death. I wonder if that's why she started being nice to her brother again."

"There's something else you should know. I haven't told a soul and I would like to keep it that way, if you don't mind," Tony said hesitantly.

"Go ahead. I'll keep your secret."

"The girl he raped—my mother—she was Marcus Ryder's daughter."

Silence seemed to descend between them. Even the constant dripping water and soft bird calls stilled at the sudden declaration. David let out a low whistle at the bombshell Tony had laid in his lap.

"So, that means you're Marcus's grandson?" David whispered and the sounds around them began again.

"Yep, and Adam is my uncle."

"Holy crap! I can see now why you didn't want that out there. Does Marcus know?"

"Of course, he does. And he knows why I want to kill him. It's not just him killing my wife and taking my son, but it's the way he treated my mother. I found her living in total poverty. Marcus had thrown her out when she got pregnant. She thought giving me up would win his favour again, but it didn't. He refused to see her and cut her off completely. Then, when I found her, he had her killed. Her twin brother wouldn't even talk to her."

"Her brother? You mean there are others out there?" David exploded with surprise at this news.

"There's just one more. He's about seventy-three now. I haven't met him, but I believe he's just as arrogant as Marcus—he's been cut off as well. He made the mistake of coming out of the closet to his father."

The sky above them was starting to lighten to a dull grey, and the birds were competing with each other for their morning song. The men sat together in a companionable silence listening to the bush come alive with the flapping of wings in the canopy.

"Shit! Marcus's grandson! You sure I can't tell anyone?"

"No. I can make you forget, but I'd rather not, David."

"All right. A promise is a promise. But shit, man, that is some secret to keep." David chuckled.

A phone ringing broke the silence of the early morning, and Beth reached across the bed to pick it up. "Hello?"

"Beth, is Hunter with you?" Charlotte's voice called through the receiver.

"Charlie, what time is it?" Beth asked in a croaky voice.

"Never mind the time, Beth. Is he there with you?"

Beth sat up and looked at the bedside clock. "I don't know. He wasn't here last night, but Tony was trying to get him home. Why?"

"Tony? What the hell is going on, Beth? Oliver and Owen have just rocked up here with a story about Hunter and Marcus. Now you're saying Tony is at your place? Are you in danger? Do you need help?" Charlie called down the line, full of concern.

"Just hang on and wait. Let me wake up first. Bloody hell, Charlie, I thought David was bad in the mornings." She rubbed at her eyes, trying to wake herself up fully.

"It must be bad if you're swearing. Do you want us to come over?"

"Why not? The house is full anyway. Bring the kids and they can help look after Dom and Cam for us."

"We'll be there soon." Charlie hung up before Beth could say another word.

As she got out of bed, the alarm went off. She hit it a bit too hard, and bits of old plastic went flying across the room. "Bloody stupid thing," she muttered to herself and got dressed. As she went down the stairs, she could hear movement in the kitchen. Knowing that everyone except Jasper, Adam, and the kids had left already, she was very surprised when she saw a woman with multicolour hair making coffee at her bench.

"Who are you?" Beth asked, her mind still befuddled with sleep and the surprising riot of colour before her didn't help ease her into the day.

The woman turned and smiled. "Sorry. I heard the phone, so I thought I would get some coffee on. I'm Tia. My brother Nikau and I brought Hunter home last night. Tony let us in. I hope you don't mind. You must be Beth."

"You're Tia? Matt said you were beautiful, and he wasn't kidding." Beth sat at the table and watched the younger woman.

"Matt said…Tony didn't?" Tia's eyebrows rose with the question.

"Give him time to get used to it. He goes a bit coy every time you're mentioned. Welcome to our home. I take it Hunter is asleep somewhere?" Beth asked through a yawn.

"In the lounge. Nikau took Tony's bed." Tia finished putting the coffee on and sat down opposite Beth.

"And you and Tony—?" Beth asked with a hint of a smile.

"Sat here at the table and talked until the others got up and left," Tia told her.

"In about five minutes' time, there will be an invasion of the Brown family kind. They think I need rescuing. Charlie is going to have a lot of questions for you, young lady." Beth tried to hide the smile that threatened to spread.

"Charlie is Claire's aunt, and she is married to Ben, who is Claire's father's younger brother. They have two children—twins Oliver and Owen, who have also been approached by Marcus's organisation."

"Very good. I don't have to worry about you. You and Tony are going to make a lovely couple." Beth smiled, and Tia looked pleased.

"Claire, get up—Marcus is on his way," James said urgently, shaking her shoulder.

Her eyes flew open at the mention of that name, and she felt herself shudder. Clutching a hand to her heart, she felt the protective love that was surrounding it and drew on it to help her face her demon. That is how she had come to think of this man: as a demon from hell sent to torment and harass her.

"When?" she asked.

"Not far. About half an hour. He's bringing some more men with him, so don't be surprised if I'm replaced." The worry of this happening was written all over his face.

"If he thinks you've gotten too close to me, he'll use it against you. I don't want you getting hurt on my behalf."

James turned his back on her so she could dress. "That's the problem. I have gotten too close, Claire. Greg and I both have. But don't think for one moment that we've regretted it or aren't willing to go through with whatever needs to be done to keep you and the kids safe."

"I'm ready. Where are the kids?" She had only just noticed that their beds were empty.

"Downstairs already. Greg got them up earlier—we decided to let you sleep."

"I would like something to eat before they get here." She stood at the door and waited for him, offering her elbow for James to take.

It was just as well, because one of the night shift men was standing on the other side of the door. He looked at them both with a scowl.

"I got a call from the boss. He wants me to stick to you two like glue until he arrives. He said he has a feeling you might do something stupid, James." The veiled threat was real, and the man seemed ready to respond to anything.

"Well, if that's what he wants, that's what he will get, Mr. Hewson. You slipped on the protocol, by the way—don't do it in front of Mr. Ryder," James told him, trying to make the point that he was still in charge.

Claire and James moved past him and walked down the stairs together. Greg made her a sandwich, and she downed it with a glass of milk. Then they sat and waited for Marcus to arrive. Bree climbed onto her mother's lap and sat holding her hand.

Cars could be heard pulling up outside, and multiple voices cut through the morning quiet. The door opened and Marcus strode in, his eyes falling on Claire.

"Mr. Carter, please take the brats upstairs and keep them there," he demanded, looking very pleased with himself.

Once Greg had left with the children, Marcus came and sat beside Claire. He took the hand that Bree had just let go, and his felt very cold compared to her daughter's warm one. He kissed the back of her hand.

"Here is my beautiful bride-to-be. I hope you are looking forward to tonight, Claire. It is going to be magical."

"And what is happening tonight?" she asked politely, trying not to rip her hand from his.

"We are going to change the world, my dear. That is what is happening. I have brought you something nice to wear, something I think very appropriate for the occasion. I can't wait to see you in it—and out of it." He winked at her. Claire felt like she was going to be sick but forced it back down.

"Mr. Boyle, I am sure you will be most desperate for a break by now, so I have brought you reinforcements. Mr. Healy will take your place for a while, though I will be needing your services again tonight—so get some rest. I want you alert and at your full strength." The grin was full of malice, and his words dripped sarcasm.

A large man with a short-cropped beard came to stand behind Claire and clamped a massive hand on her shoulder. So tightly he squeezed, she winced in pain and tried to move away from him. James reluctantly let her elbow go and left her side.

"I'll see you later," he told her, hoping nothing would happen in the meantime.

"I do hope you are not becoming friends with that boy, Claire. A few rumours have been reaching my ears about how you two have been acting." He raised a hand to stroke her face with a finger, to which Claire immediately pulled away from his touch.

"Nothing of the sort, Marcus, and he's hardly a boy—only a couple years older than me, I would think. But definitely not as old as you."

His eyes went flinty for a moment before he recovered. "There is something to be said for an older man…more experience, taking his time."

"Experience, yes, but don't you need something else to help you with the other?" She lowered her voice to a whisper. "You know, a little blue pill?" Claire knew she was goading him, and that comment was like a red flag to a raging bull, but she couldn't help herself.

"Mr. Healy, Mrs. Drummond would like to take a turn around the grounds for some fresh air. I fear she has been cooped up for far too long, and it seems to be starting to affect her." Marcus spat, not looking up at the large man that was keeping her Talents at bay.

Claire was lifted off the couch by the hand that grasped her shoulder, and she found she had no choice in the matter. Out the door and into the cold, wet day she was dragged and then pushed around outside like she was on display.

Across the gully, Matt stood when he heard cars coming up the road. He counted them as they passed through the gates and watched as large men, all dressed in dark suits, stepped out of them. Five cars, each containing four men. This was going to get messy, he thought to himself, and he nudged Addy with his foot.

"Something's happening," he told her when she woke.

"How many?" she asked in his ear as she peered over it to see through the trees.

"Twenty in all. Two are going in now. What's the bet that the smaller one is Marcus Ryder?"

"That's a stupid bet to make, Matt. Of course, that's my lovely father-in-law."

"You've never offered up an opinion on him…why?" Matt asked as he watched three men take a fence line each. The others were all leaning up against the cars, talking.

"He's a creep. He grabbed my arse once while Adam was in the room. He thought it was a great joke." She made a noise in disgust at the memory.

"Who, Adam?"

"No, Marcus, you idiot. I never liked him. When he looks at you, it feels like he's undressing you with his eyes." Addy could feel Matt tense up at her comment. "I mean, that's what I felt."

"I know what you meant, Addy," he said quietly and went back to watching the house. In one of the upstairs windows, he saw a little face looking out. "There's Bree."

"Where?"

"In the second window from the right. I'm sure it's her."

Addy squinted and peered through the trees. The window opened, and the long, dark hair of Bree could be seen more clearly.

"Do you need glasses?" Matt asked, watching her squint.

"No, I don't." Addy replied more forcefully than was needed before relaxing the muscles around her eyes a bit. She ended up squinting again. "It's the light. Are you going to contact her?"

"Not yet. I don't know who's down there and who could be eavesdropping. I don't want to risk it."

"What about Tony, could he—?" Addy started but was cut off.

"The door's opening." Matt's voice rose a bit in volume.

From their vantage point, they could see Claire emerge from the doorway, followed closely behind by a very large man. He towered over her and had his hand clasped on her shoulder. Matt watched his wife being pushed around the grounds and felt like this was a deliberate act from Marcus, trying to see who was watching, and he had to calm himself and wait.

"That's not the same guy we saw with the kids before. We didn't see the other one that is supposed to be with Claire" Addy told him. "Ask Tony if he knows who it is."

"Just wait—they're trying to find us." Matt felt the search coming and he immediately covered his cousin, trying to shield her from it both mentally and physically. The pressure from it nearly knocked the wind from his lungs, and he tried to let it slip past and around him without giving out too much of a signal. He hoped that Tony was doing the same for David.

Chapter Sixteen

Tony felt the surge coming like a rogue wave. It built up and tried to crash over the top of them. He startled David with his quick actions as he covered him bodily to deflect the search. From high above them, birds took to wing and called loudly with the sheer force of the energy the person was sending out, trying to find them.

"Wait!" Tony warned as David tried to throw him off. He gritted his teeth as he tried to keep them hidden. His thoughts were similar to Matt's—concerned about their welfare.

"What the hell, Tony?" David said, muffled under the weight of Tony's body.

"Searching...just wait." Sweat was standing out on his brow, and he closed his eyes, concentrating on hiding them. The protection of keeping them hidden harked back to his original training, when he was recruited to become a watcher for Marcus. The last time he had used it was when he was still spying on Claire in Scotland, but her search had been like a feather compared to this deliberate, forceful, and relentless push.

The waves of detection soon ebbed away, and Tony released his hold on David.

"Sorry. I didn't have time to let you know," he said sitting back on his heels and shaking his head to dispell the effects.

"Not a problem, mate." David picked himself up from the ground and tried to brush the mud off. "You do what you think is best."

Tony had managed to get himself back under control and was putting his mental defences back into place when he felt a light brush from Matt.

"You guys all right?" Tony asked him.

"Yeah, that was a bit brutal. Did you see who that was with Claire?" asked Matt.

"We didn't see them. It's a bit hard from our position. What did he look like?"

"Like a giant compared to Claire. Massive hands and a beard."

"Not sure. I don't know all of them by sight. But I would say that with that search, Marcus knows we're here. I want you both to keep your head down and don't do anything stupid. And if you see anything out of the ordinary, let us know."

"You mean like the five carloads of guys that arrived a little while ago with Marcus?" Matt replied.

"You couldn't have led with that? Yes, that's exactly what we need to know." Tony muttered under his breath, saying something unintelligible about amateurs. "Just keep your eyes peeled and report what you see."

He broke the connection and shook off the annoyed feeling that was starting to rise. Today was going to be a very long one, and he was not in the mood for mistakes. This all had to go perfectly, and he had to be ready to act when the time came. He looked at his watch: it was only nine in the morning.

"Why didn't any of you call me?" Ben asked Beth once they had been brought up to speed with what was going on.

"Because Matt wanted to limit the number of people involved so no one got hurt," she explained again. Why they thought she knew more than she was telling them was making her very angry, and it was starting to show in her voice.

"What's happening out there?" Ben demanded.

"We don't know. There has been silence since they left," Adam told him. "I'm just as mad as you for being kept out of it. My wife is out there being put in danger."

"Adam Ryder, don't you dare say she should be here looking after your sons." His mother rounded on him. "She has the Talent to help out there, so I suggest you do not say one misogynistic word about it."

"I'm not—I wasn't." Adam tried to defend himself. "I was just saying that I feel completely useless being here."

"Welcome to the club." Ben ran a hand through his hair. He looked up just as Nikau walked into the kitchen. "Who the bloody hell are you?"

"This is my brother, Nikau. He's Tony's business partner," Tia piped up.

"Is there anyone else in the house that we should know about?" Ben asked.

"Excuse me, Benjamin Brown, but whose house is this?" Beth stood up and crossed her arms. "I don't think you should be coming into my home and making any demands, do you?"

"Beth, he didn't mean it like that," Charlie said, trying to keep the peace. "We're all tired, and this has been a very big shock for us. It really would've been nice to be told what was happening."

"A lot of what has happened has only been in the last twenty-four hours, Ben. We really didn't have time to think about who to bring in," Adam said. "We aren't sure if Marcus will make a strike here, so a bit of help defending this place would be good. We have the boys, who can help as well with their Talents."

"Don't try and appease me, Adam. I've known you too long for that," Ben told him.

"I'm not. I just have no idea what the hell I'm doing."

"What makes you think that I do? Hell, I didn't do anything when you and Claire where teenagers. That was all Geoff and David."

"I can help," Nikau offered. "I mean, I do have a bit of experience in this area, and I've brought some equipment with me. Tia can help as well."

Suddenly, Adam gave a strangled cry and collapsed to his knees. His eyes rolled into the back of his head before his limp body fell the rest of the way to the scrubbed tile floor with a *thump*. He was quickly followed by Charlie, though to a lesser degree. She clasped her hands to her head and grimaced in pain and fear. Ben was at her side within seconds, supporting her and holding her while Beth staggered to Adam.

At the table, Tia's head slumped slightly onto her chest, her breathing laboured. Nikau was there beside her, wild-eyed, taking her head in his hands and calling her name over and over. From upstairs came the sounds of loud thumps and two little boys screaming. It was all too much for Beth, as she collapsed to the floor, her head pounding from an outside source. She knew they were under attack already and couldn't do anything about it.

Charlie came round first, as the waves of the mental attack began to ebb. Her breathing was hard, and Ben helped her up and into a chair, his eyes wide with concern. She grabbed his arm and tried to talk, the words coming out slowly between gasps.

"The boys," she finally managed.

Ben looked up at the ceiling and scrambled up from his kneeling position, launching himself out the door as fast as possible, taking the stairs two at a time. In one of the bedrooms he found Dominic and Cameron, staring in horror at his two sons as well as Jasper and Hunter, who lay unconscious on the floor.

Bree stood stock-still at the open window, staring out into the bush on the opposite side of the gully. Her defences were up and put into place when the search went out. The power of the one who was making it was great, and he would need to be dealt with soon. When it was all over, she checked to be sure things were okay with those she loved and pulled her mind even further into itself.

"I can't do this, Aunty Breena. I'm not strong enough," the little girl whined, throwing herself to the ground. Her fear was getting the better of her.

"You can, our wee angel. I'm sorry that you have been asked to do this now—as young as you are—but it needs to be done." Breena formed in her mind and sat beside the child.

"Uncle Adam is a Mind Touch. Can't he do it instead? He could get in. He's Mr. Ryder's son."

"No, he can't, Bree. If he comes here now, it will all unravel. Your Uncle Adam can't face his father, because, my darling, he would be killed."

"I don't want to do it, Aunty Breena." Bree launched herself into Breen's arms and started to cry, shaking her head over and over. "Please, please don't make me do it."

"My sweet wee angel." Breena's heart was breaking for the child and she held her close, trying to comfort her as best she could. Looking up and out of the child's mind, Breena sent a question. *Can I be with her?* She waited for the answer she was hoping for.

From on the hillside far away came answer. The sacred stones focused, and the message was sent. *"This is allowed, Breena. We shall aid the child. It was always there for the asking."*

Relief washed over her, and she held her niece in her arms. "You won't be alone. They are letting me be with you. I promise." She smoothed her hair and kissed her forehead. "It needs to be soon, Bree."

"Thank you, Aunty Breena," Bree replied in between hiccupping sobs.

Claire lay limply in Mr. Healy's arms as he carried her into the house, and all eyes turned towards them. He deposited her onto the couch and looked up at Marcus Ryder with a mix of fear and concern.

"What happened, Mr. Healy? Why is Mrs. Drummond unconscious?" The level tone in Marcus's voice was chilling to those in the room.

"She just collapsed out there. I didn't hurt her in any way, Mr. Ryder. One minute I was walking her around, and then the next she was on the ground," he explained, looking both confused and uncertain.

Marcus turned and looked at Mr. Hewson. "Is this your doing?" he demanded.

"You said you wanted a strong signal sent out, so that's what I did. I tried to flush them out with it."

"So why is Mrs. Drummond like this?" He rounded on the weasel-faced man.

"I don't know. It could have been a bit strong for her mind, possibly." Mr. Hewson was backing away from Marcus.

"She has more power in her little finger than all of my men put together. Why do you think I have been suppressing her with people like Mr. Boyle and Mr. Healy here? Your mind sweep should not have affected her this way. So, I will ask you again, what did you do to her?"

"I swear it was not my doing," Mr. Hewson said defiantly.

Claire groaned behind them, gaining Marcus's attention. He sat by her side and took up her hand in both of his, holding it gently. He looked up at Mr. Hewson.

"If you have damaged her in any way, you will be dying today."

As she started to come to, Mr. Healy placed his big hand back on her shoulder, and Claire's eyes flew open at the sudden and unwelcome touch.

"Claire, are you all right, my darling?" The gentleness of his voice drew her to him, and she could feel the Charm seeping over her.

"I don't…what…?" she stammered, trying to get up.

"Do you remember what happened out there?" Marcus asked her.

"A wave of pain in my head…who did that?" Claire's free hand rubbed at her temple.

"I'll make sure he will be punished, Claire."

Claire shook her head and the final effects of the rapid and harsh search was dispelled. She looked Marcus in the eye and her anger swelled once more.

"No, he won't. If I get hurt, it is down to you, Marcus, and you alone. With my Talents being suppressed, I couldn't put my defences up, and that…that solid wave of seeking smashed into my mind. Keeping that in mind, if you punish anyone for this, you will live to regret it." She pulled her hand from his and began to sit up. Marcus tried to push her back down again, but she brushed him away. "Go away, Marcus. You're annoying me," she told him as she stood up and swayed a bit. Thankful for the first time that Mr. Healy was there, she let him steady her. "I want to go lie down, Mr. Healy." She glared at Marcus as she walked past him.

Her right foot had just touched the first step of the steep staircase when a scream in the living room split the air in two.

Claire rushed back and found Mr. Hewson writhing on the floor at Marcus's feet. His features contorted, and he was scratching at his face and head, leaving bloody tracks as his nails caught at his skin.

"Stop it!" she yelled at Marcus. "Leave him alone, you bastard!"

Marcus stared at her with incomprehension, his mouth hanging open and the colour draining from his face.

"It's not me. I did not do this," he stammered, acting just as shocked as everyone else in the room.

Claire looked around her, trying to find the one with Talent who was causing this man pain—but she found no one. She looked up at Mr. Healy.

"Let me go. I can help him. Please let me go," she begged him.

"Don't you dare take your hand off her, Mr. Healy," Marcus ordered.

Claire went rigid and stood straight as an arrow as her mind filled with a buzzing noise. Her hands went to her ears to try and stop the noise from filling her mind and taking her over. The attack was softer than she thought it would be, and a scent of a rose filled her senses.

"Don't fight it, Carling." Breena's voice was in her mind. "Bree needs to finish this."

"Bree is doing this? Why are you letting her? What is wrong with you, Breena? Stop her!"

"I can't, Carling. Please calm down. It will hurt more if you fight it."

"Breena." The name escaped her lips as her eyes rolled into the back of her head and she collapsed for a second time. Like a rag doll, Claire dropped to the floor.

Greg sat on the bed, listening to the voices coming up the stairs, while Johnny sat on the floor playing with a toy car.

Breena was still standing at the window, the morning breeze shifting her hair slowly, but she didn't feel it. Her eyes gazed unseeingly off into the distance, and she was not happy.

"Now, Bree," Breena whispered to her.

The energy she had gathered to her from her surroundings was now ready to be released. Bree found the man she needed and slipped into his mind. Once inside, she released the energy like many bees. It swarmed around, breaking off bits and pieces as it went. With a sad nod, she left this horrible man with the pain she was inflicting.

The second task was a little bit more difficult. Her mother was being suppressed by someone other than James. It would have been easier if Marcus had left him with her. This new man was stronger than James, and she had to find the right angle to attack, to find a way to her mother. Just the smallest gap in his defences would be enough to gain access to her, and she found it. She wriggled her way into the gap, Breena following along with her.

"Thank you, Bree. Can you go visit your grandparents while I do what I need to do?" Breena asked the girl.

Bree nodded and ran away. She stopped just as she was about to enter the subconscious, noticing a slight hum starting to grow. She pushed in and stood waiting. There was only quiet and dark inside. She noticed that it was like this when her mother was not there.

"Grandma? Grandpa?" she called out. There was no answer, and a fear started to grow. Bree took a small step further in. "Grandpa, are you there?"

A white mist billowed towards her. Through it, John came striding out and picked her up, lifting her high into the air. Bree giggled, put her arms around his neck, then giggled some more when the whiskers tickled her cheek.

"What are you doing here? Where's your mum?" John asked her with a smile.

"She's busy, Grandpa." Bree stopped laughing and became very serious. "Breena is helping her learn a new Talent."

"Oh, is she now?" John was moving through the dark and came to a spot of light with a tartan blanket spread out on the grassy ground. Around them the landscape changed from darkness to a parklike setting, with great stretches of perfectly clipped grass and bare trees swaying by an unknown wind. On the blanket sat Jess, waiting patiently. John put her down, and she ran to her grandmother.

"Hello, Bree. This is a lovely surprise." She opened her arms and the little girl ran straight into them, starting to cry. "Bree, what's that matter?"

"I had to do something, Grandma, and I didn't want to do it," she said into her grandmother's shoulder. John came and sat by them, rubbing his large hand up and down the little girl's back.

"What was it, Bree? Can you tell us?" His gravelly voice was soft and gentle.

"I had to hurt a man so he couldn't use his Talent. Aunty Breena told me how to do it. He hurt Mummy and tried to hurt Daddy."

"What did he do, sweetheart?" Jess threw her husband a worried look over Bree's head.

"He sent out a strong search and Mummy had no defences up. She couldn't handle it and she fell down."

"Your mummy will be all right, Bree. She's made of strong stuff. She gets that from her mum," John comforted her and smiled at his wife.

"I hate to interrupt, but Bree needs to go back now." Breena was standing over the little group.

John was on his feet in a flash and faced off with her. "What are you playing at, Breena? Bree is in here crying and Claire is hurt."

"Not hurt, John—well, there was a bit a pain because she fought it until I explained. She will be fine. Bree is upset because she didn't want to do what needed to be done, and it was a task she alone could do."

"Why couldn't Matt or even Tony do it? Why a six-year-old child?"

"If Galen or Tony had done this, they would have been discovered. No one apart from those closest to the family knows that Bree has come into her Abilities. They could not suspect her, and therefore, she is safe."

"I am not happy, Breena, not happy at all about any of this." His voice deepened and became threatening.

"John, nothing is going to change what has already happened by threatening me. Especially when Claire needs your help." Breena raised a hand, and Claire appeared on the blanket beside Jess.

Bree climbed off Jess's lap and went to snuggle with Claire, picking up her limp arm and placing it over the top of her tiny shoulder. John knelt on the other side of his daughter and smoothed back the long, blond hair from her face.

"Bree, you can't stay here. You are needed back in the real world. They're calling for you," Breena told her gently.

"No. I want to stay here with Mummy. I don't want to go back." Bree's small voice was shaking.

"Bree...please, sweetheart. They can't find out. If they do, they will hurt you and we don't want that," Jess said, moving Claire's arm and gathering Bree to her again. "I wish you could stay as well, but you must. Mummy would want you to, wouldn't she? I promise we will look after her. She'll be fine."

Bree nodded, then reached up and kissed Jess's cheek.

"You can come back later and check on her. Go with your aunty now." John still looked unhappy, but there was nothing he could do about any of it.

Breena reached down and took the little girl's hand. She helped her stand, and they walked into the darkness together. When Bree came back to herself, she turned and found Greg looking out the door and another man running up to him.

"Bring the girl. Mr. Ryder wants her. Now!" the man said urgently. Greg turned to her and held out his hand.

"Don't be scared, Bree. I'll be there with you. Johnny, stay here and lock this door behind us. Only open it if you hear Bree's voice or mine, okay?" Johnny nodded his understanding and got up to shut the door behind them.

At the bottom of the stairs, Bree looked around. There were so many tall men in the room that she felt like she was in a forest, surrounded by large trees. She held on tightly to Greg's hand as they walked further into the room, stopping in front of the older man. Bree could feel his age weighing heavily on him, even though he didn't look as old as he seemed.

"Breena, your mum has had a…well, a turn. I think you should sit with her for a while. She called for you before she fell asleep," Marcus told her. "Climb up beside her. There's a girl." He gently turned her around, and Bree saw her mother laid out on the couch with a large man holding her hand.

"What happened to her?" Greg asked in a low voice, concerned.

"That is none of your concern, Mr. Carter. Go look after the boy," Marcus ordered him.

Bree lay down beside her mother, closed her eyes, and joined her again in her subconscious.

Chapter Seventeen

Matt had given the watch over to Addy and was wandering around in the bush, always keeping close in case there was another attack. This waiting game they were playing was beginning to get on his nerves. Apart from most of the men rushing into the house, there had been no more activity for over half an hour, and Tony wasn't making it any easier when Matt had reported to him, either.

"Matt, get back here," Addy said urgently, and he almost tripped in his rush to join her. "Stop crashing about! You have Stealth—use it," she told him irritably.

Ignoring his cousin, he looked toward the house and saw the men coming back out. Marcus joined them and was talking very animatedly to one man, pointing, and gesturing both to the hill behind them and at the road. The cousins watched the men get into the four-wheel drives and head out the gates. The lead car turned right to head out of the gully, and the other three went left.

"You have incoming." Matt hastily sent the thought to Tony. "Three cars, four in each. One car with four heading out of the gully."

"Cheers. Will keep an eye out. Warn Adam—that other car may be heading their way." Then Tony was gone.

"Rude bastard," Matt said under his breath before reaching out toward Adam. This time there was a difference. While

Tony was proficient and had the added benefit of having multiple Talents, Adam only had two: Charm and Mind Touch. And unfortunately, his father had neglected to teach him anything more than the basics of both. Matt pinpointed Adam before he even attempted any contact in order to make sure he was paying attention to the call.

"Adam," Matt called out and then again, a bit harder, trying to keep the noise level down as well. "Adam—pick up, Adam."

"It's not a telephone, mate," Adam replied with a chuckle.

"The way you answer, it feels like it. Got a heads up for you. Four guys just left here and headed out of the gully. Not sure if they're coming your way or not."

"Thanks. How's Addy doing?"

"I don't think she likes it here. The bugs are just as bad as Scotland. Stay safe."

"See you back here soon, hopefully. Give Ads a kiss from me."

"Yeah…not gonna do that." Matt broke the connection. "Adam says hi and I'm supposed to give you a kiss, so take it as given."

"Sweet as," Addy said in her best Kiwi accent.

Adam looked at his watch. It was just after ten in the morning. He walked into the dining room, where a map of the area was spread out on the formal table. Nikau had set up a command post in the room, and Beth and Jasper were giving him advice on where there were blind spots around the place. Tia was on the laptop, downloading terrain maps and printing them out.

"Where are the boys?" Adam asked.

"Ben and Charlie have taken them outside to get rid of some of their energy. Hunter is doing that blasted free running to keep them entertained," Beth said to him. "How are you feeling now?"

"I'm fine, Mum. Stop fussing. Just worry about the influence Hunter is having on his nephews." Adam smiled at her. "Matt just messaged. There's movement up there—a carload of guys is heading out of the gully, and he warned me that they might be coming our way."

"How long ago?" Nikau asked.

"Just now. From memory, it should only take them about ten minutes max to get here."

"Tia, check those cameras we put up. I suggest getting the kids inside, Adam, out of harm's way," Nikau told him.

"I'll go," Jasper offered, and he ducked out of the room.

"Cameras are up and running," Tia said from behind a large screen. "Nothing out there except for that horse."

"And bloody fantails." Nikau shivered as he looked at the screen. "Do you guys breed them out here?"

"Don't be ridiculous," Tia told him. "They're just birds."

"They are not. They're spirits. Harbingers of death."

"Harbingers of death? Bloody hell, has Mystic Meg got to you as well? Anyway, we were taught that they're spirits of our ancestors," she said with some exasperation.

The others in the room were looking at the brother and sister with confused looks on their faces.

"Really…with everything that's going on, you two are having a discussion about the meaning of a flighty bird?" Adam said in amazement.

"Sorry, dude," Nikau said a little shamefaced, before changing to become serious again. "Okay, so I've been around Tony long enough to know a bit about this place. What special gifts do you guys have?"

"Me, nothing," Ben told him as he came into the room, quickly followed by his wife and their boys. Jasper and Hunter brought up the rear. "I lucked out in the Talent draw."

"Good, then you can man the cameras. I need Tia on other things. Anyone else?" Nikau asked as Ben replaced Tia behind the screen and stared intently at it, trying to work out what was where.

Charlie put her hand up. "Healing."

Owen and Oliver spoke at the same time. "Healing, Seek." Their words merged together.

"Flight here," Hunter responded.

"Light," Jasper told him.

"Mind Touch, but not very good," Adam said, a bit embarrassed.

Nikau then turned to Beth when she didn't say anything. "Same as Ben—no Talent here."

"I wouldn't say that, Mum. You're the best cook I know," Jasper said with a smile.

"We have a car coming in—big black thing. Just passed Janie's paddock," Ben called out.

"Right. Here's what I want." Nikau clapped his hands together, his blood now pumping with adrenaline. This was the kind of thing he loved doing.

David was starting to feel his age, but he wasn't about to tell Tony that. The cold, damp air was seeping into his bones, and he felt achy. He hated getting old. He wished he could have stopped his life in his twenties and been quite happy, and then he thought about it a bit more. No wife, no kids, no great adventures instigated by a wayward niece. But his sister and her husband would still be alive.

Thinking about Jess, he wondered if Claire would take him to see them in her mind, and he smiled at the absurdity of it. This life hadn't been so bad. He and Beth had found a way through their problems and become a proper couple. *The kids have turned out great,* he thought to himself. *Jasper's more like his mother, but Hunter definitely takes after me, both in looks and personality.*

"Are you thinking of your family as well?" Tony asked him quietly.

"Just a bit. What about you?"

"Not much to think about. I only have one person left, and he's under his great-grandfather's protection."

"We'll get him," David said.

Out in the bush, they heard what sounded like elephants roaming through the undergrowth. David and Tony ducked back behind the bush and retreated, leaving no trace behind. They watched and waited for the men to appear, and when they did, David nearly burst out laughing.

Carrying shovels and picks came Marcus's men, all dressed like they were ready for the office, in fine suits and—David presumed—polished shoes. At least they had been polished that morning. Into the clearing beside where David and Tony had only just been standing, the men gathered. One started to give orders and pointed at the ground, while others were sent back to the car for more equipment.

They searched the ground and obviously found what they were looking for as they immediately began to dig into the wet, composited soil, scraping away the years of leaf litter buildup until they hit stone. Groups of two or three were working together, and they were all evenly spaced out in a circle. Tony looked at David and raised an eyebrow.

Only when the first two men reemerged from the trail did they begin to understand. Between the two of them, they struggled with a large piece of dark, worked stone. The man in charge consulted a piece of paper, pointed to one of the holes, and told those who worked on it to hurry up. From the same path emerged another stone, and then another. Soon, the first stone was put into place in the hole that had been prepared for it—upright and pointing to the sky.

"He's recreating the circle," Tony said in wonder. "Why?"

"It'll have something to do with Claire," David said darkly. "When they go, do we destroy it?"

"No, I don't think we should," Tony responded.

With each stone that was put into place, Tony could feel the atmosphere change in the hills. The anticipation was slowly giving way to a more domineering and dangerous feeling, and he was beginning to be confused. It was the same feeling he had when he was on that hill in Scotland with Jack.

They watched in silence until the last stone had been put in place. The circle was now complete, and the men stood around it. David could see them as confused as he was, wondering what Marcus would want with a stone circle in the New Zealand bush. It was out of place and otherworldly, but David felt an attraction to it. He wanted to go down there and touch the stones. He could feel their pull, their call to him.

Tony put a restraining hand on his shoulder, stopping David from moving forward and giving their position away. He shook his head and calmed the racing mind of Claire's uncle. He needed to get David away before he did anything stupid.

The men picked up their tools and jackets, moving back down the trail they had come from three hours earlier. In three short hours, they had created something that shouldn't belong—a mixing of old cultures and ideals. Tony could feel the maelstrom starting, fighting for control of the area.

When he judged it safe, Tony let go of David's shoulder. As he had expected, the not-that-much-older man walked directly to the stones and stood in awe of them.

"Don't get too close, David. It doesn't feel right. The energy is all wrong compared to the one in Scotland."

"The ones in Scotland don't feel of anything, but these are amazing." Before Tony could react, David reached out and touched the nearest stone. At first, his eyes widened in surprise and amazement, but soon he was shaking. His knees gave out, and he fell to the ground.

Tony rugby-tackled him away from the stone, and as soon as David lost touch with it, he gasped for air. Taking in lungful after lungful, he pushed himself up off the ground.

"I don't think you should do that again, David," Tony said as he brushed leaves and dirt from himself.

"I think you're right. Not a good idea." David was as white as a sheet, still shaking.

A tiny voice called in the dark, a small sound that floated and wafted on a faint breeze. It came again, louder this time and persistent. It wouldn't give up and kept calling. Round and round it played on the air, turning this way and that until it was still and so loud. Claire covered her ears from the noise.

"Mum! Open your eyes. Aunty Breena says it's time you woke up."

Claire pried her eyes open and looked into the dark, startlingly blue ones of her daughter. They sparkled and shone just like her father's, with a hint of mischief. The face was not his, but his sister's. Her namesake was the spitting image and for a very good reason. The little girl smiled at her mother and held her hand.

Looking around her, she found she was not in the cabin in the gully, but in her subconscious with her daughter, mother, and father surrounding her. She was lying on a blanket in the middle of a park, with trees bare and stark against the sky. There was someone else there with them, out in the darkness, just out of reach and touch. It was a weird feeling for her. For the last few days, she had been so inhibited by the Strength Talent of James and now with the other man, Mr. Healy, that the sense of actually being able to feel those with Talent was like the sun shining after days of wet weather.

She sat up and stretched. The sleep had been a deep one and relaxing. Images flashed, and she remembered Breena being there, telling her not to fight. The information was new—it must be examined and studied, learnt and put to use. But that could wait. She was with her family, bar one. With a start, she found Matt not far away from her and reached out greedily for him to join them.

He was there and she was lost in his eyes, her heart completely open to him and full of love. The yellow rose was in her hand, and she planted it in the ground. She watched it grow, coiling up and sending out new shoots until it was large and covered with the deep, buttery yellow blooms of the original.

Slowly she drew all her family to her to celebrate their love for each other and give her strength. One by one, more joined them, brought into this place to be together. Addy and Adam appeared with fascination and smiles, their children Dominic and Cameron joining Bree. Ben and Charlie, hand in hand, came to greet her, only for him to be wrapped into an enormous hug by his older brother. Owen and Oliver, so tall and so alike, gave her a wave. Jasper and Hunter emerged, unalike as brothers could be, but still so close to each other.

She held the hands of Matt and Breena as Gerry and Gran entered the light, quickly followed by Robbie and Fiona. Gran took Claire's face in her hands and looked at her with wonder. Gerry picked Bree up and hugged his son before turning to Claire. Matt walked with them, introducing them to Claire's family.

Beth and David came last. Jess stood and greeted her twin, tears standing in both their eyes. Claire smiled at them all, but there were still people missing. She could feel them in her heart, and she found where they were. At first he resisted, but then relented.

Tony came to the group, and his son Johnny ran into his arms. They were so happy and would be soon together. But still there was one missing—a piece that needed to be filled to make the set complete. She looked at Tony and found what she wanted.

A thin woman—with long hair coloured blue, red, and pink and eyes as deep brown as Tony's—came walking into the light with amazement. Claire could feel how shy and awkward she felt, and she went to meet her before Tony did. She took the woman's hands in her own and felt the energy there, just under the surface.

"Welcome, Tia," Claire said, leading her to Tony and joining their hands together. "Done," she said with a finality that took the couple by surprise.

Claire walked about them in a daze of happiness and contentment and then stood at the edge, watching them all. Breena stood beside her, and she began to cry. Her sister took her arm and held on tight. The emotion was raw and ancient. It welled up from a hidden depth inside and burst forth from her with a warm, golden light that surrounded them all. The single rosebush dropped seeds and new plants grew—one for each of them, in all different shades, a cacophony of colour and light.

One at a time they came to her and said goodbye, but there was no sorrow at their parting. They each took with them love, which would protect and help them in the coming hours. Last of all were Matt and Bree, who held tightly to her.

"You must wake up now," Breena said in her ear. "It is done. The first part of your task is complete."

Chapter Eighteen

Addy turned to Matt and found the same expression that she thought must be on her own face. The bush around them was quiet and still, and even the breeze seemed to be holding its breath. Across the stream, a car raced down the road and in through the gates, followed by two more. The clang of the heavy metal gates closing echoed in the gully, and this seemed to break the spell.

"Wow," Addy said. "Did that just happen?"

"I think so. I was just thinking I was losing my mind, but you saw it, too?" Matt sat down heavily on the ground and ran his hands over his face and through his hair.

"Oh yes. I saw. But did you feel the energy? It was overwhelming. How did she do that?"

"I gave up a long time ago trying to figure out how Claire does anything. Her mind is just so amazing. The capacity it has is just…just…" Matt made the sound of an explosion, his hands on either side of his head, spreading outward.

"It's just as well that you're the kind of man who isn't intimidated by an intelligent woman." Addy laughed.

"Oh, she intimidates me. Have you seen her when she truly gets angry?" He laughed with his cousin, and it sounded good. To Addy it felt like hope.

Addy looked out over the gully. The day felt brighter, even though the clouds were still low on the hills, and it was looking like they were in for more rain. Her heart felt light and free, and she felt like singing. Looking back, she realised it had been a long time since she had felt like this, and she silently thanked Claire for her gift.

Movement at the house brought her back to Earth, and she watched. Bags and equipment were being moved from the cars and men were stripping off muddy and dirty clothing outside before filing into the house. Matt was at her side, watching with her.

"They look like they've been busy," Matt said.

"Think it might be time to catch up with Tony," Addy suggested.

Matt didn't need another prompting, and Tony answered the call without delay. "Matt, what have you got?"

"Thought you might have something for us. What's with all the mud men that have just turned up here?"

"They had a little landscaping party up here. You know the sketch David drew? Well, it seems that he wasn't far off the mark. They have made an exact replica of the stones at your Gran's place."

"What the hell?"

"I know. It gets better. They have an energy to them. David tested it out and I don't think he liked the result." Tony's tone was cheerier than the subject should have made it.

"You come back to Earth yet?" Matt asked him.

"Just about. Don't tell David I told you, but he's a bit of a mess at the moment."

"I know how he feels. Being reunited with a dead sister is very emotional."

"Come again?" Tony asked, obviously confused.

"Claire reunited my family with my sister Breena so she could pass over."

"Did this happen under that large tree by the ford?" Tony asked curiously.

"Yeah, it did."

"I was watching. Claire climbed the hill and sat with me. I wondered why she was so sad that day."

"Didn't it ever get old—the watching, the following?"

"No, it was something I had to do. There was no question of stopping."

"Do you ever feel, Tony, that our fates and destinies are not in our hands? That we are puppets for others?"

"Claire and your daughter, you mean?" Tony answered with his own question.

"No, not even them. I mean something more, larger."

"I got that feeling on the hill that night. It was Breena I was fighting—did Claire ever tell you?"

"Yes, she told me everything. Including what she said to you. *Love is stronger than hate.*"

"She got that right. Keep your eyes open, Matt." Tony ended the connection.

As she stood at the window and looked below her at the activity and commotion, Claire was still in her haze of the family reunion in her mind. It stayed with her, and she hoped it wouldn't go away. A step behind her made her turn, and she steeled herself when she saw Marcus enter the room.

"I'm pleased to see that you have recovered, Claire. Are you feeling well?" he inquired.

"I am. Thank you, Marcus. With everything that went on this morning, I think it got to be too much for me."

"I'm sorry you were caught in the search—I should have warned you. I didn't realise that it would affect you so much." He almost made his words sound apologetic, but there was no real remorse behind them.

"With anything, knowledge is the key. If you have it, then you will know what to expect and not hurt people with your actions."

"Are you trying to lecture me?"

"No, sorry. That's my husband's job. You remember that I'm married?"

"Yes, how can I forget? But that will soon be rectified. The papers are being drawn up as we speak. I know some people who can pull a few strings for us. You will be free in a matter of weeks, rather than years."

"But I don't want to be free, Marcus. I am quite contented with the way things are. My life is a very happy one, and I don't want to change that."

"But it could be so much more, Claire…so much more. Think about what I'm offering you: the chance to be a part of the change. I have so many people who are backing me and are willing to take the risk—all except for the one person I need at my side. There is no more to be said on this, except that you will be mine. It just depends on whether you come to me willingly or I have to take you by force—again. Either way is fine by me."

Marcus's whole demeanor had changed back to his normal self. She was getting to him. Claire watched as he started to turn and walk out of the room, just as he reached the door she spoke up.

"The people who are backing me were right. I should've killed you all those years ago. I let my emotions get the better of me then, I'll make sure it won't be the case this time. But I guess that's what happens when you send a child to do the work of a woman."

"Your people? You mean that ragtag lot hiding out at your uncle's house? The ones who don't seem to want to come to your aid?" he asked, turning, and walking slowly back to her.

"My family are with me always, no matter where they are." Claire smiled at him as he approached, but there was not one bit of warmth held in it. "As a unit, we are strong and can face anything. But they're not the only ones who are behind me, Marcus. If you look carefully, you may see them looking down the ages. They are behind me, guiding and supporting me. Who do you have to lean on, to take strength from? I don't see any of your family with you. There is only Adam left—who hates you, by the way. Is there anyone else you can depend on?"

"I don't need anyone else," he hissed at her.

"But you just said you needed me. I'm hurt."

"Yes, I need you for this one thing, but it is my choice to keep you with me forever," he spat at her.

"So, you don't love me?" Her voice took on a girlish nature.

"Love is a weak emotion that can hurt to the very core. I decided long ago that love has no place in my life."

"I can see that." Claire walked towards him with her minder trailing behind. Standing directly in front of him, she looked up into his face while she bit her lower lip and placed a hand on his chest lightly. "But love can be so strong, so raw and encompassing."

The huskiness of her voice was moving him. She could see the lust building in his eyes. Marcus took a step backwards. The desire he had for her was fighting with his need to stay in control of the situation.

"There will be enough time for that later. I have to go get ready," he said, more to himself than Claire.

The sound of his footsteps heading down the stairs floated back to Claire. She sighed and returned to the window to watch. The breeze wafted in, and she breathed deeply the smell of a wet winter's day.

"You're playing with fire, Mrs. Drummond," Mr. Healy said from behind her.

"I know exactly what I'm doing, Mr. Healy. Exactly," she said with a smile as she silently made her way into his mind.

"They've spread out." Owen said, pointing at four points on the map that surrounded the house. "They parked up there and moved down the track—there." He moved back so the others could look at the map.

"Do you think they're here only to watch, or something else?" Ben asked Nikau.

"I have no idea. By the way you all reacted before, I don't think they came for a picnic," Nikau said. "But there is something else, isn't there? What happened the second time? Because there was no pain that time."

"It was nothing, Nik. Leave it. It has nothing to do with you," Tia said.

"It does, because you acted the same as them. Am I going to get an answer?" he asked the room.

"It was a family thing, Nikau. Claire called and we answered. It has nothing to do with what's going on here. She needed us and our love to support her," Beth told him.

"Claire has never met Tia, so why was she affected?" he asked with a frown.

"Because Tony was there, and Claire needed to do something that had to do with the two of them," Jasper offered his boss. "Something very important."

"This is like pulling bloody teeth," he exclaimed at the lack of anything concrete.

"All she did was put my hand in his," Tia said quietly with a shy smile.

"I give up. I'll ask Tony when he gets back. Let's get back to it," Nikau said with some frustration.

They talked about how they would defend the house if it came to it and what they could do to attack. A lot of the talk focused around Jasper and the light protection he could provide.

"I remember when you were teaching Claire how to make a light. You passed them on to her to use. Do you think I could give it a go?" Hunter asked his older brother quietly.

"What have you got in mind?"

"Well, with my Flight, I could be up there, firing light balls at them." He pointed above him. "You could pass them on, and I could fire."

"I'm not sure it would work. I mean, Claire was one thing, being a Chameleon, but you don't have any Talent for it."

"We could give it a go…it couldn't hurt." When he saw Jasper's reluctance, he tried again. "Come on, Jas. It'll be something they won't be expecting."

Jasper thought for a moment and looked around at the people gathered in the room. He was still doubtful, but not trying could put them all at risk. Hunter started to smile. He knew his brother very well, and he could see that Jasper had made up his mind.

"Where?" Jasper asked him.

"How 'bout out back in the yard?" Hunter's voice dropped into a conspiratorial whisper.

"No, not outside. I want this to be a complete surprise *if* we manage to pull it off. How about the attic? We could use Dom and Cam as an excuse—get them out of the way and use the light to entertain them."

"Brilliant. You tell them and I'll go clear a space," Hunter said, about to move off.

"Ah, no. This was your idea, little brother—you tell, I'll go." Jas grinned at Hunter and was out the door in a flash.

Nineteen minutes past three, David's watch said. He stamped around their hiding area, but it wasn't quite as satisfying when there was no sound to go with it. He thought about reining it in, but Stealth was second nature to him, and he hated it when he had to do so.

"I'm getting too old for all this bullshit!" he exclaimed to the world. "I am wet, tired, and cold, and I've had enough." His irritation was growing.

"I know what you mean," Tony agreed.

"You're younger than I am...what are *you* complaining about?"

"I'm not that much younger. Only by a few years."

"Which made your pursuing my niece even worse."

"Let's move further away from those stones. I think they're making you grumpy."

"No, they aren't. You just don't want to face what you've done. You were what—sixteen, seventeen when she was born?"

"How'd you know that?"

"My sister talked to me. She couldn't stand the idea of cutting me off completely. We are—*were*—twins."

"Yes. I was fifteen. When you look at it objectively, there wasn't that much difference in ages."

"There was when she was seventeen, mate."

"All right, so I got a bit obsessed. I thought I was looking out for her. At twenty-three, I found her very...what's the word?"

"Don't ask me. I don't want to even think about it."

"Different. Not like other women at that age. She was—and still is—self-reliant...ballsy, even. She could handle herself even without all those Abilities she ended up with. That kind of woman I find rather attractive." Tony smiled.

"Not many men do. They see a confident woman and they run a mile. Beth is like that, and oh, the fights we used to have. Sometimes I miss them. Claire is very much like her mother. Jess could be like that as well. Feisty women seem to run in the family." David looked at Tony with a little speculation. "Tia seemed nice—not that I got to talk to her much this morning."

"Yes, she is. She's a very special lady," Tony said with a smile not only on his face but in his voice as well.

"That thing Claire did with you both—do you know what that means?"

"I have a feeling. And the more I think about it at the moment, the more I don't mind being forced into it. Maddison was a sweetheart and I loved her so much, but Tia...she knows what she wants, and she goes and gets it herself. There's no subtlety about her, no mystery. I know where I stand and what's happening, and I like that."

"God, listen to us. Two idiots in the bush, sprouting on about women. I think you're right. We should move. Those stones are turning us into gossipy old women."

Sitting on the bed and swinging her legs, Bree felt bored. She wanted to be outside and playing in the puddles, out in the fresh air and running about. She wanted Johnny to chase her and laugh so hard that their tummies hurt. Being stuck indoors made her grumpy and short-tempered. She had performed her task, and now she was just waiting for her dad to come and get her. He was out there watching the house. She could feel him, but he couldn't come just yet. They had to wait.

Johnny looked up and smiled at Bree. She didn't mind him very much, and she knew what the future held for them both. That knowing was not set in stone. Things could change in an instant. She thought of her Aunty Breena, who died before her time, by a glitch in the fabric of the universe. Now she was here to right that balance.

"Do you want to play a game?" Johnny asked her.

"Not really. I'm too bored," she told him, her feet bouncing off the mattress.

"So, play a game, Bree. Then you won't be so bored," Greg encouraged her.

Bree liked Greg. She had decided that the moment they met after she had been reunited with her mother. He had kind eyes, but there was a sadness there. Looking at him for a moment, she could see the rest of his life branching out before him, with each path a different choice he would have to make. The path he was on now led to the possibility of Bree being reunited with her mother and father. But there was a fork in the road coming, and she needed to make sure he stayed on the right path. It was going to be tricky, but she could manage it, Bree decided.

"But I want to be bored at the moment, Greg. In my head, I can tell these men to go away, and they would. I could tell Marcus to go drop himself in my uncle's pig sty and roll around like a fat little piggy, and he would." Bree laughed at the image.

"That would be funny," Greg agreed with a grin.

"In my head, my dad would be running through that door and taking me away," Johnny said sadly.

"You will see him tonight, Johnny," Bree told him.

"How can you be so sure?" Greg asked.

"I just know. I know a lot of things." Bree kicked her feet on the bed a few more times. She had to be careful. This was one of the paths that he had to make the right turning on, and James wasn't with them to help.

"What things can you know, Bree? You're only six." His curiosity had gotten the better of him, and Greg wanted to know what this strange little girl knew.

"I know I love puppies and kittens. I know my mum and dad love me. I know we are going to go live in Scotland soon. I know that Johnny looks like his dad. I know that you like us." She gave him a quick look to see whether he reacted.

"Yes, I do like you. I don't want to see you hurt."

Bree jumped down off the bed, walked slowly over to Greg, and climbed onto his lap. She rested her head against his chest, and he automatically put his arms around her protectively.

"I know that you got hurt when you were little," Bree said so only he could hear, and she waited for that moment he would step onto the path she wanted him to take. But he was hesitating. "I know you tried to protect your little sister, like you're protecting us."

This time his metaphorical feet moved. The protective spirit she had felt the first time she met him rose up from inside him, and he stepped forward. Bree was happy he had made the right choice, but sad she had to use his memories against him.

She manoeuvred her way into his mind and watched as he played the memories of his little sister over and over, watching the moment she had died. Bree felt the anger he had for his father increase but find no outlet. She felt the guilt Greg had for not being able to protect her from him. The guilt he had of killing his father when he was older. The guilt of feeling no remorse for it.

"Shh," Bree told him and calmed his thoughts. She reorganised his memories and put them back. "It will all be okay."

Not realising she had not actually spoken out loud, he hugged her close. "I hope so, Bree. I hope so."

Bree stepped back out of his memories. Greg was not a bad man, and neither was James. But there were some very bad men out in the yard, and she could feel them as they geared themselves up to leave. Some of these men loved to do bad things, loved to hurt people, and they were good at it. Bree tried to block them out and keep the good energy in, the lovely scarlet rose from her mother firmly in her mind.

Chapter Nineteen

"Make sure you have that place sewn up tight. I don't want anyone getting in or out until I get there later. You do not attack. Do you understand?" Marcus said before noticing that Claire had come downstairs.

"They will resist you," she told him, walking towards him.

The room was full of large men still, sprawled around on chairs, standing against walls. Claire had come down because of all the noise from outside. Now that she had a connection with Mr. Healy, she had a better understanding of some of Marcus's plans. She had found out he wanted to be a part of this group who were supposed to go and surround the farmhouse, rather than babysitting her.

"I'm sure they will, but I will not hurt them, Claire. See, I have taken some of your views on board. I'm willing to change some of my ways." It was not a genuine smile he gave her.

"But I fear it's not enough, Marcus. If it were that easy to change you, Mr. Healy here would be letting go of my shoulder." Claire rolled the shoulder that had the constant pressure on it, trying to relax the muscles. In response, the tall man swapped hands, and Claire rolled her eyes.

"Just a little longer, my dear," Marcus said, then turned to his men. "You lot—up and out," he demanded of those who were lounging on the couch, and they moved immediately.

"Don't bother. I was going for some fresh air, if I'm allowed. It's a bit fetid in here for my taste." She stared at him, hoping he would let her go and not demand she stay inside. It would be easy to do what she must inside, but visually it would be better out.

"Of course, you can. They won't be here much longer," Marcus said, distracted as another man came to him, demanding his attention.

"Thank you." Claire did not need to be told twice, and she was out the door before he could change his mind.

All this bowing and scraping was getting to her, but she kept her emotions in check and held on, even if it were by her fingernails now. Outside, the clouds were lifting, and a weak sun struggled to break through. Claire thought that it was very much like her at the moment.

Walking to the middle of the yard and then stopping with Mr. Healy still at her shoulder, she lifted her face to the golden orb in the sky, feeling the slight warmth it was giving. Then she sent out her thought to her husband.

"I'm okay. It will only be a matter of hours now, my love. Warn Adam that there are men on their way to the house."

"I see you and I can hear you. How can you talk when that man is suppressing you?" His thoughts floated to her.

"Another gift to help me."

"Then why not obliterate them all and come back to me? Why stay there?" Matt's frustration at not being able to do anything was in between them now.

"Because it's not time. I have one more task to complete. Matt, please believe me when I say I would gladly get the children, reduce this house to ashes in a second with all of them inside, and be with you. But I would only have to start all over again another few years down the track. What I started when I was seventeen must now be finished. Marcus is going to die tonight." The finality of it was like a large bell tolling.

"I just want you and Bree back safe. That's all. I miss you," he said quietly.

"I miss you, too, Galen." Claire hung her head when she felt tears seep from under her lashes. A squeeze on her shoulder warned her. "I have to go, sweetheart. It will be soon. I love you."

Opening her eyes, she was not surprised to see Marcus striding across to her. This man was not hard to look at with his chiselled features, but the years of shutting people out and denying himself the ability to feel love for anyone had hardened and distorted what might have been handsome. There was also something else that was becoming more prominent in him—a darkness that was starting to consume his soul. She felt pity for him, she realised. Anger, still, and hatred, but pity was fast becoming the dominating emotion.

"The men are ready to leave, Claire. Shall we wave them off together?" He placed his arm around her waist and pulled her to him.

"This is not something you'd normally do. What else have you got in mind?" she asked, trying to pull away from him.

"Just wave, Claire." He held up his arm as the cars started up and pulled away from the house. They watched them go down the drive and out the gate, which slammed closed with a *clang* once they had passed through.

"I know that your soon-to-be-ex-husband is not far away, so I was hoping to send him a message," Marcus told her. Then, he turned, took her face gently in his hands, and kissed her—a lingering, soft, almost loving kiss.

As she placed her hands on Marcus' chest to push him away, Claire could feel Matt battering at her mind, and she kept him out. This was not something she had wanted him to see, and a small piece of her died inside with the shame of hurting him.

Up on the hill opposite, Addy was having a hard job holding Matt back. She had also seen Marcus kiss Claire, and when Matt started to head down the hill, she grabbed at him. She was now pushing against his chest to keep him from making the mistake Marcus wanted him to make.

"Snap out of it, Matt. This is not what Claire wants. She knows what she's doing." Addy tried to reach him.

When words failed, she put all her might behind a very large slap, the noise of which echoed around them. This did nothing, and she raised her hand to do it again when Matt caught her wrist.

"Don't." His teeth were clenched, and his eyes looked as if they could burn holes through her.

"Matt, I—"

"I know. Let go, Addy. I can't let him touch her. She won't fight back against him. She is in full use of all her Abilities, despite that giant behind her. But still she won't fight back."

"There must be a reason. Did she say anything else?" Despite Matt's request, Addy still had a hand placed firmly against his chest.

"Yes, this bloody task that the Guardians have set. She said only a few more hours. If we hadn't gone to those stones that morning, this wouldn't have happened."

"Yes, it would have. Matt, do you trust Claire?" Addy demanded.

"With my life. How can you even ask that?" He pulled away from her.

"Then trust her. We can only do what we can. It's frustrating, I know, standing here in the bush, but we have to trust that Claire knows what she's doing. You can't go off and confront them now. What would happen if you were hurt?

How could you help her afterwards when she's going to need you the most?"

"But he—"

"That monster did that knowing you were watching. It was a deliberate act to unsettle you. Just focus on Claire and Bree. They are the goal—getting them out unharmed."

Matt nodded his agreement, but he was still looking down on the house. The yard was clear now. Only the men patrolling the fence line could be seen. It was silent, and the sun was going down behind the hill. The air chilled and a cloud parted, letting in a small piece of deep blue sky the same colour as his eyes.

Time was racing away for those in New Zealand, but in Scotland it was more sedate and calm. Sitting in the house in her new bedroom downstairs, Gran was looking through an old photo album. People who had been before but were long since passed now. Parents, brothers, sisters, uncles, aunts, and cousins. The People were dying out in Scotland at a very fast pace, and there was nothing that Gran could do about it. There was still hope for the future with the children coming back to live in Scotland.

"Your turn will come, Gran." Pressure on the bed next to her made her smile, and she looked up at Breena.

"I know, but still a while off. What is it like with the Guardians?"

"Beautiful and calm. It's not much of a description, but that's how it is for me."

"And your mother? How is it for Leana?"

"Peaceful and full of roses," Breena smiled. "It's different for us all."

"So, once we pass over with them, that's it forever?"

"No. You can choose to come back if you wish, or only a part as I have. The choice is yours, Gran, as it always is. We are not forced to do anything we don't want to do. Free will is ours."

"That's good to know. I had the strangest dream last night. We were all together, but there were others," Gran told her, remembering how calm the dream made her feel.

"That was not a dream, Gran. Claire needed us, and I helped you and Da go to her."

"She is so strong. I hope she survives this."

"That's what we are working towards. Gran, you and Da need to be at the stones by eleven this morning. I will meet you there and guide you."

"So soon?" she asked quickly.

"In a few hours. Get Da to take you in the car."

"Don't you think I can manage the hill?"

"You probably could, but why not take the easy way?" Breena took her grandmother's hands in her own. "Please, Gran. This is really important. We need both of you there to lend your energy."

"We'll be there. Why come to me, and not your Da?"

"It hurts him every time he sees me. I remind him of what he missed out on. When he is in pain, I am in pain."

"You had better go, then. I will tell him and bully him to take me up. We will be there, Breena."

"Thank you, Gran," she said leaning over and kissing the old woman on the cheek.

"We have incoming!" Ben cried out from behind the monitor. "One, two, three...there are three more vehicles heading this way."

Adam came running in at that moment. "So much for the warning system! I haven't heard from Matt or Tony about this."

"They may not have come from the gully," Nikau said as he scanned the monitor.

"Try them, Adam. Find out what's going on," Beth told him. "Where are the boys?" She looked around the room.

"Hunter said they were going to entertain Cam and Dom to keep them out of our hair. I'll go get them," said Charlie from where she sat beside her husband.

Out in the hall, Charlie could hear laughter from above and climbed the stairs. On the landing, she waited to hear which room they may be in, but still the sounds came from above. The drop stairs to the attic space were down, and she climbed them slowly. Poking her head through the ceiling, she had to duck fast as a bright ball of light came hurtling towards her.

The two little boys began to squeal with laughter, and she heard a deeper voice over them.

"Oh, shit!"

"Shit is right, young man. What on earth are you doing up here, and since when can you produce light?" Charlie asked as she entered, spotting Hunter up in the rafters.

"I can't. Jas has been feeding them to me. Watch. Go again, Jas."

"I'm not sure if that's a good idea, Hunter," Jasper said, hesitating and watching Charlie carefully.

"Do it, Jasper. Call it a curiosity," said Charlie as she entered the room fully.

"If you're sure. Here—catch, Hunter." With one motion, he produced a small light and sent it flying to his brother. Hunter caught it deftly and then fired it off down the length of the attic. At the other end, Dom and Cam stood waiting to chase it and return it to Jasper.

"Except…when we fire them at those idiots out there, they'll be flaming hot by the time they reach them," Hunter told Charlie eagerly.

"And have you practiced with the fire lights?" she asked the pair.

"We haven't used one of those yet. I didn't want to start a fire," Jasper said, walking towards her, and Hunter came back down to the floor.

"You can always take it back if it gets too hot. Try it." She crossed her arms and waited for the inevitable burn that would come with it.

"Charlie, I don't think—" Jasper started to say.

"Do it," she insisted firmly, cutting across him.

"Okay. You ready, Hunter?" His brother nodded and held out his hand confidently, trusting his older sibling.

Jasper produced a small light ball and let it linger on his palm. Then, slowly, it started to burn. Tiny blue flames licked up from it, and the core began to burn bright white. The glare from the ball became intense, and they all squinted at it. Jasper looked at his brother and Hunter nodded back, noticeably nervous.

Hunter held out his hand and waited for Jasper to upend it onto his palm. The moment it hit, the skin began to sizzle. Hunter let out a cry of pain. Jasper retrieved it straight away and extinguished the light with a small popping sound. Hunter held his hand, looking at the small, round burn mark, and blew on it.

Charlie took his hand in one of hers and swiped the other over the top. When he examined it, there was only a little silvery scar left behind.

"That is so you remember not to be so stupid. I suggest when you use this properly, you have gloves on—ones that will protect you, Hunter, not woollen ones."

"Yes, Charlie," he said, looking shamefaced.

"Now, the lot of you downstairs. We have more visitors arriving." Charlie waited until they had all filed down the stairs to shake her head at their stupidity before following after.

As she entered the dining room, she heard Hunter telling them about their little plan, and she also noticed him rubbing his palm. An excited ripple went through the group as they all discussed the possibility of its uses—until Adam called for calm.

"If we can use it like that, then so could they. We know Marcus has Talented in his ranks. That attack was proof of that. We're going to have to be ready for anything. This is one aspect we can use, but we need to know what could be used in retaliation. Do you and Tony have files on Marcus's men?" he asked Nikau.

"Of course we do, but the files are incomplete. Tia, can you get them up for us?"

"On it." Tia started to tap at the keyboard. "Right. I'm printing out the ones we know have Talents. As Nik said, these are not complete."

"Sorry, I never got all of the files for you," Jasper said regretfully.

"Hey, we're far more informed now than we ever were before you started there, Jasper. You did a great job."

The printer in the corner started to buzz and hum, then began to spit out page after page of profiles. Beth collected them, then sorted each page into the categories of Talents, Mental, Physical, and Life State. As each page spewed forth, the piles became larger in the two most common. Only one page lay in the Life State pile, and that was Marcus.

Nikau looked at Adam for a moment, as the younger man was staring at the solitary page. He came and placed a hand on his shoulder.

"I noticed you didn't use the words *father* or *dad*," he said quietly.

"He was never a father to me or to Jack. He doesn't deserve the title," Adam replied.

"What about his other children?" Nikau asked.

"What other children? I only know about Jack."

"He has had two others that we know of. A girl and a boy—twins. Only the boy survived. The girl was disowned after she fell pregnant when she was raped. She stayed alive long enough to meet her child when he became an adult. Marcus refuses to acknowledge him."

"How do you know this?"

"It is our business to know, Adam. In our line of work, we need to know everything about our targets. We treated your father in the same manner."

"He is not my father anymore. Please stop referring to him in that way," Adam said through gritted teeth.

"If you want, I can tell you who your nephew is," Nikau said in his ear.

"Let's just get through today, shall we, Nik? Then you can tell me whatever you want." Adam shrugged off the hand and walked away from Nikau.

Chapter Twenty

Dinner was over and the table cleared. The children, along with their minder, Greg, had already been sent upstairs for the evening. Now, Claire sat at the table with Marcus sitting across from her, with Mr. Healy and James on either side. Her fingers were tapping on the table, drumming out a rhythmic tune as she stared at Marcus. Mr. Healy shifted in his seat in discomfort.

Marcus lifted his drink to his lips and sipped slowly, watching all three of them. His mind was working all the time, trying to play all the angles he could to keep on top of everything. He discovered that James had become very fond of Claire, and he was looking forward to taking advantage of that. Claire could hear every thought he had and tried hard not to show it.

"Very shortly, Mr. Boyle, I would like you to take Claire upstairs to get ready." Marcus took his time with every word, enjoying himself. As he was talking, Mr. Healy was shifting in his seat. "Is there a problem, Mr. Healy?"

"I have a bit of pain in my stomach, Mr. Ryder. Sorry," the large man answered.

Claire increased the tapping on the table, changing the tempo. Mr. Healy continued his fidgeting and now was grimacing. Marcus finally had enough and pointed at James.

"Take her arm, Mr. Boyle. Mr. Healy, go away and do something about your ailment," he said impatiently.

The switch was made, and Claire stopped her tapping. "I hope you feel better soon, Mr. Healy," she told him and watched as he hurried away.

Her eyes reverted to Marcus and bored into him, making him feel very uncomfortable. He finished his drink and stood, pushing the chair back behind him. He seemed to want to say something but then stopped. Gaining control again, he spoke curtly to them.

"Upstairs now. We have a lot of preparing to do, and I would like you to be ready by nine." He looked at his watch and then walked to the lounge without a backwards glance.

Claire was sick of these stairs. She felt like she had been up and down them so many times that day, but she trooped up them once more. At the door to the bedroom she shared with the children, she paused, but James shook his head and guided her to the other room.

Lying on the bed was a white garment bag she was not expecting. They entered the room, and James shut and locked the door at the same time as releasing her. He turned and put a finger to his lips to keep her quiet, then swept the room for listening devices.

"It's okay. We can talk."

"Thank God that beast has let me go. I think I have bruises on my shoulders from where he was gripping me."

"But he didn't need to grip you at all, did he?" he asked her with a slight grin.

"He was doing what he was ordered to do: suppressing my Talents."

"But there was no need. I could feel them fighting me. How come he couldn't?" He sat down on the edge of the bed.

"I may have put a small suggestion on him—plus, I'm very good at hiding them. Can you remind me when I next see Mr. Healy—without Marcus around—that I must apologise for his stomachaches?"

"That was you as well? What are you?" he asked, shaking his head in wonder.

"That's not a nice question to ask a lady, James. I am me. That is what I am. I hope this doesn't change anything."

"Not a thing, Claire. I will help you as much as possible."

"Good. That, I suppose, is for me?" She pointed to the garment bag and began to open it. Silky white material started to spill out, and her heart sank.

The zip now fully open, she picked up the bag and pulled out the dress. The material draped down to the floor, and she held it up high. Sequins and pearls were sewn into a delicate pattern, but there was no denying that it was intended to be a wedding dress. She made a face and threw it onto the bed, then searched the bag for anything else.

"Thank God there's no headdress. I would have thrown it in his face," she exclaimed.

"I really can't tell you anything of his plans, Claire. He hasn't told anyone what's really going on."

"Don't worry about it. I have a feeling I know what's going to happen. I better get dressed…don't want to keep him waiting. He will only take it out on you." She stood and picked the dress up.

In the bathroom with the door shut, she finally had a moment to herself. The indignation of having every private moment scrutinised and invaded was almost—but not quite— as bad as what Marcus had put her through a couple of nights before. She let out a deep breath, sat on the toilet seat, and put her head in her hands.

The events of the coming night were laid out to her, and the role James was to play was going to be a difficult one for him. She just hoped that he would act the way she needed him to. It was one thing she could have no control over. His split decision was going to determine which way it would go. It had irked her when she found that little piece of information out, as she didn't want to leave it to chance.

Slowly she undressed and got under the shower. The warm water washed over her, clearing her head as it dripped from her hair. She didn't stay under it long, as it was not the time to relax and enjoy it. She stepped out and dried herself off, all the while staring at the dress. When she pulled it off the hanger, she found a small mesh bag. Inside was white underwear. Holding up the bra with two fingers, Claire looked at the lacy number. It was not something she would have picked out for herself, and neither were the knickers.

Claire dressed and was having trouble with the zip at the back. She opened the door and stepped out into the bedroom. James stood up when he saw her, his mouth open a little in amazement. She had to admit that it was a lot different than what she normally wore—jeans and a T-shirt with a jumper when it was cold.

"Can you zip me up, please?" She turned her back to him and he obliged her.

A knock came at the door, and the handle moved just as he finished zipping up the dress. James jumped and took Claire's elbow at the sound. He walked her to the door, unlocked it, and then opened it. Standing outside was a woman with an obviously fake smile stretched across her face, showing overly white, straight teeth, all framed with her dark hair cut into a very neat and short bob.

"Hello. I'm here to do your makeup and hair. I'm Susie," she said to Claire when they didn't say anything. She held up a case she carried as proof.

"Come in, Susie." Claire invited her in with a fixed smile and nudged James into action.

He opened the door wide to let her in and then shut it behind her. Susie placed her case on the dresser and opened it up. Inside were all the tools of her trade. She turned and looked at the light above them, frowning slightly.

"What's the lighting like in the bathroom?" she asked Claire.

"A bit better than out here," Claire replied.

"Mr. Boyle, can you please take that chair into the bathroom for me?" she asked him stiffly.

"You know I can't, Miss Foster. You will have to manage it on your own," James told her.

"You two know each other, then?" Claire asked James, detecting a decidedly icy undertone to the conversation between the two.

"Yeah, not going to share that info with you," he replied testily.

"I'll end up getting it from her, and I have a feeling that it is going to be a bit more colourful."

"Later." It was the only word he would give her on the subject.

After much heaving and straining, Susie managed to get the chair through the doorway of the bathroom, and she positioned it where the light would be most favourable to work in. She waved Claire to sit, and she did so with reluctance, as she hated makeup.

"This is a big night for you. You must be excited!" Susie draped a cloth over the sparkling white gown before getting to work, brushing Claire's damp hair back from her face and pinning it to stay there.

"Not really. How would you feel if the man who raped you only a few nights ago insisted that you wear a wedding dress and get made up like a china doll?" Claire asked as she waited.

"Ouch…someone didn't get the memo. Do you realise how many women in the organisation would kill to be in your shoes?" she asked a little frostily, as she pulled on Claire's hair, running a brush through it.

"They're welcome to have the opportunity." Claire was beginning to see why James was a bit testy with her.

"Mr. Ryder is such a lovely man. When I started with him, I was so plain. He sent me off and I came back stylish and beautiful, with qualifications to boot."

"Does that mean he gets you to do up all his girlfriends?"

"No, I run my own salon. I pass information along to him. Unfortunately, I don't have any dealings with his personal life apart from cutting his hair."

"No, I suppose you wouldn't." There was something about this girl that was setting Claire's teeth on edge. It may have been her rabid devotion to Marcus.

Claire sat there enduring the primping and preening. All the while, James sat at her side holding her elbow. Her thoughts drifted through his memories and found Susie tucked away inside. Unlike Tony's beautiful, boxed method, James's was more like books, each part of his life written meticulously into leather-bound journals and then placed in dark wooden shelves.

The pages flicked through her fingers, and she read the last entry on this subject. James had been thinking about leaving the organisation for a while but was hopelessly in love with Susie. When the time had come and he built up enough nerve, James asked her to leave with him. She had refused.

Why would I leave when I finally have it all? A life, a business of my own…and how could I betray Marcus like that? she had declared to him with a derisive laugh.

You have more feelings for Mr. Ryder than you do me, James had accused her.

The words she had said were large on the page, much larger than the others. Of course, I do. Marcus is a powerful man, and that's a great turn-on for me. You are just a—what? A lackey, a gofer, a bodyguard. Someone to be ordered around. What we have is fun, James, but no more. My eyes are on the prize. I want Marcus.

Claire put the book back where she found it and tiptoed out. The silence she had left to do her searching was still surrounding them, and she was grateful. James's reaction was understandable. He didn't trust this woman.

Susie put the last pin in her hair and stood back to look at the results. She tweaked a curl back into place, then sprayed copious amounts of hairspray in a great mist around her head to hold it all into place.

"There. You're all done," she said, packing her things away.

"Susie, thank you. I can see that you didn't really want to do this, but you're amazing," said Claire, looking into her eyes and shaking her hand. "When you go down to Marcus to make your little report, I want you to tell him that it all went fine and there was nothing out of the ordinary. That we chatted about silly girl things and James got in the way, always being there. Are we good?" Susie's eyes were glazed for a moment, and she nodded. "Right. If there's nothing more, enjoy your evening. Goodbye, Susie."

"Miss Foster," James said stiffly as they walked to the door. As soon as it was shut, he let go of her arm and locked the door once more.

"That wasn't really necessary, was it?" he asked Claire.

"The fact that the door was locked would have sent up red flags to Marcus," Claire told him. She sat on the bed and put the shoes on that had been provided for her—another thing she hated. High heels. "When we get to where we're going, I don't want you to do anything to stop it until I give you a nod. You will know what to do. I promise you. Now I need your promise that you will do as I ask."

"If he is going to do…" he struggled with the words, "…that again, then I won't hesitate whether you say or not."

"James, this is important. You must wait. Something is going to happen, and it all has to do with timing. I need that promise."

"Or you will put a suggestion into my head?" he asked.

"No, I will never do that to people I consider friends. We are friends, aren't we?" she asked him carefully.

"Yes, we are. All right. I promise I won't interfere until you tell me." He stood straight as he made the promise she had asked him for.

"Good. Now I think it is time to go downstairs, Mr. Boyle," Claire said formally, trying to get her nerves under control. She held out an arm and he took it and kissed her cheek.

"For luck," he told her with a wink.

"They're moving in," Owen told the others quickly, looking up at Adam. "They're surrounding the house."

"I can't see anything out there," Ben answered his son.

"They're there, Dad. I promise you." He sent another search out. "There are quite a few. Some have Talent, but nothing we can't handle."

"Can you tell what the Talents are?" Adam asked curiously.

"Not really. I can feel one Mind Touch out there, but everyone else is a blur—sorry, Adam."

"You've done a great job. Keep an eye out, Ben. They should be coming near the cameras soon," Nikau interjected before Adam could speak. "Adam, can I have a word?"

The younger man followed Nikau out of the room and into the entryway. He made sure no one was around before he broached the subject.

"I know that you think that your Talent isn't fully complete. Tony told me. But he also told me that you're far more capable than you give yourself credit for. Have you thought about getting Tony to help you with it, to open it up?"

"No. I've never liked this thing that I can do. It was thrust upon me and has been the cause of me losing my family. That's why I've never pushed myself to learn it. Claire was always on at me, but I couldn't."

"It's not your fault you had a prick for a father. But we need your Talent more than you know. Please, talk to Tony. Get him to help you."

"If I do this, then I will be able to do unspeakable things to people."

"Adam, you are not your father. You're you. How can a man who obviously loves his kids so much become like your father? It's not in you to be cruel. Just talk to Tony, please, before it's too late. And that time is coming pretty fast."

"I'll think about it," Adam said.

"Don't think too long," Nikau warned him and walked back into the dining room.

Adam sat down heavily on the stairs and chewed on a thumbnail. Nikau had told him exactly what he thought all his adult life, since the Talents had come to him. The fear of becoming like Marcus was in him and clouded his judgments every day, making him second-guess himself just to be sure the outcome was fair and just.

"Nikau is right, Adam. You're nothing like him. You're better." Beth stood leaning against the dark wood bannister. She went and sat beside him, taking his thumb away from his mouth. "If your father was like you when I fell pregnant, he would have been more kind, and he probably would have married me. That's something you would have done. When I first met you properly, I could see immediately that you were more mine than his. Your laughter is genuine, the love you have for your family is real, and you have more emotions in your little finger than Marcus could ever feel."

"Mum, I'm scared of opening it up, of having more."

"You weren't scared the first time you used that name for me, of opening your heart to me—the woman who had given you up."

"But you had no choice. I wasn't given up. I was taken from you."

"Marcus had told you all those stories about me, but you still welcomed me into your heart and believed my side of the story. Was that a hard thing to do?"

"No. It wasn't." He smiled at her.

"Then, my boy, talk to Tony. If he can help you, then you should take the opportunity. You better yourself every time you learn something new for business. What's the difference here? You'll only be becoming the man you were supposed to be. I believe in you, Adam."

"Will you sit with me when I do?" His eyes and voice were almost like a little boy once more.

"Yes, I will." She linked her hand with his and gave it a squeeze.

Finding Matt earlier had been easy. They had been friends for a very long time, and they also had Claire as a common connection. Sending out his thought to Tony was a different matter. For years, he had only thought of him as someone in the shadows and an enemy to them. Adam's change of attitude towards him was still coloured by this, and it made finding him difficult.

"I'm here, Adam. You can stop trying," Tony said in his mind. "What's happening?"

"There are a lot of men descending on the farm. I can't protect everyone here if I can't use my Talent properly. Nik suggested you might be able to help."

"I could, but you have to be willing first. You will have to trust your mind to me completely. I don't just mean the part the Talent is used from, but your entire mind. It's limited in you because you choose to hide it away in that tiny spot. To help you, I need to expand it so that it encompasses all. Are you willing to do that? Are you ready to trust me completely?"

"I know what you're asking. Claire asked me the same thing when she implanted the way to make a suggestion. I am ready."

"Adam, you're not ready. You don't trust me enough."

"What about Matt. What about Claire? Could they help me?"

"Claire is being suppressed, and Matt has only just learnt what he can do. I'm your only option at this point," Tony told him directly. "Who's with you? I can feel someone with you."

"My mother is here beside me."

"She has no Talent. Is that right?"

"Yes, but I don't see what that has to do with anything."

"She has no Talent because she suppressed it herself. I feel a great deal of Talent in her if she would just let it out."

"What are you talking about? Mum has no Talent. She even hated it at one point."

"Ever wondered why all of her sons have Talents when it's passed down the female line?" Tony asked him slowly.

"I…um…hadn't thought about it. But that still isn't helping now."

"But it is. I can feel the trust she has in my helping. I can't do this without yours."

Adam thought about it for a moment. Questions of Talents formed a queue to be answered, but he had none. This revelation that Beth was suppressing her own Talent was a big one. He came to his decision.

"I trust you, Tony," he told the man confidently.

"Okay. Let's get this done, then. Just open yourself to me, Adam, and I will do the rest."

Adam's mind felt hazy as Tony completely took it over. His thoughts were not his own, his memories shuffled through. It was a weird sensation, and he now knew what Claire had meant when she described Lilith and her father talking inside her mind. She had said she felt like a bystander listening in to a private conversation in her head, a conversation that had nothing to do with her. He waited as Tony riffled through the different parts of the mind and put them into order.

Finally, Tony came to that tiny space where Adam kept his Mind Touch Talent, and he took it into his hand. A spectator watching some bizarre performance on a stage was how it seemed, very surreal and unnerving at the same time. Tony looked hard at the small space, and it started to grow outward. The constraints Adam had put on it were bursting at the seams and then shattered into tiny fragments, smaller than a dust particle.

Tony now was holding it in both hands as it swelled and grew until he had to place it on the floor and control it from there. Adam felt the pressure of it growing inside him. The knowledge pushed its boundaries, and the limits were endless. On and on until it surrounded himself and Tony, and then more. There was a single note of music as his Talent inserted itself into every aspect of his consciousness, and then it changed when it came to the subconscious.

"This is yours now, Adam. You need to fix it in your subconscious in order to control it yourself," Tony prompted him.

Together they walked to the space and Adam stepped inside. Uninvited, Tony followed him. Around him was bare and empty. The darkness was not quite complete, but the dimness made the features on Tony unsubstantial and misty. Adam compared it to Claire's and found that hers always felt like a park in autumn, just turning to winter.

"We make our subconscious what we want of it," Tony told him and led the way to the very heart of the space. "In Claire's, this area is where her parents reside. There's a picnic blanket and the sun is shining. Don't tell her that I know that." He smiled.

"I've never seen it," Adam told him.

"That's because her parents never trusted you fully. But this is a blank slate. Is there nothing or nowhere in your life that you feel centred to?"

"My childhood growing up was never stable. I never knew from one moment to the next where I was going to be. The only constant was Claire, but that seems wrong now. There's my own little family, but I'm always afraid that they are going to be taken from me, that I will let them down somehow."

"It's a place to start. Your home."

Adam didn't know if it was just the place they were in or the way Tony moved at that moment, but it triggered a flash of memory to him. He staggered at the force of it and bent over as the breath escaped his lungs. Looking up at the tall man, he remembered those dark eyes with the same expression from when he was a teen. The beating he had been given that day was lighter than all the others, but still a beating.

"You remember," Tony simply stated. "I'm sorry. I tried not to hurt you too much."

"You still did. But not as much as knowing who told you to do it. I forgive you, Tony."

Tony's eyes closed, and Adam could sense he was closing something off from him. There was something else in Tony's mind that he was keeping from Adam, but at that moment he didn't care what it was. It had been important for him to forgive this man of the transgression that was not fully his to own.

"I have helped you as far as I can go. The rest is up to you. The Talent must be grounded here in the centre for you to harness it fully. You need to reach out to someone and bring them in with the touch alone. I cannot be that person. In a normal situation, it would have been a mother or father."

"What about you? As I understand it, you didn't know either of your parents."

"That's a dangerous question to ask me, Adam. I came to this Talent late; my first were Strength and Light. The person I drew in is none of your business."

"Fair enough. If I bring in the person I'm thinking of, will you stay?" he asked, hoping that Tony would agree.

"You're up to something, Adam."

"Yes, and I'm hoping that it will work out. Please, can you?"

"I'll stay," Tony agreed, though Adam could see he was being cautious.

"Thank you," Adam said. He felt nervous again. This was going to be hard to explain, but he had to do it.

The call left his mind, strong and pure. *This is how it's supposed to work,* he thought, concentrating on what he was trying to achieve. Then he found her. Her mind was alert and concerned. She was startled at the call that resonated inside, and she grasped it with both hands, swept away by it.

Adam stood and watched as Beth appeared inside his subconscious with him. She looked around and smiled, then walked towards him. Tony stepped between them and held up a hand to stop her.

"In here, he cannot touch you. It would mean a permanent connection that wouldn't be appropriate for a mother and son. Do you understand, Beth?" Tony asked her.

"I understand. Thank you for the warning. But why has he brought me here?" Beth looked past Tony to her son.

"I brought you here, Mum, because you are my mother. I understand the love you have for me never went away after I was taken from you. I always wanted you when I was small. I always knew the lies that my father told me about you were just that, lies. I brought you here because, I love you, Mum."

The words he had finally spoken to her rang like a bell in his mind, and he felt elation course through him. He felt complete and recognized acceptance in those three little words. So simple to say and often said when not meant, but those words had a power of their own—the ability to heal old wounds. Around them a scene was forming of the one place he felt calm and at peace: his mother's kitchen.

"There's also another reason. Tony has sensed something in you that you may not be aware of. He has sensed a suppressed Talent. He doesn't know what it is, but it's there."

"I have no Talent, Adam. I've never had one," Beth replied calmly.

"Beth, what happened when you were young?" Tony interrupted her.

"That is none of *your* business." She bristled against this question.

"Something happened when you were twelve. There was some trauma you experienced that made you suppress what should have been yours. It's all right now. You can release your hold on it. Let it free to emerge."

"My mind is not yours to fix. Leave it alone." Beth's anger was building.

"I just thought it was such a shame that for all these years you've missed out on being you," Tony said gently.

"Leave it alone," Beth repeated. "Adam, I would like to go now. Thank you, my son, for bringing me here, but please let me go."

"Yes, Mum." He pushed her thoughts away and was left standing with Tony. "I shouldn't have done that."

"Do as she asks and leave it. She will find her way," Tony told him, and then he, too, was gone.

Adam blinked in the light as he came back to himself and saw his mother walking away from him. Placing his head in his hands, he hoped that he hadn't damaged their relationship. It had taken too long to get through all the defences she put up to protect herself from hurt.

"You got what you needed?" Nikau asked, leaning against the door frame.

"Yeah, I think so," Adam replied, his eyes still on the doorway his mother had passed through.

Chapter Twenty-One

At the bottom of the stairs, Claire stopped for a moment before turning into the living room. She took a deep breath and then went to face Marcus with James at her side, his reassuring touch on her elbow helping her along. She looked up as Marcus rose to meet her, a smile upon his face and arms open wide. He had changed also and was now in a very dark suit with a black bow tie. Claire tried not to laugh, as she thought he looked like a penguin.

"I knew that dress would look beautiful on you. You have such a lovely figure. It is such a waste to hide it beneath all the baggy layers you normally wear."

"Wrong thing to say, Marcus. You should've told me I look beautiful in anything," she said, sitting down before he could touch her.

"You do, Claire, and from now on you don't have to worry about dressing the way you do. You can have the pick of the new season's fashions and be the most stylish woman in the country."

"I like the way I dress. It's comfortable and practical. I can't keep up the charade anymore." She paused when she felt James's grip tighten on her elbow. "I will never like you and will always be trying to get away from you."

"That is why Mr. Boyle here and Mr. Healy will be your constant companions until I can work out a way to suppress your Talents permanently. I will have you, Claire, and it all starts tonight."

"When tonight? I'm tired and would prefer to go to bed."

"Not long now. Only a matter of a few hours." He looked at his watch. "There is no rescue coming, if that is what you were hoping. I have the farmhouse in complete lockdown. No one is getting in or out of that place in one piece."

Claire would have liked nothing better at that moment than to wipe off the grin that was spread over his face. Instead, she took a deep breath and calmed herself once more. It was only the nerves trying to overtake her rational thinking, and she pushed them down again. She was going to have to concentrate harder than ever. She thought about everyone and hoped they would be in place and safe from harm.

While she continued to chat with Marcus, in her mind she could see Adam leaning over the table at the farmhouse, talking with Owen and another man she did not recognise. From there, she saw Bree and Johnny, fast asleep in their beds upstairs. Both were slumbering the peaceful sleep of the innocent, with Greg watching over them. Then to David and Tony: two men who featured a great deal in her life and whom she loved. They were cold and tired, but still alert. She saw Tony seemly nod to her as she watched them.

Her final check was on Matt and Addy. Addy was asleep, wrapped in a blanket, while Matt still watched the house vigilantly. She whispered in his ear as she passed, "I love you."

He heard her and smiled and replied just as softly, "Love you, too, Claire."

Floating back to the house and rising to the window the children were in, Claire created a very delicate, light protection that could only be broken by one person. She sent it into the room, and it surrounded Bree and Johnny. She pushed it out to Greg as well. If any of Marcus's men should enter, they would see nothing out of place and would immediately have a strong compulsion to leave the room.

When she returned to the real world before her, Claire found Marcus looking at her funny.

"I'm sorry. What did you say?" she asked, her irritation at his mere presence growing.

"I asked if you would like something to drink, but I don't think you should. You have been very vague tonight."

"I told you, I'm tired. Having someone attached to you at all hours of the day and night and during very private moments is draining. Especially when I have no energy to draw on."

"I have been reading about pregnancy. As I understand it, women do get quite tired as it progresses. You see, I am willing to be very supportive of you during this time."

"I'm not pregnant," Claire said with some force. "If I haven't become pregnant in the last six years since Bree was born, then it's unlikely that it will happen now. Therefore, there's nothing for you to be supportive of."

"Good. Then the child we will conceive tonight will be all mine, fully. It doesn't matter either way. Because if you are carrying, just as I believe you are, then he will become mine." He was so serious that it frightened her, but not as much as the hint of darkness that lay within his voice. A darkness she had heard once before coming from Jack. "Mr. Wilson," Marcus called out, and hurried footsteps came from the back of the house.

"Yes, Mr. Ryder?" His fawning behaviour left no doubt in Claire's mind as to who had been secretly reporting to Marcus.

"Make sure everything is ready and we have all that we need in the car, please."

"Right away, Mr. Ryder," he said and hurried out the door.

The Rover bounced and swayed as it made its way over the pitted and half-lost track leading up the ridge to the where the stones were located. Gerry tried to make sure the ride was smooth for his mother-in-law, and he was constantly looking over at her to make sure she was all right.

"Keep your eyes on the track and stop worrying. I'm fine," she told him as they swayed some more. She gripped the dash and increased her handhold on the door.

"We're just about there," Gerry reassured her as he wrestled Matt's old Land Rover through the rocks and ditches.

Summer was just about done for the year, and autumn was not far off. Gerry once again thought about tackling the subject of Gran leaving the house for the winter and coming to live with him in Glasgow. He knew she would put up a fight, since the house was the only home she had ever known. She had been born there. Her children and then their children were all born in that house. But she was getting on now, and she was alone. Winters could be harsh in this part of Scotland, and she could be snowed in for days.

As he made the final corner, the large rocks stood in their way—rising from the earth, cloaked in thousands of years of lichen growth. He came to a stop and turned the engine off. The silence that descended was all-encompassing, and even the sound of the motor cooling in the breeze that buffeted the car was muted. Gerry didn't know what to expect next. Were they supposed to stay in the car and wait, or get out and wander around?

"Let's stay here. That wind is too cold for my old bones," Gran said in her matter-of-fact voice that decided everything.

"What is it we're doing up here?"

"Helping Claire—I told you. Breena wants our help at the stones."

"Have you noticed that since Claire has come into our lives, none of us have questioned anything she's said? Not even you," Gerry asked, still looking at the stones that rose up out of the ground.

"That's because she has told us nothing but the truth."

"Do you really believe in these Guardians?"

"I thought you believed in the old ones. What has brought all this hesitation and uncertainty on?" she asked, looking at him.

"I don't know. We have not heard one word from them all since they left. I suppose I just feel left out and am looking for someone to blame."

"When I was little, I used to dream I saw a procession of people in hooded cloaks marching up the valley and taking the path to the stones. They would stop at the spring and then place themselves in between each stone. One night, I snuck out of bed and waited in the field for them to come. It was such a cold night, but I was stubborn and stayed out there all night. My Granny was waiting for me in the kitchen when I finally came in, frozen and wet through. She wrapped me up by the fire and gave me a cup of tea, then calmly asked me what I was thinking of. I can still remember the smells of her kitchen." Gran was lost in her past.

"What did you tell her?" Gerry asked, interrupting her thoughts.

"I told her of my dreams, of seeing the procession and wanting to join them. She shook her head and told me that I was being foolish, and that I would not be joining that procession for many years to come. She had Foresight, so I believed her. I think that day is coming soon."

"Not for a while yet, Ma. I was thinking you should come to Glasgow this winter."

"Now, what would I be wanting to live in that noisy place for? Thank you for thinking of me, Gerry, but I will be fine at the house. Gordon has always dug me out of the snow before. I'm sure he will do it again this winter. The sheep and cows are all set to go to the next farm for them to look after, so I will be fine."

"I just worry, Ma," he began to protest.

"I know you do, and you're very sweet to look after your difficult mother-in-law the way you do."

"You're all I have left...my own Ma and Da have left this world already...Leana, Breena." He became quiet as he thought of them.

Gran reached over and placed her gnarled, arthritic fingers on his arm. "You still have Matt, Claire, Bree and—" she stopped short.

"And who?" he asked her.

"It's not my place to tell you."

"But you're bursting to anyway. Claire is pregnant, isn't she? Why didn't they say?"

"Because of everything else that was happening, and she was only just pregnant."

Gerry smiled and gave a little chuckle. "I'm going to be a granda again. I wonder how Bree will take it."

"And you won't have to wait long to see the wee bairn. They are going to be living in Scotland very soon. I've seen it." She touched her temple. Gran didn't regret telling the news to Gerry. It made him happy and gave him joy.

"What are they doing?" Nikau asked Owen, checking on the mark he had placed on the young man's face. Oliver and Owen had been up to their old tricks of switching places, and Nikau had found a good solution to work out who was who.

"Nothing. Standing around, watching the house. Some are smoking and some are just pissed off that they have to stand in the rain. They're not very comfortable out there." His grin was evidence of how much he was enjoying these trespassers' misery.

"Keep up the good work," Nikau praised him.

"When are we going to unleash the fireballs?" Hunter asked enthusiastically.

"Only if necessary, little bro," Jasper told him.

"Jas, can you isolate that one guy out there who has Mind Touch? He's their communication to Marcus," Adam called from the corner, where he sat with his feet up on another chair.

"How? A light binding would be obvious. They have this unfortunate tendency to glow a bit. Plus, I need to see him to do it. If he sees me before I can release the light, he will attack me."

"I can protect you until you do it. I've been working on it—up here." He pointed to his head. "I can shield you away from him, and he won't know what hit him."

"What if I used my Seek, the way they did earlier? I could knock a few out, confuse some more, maybe," Owen offered.

"Can you do that?" Ben asked his son, taking his eyes off the monitor in front of him briefly.

"Yeah. After it happened, I sort of examined it. I'm sure I can reverse the process. It's worth a shot, Dad."

"If we do this, Adam, we can't tell Mum. She would freak out," Jasper said quietly, as he looked out the door to see if she was close.

"No...I won't do it behind her back, Jas. She has a right to know, but we will do it. If we can get rid of their communication, we'll have the upper hand," Adam told him, chewing on his thumb nail once more.

"You can tell her, then, because I'm convinced she still thinks I'm ten. You only met her when you were already grown." Jasper grinned. It was a common excuse for him when he wanted his older half-brother to ask for something from their mother.

"That's getting very old. You're going to have to stand up to her sometime, Jas. She just might surprise you." Adam got up from his chair and left the room.

In the kitchen, he found her sitting at the smaller family table with Tia and a cup of coffee in her hands. The immediate silence of the room made him suspect they were discussing something not for his ears. Tia did look a bit embarrassed and wouldn't meet his eyes.

"Yes, Adam, was there something you wanted?" The tone was tight and still had an angry note to it.

"We have a plan, and I thought you should know about it. It involves Jasper and me."

"Go on." She placed the cup back onto the table and crossed her arms.

"There's a man out there who is vital to Marcus. I'm going to shield Jas as he gets close to him, and then he's going to bind him so he can't use his Mind Touch. Owen is going to try and confuse the others out there while we do it." He waited, holding his breath for a long time. The clock on the wall loudly ticked away the passing seconds until she finally answered him.

"Are you asking my permission or telling me?"

"Telling. I don't want to leave anything to chance. If we take him out, then we will have the upper hand. Marcus can't get his messages through."

"Why tell me? You could have just gone out there and done it, then told me after."

"Because you are our mother, and you deserve to know beforehand."

"Just so I can rant and rave about the safety of my sons? No, Adam, you are grown-up enough to make your own decisions. I know you'll protect Jasper. But I would suggest that you get Charlie and Oliver ready in case you need them." She dismissed him, and he left feeling very unnerved by her answer.

Adam was still wondering about Beth's response when he collected both Jasper and Owen. He sent Hunter to tell Charlie and Oliver what was happening while the three of them went upstairs to change into some dark clothing.

"This is a bit of overkill, isn't it?" Oliver asked when they came downstairs. "You three look like you're about to break into some secret government facility."

"Shove off, Olly." His twin pushed him.

"Don't come crying to me when you want something mended."

"No, I won't. I'll be going to Mum," Owen said with a wicked grin.

"Knock it off, the pair of you. Do you want to go over it again?" asked Adam when they gathered at the back door, his hand already on the doorknob.

"No. Let's just get out there." Jasper had a sudden attack of nerves. This was the first time he would have to use his Talent as a weapon. Before, it had all been fun and games with Hunter.

"Okay, Owen—where is he?"

The younger man closed his eyes and concentrated on the spot where he had found their target before. He locked onto his position and pointed in the direction. "He's standing under the large willow we use to jump off into the river…you know the one?" Owen asked Jasper.

"Yeah, I know it. There's some good cover on the way. How do you mask me?" he asked, turning to Adam.

"Don't worry about that. Just don't run off from me. I have to be touching you until we get close enough. Let's go."

Adam didn't want to wait anymore. The need for action was finally on them, and he wanted to get it over with and get them back without any incidents. He opened the door, and a gust of wind blew in along with the rain that was now falling. The weather was worsening as the night progressed. Adam hoped that it might help disguise their movements from the men out there.

The door shut behind them, and they were under the old tree in the backyard getting their bearings once more. Adam followed Jasper as they leapt the fence and ran through the field beside the house, keeping close to the hedge that made the border. The rain had made the ground muddy, and they slipped and slid along, trying to keep their footing while attempting to be as quiet as possible.

Water streamed down their faces, creeping under their collars. It seeped through their clothing and chilled their skin with the help of the bitter increasing wind. At the next fence line, they waited while Owen sent a small search out again. After he nodded that he was still there, they crossed the fence and Adam put his hand on Jasper's shoulder. "Owen, stay here. I'll get Jas closer and signal you when we're ready. Just don't include us in it."

"Right—but make sure you put up defences, just in case." Owen pushed himself into the hedge to get out of the rain as Adam and Jasper headed away.

They stuck close to the hedge, and Adam trusted Jas to keep them hidden from eyesight while he concentrated on anyone looking with a Talent. The process was not the same as using the Hide Talent, but more keeping their thoughts hidden. Trying this for the first time, he had to adjust a few things as he went. Hiding his own thoughts was easy with the defences he put up, but hiding those of his brother was harder. Jasper's thought patterns were alien to him—they jumped from one subject to another.

"Hey! Concentrate on what we're doing and not a girl. You can think about her later."

"Jealous?" Jas laughed at being caught out.

"Not my type. Just concentrate." They moved forward, trying to keep silent.

At the end of the hedge, they stopped. The river was only metres away, and they could hear the rushing water. The rain in the hills was swelling the river fast, and the roar as it flowed down the valley was increasing. Looking over the expanse of wasteland, they made out the willow and saw some of its branches already trailing in the swift water.

"He's not there," Jasper hissed. "Owen said he was here."

"Well, he must have moved. I wouldn't stay there if I were him."

From behind came squelching footsteps. Adam turned and saw a dark figure working their way towards them. As it got closer, he could hear Owen swearing profusely at the weather.

"If we get caught, it will be because of him," Jasper said, concerned, looking around for any hint of Marcus's men.

"He's moved," Owen told them.

"We figured that. Where has he gone?" Adam asked impatiently.

"That direction, and I know…I'll stay here." He pointed to the right.

Jasper and Adam once again moved off in the direction Owen was sending them. It was a bit harder this time, as there was no shelter to hide against. They crept low to the ground, moving amongst the long grass, and stopping when a bush would give them cover. The effort Adam was putting in was starting to take its toll, and he was faltering in his steps.

"There." Jasper stopped suddenly, and Adam almost lost his grip on his brother. He peered into the gloom and saw a dark shape moving against the lighter shade of the ground.

"Do you want to get closer?" Adam asked Jasper.

"A bit. The less time the light has to shine before it reaches him, the better." Slowly, they inched forward until Jasper stopped him again. He held up his hand to Adam and started to count down with his fingers. The last finger was up, and when Jasper lowered it, Adam released his brother.

With a speed Adam could hardly comprehend, Jasper released the light to make a binding around the man they had been seeking. The light snaked along the ground, and they watched it stalk its prey. The glow it emitted was low, but it was still evident in the darkness of the stormy night. It managed to circle around the man and up his back it went, sending out shoots to encompass the body before he had a chance to realise what was happening. It snapped shut around him and he fell to the ground. Jasper and Adam could see him trying to release the bonds without success.

The wave of Seek was bearing down on them, and Adam could feel it. He grasped his brother in his arms and they landed on the wet, soggy ground, with Adam covering and encompassing his mind over Jasper's. The wave was strong, and it almost broke through the defences Adam had hastily erected to protect them.

In the distance, they could hear cries of surprise, but the noise coming from in front was the most terrifying scream Adam had ever heard. It cut the air like a knife through butter and sent birds flying from their soggy night perches, crying out into the darkness. When the waves of Seek were over, the man cried out once more with a grunting sound of agony, and then there was silence.

The noise he had made brought running feet towards them, and Adam pulled his brother up and they made for the hedge. They were panting by the time they reached Owen, and they skidded to a stop on the muddy ground. Jasper fell on his back in the mud, and Owen reached down to help him back to his feet.

"Get in the hedges and be quiet. Jas, release the bonds. We don't want to give the game away," Adam told them and forced his way through the branches and foliage.

They stood, trying to make their breathing quiet so as to not attract attention. Men running rushed past them, searching the area. A cry went up as they found their man and called for assistance. Adam judged that they would be safe enough to make it back to the house and started to step out of the hedge.

"What's that?" someone quite close yelled.

Adam froze on the spot and pulled his leg very carefully back under cover, holding his breath for what seemed like a long time. A beam of light shone where he was about to exit and scanned the hedge for signs of any disturbance. He was grateful for the times that he had played with his brothers when they were younger here, burrowing into the hedges and hiding until they were found.

The torchlight skimmed over again and down on the mud. "Are those footprints?" one man asked.

"How should I know? They could be cattle prints. This is a farm. Do you want to get even muddier checking them out?"

"No chance. This has to be the stupidest bloody job there is. We're guarding a house full of those with Talents we have no hope of defending ourselves against."

"Just keep your head down and do what you're told. You'll get paid nicely for it. Come on, let's get back to that tree. I'm sick of being wet."

Adam heard them leave and waited a few more seconds before whispering to Owen, "Any others?"

"Nope, all gone. You should've asked earlier. You almost landed us in it," Owen told him off.

"Piss off, Owen. Let's go." Adam pushed himself out of the hedge, and making sure they were all together, he led the way back to the house.

Chapter Twenty-Two

God, when is it all going to kick off? This is getting ridiculous! David thought, pulling the collar of his jacket tighter around his neck.

The rain was getting heavier and was now pouring through the trees. The sound of the drops hitting the foliage and the wind rushing through was making for a very miserable night for the pair. They had long ago stopped talking, having run out of things to say, and were fully occupied with their own thoughts. David had a suspicion that Tony was talking to the others, but he didn't want to come out and fully confront him. It was bad enough those stones were having such a bad effect on him. The last thing he wanted was to fall out with Tony.

He looked at his watch quickly, pressing the light. It read eleven-thirty. If he were home, he would have been in bed already for a good two hours. Years of early rising to feed the animals before a hard day's work in the fields had firmly set his body clock, and it did not like this at all. Not to mention the wet and damp clothing that clung to his body and cooled with every breath of wind.

"I wish I knew what was going on," he finally said, and his words felt loud in the bush.

"Adam, Jasper, and Owen have just taken out the means of communication for the men surrounding your house. They are very resourceful boys. Addy is asleep, and Matt is watching the cabin. Bree and Johnny are asleep, and their watcher is dozing. And Claire—well, that's interesting." The surprise in Tony's voice caught David's attention.

"What? What's interesting?" he demanded.

"I can feel Claire. She isn't being suppressed." Tony shut his eyes and concentrated. "Her minder is there, holding on to her, but… My God, she is amazing."

"Will you just bloody well get on with it and tell me what is going on?" David cried out angrily.

"Claire has full use of her Talents. She can use them even if they're trying to suppress her. Hang on."

He sent a thought her way and felt her brush it aside. He tried one more time, but again she turned it away, refusing to answer him. There must be a reason she would not talk, so he removed the thought and opened his eyes. David was standing in front of him with hope in his own.

"Claire didn't want to talk. She could if she wanted, but she wouldn't. It was almost as if she was in two places at once."

"When this is all over, we're going to have to have one hell of a debriefing from everyone. I'm tired of being kept out of the loop. Do you have the same Talents as Claire?"

"No, I don't even come close to her." Tony almost sounded jealous. "Claire's Talents and strength are off the charts. I don't think there has ever been a person like her before."

"I know her. She would never use them unless she has to," David said, rubbing his hands together to get them warm.

"No, she won't. That is why she's the best person to have them," Tony agreed.

A beeping came from Marcus's wristwatch, and he turned it off. He stood and walked to the rear of the house. Claire could hear him talking but couldn't pick out the words. She looked at James, and he gave her an encouraging smile. The time was coming. She could feel the energy increasing in the gully. Like static electricity, the air was alive with it.

"It's time to go," Marcus called out as he walked back into the room to stand in front of Claire.

He held out his hand to help her up, but she refused it. Instead, she accepted the help from James. Claire knew this would provoke Marcus, but she couldn't stand the thought of his touch just yet.

"Put her in the car, Mr. Boyle," Marcus said darkly and then followed them out. Just as he was about to shut the door, a cry came from the house. He stopped and waited for whoever it was that had called to him.

Claire watched from the back seat of the car and wondered what was happening. She sent out a thought and found an incredible mind hidden by the door. She pulled it back immediately, hoping they had not discovered her. The door was pushed open a bit more, and Claire saw Susie standing in front of her boss. Even Claire could see she was flirting with him and trying to lessen whatever bad news she had just given him, and she felt the sting on her own cheek when Marcus backhanded the woman and sent her flying.

"That bastard," James muttered and made to launch himself from the car.

"Not yet." Claire restrained him from leaving her side. "Not yet, but soon."

He settled back down in his seat, and she could still feel the tension of his muscles bunched up under her hand as he clenched his fists. His eyes never moved from Marcus as he shut the door and made his way to the car.

The silence in the car was palpable. Marcus was definitely angry at the news he had received, and it radiated from him. He started the car and pulled out of the parking space very aggressively, then rushed down the drive. The gates took a long time to open enough to make it through, but as soon as the car could fit, he was out onto the road and turning left to head further up the gully with a screech of the tyres.

The sound of tyres squealing brought Matt's head up in time to see the car hurtling up the gully. After shaking loose the effects of the light sleep, he quickly sent a thought to Tony.

"Someone heading your way." The message was sent so urgently he wasn't sure that the man had understood, but he hoped that he did. He sent a searching quest towards the house and found Bree asleep. There were others in the house as well—one in the same room as Bree, and two downstairs.

He immediately retracted his search when someone was alerted to it and had tried to grasp on to him. They knew they were there. He nudged Addy with his foot, trying to wake her, finally crouching down and shaking her when she didn't.

"We have to go," he told her when her eyes finally pried themselves open and she looked at him blankly. "No time. We have to go. I want to get Bree out of there."

Matt grabbed Addy's hand and hauled her up from the ground. She shook out the blanket, starting to fold it. He gave her a strange look and took it from her hands, then hung it up on the branch he had just been leaning against.

"Don't worry about that. Let's get down there." He moved out through the bush. The wet branches and leaves slapped at his body and face, but he did not give them a second thought. His sole focus was his daughter. There was nothing he could do about Claire, and he knew she could look after herself, but Bree needed him.

They hurtled down the hillside. Matt came to a skidding stop just short of the stream, which was now running high, its waters a murky colour in the dark of the night. Matt held out an arm to help Addy come to a halt, and they both watched the water tumble over the rocks that they had used as stepping-stones hours earlier.

Without thinking, Matt took his cousin in his arms, then lifted them both off the ground and up through the canopy above. The rain pelted them as they rose higher and higher into the sky, racing through it towards the house. Addy clung to Matt with her hands firmly clasped together around his neck, refusing to look down at the space below them. Matt landed on the roof and steadied Addy as she found her feet and finally opened her eyes.

"Give me some warning next time," she scolded him.

"I'll try to remember," he replied grimly. His mind was already searching out the men on the perimeter of the fence. "Stay here," Matt said as he took off once more.

"Where else would I go?" Addy said into the darkness, trying not to slip off the wet roof.

One by one, Matt took care of the security detail outside the house by making them sleep. He came from above, knocking each man to the ground and then placing a hand on their heads before they could move, suggesting a long nap would be a good idea. The sleep he suggested was one that a jackhammer by their heads would not even rouse them from.

Flying back to the house, he faded out using Hide and made a circuit of the building, investigating where everyone was located. He found Bree in a room upstairs, along with a man he presumed was the Greg she had told him about and Tony's boy. At the back of the house, he found one more man and a woman. His defences were up, and he was glad when he sensed her searching for the touch she had felt.

They were next to be taken out. He wanted to try and separate them, attacking each one on their own. The woman was the first he wanted to disable. Her mind was quick and sharp with Mind Touch. She had been trained well in her Talent, and he decided that she was the main threat to their rescue.

Rising up the side of the house, he found Addy where he had left her and came to rest beside her. "You all right?" he asked.

"Just wonderful. Are you going to get me down from here?" There was a note of panic coming from her, and he tried not to laugh.

"There are two downstairs. A woman and a man."

"I'll take the woman," Addy interrupted him.

"No—she has Mind Touch. I'd better deal with her. You can have the guy…I couldn't detect any Talent with him."

"No fair. I get the easy one," she replied in a pouty voice.

"Any more turn up and I will gladly leave them to you," he reassured her.

"Divide and conquer?" she suggested.

"You read my mind. You take the back and be careful. If that woman comes out your way, get out of there quick. She's good."

"Now get me down before I crumple into a heap."

"Are you afraid of heights?" Matt asked his cousin with amusement.

"Not of the heights, of the falling! Now get me down!"

Matt chuckled as he lifted her up again and they moved towards the back door. They landed and immediately pushed themselves into the shadows to hide.

"Give me a couple of minutes and keep your ears open. When you hear the front door, try to get in this one."

"Just go do your thing and leave this to me," she said and pushed him away.

Up and over the house he flew, landing by the front door. Thumping on it with a fist, he waited until he could hear footsteps on the other side of the door. It was the woman, just as he thought it would be. The defences on his mind were now slammed into place with more energy thrown in for good measure.

The door flew opened and a young woman stood before him, dressed impeccably. He noticed one cheek was bright red.

"Who are you?" she demanded.

"I've come for my daughter, you bitch." He stepped inside and used her surprise to his advantage. She was not ready for the great ball of light and energy he threw, making her stagger and then fall to the polished wooden floors. When the woman tried to get up and use her own mental Talent, he sent another and another, pushing her along the slippery floor until her body was slammed up against the wall.

The next ball covered her head and she tried to shake it off, but it refused to budge. Matt could feel the energy she had compiled inside herself trying to escape and be released against him, so he clamped the light harder around her, binding both mind and body with no escape for the energy. Her eyes went wide with fright when she realised that she was up against someone she could not best.

With a twist of his hand, he closed her mind down—turned off the metaphorical light switch—sending her into a darkness that he hoped she wouldn't return from anytime soon. He stood over the inert body, panting with the effort he had used.

A cry from the back of the house reminded him of his cousin, and he ran in blindly to find her. He burst into a room and found Addy kicking with her foot to smash the face of her opponent, dropping him like a stone to the floor in a bloody mess.

"You okay?" he asked, noticing a cut on her cheek.

"Yeah, I'm fine." She wiped the blood and smeared it across her face.

"How did you—?"

"When the boys took up karate, I decided it was probably a good idea I honed my skills. Pleased I did." She grinned.

"Why did I bother worrying about you? Come on." He headed out of the room and reached the bottom of the stairs.

Climbing them two at a time, he reached the top and walked down the hallway until he found the door he wanted. Standing outside, Matt reached in with his mind to find Bree. The sleeping child rolled over on her bed and smiled. Inside her mind, she ran to her father and into his arms.

"I'm here, my wee angel. Open the door for me. It's locked." He held her close.

"I can't—Greg has the key," Bree told him.

"Can you get it from him?"

"I'm sure he will let you in."

Matt could feel her get up from the bed and walk on silent feet to the sleeping form in the corner of the room. Through his daughter's eyes, this young man looked like he wouldn't hurt a fly, but he wasn't so sure. She reached out and shook his arm.

"Greg, you have to get up. Dad is here. He needs to get in," she called to him.

Greg grunted in his sleep and shifted in the seat, but he did not wake up. Bree came back to Matt and looked at him solemnly.

"I need you to leave my mind, Daddy. I have to do something, and I can't do it when you're in here."

"Be careful, Bree," Matt told her and drifted away to stand outside and wait with Addy.

It was only a matter of seconds before the key was being inserted into the lock on the other side of the door and the bolt was sliding back. It opened, and the young man Matt had seen was standing before them. He immediately stepped back and out of the way.

Bree launched herself into her father's arms for real, and Matt kissed her little face and held her close, reconnecting with her. He looked over her shoulder at Greg, who was sitting on the bed, unsure of what to do or how to act.

Still clasping Bree in his arms, Matt held out his hand to Greg, who looked at it suspiciously. "I just want to thank you for looking after Bree," Matt told him, and they clasped hands with a smile.

"She's pretty special," Greg admitted.

"I know that." Matt grinned back.

"Matt, I need you. I can't get to Johnny," Addy called from the other side of the room. Her hands were up and moving like she was miming an invisible wall.

"Mummy put it there to protect us," Bree told him in his ear. "You have to take it down."

"How did you get out of it, then?" The only response Matt got from her was a small smile. He put her down and went to stand by Addy.

In his mind, he went to find the information on light that he knew was there. Opening his eyes again, he changed the way he saw and there it was: a shimmering and swirling golden light barrier. Matt laid his palm on it, feeling it move and undulate. It began to swirl faster and faster until it ripped apart and shattered, falling to the ground in a curtain of sparks.

Addy, who was still pushing against it, fell forward, stumbling and catching herself on the bed before she landed on the small boy. The jolt woke Johnny, who immediately curled himself into a ball, a whimper escaping from his lips. Bree was at his side straight away and held his hand.

"It's all right, Johnny. It's my dad and aunty come to rescue us," Bree tried to give him reassurance.

Greg was there instantly, picking him up and holding him. "They aren't here to hurt you. I promise. They're here to take you back to your dad, Johnny."

"Can you help us get them out of here?" Matt asked Greg.

"Yeah, I can. James has gone with Claire. Do you want to go get her first?" Greg asked him, seeking some guidance.

"No, this is my job—to get the kids to safety. As much as I want to go tearing off after her, I know my wife can look after herself." The tight smile Matt gave belied his words.

Downstairs, they were headed to the door when Addy stopped suddenly over the woman and looked at her.

"I know her! She's my hairdresser!" she exclaimed.

"That's Susie Foster. James had a thing for her once. But she wanted Marcus more," Greg said, not even stopping to look at her. He was still carrying Johnny when he opened the front door and rushed out into the night.

Matt handed Bree to Addy and told her to get to the car. He waited until they had left the house to try and reverse some of what he had done to this woman. Banishing the light bindings, he checked her pulse and was relieved to find one. Placing a hand on her forehead and pushing into her mind, he found a mess. It was all confusion and clutter, as if he had shaken her mind like a snow globe.

He searched everywhere to find her life force and was just about to give up when he found it. A pathetic-looking thing crawled towards a large black mass in the centre of her mind.

He picked it up and fed it energy. He could feel her reviving and restrained her carefully.

"You will recover slowly. I don't know if you will have your Talent after this, but I had no choice. You had my daughter captive, and I needed her back."

He pulled her away from the blackness and set her into her subconscious to heal, then checked her again once he was out. Standing up, he turned and didn't look back, feeling guilty for having to hurt her. If this was only half of what Claire went through with Jack, he now understood why she felt she had to run.

The worry now was her facing Marcus. He looked up the gully to the hills silhouetted against the cloudy sky, and his mind sought her out as the heavens opened up in a large downpour of rain. She was there somewhere. He could feel her, but she was blocking him. Matt sent a feeling of love and understanding and then got in the car beside Bree.

From around the large rocks Breena strode, the wind pulling at her hair and dress as she approached the car. Gerry got out and ran around to help Gran from her seat before they greeted her. She led them to the stones, and they stood in the shelter of the rocks, looking at the circle.

"What is it that we have to do, Breena?" Gerry asked his daughter.

"All we have to do is stand in the centre of the circle and join our energy. The stones will help us, but we must be the focus for Claire. I don't like this, Da. Claire is going to get hurt and I can't be there. I'm tied here." Her frustration at the situation was evident, and he put his arm around her.

"If this is all we can do, then do it we must, to the very best of our abilities. Claire will have help there. She has support."

"When do we enter?" Gran asked, hugging herself against the cold wind.

"Soon. They should be here soon, Gran." She left them to stand by the spring and look down the hill. "They're coming up now."

Gran went to her side and stood watching the procession coming up the hill. The sight of it brought her back to her younger years, and she gasped at it.

"I never thought I would see it again." She clasped her granddaughter's hand.

"You will see it one more time after this, Gran, but not for a few more years yet. Come. We'll wait for them by the rocks." Hand in hand, they walked back to Gerry and waited for the Guardians to join them.

They broached the hill and walked to the spring, chanting softly as they moved, then turned to the stones. One by one, the hooded figures entered the circle and took up their places in the gaps. Breena led them into the circle, and as Gran and Gerry passed through the entrance, they could feel the power of the stones for the first time. They felt the energy rushing through them and could hear the humming noise they made. Gran's eyes opened in surprise at the feeling, and she stood more erect and walked more freely than she had in a few years, the aches and pains that had become a daily occurrence eased and abated.

Breena turned to them and held out her hands, and they clasped one each, completing the circle. The Guardians began their rhythmic chant in an ancient and long-forgotten language, their arms reaching into the circle, blessing the three who stood there.

The air around them was still, but outside the stones, the wind was starting to increase. The clouds were darkening, thickening, dropping lower onto the landscape until they enveloped the hillside. The mist became so thick that the rocks, which only stood a few steps away, became lost in the grey light. The air became charged with not only the energy the Guardians were feeding it, but also the buildup of static electricity.

Gran and Gerry closed their eyes to the sights around them, wishing they could close their ears to the roaring of the wind as it now tore around them, bending the long grass over on itself. Breena was watching outside the circle and a half a world away, waiting for the moment when they were to fully release their combined efforts and send them in aid of Claire. The images swirled in front of her eyes as she watched the white figure of Claire walking through a deeply wooded forest, a man on either side of her.

A bolt of lightning split the air as it landed close to them. Their handholds nearly faltered at the shock of it, but they held firm and gripped each other tightly. The tempest was rising, and the rain began to fall heavily in large, fat drops, which thumped onto the ground as they exploded. Inside the circle, they remained dry.

The air crackled and sparked around the circle. Little bolts of electricity leapt from one stone to the next, arcing blue and gold down the faces. The force was almost too much for Breena to bear. She tried to keep it in check for the moment it was needed. She looked up at the sky above her, and it shone down through a tunnel of circling and swirling cloud. The moment was coming, and she prepared herself for her final act on this mortal world.

Chapter Twenty-Three

The car came to a halt at the end of the road. Marcus got out and opened the back door for Claire and James to exit. He slammed the door behind them, shoved a blanket into the free hand of James, and then held out an arm for Claire to take. This time she didn't hesitate at the touch, and he guided her to the start of the new track his men had cleared. Her impractical high heel shoes already sunk into the soft earth. They walked under the canopy of the trees, and the water eased slightly.

The rain was picking up and the wind was blowing the tops of trees, bending them, and shaking the water from their leaves. They walked carefully, with Claire in the middle of their little procession, the ground wet and slippery under their feet. The further in they went, the more it rained. The clouds were now down on the hill and the mist through the trees gave it a mystical look as it swirled and eddied around the trunks and bushes.

Finally, they came to the edge of the clearing, and Claire gained her first look at the stones Marcus had erected. Each one was so close to its twin in Scotland—so much so, it looked like he had transported it from its sacred seat in the hills to this little gully in New Zealand. Each large stone had replaced the original green that the guardians of this land had brought forth, and the energy they emitted was dark.

A flash of lightning from somewhere on the hill lit up the area in a stark white light and the wind kept increasing, tearing at her dress and hair. She breathed in the smell of the electrical storm, and an image of three people standing together came to her. They were there. She sighed in relief. She was not alone. Inside her chest, the yellow bloom opened more, and the golden centre was exposed—the heart of the flower from which the seeds were made. The scent from it poured out the love that was stored there.

Marcus pulled her across the cleared ground. Claire tripped, and he dragged her up, impatient to get to the circle. He could feel the power of it increasing with each second, and it aroused him. He would have her completely that night—in mind, body, and spirit, and his plan would be almost complete.

At the entrance to this circle, they stopped briefly before stepping over the threshold. Once inside, there was no storm. The winds had died, and the air was crackling with energy. Claire looked around her and could see the stones sparking with it, impatient for release and condoning the union that should not be. It was an evil-feeling place, so dark and foreboding that it chilled the spirit. She trembled—not from the cold air of the depths of winter, but from the feeling in the stones.

Taking the blanket from James, Marcus laid it out in the direct centre of the circle. He led Claire to it, pushing her to lie down on the rough wool, and stood over her. With arms raised to the sky, which showed the stars in a tunnel of cloud, he called out in a guttural voice that was not his. He turned lust-filled eyes down, devouring her hungrily with them. Marcus was no longer there. Behind his eyes now lay another entity.

"Don't do this, Mr. Ryder. Please, don't do this," James cried out to him, but Marcus could not hear his pleas.

"Take my hand, James." Claire looked into his eyes. "Just hold my hand and don't look. You will know what to do."

Marcus lowered himself down onto his knees and pulled her legs apart. He fumbled with the zip in his trousers as he pushed the muddied dress higher up her legs, feeling her thighs as he went, and then ripped the underwear from her body. She cried out with disgust and horror that it was going to happen.

From outside the circle, a call could be heard along with the sound of bushes cracking under the weight of men. Bursting into the clearing, two shadowy shapes emerged, and they ran to the circle. One faltered and stumbled to his knees. Unable to get any closer to the stones, he cried out in frustration. The other was there, stalking around it, his body buffeted by the winds and rain. A flash of lightning lit up his features, and Claire recognised Tony.

She turned her gaze from him and looked to James. He had his head down and was sobbing. She felt his frustration building and knew it would be soon. The stones were now racing with dark energy, arcing like their counterparts in Scotland, and she looked up into the heavens as Marcus started to mount her.

Her mind exploded with the energy she had pent up, waiting for this very moment, and time seemed to slow down as she watched everything happen at once. Breena came into focus and Claire saw her release the combined efforts up into the clear blue sky of Scotland, sending it forth with all the love they could spare.

Into the very centre of the circle, a great blue bolt of lightning and energy crackled and burst over Marcus. His body arched, and he fell from Claire. James, leaping back to save himself, grabbed the remains of one of the original stones someone had carelessly left behind, and brought it down hard on Marcus's exposed head. With their energy broken, the stones fell backwards and shattered into small pieces. Tony ran to Claire and picked her up, carrying her out of harm's way. Beside them in short order was David, sweat and rain coursing down his face as he took Claire from Tony.

Tony walked back over to Marcus, snarling at the man. He was already gathering a killing light to his hand when Claire called out. He stopped, and breathing heavily, he dispelled it and clenched his fists.

"Not yet," Claire told him, freeing herself from David's arms. She walked over to his side and took his hand. "Not yet. I want him awake and fully aware of what is happening to him first."

Her anger was spilling over, and she was squeezing his hand tightly. He nodded his agreement and knelt beside his grandfather. The man had disowned and killed his mother, refused to acknowledge him, murdered his wife, and taken his son from him. This man created nothing but misery and heartache for anyone he knew and could not love anyone but himself. This man could not see that love was stronger than hate.

Placing a hand over the wound James had inflicted, he healed the bleeding gash and then sank deeper into the skull. The bones he knitted back together so well that no one would be able to tell that they had been broken. Further in, Tony dispelled the bruising and bleeding on the brain, reconnecting the neurons. He then set about waking him.

The breathing that had been ragged was now easing into a normal rhythm, and his eyes fluttered. Opening them up, he saw Tony first and he grew angry. With difficulty, he stood and faced the man who was his grandson, the same height and colouring. Only the eyes were different.

"James, attack him," Marcus ordered.

"No. I am done taking orders from you," James said, dropping the bloodied rock that was still in his hands.

"I will kill your sister!" Marcus screamed at him.

"I don't think you will be doing much of anything after this." James looked at Tony. "Do you want me to hold him?"

"Thank you. That would be very kind of you," Tony said with a nasty smile, still staring at Marcus.

James came up behind Marcus and grasped his arms behind his back tightly, making the older man grunt in pain. He pushed him back onto the trampled blanket and stood him directly in the centre of the broken stones.

"Nice touch. When we're done, I'd like to talk to you about your future job prospects," Tony said.

James just nodded and held on tighter to the wrists of his tormentor.

Claire came to stand in front of the older man, and he smiled at her. "You don't have the guts to kill me. All that talk back at the house was only bluster. I could see through you. You don't have it in you to hurt me."

"Don't I?" She waved her hand in front of his eyes and watched them open as big as saucers.

The image she showed was that of Jack being held by Tony, just as James held him now. The ghost of Claire produced a spark and slipped it into Jack's chest, the light fading from his eyes as the life left him. Then Tony lifted and threw the limp form off the hill, down the brook that emerged from the sacred spring.

Marcus's head shook in disbelief. "No, you lie. You are too gentle and soft to do such a thing. You wouldn't do the same to me. I don't believe it," he spluttered. Claire could feel the dark presence ebbing from his mind and body, already deserting the condemned flesh of his puppet.

"You're right. This time it is not my turn. This time is a time of direct family. I do not belong to your family. But there is one here who does." She turned and looked at Tony.

"How did you know?" he asked her.

"Is there really any need to ask that question? You are a descendant of his, and it's your right to take his life if you so choose. What do you choose, Anthony Marcus Benning?" There was no demand in her voice, no hardness, only the gentleness of one who had been in a similar position.

"It is my choice, and for the sake of those who descend from Adam and myself, I choose to rid this world of his evil."

"Done," Claire intoned. She pulled off the ring Marcus had placed on her finger, turned back to face him, and threw it at his feet.

The desperation was written in his eyes as it dawned on him what his fate was to be. Marcus began to shake. His knees went weak and sagged against James's hold. The younger man jerked him back to his feet.

"Face it like a man, you bastard," James whispered in his ear. "For all those innocent people you have killed."

"Well said, James. I would like to add my own to that. Enjoy your death, Marcus. It is long overdue." Claire walked away from them, back into the reassuring arms of her uncle, and buried her face into his shoulder.

The moment had come. She thought she could watch with great satisfaction the death of this man but found she couldn't. The idea of killing was still abhorrent to her, and she was glad that it wasn't up to her to do so. It would have ripped her apart, shredding her soul to the wind.

Claire heard a gasp from behind and then a gurgling sound of breath escaping the body for the last time. Images of Jack floated back to her, and she squeezed her eyes harder, trying to block them. She clung tightly to David, who gave comfort as much as he could, lending support for her weakening legs and quietening the sobs when they came.

The clearing was quiet and still. The sudden storm had blown itself out with the final act from Tony. It was as if the world celebrated the passing of the evil by being calm and taking a sighing breath. Droplets of water still escaped from the canopy above, dropping down with a song of their own, racing to the brook that would carry them away to the river in the main valley and out to sea.

When she took courage and looked up, Claire saw James standing over Marcus's body, giving it a swift kick, then stalking out of the stones to stand with her. Tony was still where he was, his own body now shaking. He let out a great cry of loss. His pain enveloped him and was released in that shout. He stood breathing heavily, then stooped, picking up the edge of the blanket. Tugging at it hard, he rolled the shell that had been Marcus off it and then turned, carrying it over to the group watching him.

Covering Claire with the damp blanket to protect her from the winter air, he then picked her up in his arms.

"We'll pick the ute up tomorrow, David. James's car is closer. I want to get back to my son."

"James, please lead the way," David urged.

They turned to leave and found their way barred. A group of seven in dark robes stood before them, their hands clasped in front and their faces hidden under the large cowls.

"Greetings to the One True Child, Carling. The task is not yet complete. There is still one thing to be done," the middle figure spoke.

Tony placed Claire down on her feet once more and pushed her behind him. "No. She is finished. There is nothing else," he cried out to them.

"The body of Marcus, last of his name, must be disposed of. It cannot lie here—it must be scourged from the earth. As long as there are the bones of his body, the evil that was contained in him shall have access to the world."

"You want us to burn him?" Claire asked, coming to stand in front of them.

"We do, Daughter," a woman spoke sadly.

Claire looked back at the broken circle and the body that remained there, and then back at the Guardians. "Can you promise me one thing before I do this?" she asked them.

"If it is in our power to so grant it, then we do," another spoke.

"When this is all over and everything is finished, will you please explain it all to me?" she asked.

"Daughter, we will do so willingly," the woman said.

Claire shrugged off the blanket and handed it to David, then made her way over the slippery ground to the circle. When she stepped back inside, there was no feeling of power or energy remaining, and she breathed a sigh of relief. The husk of Marcus's body was lying faceup, his eyes staring blankly up at the now clear and starry sky. Claire leaned down and shut them carefully. His flesh was still warm to the touch, and she shivered from it.

Standing once more, Claire drew energy from the surrounding bush, pulling it from the earth and from those standing near. Carefully, she created a light in between both of her hands. It glowed brightly with golden sparks hidden in its depths. The light grew and became more intense—so much so, the others all shielded their eyes from it.

Claire released the light to encompass the body, binding itself to it and burning away the flesh. Great golden and white-hot flames flared into the sky, reaching high—but Claire stayed where she was, unaffected by them. Her concentration kept the flames going, pushing them on to consume everything and leave nothing but ash in their wake.

When she was done, when the body had gone to dust and was now blowing on the wind, Claire collapsed to her knees. Her hands rested on her thighs, eyes streaming with tears, back bent with sobs. It was done.

Tony was there with the blanket, wrapping it around her shoulders once more and picking her up, carrying her away from the ash remains. The Guardians each lined up and laid a hand on her head in blessing as Tony passed them.

In their own little procession, the small group left the clearing without a word. James, then David followed, with Tony holding Claire in the rear. He held her close, and she wrapped her arms around his neck, finding comfort in his embrace. But it was not his comfort she was wanting, was yearning for. His were not the arms she wanted around her.

The drive back to the farmhouse seemed to take forever to Claire. The dark clouds were breaking up and the moon began to show her face, illuminating the landscape around them with its gentle silvery glow. The village was there with sparkling streetlights and windows long dark, as the residents were all abed. She felt their dreams as they passed them by, and her spirits began to soar as they headed out the other side.

Along the road they travelled, this well-worn road she had run down so many times on her way to her uncle's house. Past Janie's paddock, the horse looking like a ghost standing in the dark. Past the many fields, fences, and hedges, past the ditch where she had been hit by the car so many years ago now. Then the gates of the farm. Up the gravel drive, taking them straight to the door.

The porch light glowed warmly to welcome them home. The door burst open and he was there, running down the steps and up to the car before it had come to a full stop. The door was wrenched open and Matt had her in his arms—his strong, loving arms. The love had sustained her through everything she had gone through. He carried her out of the car and up those worn steps and into the house, not waiting for the others to join them.

By a roaring fire he placed her and held her close to share his warmth. Matt gazed into her eyes and held her face in his, then gave a kiss, so gently, so softly that it was barely a kiss. He smoothed the hair from her face and caressed her cheek, drinking in her beauty, feeling like they had back when they first met—so nervous, but so in love. Then he kissed her again stronger and harder, wrapping his arms around her tightly, bringing their bodies closer. When he finally broke the kiss, Claire was crying. The emotions had broken inside and spilled out softly. These were not the horror-bound sobs that David and Tony had calmed, but a happy and love-filled acceptance Matt had given her.

There would be plenty of time to talk later. The truth of what had happened would be laid bare between them, as it always was. She would hide nothing from him, and he would accept it all and help her heal, caring for and loving her as he always would.

On the hill so far away from the farmhouse stood three people, their hands still clasped together, a small family united. The Guardians had left when the last of the blue lightning disappeared, along with the storm that had blown in. The sun now shone down on them, and the wind was gone. It was a warm afternoon, and it was reflected in the love they felt for each other.

Breena smiled and hated to do what she must. After her last act on this mortal world, she was now expected to leave and join the Guardians permanently, along with her mother. She hugged her Gran to her and kissed her cheek, wiping the tears from the old lady's eyes.

"I will be here when it is your turn, Gran. I will be your guide to the other side as I was with Mum. But that is not for many a long year. There is still one more thing you have to witness before you join us. My love will be with you until we meet again." Breena hugged her once more.

"I look forward to it, Breena. I look forward to it." Gran fished around in her pocket for her handkerchief and dabbed at her eyes.

"Da. We have to say goodbye again." Breena's eyes were filling at the thought. "I had hoped I could stay longer with you."

"Ah, lass, you are called where you must go. We will all be together again." He took his daughter in his arms, making the most of the time they had left together. "Tell your mother I love her and always will."

"I will, Da. You will have visitors soon," she told him.

Giving him a quick kiss on the cheek, she turned and started to walk from the stones. When she reached the entrance, she turned and waved at them both, a glistening tear falling from her cheek and down into the grass. As she left the stones, she faded from view with not even a footprint to say she had been there.

Gerry sighed and took Gran's arm, helping her from the stone circle. Something sparkling in the grass caught his attention, and he stopped to look. Lying on a blade of glass, glittering in the sunlight, was a perfectly clear gem in the shape of a teardrop. He smiled, picked it up, and held it up to the sun. A flash of a ring came to his mind, and he tucked the gem into his pocket. Gran smiled up at him, nodding her silent agreement, and then they made their way to the old Land Rover.

Claire lay in the bed she shared with Matt, staring into the darkness of the room. She was clean, dry, and warm and could feel sleep knocking on the door, but she just couldn't seem to get there. Matt rolled over and placed an arm over her, drawing him to her as he did.

"I know you're awake. I can hear the cogs going around," he murmured in her ear, kissing her neck.

"There's something missing."

"Nothing is missing…you are here, and Bree is safe."

"Breena," Claire said softly back. She slipped into her mind and called out for her sister-in-law. As she did, she drew in Matt and Bree. The tired girl was rubbing her eyes and demanding her father pick her up.

"Claire, can't we do this later?" he asked her as Bree laid her head on his shoulder.

"No. It needs to be now. I can feel her slipping away from me." The urgency in which she spoke brought him fully awake. "Breena, where are you?"

"I am here, Carling. I was always here." She came out of the darkness and joined them. "My time is short now. We must make our farewells quick."

Claire took Breena's hand in hers and felt the cool touch that came with them. "Thank you for your help tonight. I couldn't have done it without you."

"My sister, it was you who did most of it. I was just the conduit for the energy. All will be well, Carling. You will have the quiet life that you wanted. I wish you all the happiness in the world." Breena kissed Claire and held her close briefly before taking her brother's hand.

"You, Galen, look after these two and the one on the way. I shall miss you, my brother. I wish we had grown up together as it was planned. I could have had a lot of fun teasing you." She smiled at him.

"And I you," he said with a choked voice. "Is this really goodbye? You won't be visiting at all?"

"No, Galen, I won't. This is goodbye. If I see you again—" Her voice was lost in a sob, and she gathered him and Bree up in her arms. Bree lifted her head and kissed Breena on the cheek.

"Goodbye, Aunty Breena. I will look after them," the little girl said softly. "And you will be with me in my heart."

"Goodbye, my wee angel." Breena pulled away and looked at the little family. "Take care."

As she backed away, Breena kept her eyes on them for as long as possible before she faded into the dark. Matt, Claire, and Bree held on to each other for the longest time afterwards before Claire let them slide back out of her mind.

Matt sniffed in her ear, and she rolled over in his arms and kissed him, holding him close and letting him grieve once more for his sister. It had been a cruel thing that he had to endure this process three times now, and each was as raw as the last. She held him until he fell asleep, and she was sure he was dreaming, then kissed his forehead once more and closed her own eyes.

Dawn was not that far away, and it broke over the valley with a bright golden light. The world felt fresh and new after the storm of the night before, and the birds sang from the treetops with a vigour that talked of a promised spring. The familiar sound filtered through to the unconscious brain of Claire and she lay there enjoying it, thinking back to another time when it wasn't so well-loved by her.

Careful not to wake Matt, she left the warmth and comfort of the bed and got up. Dressed in only one of his old T-shirts, Claire looked in his bags to find something else to wear when she noticed her own luggage up against the wall. Gently she opened it and pulled out her own clothes and dressed, then quietly left the room, and went downstairs.

Out on the steps of the porch, she stopped to put her sneakers on and then headed down the drive without a noise to alert anyone she was going. The run was cathartic and renewed old memories. The road passed under her feet at a quick pace, and she soon was at Janie's paddock. The old horse was on the other side and whinnied a greeting to Claire, who waved at her and kept going. On and on she ran, feeling the sun warming her face and dispelling the nightmares she had experienced during her sleep.

The Village came into view and she stopped just short, not wanting to run into anyone she knew. She turned and ran back down the road she had just passed. Janie was waiting for her at the fence when she returned, and Claire stopped to greet her old friend, pulling a red apple from her pocket that she had grabbed before leaving.

"You didn't think I would forget, did you, old girl?" It took the horse a while to eat the apple she held out for her to take. Claire patted her neck and leaned her head against the warmth of the horse she had known for years.

"It is a good thing you do for me, Claire," the horse responded in her head. "I have missed our talks."

"As have I, Janie. Are you well?" Claire asked, rubbing her ears and neck.

"As well as an old horse can be. It has been a good life here, and I am grateful for it." Janie nudged her.

Claire looked up. "I think you're about to get another apple," she told her old friend as she felt the presence of her uncle coming down the road. She was impressed by how fit he still was at his age and wondered if his Talent had something to do with that—or whether it was just the work he did around the farm. Claire looked around Janie's long face and waved at him.

"I thought I would find you here," he said as he joined her and fed the horse another apple. "There you go, you old thing." He rubbed one of her ears and patted her nose. "I introduced Matt to Janie the other day. He was getting frustrated that we weren't doing anything, so I took him out for a run. We ended up here."

"I always seem to end up here, talking to her. She has been a great confidant all these years."

"She has indeed. I didn't think you would be up for hours yet after last night." He watched her carefully.

"I'm fine, Uncle David. I needed to run, get rid of it all."

"As long as you are, we are all here to help and talk to if you need us."

"I know, but there is only one I need to talk to right now, and he's still fast asleep." She brushed her thoughts over Matt's dreaming ones. "What about you? You must be exhausted, old man!"

"Less of the *old*, please. Although I did feel it out there last night. Those stones were awful. Their effect on me was not nice." He shuddered at the memory.

"Those stones are going to have to be dealt with. We can't leave them up there. It all needs to be destroyed and taken away." There was anger in her voice again, and she tried to push it down.

"I'm thinking it would not be a good idea for either of us to go back there. I'll talk to Tony when he gets up. *If* he gets up."

"Is she that beautiful?" Claire asked curiously.

"Is this coming from just curiosity or from somewhere else?"

"Curiosity only. I love him like a brother, and I'm just interested in who he's seeing."

David processed what she had said and tried to see anything else in it. "She is beautiful, inside, and out. Tia is a lovely girl, and I think she's well-suited to him. But you know this already. Why ask me?"

"Doesn't hurt to have confirmation, Uncle David." She smiled at him. Claire gave the horse one more pat. "I will see you tomorrow and bring you another apple," she told the horse.

"I would be grateful for that," the horse replied eagerly with anticipation.

Claire and David started to walk back to the house. "How did you know about Tony?" he asked, his own curiosity driving him. Since the night before, he had tried to puzzle it out. He felt certain it was not something Tony himself would have offered up to her.

"It was one of those flash moments when everything seemed to fit. He told me he hadn't known his parents, but that he met his mother before she died. Plus, I did have a bit of help with other things that had been planted in my memories. When I saw them standing opposite each other, the resemblance was uncanny, except for the eyes. Tony's are much kinder than his grandfather's. Does Adam know?"

"I haven't told him. Tony asked me not to. Though if it were up to me, I would tell him in a moment."

"It's not up to either of us to spill that particular can of worms." She sighed and looked out over the fields. Janie was keeping pace with them along the fence line, still hopeful for more apples.

David placed a comforting arm around her shoulders, and they walked back to the house. There was no need for words. He could feel she wasn't ready to discuss anything. It was a pattern Claire had formed whenever something unpleasant happened to her. But this time, the things that had happened to her were worse than she had ever experienced, and he felt the change.

At his touch, which she had always accepted unquestioningly for comfort in the past, there was now a tenseness in her stance. There was a piece she held back from him that she never had before, and it worried him, but he refused to pull back from her. He would be there for her no matter what. He owed his sister that much, to look out for her child.

They reached the front steps to the house, and David stopped her before they started the climb up to the front door. He held her by the shoulders and pulled her into a big bear hug, dropping a kiss on her head.

"Remember, we love you, Claire. We all do," he told her.

"I know—I do know. Just give me time, Uncle David," she replied into his chest.

"I can smell Beth's French toast. Come on. Let's get some breakfast." He smiled down at her and they entered the house.

The kitchen was crowded with people crammed in together around the small, round table. Chairs from the formal dining room had been brought in, and Dominic and Cameron sat on their parents' laps to eat. It was noisy and comforting, and as they entered, David and Claire were greeted warmly.

"We were just about to send out a search party for you," Adam called out to them both.

Matt caught Claire's eye, and he didn't need to reach her mind to find she was still dealing with the last few days. He gave her a small smile, and from his knee, Bree smiled as well. She walked over to them and leant down, giving them a kiss each. Nikau stood up and offered his seat to her, then left the room.

When he returned, he gave a file to Adam to look at.

"You wanted this when things had settled down. I thought you should see it now." Nikau gave Adam a wink, leaning on the kitchen counter with his arms folded across his chest.

Adam opened the file carefully and looked at the contents over the head of Dominic on his knee. He gave no indication of what was inside, and he closed the file and looked at Nikau.

"Is this all true?" he asked him.

"Yep. Every word. It's up to you what you do with it." Nikau replied.

Adam handed it over to Tony, who took the offered folder without even thinking of it. "You dare call me uncle and I will kill you," Adam said to him with a deadpan face.

Tony looked at Adam and then at Nikau. "You gave him this?"

"Of course. I told you that if you mess with my sister, I would have to do something drastic in return." Nikau was smiling at his business partner, but it wasn't in smugness or with any ill intent. It was a genuine, happy smile.

"Would someone like to enlighten the rest of us?" Addy asked, looking around them.

"Tony is my nephew," Adam said simply. "His mother was apparently my sister, Marcus's daughter." He looked to Tony for confirmation.

"Yep, something like that. I was going to tell you at some stage, but—well, you know."

"Your family is fucked," Jasper said with a smile to his half-brother. "No offence."

"Jasper Curtis Fuller!" Beth called out, wagging a finger at her eldest son. "He's your family as well, remember."

The tension was broken, and everyone laughed. They had all been waiting for Beth to explode at the use of bad language in her house, but this comment of hers was the tonic that was needed for them all to remember that in one way or another, they were all related.

"Well, I hope the family troubles are all over and everything is settled soon," Claire called out and looked at Matt, who nodded back to her. He couldn't have thought of a better time to tell them all.

"Because we have some news of our own," he finished for her, and then looked around the room. "We have two pieces of news. The first is that we are moving to Scotland. I have a new job there. And the second—"

"Is that I'm going to be a big sister!" Bree piped up from his lap.

There was silence as everyone stared at her, then at Matt and Claire for confirmation of her words. They nodded their affirmations, and then they were swamped with congratulations.

Later in the afternoon, Claire was outside enjoying the cool winter sunshine. She needed some time by herself after the frenetic past week. She had told Matt what happened, and all that Marcus had put her through, and he was now in the process of digesting it himself. Not once during her telling did he accuse her of not fighting him off or not trying hard enough to get away, but he held her gently in his arms to try and help her deal with the intense feelings that were still with her. He was her rock, but he still needed to come to terms with things as well so they could move forward with their life together and put it all behind them.

Claire was standing under the large tree in the backyard, her back against the rough bark, and was looking out over the fields when she heard the back door open. She remained still and felt for whoever it was that was heading her way. It was Tia, and she became curious as to what this woman wanted.

"Hi," Tia called to her. "I was looking for Tony. I thought he might be out here."

"He took the kids down to the river with Adam a short time ago. They have a lot to discuss," Claire said with a smile.

"That was a cruel thing my brother did." Claire could see that she was ashamed of his actions.

"No. It needed to come out. That family needs to heal itself after all the damage Marcus did, and the only way that can be done is with truthfulness." Claire cocked her head to one side and looked deep inside Tia's heart. "You love him, don't you?"

"Yes. I do. Do you have a problem with that?" Claire felt Tia's defences immediately come up between them, and she smiled at her.

"No. Just treat him right. He deserves to be happy, and you will make him happy. I can see that." For the first time since all the Talents had been given to her, Claire used one that she had promised herself that she wouldn't, and her eyes opened wide with what she saw.

"Wow, you are going to have some life together. I hope you and I can be friends, because I want to be there when it all happens to you two," Claire grinned.

"Oh great. Another Mystic Meg. I don't believe in all that bullshit, Claire, so don't start spouting off about how happy we're going to be." Tia turned to go but stopped and looked back at the woman she had been jealous of for years.

Claire closed the gap between them and took her hand. In a moment, she was showing Tia exactly what it was she had seen for them.

"You were there in my mind. I joined your hands. This was meant to be, Tia…enjoy it, enjoy him. His love will be boundless with you. You are the only woman that can make him happy. Maddison and I were just the warmup. With you, he will be a complete person again. Don't hold yourself back because you think he will hurt you—he never could. I never understood him properly, could never see the kindness, the gentleness inside him, but you do. Love him, Tia."

She let her hand go, and the two women stood looking at each other. Tears sprang into Tia's eyes just as they did in Claire's. Claire embraced the woman before her and held her close. "Please don't shut us out of your lives. I would like to get to know you both as friends—very good friends."

"I don't think I would have a choice in that, Claire. He still loves you deeply."

"That is what worries you, but it's a different love. He made a very solemn vow to my parents when they died to keep an eye on me. Tony still means to keep that vow. I never wanted his love, never accepted it. The only way I can love and accept him is like a brother, Tia, and he knows that. But I'm not the light in his heart. I'm not the woman he looks at with such intensity. That *is* you."

"But he doesn't look at me. He avoids my gaze every time I'm in the same room as he is." She pushed herself out of Claire's arms and dashed the tears from her eyes.

"Are you so sure?" Claire smiled. "Just wait until tonight. Addy and I will be on his case, and you will see who he looks at the most."

"You lot are really interfering, aren't you?"

"Of course—how do you think we got our husbands?" Claire laughed and linked arms with her, and they walked back to the house. "Believe me when I say that Tony hasn't got a chance in hell of getting away from you."

Chapter Twenty-Four

Claire stared into space, stirring the gravy she was making to go with the delicious-smelling lamb roast that filled the small kitchen. She didn't know where the years had gone. One minute she was a gangly seventeen-year-old living in New Zealand, having her world shaken to its core, and now she was turning forty-five, with two children and living in Scotland with the most wonderful man.

Her eldest daughter was now twenty-one and was doing well in her own life. Bree had another year at university until her degree was done, and she was a free spirit who enjoyed every moment of her life. Claire looked up and was startled once more to see the beauty she had grown into, so much like her aunt and namesake. Claire had often caught her husband looking to see any sign of the sister he still missed so terribly.

The son who was born shortly after the move was so different from his sister in looks. While Bree had dark hair and the bright blue eyes of her father, Callum was blond and had his mother's kind, gentle eyes. At fifteen years old, he towered over her already and was soon going to be even bigger than his father. He was built more like a Brown or a Fuller, her Uncle David had declared when they last visited. He had also inherited other traits from his mother, as well.

"Bree, you are getting it all wrong. Mum! Bree hasn't set the table properly," Callum called out in his deep voice that had just developed to go with his height.

"I have not, you snot!" Bree exclaimed as she looked at the table and then began moving the cutlery around to where it should be before heading quickly up the stairs.

Claire looked carefully at her daughter and a small smile crept over her face. Bree had tried so hard to hide her nervousness at who was coming to dinner. She thought her secret was safe. But Claire had seen this secret years ago, had been shown signs of it when she was still six.

The door opened behind her, and Matt walked in. His hair was now tinged with silver that made him more distinguished, with some of it tipping the edges of his ginger beard. His eyes immediately began to twinkle the moment he saw her, and he came up behind her to give her a squeeze, planting a ticklish kiss on the space between her neck and shoulder.

"Aw, yuck, you two. Get a room," their son yelled out to them from the living room.

"Sounds like a good idea to me," Matt said into her ear.

"We don't have time for that—they'll be here soon," Claire said, carefully extracting his arms from her. "Did you get the wine?"

He picked up the bags he had deposited on the counter and held up two bottles, then indicated a third. "And I got a new bottle of that Scotch you two like."

"Good, because you drank the last of the other bottle the other night," Claire threw at him good-naturedly.

Matt opened the bottle of red to let it breathe and placed it on the table. The doorbell pealed through the house, and he turned to go answer it. From upstairs, there came thumping feet and Bree flew down the stairs, reaching the door before her father could.

"What's the hurry?" he asked her. But the only reply he got was a tight smile as she smoothed her wayward hair from her face, and then opened the door for their guests.

Standing before them was a tall man with wavy salt-and-pepper hair and a crinkled smile that reached his dark eyes. He stepped in and caught Matt up in a hug of friendship and was soon followed by his family.

"Tony, so great you could make it," Matt greeted him, taking the offered bottle from his hands, and looking at it. "Claire's in the kitchen. Hello, Tia. Come in, you lot, come in." He shut the door behind them.

"Tony…Tia." Claire came out and hugged them both. "Go through and sit down. Callum, go get some glasses, will you? I'm sure your Uncle Tony would like a drink."

"You know me too well, Claire," he told her and held out his hand to shake Callum's. "God, you're getting tall. You don't get that from your mother."

"Nah, I don't. Sometimes I think I was found on the doorstep." He smiled at his uncle and godfather.

Tia walked into the kitchen after Claire. "Is there anything I can do to help?" she asked.

"You could work your magic on the roast. I think I've overdone it again, but don't tell Matt," she said and smiled. "How have you been?"

"I'm good. And you?" Tia's words made Claire stop, and she looked at this woman who had taken Tony's heart.

"You know, too, don't you?" They both looked into the living room and watched Bree and Johnny, Tony's son from his previous marriage.

"He thinks he has hidden it from us. Do you know how they met up again?" Tia asked softly.

"A little. But she hasn't come out and said anything."

"What are we talking about?" another soft, feminine voice said beside them, and Claire jumped.

"Nothing that concerns you, Aroha. This is a private conversation between your aunt and me," Tia told her daughter.

"Is it about Johnny and Bree? Because I know all about it. He proposed," she answered with a large smile.

Tia and Claire looked at each other, down at Aroha, and then out into the living room with complete shock.

"How on earth did you find that out?" Tia demanded.

"I can get Johnny to tell me anything. You must know that by now, Mum." The girl smiled and left them to go sit by her father.

Claire noticed something else that she wasn't sure Tia would approve of. "Heads up on my son. I think we might have trouble there, too."

"Would that be a bad thing?" Tia smiled. "They would make a formidable team."

"He's only fifteen and she's only fourteen. How about we don't rush things between them yet?"

"Use your Talent, Claire. What does the future say?"

"No, I won't," Claire said and laughed. "Have a look at the roast, will you? I'm sure it's dry."

"Stop changing the subject." Tia chuckled.

The dinner was a great success, and Claire and Tia couldn't help but smile at each other from across the table and at their respective children's discomfort. The end of the meal was cleared away, and they all convened once more in the tiny lounge. Coffee and glasses of stronger drinks were handed around, and then Claire nudged Bree.

"Get on with it. You're killing Tia and me. I want to see the look of surprise on your father's and Tony's faces," she said under her breath.

"You know?" Bree was shocked at the statement.

"Of course. I'm your mother; now get on with it," Claire urged her.

Bree looked over at Johnny and nodded to him. His face suddenly turned a bright shade of red, and his nerves were clear to see. Claire's heart went out to him.

"Um, I have a bit of an announcement to make," he said quietly, then waited. Bree nudged him and gave him an encouraging smile. "Can I have your attention, everyone?" His face was going an even deeper shade of red as he raised his voice higher.

The room stopped, and now all attention was on him. He was the spitting image of his father, tall and very good-looking with the same eyes and hair. They waited for him to go on.

"Um, Bree and I have something to tell you all." He stopped and gulped as he built up the courage to go on. "We're getting married," he said quickly, the words tumbling over each other.

Claire's eyes darted from Matt to Tony to watch their reactions, and she wasn't disappointed. Matt turned to Tony first.

"Did you know about this?" he demanded.

"No, did you?"

"No, I had no idea that they were even seeing each other. When did you—?" Matt turned to his daughter.

"Last year, here in Glasgow," she said quietly but defiantly to her father.

"I recognised her from across the pub, and she walked up to me," Johnny said to his own father. His hand and Bree's were clasped tightly together.

"I think it's wonderful news. Callum, in the fridge you will find a bottle of champagne. Go get it, will you?" Claire asked before Matt and Tony could make any more comments.

"You knew?" Matt demanded, still shocked.

"I had an inkling something was up." Claire smiled at him. "And you two, don't pretend that you're not happy for them." She hugged Johnny and Bree.

The pop from the bottle broke the tension, and they all grouped together to congratulate the young couple. The evening became an even happier one. The chatter went on into the night as they rejoiced at the news. From over the noise, a phone rang, and Matt pulled his out of a pocket, heading to the relative quiet of the kitchen to take the call.

When he returned, Claire could see that it was not good news and was at his side in a flash. "It's Gran?" she asked quietly.

"Yeah. That was Dad. He said she is not good, that we should go up tomorrow."

"We'll pack tonight and leave first thing," she told him, her arm now around his waist.

"What do we tell them?" he indicated the happy group.

"The truth. Bree and Callum will want to be there, Matt." She looked at her daughter, and the insight she had knew that Bree should be there, that her happy news was what Gran was holding on for. "Do you want me to tell them?"

"No, I will. We'll wait for Tony and Tia to go."

"They are just as much family, Matt." Another little flash came to her, and she shook her head.

"You okay?" Matt asked, full of concern.

"They have to know, Matt. They have to be there," she said seriously, and he understood. Matt gave Claire a quick kiss, then moved into the group to give them the news.

The old Rover splashed through the ford, sending up sheets of water in its wake as it turned onto the gravel track. It made its way slowly up and stopped at the old oak. The great gnarled tree was resplendent with its new spring foliage, and it sat waiting for her. Bree jumped out and ran to its trunk, placing a hand on the rough bark. The tree still remembered her and welcomed her home. It was something she had always done since she was a little girl. The memory of another child was with her and this tree.

With great reluctance and a promise she would return, Bree walked slowly back to the car and climbed into the back seat. In front of her and behind the wheel, her father smiled and gave her a wink. Matt put the car back into gear with a crunch and drove up the track towards the house. He slowed for a moment as he reached the top of the hill and looked down into the hidden valley. It always made him smile to see the house that was his home, and he noticed that his family felt the same.

Down the hill they went and pulled up outside the house. The door opened wide as his father came out to greet them, his face now old and his hair wispy white. Matt watched as Claire, Callum, and Bree each took a turn to greet him before he alone stood before him. They hugged and slapped each other's backs. Then Gerry led them inside before stopping and noticing the other car that was entering the farmyard. He frowned.

"It's okay, Dad. They have to be here, apparently," Matt told his father as the car came to a stop, and Tony and his family exited the vehicle.

"Where's Gran?" Bree asked quietly of her grandfather and placed a hand in his.

"In her room. She's waiting for you." Gerry smiled down at her.

The room that used to be Leana's studio had long since become Gran's room. The large windows that let in so much light were open, and the cool breeze blew in, with the smell of wildflowers faintly on the air. Lying on great stuffed pillows was the frail frame of Rowena, Bree and Callum's great-grandmother. She was very thin and frail, her fingers twisted with arthritis and her breath shallow. They each came to stand beside her and lay a kiss on her brow. Bree sat on the bed and took up Gran's hand, raising it to her face.

"I told her you were coming," Gerry said quietly. "She's been waiting for you."

"I know. I've been with her since we crossed the ford," Bree said softly. "She still has fight in her." A tear ran down her cheek as she once more talked in silence with her Granny.

"Don't be sad on my account, lass," Granny admonished her inside her mind. "I have lived too long."

"Never long enough, Granny," Bree told her.

"You have news for me, don't you?" The old woman had a twinkle in her eye. "News that I have been waiting for."

"Canny as ever, Granny. Yes, I do. He proposed to me last week," Bree said with a smile. "He's here with us now. If you would just open your eyes, you'd see him."

"I have seen him in my last vision. You and Johnny have brought great joy to both of them, Bree. With your wedding, their story is now complete."

"I know, Granny. I have always known."

"Your Granda has something for you. He will give it to you when I'm gone and explain what it is. He knows, too. I had to tell him, my dear. Are they all here now?"

"Yes, they are all here—those who can be."

"I want to say goodbye properly."

"Yes, Granny," Bree said, and she moved her mind from her Granny's. She laid her hand gently down and stood back for the others to say their farewells.

Gran looked at each of them. Their hearts were open wide to each other, pouring support and love to her, and she kissed each one goodbye. Matt was last, and she held his hands in hers she looked at him.

"Take me to the stones, Galen. I want to be there when I leave this world. I have not much time left. Take me now. And tell the others to come as well. They need to be there."

"Yes, Gran. I will." He kissed her again and then left the mind of his grandmother to stand at her side.

Each one came back to themselves, and Matt lifted the old woman into his arms. She weighed next to nothing. Claire bundled her up in a blanket, and they made their way out to the bottom of the hill. The brook danced and played in the spring sunshine, a beautiful music that never failed to fill each heart.

Slowly they lifted off the ground, Matt leading the way. Claire took Aroha in her arms, followed by Tony and Tia. Bree lifted Johnny up and he held tightly to her. Lastly came Callum, bringing with him his Granda. They rose into the afternoon light up to the top of the hill and the rocks that pushed up from the earth, hiding the stones from view. Carefully carrying her around to the stones, Matt stopped at the entrance for the others to catch up. In procession they entered, and Matt knelt with Gran still in his arms in the centre of the circle. The others gathered round and held hands.

From around them, they appeared, each one standing in the spaces between the stones. Seven tall figures with long, hooded robes that hid their faces, soft singing floating on the air accompanying their slow chant. In through the entrance two more came—one was cloaked as the others, and the second was in a long, sapphire-blue dress, trimmed in silver. Her dark, curly hair hung loose about her shoulders, and her eyes shone as blue as the dress she wore.

The woman joined Matt in the centre and placed a cool hand on the forehead of Gran. She looked up at her brother and gave him a small smile and nod. It was time. Gran took one last shuddering breath and let it out. With the silence now complete around them, the Guardians were gone. Only Breena and the Guardian she entered with were still with the family.

Matt laid the body of his grandmother on the ground and pulled the blanket tighter around her. He looked up at his sister and took her hands in his as they stood over Gran.

"I will look after her, Galen," she said softly. "As I still watch over you all."

"I wish we could see you more often," he told her, his voice low and husky with emotion.

"You see me every time you look at Bree. I know you do." She smiled. Then, looking past him, she nodded to the Guardian. "I must go now. Gran doesn't want to make a fuss."

Breena released his hands and took one more look at her family, then moved out of the circle they still made with their hands. She stopped by her father and kissed his cheek.

"Mum says hello and she misses you," she told him quietly.

Gerry planted a kiss on her forehead. "Tell her I love her still."

The Guardian moved off towards the entrance and waited for Breena to join him. At her side, the hazy figure of a woman emerged, her white hair pulled back into a bun at the nape of her neck. She turned and waved farewell, then walked through the entrance and vanished like a morning mist. Breena followed her grandmother, but there was no last look from her. Each time she left them, it hurt her a little more.

The group still stood silently together, their hands clasped and feeling the loss of one of their small family group. Matt bent down once more and picked up Gran's body, and as one, they lifted off the ground and floated out of the circle. Carefully, they lowered themselves down the hill and back to the house. He carried her back inside and to her bedroom, laying her back down and covering her up in the bedsheets.

Claire was at his side with her arm around his waist, holding him to her. Tears coursed down his cheeks at the loss of this woman who had been a constant in his life. She had become the mother he needed when his own was so lost in her grief that she couldn't care for him. The woman was the centre of this house. She had been born here and lived her whole life in this place.

Slowly Claire guided him from the room. Taking his arm, she took him into the living room and sat him down. Callum was there with glasses already poured, and he handed one each to his parents. Gerry raised his in the air and took a breath.

"To Gran," he said, and downed the drink in one.

The others followed, with each calling her name and drinking the whisky in one. They sat for a while before Matt realised his son was pouring himself another glass.

"No, you don't. You're only fifteen. Pass that to your Granda," he told him.

"It's not every day that your great-granny dies, Dad," Callum said in his strong Glaswegian accent.

"No. I let the first one slide, but no more. Pass the bottle and go ring for the doctor," he said carefully, not wanting to get into an argument, as they so often did these days.

"Yes, Dad." He passed the bottle to his father and left the room to make the call.

"He's just like you at the same age." Gerry laughed and sat down.

"I was never like him," Matt said, pouring a generous measure into his own glass.

Claire took the bottle from his hands and placed it back into the cupboard that it had come from, shutting the door firmly.

"We were drinking that," Gerry protested to his daughter-in-law.

"*You* were, and I would like some still there—and for you both to be functioning normally when the rest of the family arrives tomorrow. I wish they had been here," she said, thinking of Addy and Adam and their two boys and Robbie and Fiona.

Looking up, she could see the uncomfortable looks coming from Tony and his family. The little ceremony up on the hill had disturbed Tia, and she was as white as a sheet. Claire went to her and took her hand, then led her into the kitchen that was once the sole domain of Gran.

"Let's make some tea, shall we?" Claire said.

"I don't understand why we had to be there. It was a special moment for your family," Tia said to her.

"I'm not sure, either, but I do know that it was important that you all were there to witness it. Have you fully accepted who your daughter is?" Claire asked as she put the jug on the hob to boil.

"Yes. I did a long time ago, Claire. I still don't understand why she is so special, though."

"This evening, I think we need to make our own pilgrimage back to the stones," Claire said wistfully, looking up the hill to where that mystical ring stood. "You, Tony, Aroha, Matt, and me."

"What about Bree and Johnny?" Tia asked.

"Their story is their own now. This is something different."

"Doesn't it ever get tiring, being so mystical?" Tia asked her friend.

"Yes. I'm hoping that this is the end," she said as she smiled.

The tea made, they brought it into the living room and laid it out on the coffee table. When Gerry saw that everyone was gathered, he pulled a small box out of his pocket and handed it to his granddaughter.

"Your Granny told me your news, and I thought that you could use this," he said gruffly as Bree opened it.

Nestled inside was a simple gold band with a teardrop-shaped diamond set on it. It picked up the light and sparkled brightly. Bree showed it to Johnny, who immediately picked it up and placed it on her left ring finger. A click sounded in Claire's mind, and she was curious as to where he had got the ring from.

"The band was your Gran's wedding ring," Gerry started and sniffed loudly, pulling out a handkerchief and blowing his nose. "The diamond is something very special. It was left to you by your Aunt Breena the last time we saw her up at the stones, the day we were there to help your mother. She cried a tear, and it fell." He stopped, unable to go on.

Bree looked at the ring and ran to her Granda, throwing her arms around him. There had always been a special bond between them, and this just cemented it further.

After the small dinner, Claire walked up the hill with Matt holding her hand. Behind them came Tony, Tia, and Aroha, complaining she didn't want to go anywhere near the stones again. Her mother told her to be quiet and just behave.

When they reached the top, Claire started to walk around the outside of the stones as she usually did, taking in their energy and communing with them. She returned to the entrance as Tony and Tia reached the spring, with Aroha joining them. The girl looked at the stones with distrust, turning her back on them.

Claire stood by her goddaughter's side and took her hand. "Come join me in the centre, Aroha."

"I can't, Aunty Claire. It feels wrong," the girl said with no whining or pleading.

"It feels wrong because you haven't accepted both sides. Please let me guide you." She looked into her hazel eyes, and a spark of recognition shocked her.

"All right," Aroha said carefully, and Claire led her away to the circle.

At the entrance, the girl hesitated. Claire stopped, waiting for her to get accustomed to the feeling the stones were sending out. She gave her an encouraging smile, and they moved into the centre of the circle. Matt and Tony were behind them, along with Tia.

Claire placed the young girl into the centre, and the others all joined hands around her. From the hill path, the Guardians came to fill in the spaces between the large stones. And from around the large rocks another procession came—a people equally as old as the Guardians. They were born of the same spark of life, one for the north and one for the south. They joined together and faced inwards.

Sparks of energy, in all the colours of the rainbow, grew and floated around the stones as their chanting increased. The ancient language complimented each other and danced around on the wind. Through the entrance of the stones came one more, with hands held high and giving their blessing to this child of both. A nimbus of light grew around Aroha, whose very name was a symbol for all that they stood for. Love.

The golden light grew brighter and swelled to encompass her parents and godparents. The love they had for this child was the key to her acceptance, and she grabbed it hungrily. A shot of black sparked amongst the golden light, and Claire reached out for it.

She had seen a look in Aroha's hazel eyes and knew that she needed to rid this bad energy for the child to survive. She grasped it and wrestled with the spirit that she had felt dwelling deep inside Aroha's mind, expunging it from the girl. She pulled at it from its roots and tore it from her, cauterising the wound it had left behind with the balm of their collective love and setting her on the path she knew she needed to be on.

"Done," a voice rang out over, around, and through them.

Claire relaxed and felt at last her tasks were all done. She was free now to live the rest of her life in peace and happiness. This was the reward gifted to her from the Guardians until her time was ended.

The light dimmed and the ghostly figures departed. The stones were quiet once more, and they stood surrounding this child of both north and south. Aroha looked at each in turn, and a smile came to her face. The understanding of what she had to do was set in her eyes, the hope of the future of both peoples in her hands. A changer, a healer, a teacher, and more. This young woman accepted her fate and looked forward to seeing it through.

Into her mother's arms she went gently, taking her father's hand and pulling him into their embrace. Matt held on to Claire and watched them. He was happy knowing that he finally had his wife to himself, that there would be no more rushing around the world to fight unknown forces.

Aroha left her parents and stood before her godparents. "Thank you," she said simply and then kissed and hugged them both. She then turned and exited the circle, with Tia and Tony closely following.

Claire walked with Matt once again through the stones, then dropped his hand and traced her own over them. Matt smiled at her and followed the group past the spring and around the rocks.

When Claire had finished her final round, she headed towards the rocks, the small smile on her face reflecting his as she stopped at the spring to look over the valley below. The sun was setting behind her, and the clouds were a bright orange colour, with violets and pinks splashed in for good measure. The wind that almost constantly blew up here in the hills was calm and at ease, and she felt him before she heard him.

"It's all done, Tony. The future is in your daughter's hands now." She sighed deeply.

He stood beside her and took her hand in his. Once she would have pulled it away, but now she relaxed into it. It was the companionable touch from a man who had become her brother.

"Our children are grown. Their lives are their own now. I am so happy Johnny has found love with Bree," he said softly.

"A happiness you once hoped for us?" she teased him.

"No—more. You were right. We would have been wrong for each other."

"So pleased you can see it from my point of view now."

They stood in silence, watching the light fade in the clouds and the shadows deepen in the valley.

"He was there, wasn't he?" Tony asked, concerned.

"Yes. She has his eyes. It's not surprising, Tony. She is of his flesh, and he would do anything to be back."

"Thank you for taking him from her. I didn't even see it until you had finished."

"Sometimes we're blind to what is in front of us," she said and squeezed his hand affectionately. "It's been a long day. The others will be waiting for us."

"Tia suspects that I still have feelings for you," Tony told her.

Claire turned to Tony and looked him square in the eyes. "So does Matt."

The One True Child saga continues…

A young boy lost and alone, is given a
home and family.

Now, the only parents he's ever really
known are gone…murdered. Their young
daughter, Claire, survived. His graveside
promise to watch over and protect her,
becomes more than he bargained for.

WATCHER

Book 6 of the One True Child Series

The storm enfolded the harbour city in its wrath as it turned day into night. It created slick roads with its driving rain, which funnelled through the narrow streets and back alleys. Its whipping wind moaned and whistled as it passed the tall buildings, buffeting the brave or unfortunate souls who found themselves out in the chaotic elements. Hail stung any exposed skin and made uncertain footing for those outdoors as they ran for cover, trying get to shelter or get home. For hours, the skies had been stirred up into a great frenzy from the south. Rolling black clouds had come barrelling in through the harbour entrance and blanketed the city with their ferocious power. Lightning and thunder completed the set and punctuated the air with forceful, crackling energy.

Cars raced through the streets, the rain and hail glinting in the headlights; water sprayed up from their spinning wheels in great plumes, drenching those unlucky enough to be nearby. They were left with no choice but to push on and curse the careless drivers. The lights flashed brightly, reflecting off the storefront windows and growing puddles on the ground, illuminating the dark streets. The sounds of their engines were not enough to drown out the rumbling of the thunder, and the lightning spread out like fingers in the roiling, low-lying clouds.

Lost in the cacophony was the sound of running feet, pounding down the footpath and splashing through the puddles. Arms pumped beside a thin-framed body wrapped in a stained, old, and smelly overcoat, which was trying hard to protect the boy inside. His dark hair was plastered to his face and running with water. His dark eyes were bright with fright that had nothing to do with the tempest that raged around him. Streams of condensed air billowed out from his burning lungs and were lost to the storm almost instantly. The badly shod feet skidded on the wet concrete as they rounded a corner. Grimy fingers grasped at the edge of the grey concrete building to steady himself before heading down to the end of the alley that opened to the back of three buildings.

The boy threw himself into the small gap between a large rubbish bin and a wall, the only shelter offered in the deserted area. He squeezed his small frame into the space and pulled the coat up over his head, trying desperately to use it as a shield against the rain and wind that made its way down to him. He struggled to catch his breath, laying his head on shaking bare knees. He strained to listen for any pursuit from the three older teens who were after him, but the only thing he heard was the pounding of his own heart.

A loud growling came from his stomach along with that familiar hollow feeling, and he cursed the luck that had stopped his nightly food scavenging. The best food from the supermarkets and restaurants would be gone soon and he would spend another night hungry, probably becoming desperate enough to eat the dodgier things he could find. Unless—he fervently prayed—the weather kept the other street people away from the more likely spots, and he could hide himself long enough to get away from the gang of brothers pursuing him.

Tony Benning remembered a time when he was happy, when he had a home and parents who loved him. He remembered a normal life with friends and going to school. Life had been good then. He hadn't wanted for anything; he had a full belly every night and warm, safe place to sleep. But it wasn't like that anymore. Now he was cold and hungry all the time. He didn't feel safe at night and there was no family to turn to.

His parents were dead, and he had been placed in a foster home. It had not been a nice place to live. The couple whose care he had been placed into should never have been left in charge of children. They gave them little to eat, taught them how to steal, and beat them when they came home empty-handed. But the days they had the inspections from the social workers were the best. They had clean clothes, food on the table, and were spoken to like they were human beings. Tony left there as soon as he could escape.

He planned it so well. Every time he was sent out on an *errand*, he would take some money he'd stolen and hide it in a special place. One night he decided he'd had enough, and he didn't go back. Tony had spent nights on the street before when he knew he was in trouble, but now he was on his own.

The only problem was, he really didn't have the street smarts to keep the money he had held back for long. A group of older boys—the ones he ran from now—picked on him immediately and took his precious resources. They had beaten him and threatened him; now he was running scared. He knew where they liked to hang out and avoided it like the plague, sticking to the outer edges of the city—that was, until that night. He didn't know why they had decided to head to his patch, since there were no real prospects for them in that area.

Voices echoed around the streets amongst the rolling and rumbling thunder. They were closing in, and he pushed himself against the wall, hoping they would pass and not see him in the shadows. This was one of his favourite hiding spots. Not many people came down this alley; there was not much shelter to be had and only one place to hide from prying eyes.

Tony heard their footsteps entering the alley, followed by their cruel laughter. They were out for sport that night, and the chase thrilled them. What was one more dead street kid to them?

"He's not here, Andy; he's probably long gone."

"No, he is here. I can smell him." The roughness of Andy's voice sent a shiver down Tony's spine.

Hugging himself tighter, Tony tried to squeeze into the corner of the wall. He heard them coming closer to the bin, and the lid lifted as they checked inside.

"Not here, Andy. I told you." The lid slammed down with a loud, reverberating bang. Tony flinched at the sound.

Large, scuffed black boots appeared in front of him, and he was lifted from the ground and hung there by the old, smelly coat. A grinning skinhead leered at him with sharp, maddened eyes. The piercings in his eyebrows glinted in what little light made it down the alley, and water droplets meandered over his scalp and down his brutish face.

"Told you I could smell him. We have you now, kid, and we are going to play a little game. One I like to call *How many times can Andy and his brothers hit you before you die.*"

Tony struggled to gain his footing, to get away from these three who took delight in the pain of others, but the one called Andy held him fast in his grip. He dropped Tony to the ground and pushed him into the centre of the alley. The brothers surrounded him, taunting and playing a dangerous game of cat and mouse. While tall for his age and skinny to boot, Tony was outnumbered and scared. The only exit from the alley was tantalisingly close, if he could only get past them. He watched closely for an opportunity.

At first, he made a move to the left, but he was pushed back by the rough hands of one of Andy's younger brothers, who laughed at Tony's feeble attempt. All three were of a similar build and mind, led by the oldest and the nastiest of the three, who tried to run the streets under his large boot. They called to Tony, taunting him with hopes of freedom, only to close in again and push him back down onto the wet ground when he tried to pass.

Once more he tried to push through, making a break for the entrance via a gap that had opened between them. Large hands grasped his shoulder and a fist connected with the sparse and unprotected belly of Tony, knocking the wind out of him. Doubled over, he struggled to breathe, and Andy pushed him back into the middle of the group again. His laughter at the game boomed over the next lot of thunder as it crashed overhead. Tony stumbled and then stood up straight again, looking for his opportunity to get past and run for cover. Making another move, one of the other brothers grabbed him and twisted Tony around, holding his arms behind his back as the third landed a blow in the ribs. The sound of bone breaking was followed closely by a breathtaking, intense pain, and Tony screamed out as they flung him to the ground.

Tony got to his knees, his breathing coming in short, painful bursts and intense anger starting to well up inside him. He had run from one bad situation into another, and things didn't look like they were going to get any better anytime soon. The world had gobbled him up and spit him out, abandoning him to this fate. The feeling swelled inside him now, and he stood up with clenched fists and jaw. The brothers surrounding him laughed, but their laughter dissipated as Tony launched himself at the oldest of the three.

His vision pinpointed the face of Andy, and he was the sole focus. There was no storm raging above him; there was no one else in that alley, only the bald teen who was making Tony's life hell. Putting his whole weight behind him, he landed a punch fair and square on Andy's cheekbone, and he could feel it give way as his fist connected with it. With a sickening crunch, it collapsed, and Andy was down on the ground; blood poured from his crushed and crooked nose. Tony rounded on the other two, water whipping off the old coat as he turned. They tried to outflank him, rushing at him; he stepped out of the way at the last moment, grabbing their heads and smashing them together with a satisfying thud and underlying crack. They landed at his feet, unmoving but still breathing.

For a moment, Tony stood there amongst the three, breathing heavily and in pain. He let go a scream of hatred for the world; of self-pity; of loathing at these three. His fists were still clenched, anger still in charge of his mind and body when someone else stood before him. This man held his hands up and spoke calmly. It took Tony a few minutes before he calmed enough to take in what he was saying.

"It's okay; they aren't going to hurt you anymore. Shall we just step away from them?" He beckoned Tony away from the three bodies, his blue eyes piercing.

Tony took a step closer to the man, then stopped. He didn't know who he was. Was he a danger? Was he going to hurt him? Was he going to turn him in to the cops? Was he going to take him back to that place? Questions fired through his brain.

"I'm not going to hurt you, kid. I want to help you. Look, at least come in out of the rain." The man motioned to a lit doorway in the back of one of the buildings. The soft light that splayed out on the wet asphalt was warm and inviting, and he took another step.

"Who are you?" Tony found his voice in between breaths and the pain they were creating.

"My name is John, and that's my workshop. Come in and get dry. Please; I promise I haven't called the cops. I don't care what happens to them."

Tony took a few more steps towards the open door; he could feel heat coming from inside, and it lured him. The memory of being warm was such a distant one. He watched the man carefully as he led Tony into the light and then through the doorway. John stood to one side and shut out the storm behind him; Tony stood there, dripping wet and suddenly feeling trapped.

The tension was evident in his face and clenched fists, and John watched the boy. "You can leave anytime you want. What's your name?"

"Tony."

"Do you want to get that wet coat off? We can hang it here by the door, so if you want to leave, you can take it with you."

Tony shrugged the tattered coat off his shoulders and handed it to John, watching suspiciously to see where he hung it. When he was sure that it was as the man had said, he relaxed a little. John took one look at the boy and felt pity for him. He was very skinny, his bones showing through the sallow skin that should have hidden them. He was wearing clothes that were more suited to summer than winter. He led the boy through the darkened workshop, which smelled of grease and car exhaust, then into the staff room.

It was warm in there, and Tony moved straight to the heater and stood over it, savouring the warmth that it put out and shivering harder. John grabbed a clean towel from the washroom and threw it to him. Tony winced as he caught it and started to dry his hair.

"Are you hurt?" John asked, concerned.

"I'll be all right," Tony said, trying not to let the pain show.

"Let me have a look." He stepped towards the boy.

Tony pulled away from him, looking like he was about to run. John put his hands up, stepping back. He went to the bench instead and got two cups out of the cupboard.

"You want tea or coffee, Tony?" he asked him.

"Coffee." Then he remembered his manners. "Please."

John set about making them both a coffee and then told him to sit. Tony lowered himself down onto the seat gingerly and accepted the steaming cup. John was amused when he noticed how much sugar the boy spooned into the cup before stirring it briskly.

"Do you want milk?"

"Nah, thanks." Tony lifted it to his mouth and took a gulp of the hot liquid. Anyone else this would have burnt their mouths, and this only seemed to confirm something to John.

"Where do you come from, son?"

"I'm not your son," Tony retorted and drank the rest of the coffee.

"All right; fair enough. So, are you going to answer the question?"

"I don't know. I was adopted."

"Is that why you're on the street?"

"No. My parents died, and I was put in care. Are you going to have me sent back?"

"Why would I do that? It obviously didn't agree with you. How long have you been on the streets?" John stood up and went to the fridge. He pulled out the lunch he had not eaten that day and put it in the microwave, punching the numbers.

"Most do-gooders want to. I can't remember how long." The smell of the warming food reached his stomach, and it growled hungrily.

They remained silent, the only sound the microwave working until it beeped, and John pulled the container out. He placed it in front of Tony and handed him a fork.

"My wife always makes me a lunch. You're lucky today; I forgot to eat it. I get so busy that time gets away from me. Eat up."

Tony didn't need to be told twice, and he shovelled the food into his mouth as if it were going to be taken away from him. In very short order, it was all gone, and he pushed the container away, wondering how a person could forget to eat.

"Your wife is a good cook. Thank you."

"How old are you?"

"Sixteen." The bravado Tony was trying to display did not fool the older man.

"No, you aren't. How old are you really?"

"Fourteen."

"Right. Well, we will have to fudge the papers, but I know someone who can help me there. How would you like a job?"

"You don't know me. For all you know, I could rob you tonight and take off," Tony said, a lump forming in his throat.

"I don't think you will. And believe me, when I saw what you did to those three out there, I did have reservations about even inviting you in. But there is something about you that I trust, Tony."

"You've only just met me. You know nothing."

"I see a boy who is in desperate need of a home, guidance, and some general care. Look, you can try it for a couple of days; if you don't like it, then you can leave. No questions asked. Okay?" He held his hand out to him.

Tony looked at the man's hand for a moment, then took it and shook on the deal. The movement aggravated his ribs, and he winced in pain.

"Now are you going to let me look at those ribs or not?"

He nodded and started to pull up the thin T-shirt to expose the quickly bruising chest where he had been punched. John carefully pressed and felt the ribs, but the boy was so thin he could see where they were broken. He sat back down and pulled his phone out.

"I know someone who can help you with those, but you're going to have to trust me. They will not tell anyone you are here or report you to any agency. You have my word on that." When Tony nodded, John punched in a number and waited for an answer.

"Hey, George; John here. Can you come to the shop? I need your help." There was a pause for a moment. "Yeah, now. I promise it is important. Good; see you soon."

"Who's that?" Tony asked.

"That is a friend of mine, a sort of doctor." John put the phone back in his pocket and then got up. He riffled through a locker and pulled out a sweatshirt and overalls, then glanced at the towel that was draped around Tony's shoulders and got another clean one out.

"When George has helped with the broken bones, you can use the shower and change into these things. Then we'll take you home. I'll ring Jess while George looks at you."

They sat and waited for John's friend. Outside, the storm was passing, the lightning and thunder becoming more distant as the minutes passed. The rain and wind were also subsiding.

"Have you ever done something like that before?" John asked him.

"Like what?"

"That fight. Do you get angry easily?"

"Not usually. I don't think I've ever been like that before."

"Good. Did you know you had that strength inside you?"

"What strength? All I did was throw one punch and hit two idiots' heads together."

"Not every man can do that. I know I can't." There was a knock at the front door, and John got up to let his friend in.

Tony was standing by the back door when the stranger walked in behind John. George was shorter than John and was almost as round as he was tall. A severely receding hairline only highlighted his ginger hair, and glasses were perched on the end of a short, stubby nose. He looked Tony up and down, pushing the glasses higher up on his face.

"You can trust him, Tony. He'll help with the pain those broken ribs are causing." John waved him over and guided him to stand in front of the man, who had lowered himself into a chair.

"Pull the shirt up, boy; let's have a look at you," George ordered in a deep voice. Tony reluctantly did as he was told and watched as the man placed his pudgy hands over the bruising and waited. His hands were cold, and Tony wished that he would hurry up.

"Okay, two broken. This shouldn't take long, John. Then I think you should shove him in the shower." He wrinkled his nose and then knitted his brows together in concentration.

Slowly, the pain ebbed away in Tony's side and he could breathe easier. The bruising started to fade out under this man's touch, and Tony's eyes went wide. When George pulled his hands free from the emaciated ribs, Tony took a step back from him, watching John and the balding man carefully.

"What are you?" he asked quietly.

"We can answer that later. Take those things and go through that door. You'll find a shower and some soap; use plenty of it. Get changed and then we will go," John told him gently.

As Tony was about to close the door behind him, he saw the two men talking quietly; the bald man raised his eyebrows and looked his way. The door blocked the pair from his sight, and he slipped the bolt into place, making sure that the room was securely locked. He turned the shower on, stripped off, and stood under the wonderfully warm water. It was the first time he had enjoyed being wet since he left the foster home. Grabbing the soap, he started to wash, and the water ran grey before it swirled down the drain hole in the floor.

As he dressed, he looked in the mirror and almost didn't recognise himself. His hair was long and lank, his eyes sunken dark holes in his head, ribs sticking out from his skin. There was no sign he had been attacked, no bruising or tenderness.

This whole night was so strange, and he wondered at it. To be taken from a situation that he felt like he had no control over only to be thrust into another that was equally weird felt surreal. He didn't understand why this man would do this for him.

There was a knock at the door, and he quickly finished getting dressed and left the bathroom. There was only John now in the staff room; there was no sign of any cups or containers of food, or of the strange man named George.

"Come on; Jess is waiting for us." John led him out of the room, turning lights off as he went, and then through the front door. He locked it behind him and then unlocked the last car sitting in the car park.

Tony got into the passenger seat, and when the door shut, he felt hemmed in again and almost opened it in his sudden desire to bolt. His body went tense, and his eyes widened; the fists he had used earlier to maim were once again balled and the knuckles white. John was watching him and gently rested his own hands on the steering wheel.

"Anytime you want to get out, just say the word. I won't stop you." His voice was calm and low. It was soothing, and Tony's fears eased slightly. Consciously, he relaxed his hands and put the seat belt on while John started the car and drove off.

It was not a long journey to his home, a small house in the outer suburbs tucked up against a hill. John pulled up the short driveway and led him to the front door. It opened before they could get there and silhouetted in the doorway was one of the most beautiful women Tony had ever seen. She had long, blonde hair that gleamed golden under the porch light, a welcoming smile, and sparkling blue eyes. Her smile only lasted until her gaze shifted from her husband to Tony. She sized him up, and he had a feeling that he came up short in many ways.

As she stepped aside so they could enter, he noticed that she was pregnant—not heavily, but the bump was visible, and again he wondered why this man had brought him to his house. Tony followed him into the kitchen, feeling lost and unsure of what he was supposed to do. He could feel his stress levels rising.

"Jess, this is Tony," John introduced him, and Tony nodded to her.

"Hello, Tony. Please sit; dinner is ready. You'll have to find something for lunch tomorrow, John, since Tony is eating it."

"No problem, sweetheart." He motioned for Tony to sit, and he obeyed, waiting while Jess placed a plate of food in front of him.

The food smelled even better than the smaller amount he'd had earlier, and he began to eat, making sure he did not inhale it too quickly. He did not want to do anything to annoy this woman with her steely gaze. Tony could tell that John had needed to do some very fast talking to get him even this far, judging by the way he saw the man give Jess sideways looks, checking to see how she was taking this interloper. They ate in silence and wondered what would happen. When they were finished, he helped John do the dishes. John showed Tony where he could sleep and told him they would sort things out in the morning; then he closed the door, leaving him on his own.

As Tony sat on the bed, he heard the couple talking, and their voices became louder and louder. The fear that John would walk into the room and tell him he had to leave grew, and he turned to the window. Pulling the curtains aside, he checked to see how far it was to the ground. Foremost in his mind was the thought that he should just leave before he was asked. His old and dirty clothes lay on the bed where he had left them, and he bundled them up into his arms. Returning to the window, his hand was on the latch to open it when the door opened behind him. He spun around, expecting the worst. His breath caught when he saw Jess standing there.

"That's not going to solve anything, Tony. Stay the night; at least have a decent night's sleep in a warm bed."

"But you were fighting about me." His fear was written all over him, from his face to his posture.

"Yes, but only because he didn't give me any notice. You are welcome here, Tony; please stay. I'll take you shopping in the morning and pick a few things up for you to wear, and then I'll drop you at the workshop. But if you decide you need to leave, then I would prefer you did it through the front door and not the window. I don't want the neighbours talking." She flashed him a genuine smile, full of care and sunshine. Jess placed a T-shirt and pair of pyjama bottoms on the bed for him.

"Thank you."

"Get some sleep." She left the room and closed the door.

Tony got the best night's sleep he'd had in months. The bed was soft and warm, and his dreams were pleasant—even if he couldn't remember them in the morning. When he woke, he had to pinch himself to make sure he wasn't still dreaming. He rose into the fresh winter air to get dressed back into the overalls and sweatshirt John had given him the night before.

There was a knock at the door just as he was pulling the sweatshirt over his head, and John walked in. In his arms was a bundle of clothing, which he laid out on the bed.

"These don't fit me anymore; I thought you could use them. There's a belt in there to hold the jeans up. Did you sleep well?" John looked at him and Tony nodded, not trusting his voice. "Good. Well, breakfast is ready when you've dressed." He left him to it and shut the door behind him.

The jeans most definitely needed the belt, as they felt about ten sizes too big for his thin frame. As he went to pull the belt in, it ran out of holes to fasten. Quickly he finished dressing and held up the jeans in one hand and the belt in the other.

Tony found them both in the kitchen at the table. "There's not enough holes for me to fasten it," he said simply as he held the belt up.

"Easily fixed. Sit down and eat." John stood and took the belt from him, and Tony took the seat he had the night before.

When John returned the belt to him, it had a new set of holes. Without thinking, Tony stood and lifted his shirt to thread the belt through the loops. He heard Jess gasp, and he dropped the shirt immediately, feeling very self-conscious. He bowed his head, hair covering his face.

"I'm sorry, Tony. I didn't mean to; it's just you are so thin," Jess told him quickly.

"I haven't exactly had three meals a day recently," he said quietly as he sat back down.

"Well, you will from now on."

Watcher available August 2022

PREORDER NOW FROM ALL MAJOR

BOOKSELLERS

Loraine Conn grew up on the outskirts of Upper Hutt, New Zealand. Her backyard encompassed the surrounding farmland, river, hills, and mountains which she wandered with her brothers and fed her imagination. After discovering a love for writing in English class at the age of eight, she continued to write in secret. It was not until much later in life that Loraine turned what she thought was a hobby, and something fun to do, into her first completed novel. Now married, Loraine moved from New Zealand to Perth, Western Australia in 2008, and became a stay-at-home mum. While caring for her family and after battling breast cancer, a series was born from a kernel of a dream. Loraine has now published the seven book fantasy series, The One True Child Series, and Realm of Dragons, Fight for the Crown. Both the series and book have been released with the American based indie publishing company Between the Lines Publishing, under their Liminal Books branch, using the pen name L.C. Conn. She continues her career with many more stories waiting in the wings to be released, and even more ideas to be written.

CONNECT WITH L.C. CONN

Email: raindropc1970@gmail.com
Facebook: http://www.facebook.com/LCConn
Twitter: https://twitter.com/ConnLoraine
Instagram: https//www.instagram.com/l.c.conn
Web Page: https//lcconnwriter.wordpress.com/